Finding Rosamond

Finding Rosamond

Published by The Conrad Press in the United Kingdom 2023

Tel: +44(0)1227 472 874
www.theconradpress.com
info@theconradpress.com

ISBN 978-1-915494-58-0

Copyright © Jackie Wallis 2023

Although every precaution has been taken in preparing this book, the publisher and author assume no responsibility for errors or omissions. Neither is any liability assumed for damages resulting from the use of information contained herein.

All rights reserved.

Front cover design by Mike Wallis.

Typesetting and cover layout by: Charlotte Mouncey, www.bookstyle.co.uk

The Conrad Press logo was designed by Maria Priestley.

Printed and bound in Great Britain by Clays Ltd, Elcograf S.p.A.

Finding Rosamond

JACKIE WALLIS

This book is dedicated to my precious daughter, Allison.
(1960 – 1996)

Introduction

This is the tale of two women and an old diary.

The writer of the diary, a twenty-one-year-old lady, received it as a present in the year 1835. It provides a fascinating glimpse into her social activities as well as her hopes and fears, loves and losses during the reign of William IV.

More than 160 years passed since she wrote her last entry, until somehow this charming little diary found its way into an antiquarian bookshop in the Yorkshire town of Harrogate. How it arrived there is a complete mystery.

The second woman in the story is me.

I came into possession of the diary in 1996, just after my life fell apart due to the most personal of tragedies. As the new owner of this wonderful piece of social history, I had no idea as I held the little leather-bound book in my hand that a voice from the past was about to take me on a journey that would change my life forever. As this particular year in Rosamond's life begins to unfold, you will read her exact words as she tells us of the daily occurrences taking place so long ago.

The story woven around her daily entries is my fictionalised account of Rosamond's struggle as she tries to make sense of events as they happened.

My own story, however, is an accurate, absolutely non-fictional account of my life since Rosamond came into it.

Overall, *Finding Rosamond* is an account of the lives of two women, separated only by time. It involves love, despair, their respective families, and, ultimately, their mutual realisation that they need to accept what cannot be changed, and to make the most of their lives.　　　　　　　　　　　　Jackie Wallis, June 2023

Jackie

26th February 1996

Looking out of the car window on a cold February morning on the way to Leeds, I began to feel sick. 'Please be there,' I silently pleaded to a God I didn't really believe in. The feeling of dread that had kept me awake for most of the night began to intensify as we approached our destination.

'Nearly there, love,' I heard my husband Mike say. He had tried so hard to keep my spirits up on the drive to the hospital, but I knew in his heart he too was worried. As we pulled into the car park I quickly got out, leaving Mike to park the car. I pushed open the heavy door, with the rising panic I had tried so hard to ignore since my last conversation with my daughter now threatening to overwhelm me.

Allison had called on Saturday to make sure I hadn't forgotten the arrangements we had made for the following Monday. 'Do you remember where to go, Mum?' she had asked.

'Of course I do,' I replied, having been there only last week. Something in her voice disturbed me. 'Are you okay love?' I asked, for I was aware that the treatment she had recently been undergoing for her depression made her tired and anxious and having read about the possible side effects of electric shock therapy, I worried about her coping as she lived alone in Leeds. Several times I had asked her to stay with us during the treatment so I could look after her, but my independent daughter would not hear of it. 'You shouldn't be on your own love,' I pleaded.

'Stop fussing, Mum,' was the expected answer. 'I am thirty-five years old; I can look after myself.' So reluctantly I gave up, but it didn't stop me from fretting as her false cheery voice worried me.

'How about Mike and I come over tomorrow?' I said 'We could take you out for Sunday lunch if you like.' My heart was telling me that we should go and see her as soon as possible but I didn't know why.

'Sorry, Mum, I'm spending the day with Sandra tomorrow.' Sandra and her daughter Shelley were good friends of Allison, so I should have been reassured by this, but for some reason my maternal antennae, now on full alert, wouldn't give me peace.

'I'll see you on Monday anyway, Mum,' she said, 'when you pick me up from hospital.' So once more, I had no choice but to leave it there.

The rest of Saturday went by slowly with the urge to go to Leeds constantly nagging at me.

'She won't be there, Jack, she will be at Sandra's, so there's no point,' Mike said.

'I know,' I reluctantly replied but the uncomfortable feeling that something wasn't right just wouldn't go away. I called several times on Sunday evening, but she didn't pick up.

'She's probably trying to avoid your fussing,' said Mike. So, I gave up, knowing I would have to wait until morning. After a sleepless night, morning was now here, and I was hurrying along the corridor towards reception feeling sick and with my heart pounding.

'Can I help you?' the young woman at the desk asked.

'I have come to pick up my daughter, Allison Ashby.' But as soon as I said her name, I knew she wasn't there, and that my instincts over the weekend which I had tried so hard to ignore were true. Before the receptionist could even look in her book I said, 'She isn't here, is she?'

Mike, now standing beside me, said, 'What are you talking

about, Jack? Of course she'll be here.' The receptionist, having had time to check her appointments, confirmed that Allison had in fact failed to arrive. With my legs now shaking, I felt faint. Mike produced a chair and urged me to sit down.

'Something's happened,' I remember crying. 'We must go to her. I think she's taken an overdose.'

As we headed towards the door, a doctor who had overheard this exchange stopped us by saying, 'I don't advise you to do that, we'll send the police to her house, and if what you say turns out to be true, they can get her to hospital much quicker than you could.'

Not convinced by this, I reluctantly agreed to stay where we were. 'I promise we'll get back to you as soon as we have any news,' she added, before hurrying away to make the call.

We then found ourselves ushered into a side room by a nurse who told us to take a seat. 'I'll bring you a cup of tea,' she said, shutting the door. I wanted to scream.

'I can't wait here, Mike,' I cried. 'I need to get to Allison.'

'I know, love,' he said. 'But we've agreed now, so we'll just have to wait, I'm sure they won't keep us waiting too long.' Sitting down on a hard plastic chair I told him that I felt in my heart she wouldn't be here, so why had I not listened to my instincts; if I had we may have been able to stop her. Mike, trying to console me, said, 'You couldn't have known, Jack.'

'But don't you see, Mike, it all makes sense now. Do you remember how surprised we were when she asked us last Monday to pick her up from her treatment, and then asked if we would do it again this week after refusing all help from us before?'

'Yes, I do, but what are you saying?' he asked.

'She never intended to keep this appointment,' I cried. 'She's planned it very carefully, last week was a rehearsal so we would know where to come.' I did wonder at the time why she had asked us to go inside the department to collect her.

Mike, looking very confused, said, 'I still don't understand what you are getting at.'

Looking at him with my heart breaking, I said, 'She's taken another overdose, and this time I know she really meant to go through with it. We're here because she didn't want us to find her. I know she's gone, Mike. I can feel it.'

There were no words to describe my feelings as we sat in that narrow windowless room, with Mike trying to convince me that they would find her in time. Two cups of tea arrived, the first of many. 'It won't be long now,' the nurse said cheerfully as she left the room and closed the door on us again.

Trying to stop myself from shaking, I began pacing up and down. Not knowing what was happening to my daughter, I just had to get out of this hospital. I tried several times to leave but someone stopped me every time. Eventually giving up, I slumped back down into the hard plastic chair. Every sinew in my body was now rigid with fear, and I began to think I would go mad. Perversely, humour can be found in the darkest of moments as I found myself thinking, 'Well, I'm in the right place if I do.' A bizarre thought considering there wasn't anything funny about the situation we were in.

We continued sitting together in that small narrow room, with its four hard plastic chairs along one wall, and a little table in the corner holding several cups of undrunk tea and a few old magazines. There was a door at either end, one opening to the corridor where we came in, and the other leading into a treatment room which contained four beds, each with an electric therapy machine attached to it. I discovered this when I tried to escape and was horrified when I realised it was the room in which Allison received her treatment and that our tiny prison was clearly the waiting area for the patients. I could imagine her sitting nervously in this little airless room, waiting for her name to be called. I am not saying that electric shock treatment is anything to fear, and possibly of great benefit to many people, but at that moment in time with my imagination in overdrive I just saw it as a terrible thing for Allison to endure.

Time went by in slow motion, with me pacing up and down and rocking backwards and forwards on the hard chair. Three hours had passed with no word from anyone except the nurse. Every time the treatment room door opened my heart jumped, but on each occasion, it was only the nurse with yet more unwanted cups of tea. It might have helped if I had been able to cry, but the tears just wouldn't come.

The door eventually opened, and a doctor entered the room; kneeling in front of me she took my hand and told us that the police had found Allison unconscious in her bedroom. My heart soared when I heard this. 'Is she still alive?' I asked.

'Yes,' she replied, and I immediately asked to see her.

'Oh, she isn't at this hospital, I've been asked by the police to keep you here until they can come and speak to you, but they shouldn't be long,' she said as she left the room. So, the nightmare was to continue. I really believed that Alison had died but now a new worry was invading my mind – what if they can't save her?

Unbelievably, another two hours passed before another doctor appeared, this time an older woman who also knelt in front of me and said, 'I am sorry to have to break this to you, but when the police went to Allison's house this morning, they were too late to save her.'

I remember saying, 'What are you talking about?'

Mike, now on his feet, said, 'I don't understand, a doctor came to see us two hours ago and told us that Allison was unconscious but alive, and we have been sitting here, waiting to be told when we can go to her.'

The doctor, looking puzzled, replied, 'I hadn't been told that someone had already been to speak to you.'

Mike, now quite angry, repeated, 'A doctor, kneeling where you are now two hours ago, told us that the police had found her alive and taken her to another hospital.'

Shocked by what Mike had said, she didn't know how to respond. After a strange silence that seemed to go on for ages, she finally said, 'I don't know who came to see you, but I have been told directly by the police that when they arrived at your daughter's home, they found she had passed away, and I have just been informed that she died sometime in the early hours of yesterday morning.'

'Oh my God!' Mike shouted, trying to keep his temper. He then said to the poor woman, 'How could such a terrible mistake happen? Don't you realise that giving my poor wife false hope is just cruel?'

'I am so sorry,' she said, 'but rest assured, I will find out.'

I had watched this exchange in silent horror, but now I quietly said, 'Please can I go to her?' Once again, she repeated that we had to wait for the police to pick us up.

Mike's temper now exploded. He shouted, 'This isn't good enough! Not only have we been locked up for five hours in this miserable little room, but now you're also saying that my wife, who's already in shock and needs treatment herself, can't go to her daughter?'

'I am so sorry, sir,' she repeated. 'We cannot keep you against your will, but your best chance of seeing Allison is to wait for the police to contact you.'

So, the choices were to go home without seeing Allison or wait for the police to take us there. As far as I was concerned there was no choice, so in my naivety I said, 'We will stay here,' and with that the doctor left us.

Once again, we were left alone in that miserable room with no idea how long we would be forced to stay there. I still couldn't cry or even speak; I just felt frozen. Mike decided to go and ring my son David to tell him what Allison had done.

So, standing up, we made our way out of the door to find the nurses' office, but to get there we needed to pass through the treatment room. Ten minutes ago, I had been completely numb, and now as I looked at those beds all I could see, in my imagination, was Allison lying there, alone and scared as they connected her to a machine. The nurse, seeing us approach her office, asked if she could help. 'I need to make a phone call,' Mike said.

'Of course, Mike, please help yourself,' was her reply, now knowing our names as she had been the only person apart from a brief exchange with two doctors that we had had any contact with during our incarceration.

Standing in the anteroom between her office and the treatment room I began to feel faint, so I leant against the wall, and as I did the enormity of what had happened suddenly hit me like a punch in the stomach. I could see the nurse watching me and heard her say how sorry she was for our loss, and that she had been Allison's nurse when she came in for her treatment. 'You knew her?' I asked,

'Oh yes,' she replied. 'A lovely young lady, it's such a tragedy.' Hearing those words seemed to flick a switch inside me, and my whole body, once so rigid with shock, now began to shake and I could no longer hold myself upright. As every part of me began to collapse I found myself falling. Literally. Fortunately, the nurse managed to grab me before I hit the floor, and as she held me all the tears that had been locked away began to pour out in a great torrent of sobbing so intense it took my breath away. I could feel her arms holding me tight as she said, 'Thank goodness, you're crying at last, Jackie. I have been so worried about you.'

Looking back on that unspeakably dreadful day, I realise now that some of those tears were for the years spent worrying and watching helplessly as she tried to cope with her difficult life – when I had been completely powerless to stop the many attempts she had made to end it. The last few years as far as Allison was concerned had been torture for all of us, and in my heart, I always felt it would end this way. I foolishly believed that with enough love, I could heal her. This thought kept me going for nearly twenty years. How naive was I?

My tears continued to fall as the nurse held me, but eventually the sobs receded. By this time, Mike was by my side, his own tears now falling. 'I'll take her now,' he said. 'Thank you for your kindness.' Back in the room, two more cups of tea arrived. What else could the poor woman do in such terrible circumstances but make tea? Mike told me that David was on his way to the hospital.

'What if the police arrive to take us to Allison?' I fretted, but he assured me that the nurse would tell him where to find us if that happened.

Another hour passed, until at last the door from the corridor opened and David and Carole walked in, quickly followed by my ex-husband Don, Allison's father.

As soon as I saw my son, I ran into his arms crying. 'We've finally lost her, Dave, and they won't let me see her.' More tea arrived along with an extra chair, as there were now five people in our tiny room. Mike told them about our enforced imprisonment, and about the differing information given to us by separate doctors.

'That's disgraceful,' said Dave. 'We need to get you out of here.' By this time, I was utterly exhausted. Mike had eaten nothing since breakfast and I had been unable to face food this morning, so my breakfast had been a cup of tea. The hospital had not offered us anything to eat, just endless drinks; not that I could have eaten anything, but I worried for Mike.

Yet another hour passed by. We had been in this hospital for seven hours without any sign of release, but finally the nurse put her head around the door and informed us that the police were on the phone and wanted to speak to me. So, taking the call in the office, I was horrified when the police officer told me they would not be coming to the hospital after all; they wanted us to go to the police station instead. When I told Mike, he exploded. 'Is this a joke?!' he shouted.

I remember saying, 'I can't do this anymore. I need to see Allison.' So, taking charge, Mike went to tell the police we intended going straight to the infirmary, but they told him that Allison had been taken to the mortuary which was now closed until the morning and that they needed us to call into the police station, telling him they had 'something to give to your wife'. I couldn't believe it; I had waited all day to see my precious daughter and now it was too late.

Nightfall had descended when we left the hospital and snow had begun to fall as we slowly made our way through heavy traffic towards the police station. Once inside, we were escorted along a corridor and into another room, this one an improvement on the last as it had a window and soft chairs. 'Please take a seat,' a young policeman said. 'I am sorry to tell you that the officer you need to see has gone out on a call, I hope you don't mind waiting?'

'That's what we have been doing all day, young man,' Mike sarcastically replied. 'Why on earth would we mind waiting again?' he continued, his patience clearly gone.

'I'm sorry to hear that, sir,' he said. 'I'll bring you some tea while you're waiting.' Sitting at the head of a large table with tea and biscuits in front of me, it felt as though I had slipped into another universe. My child had just taken her own life and here I was pouring tea as though we were at a tea party.

Another hour passed before anyone else came in. The long hours Mike and I had spent trapped in a hospital and now here had rendered us speechless. My body sank down into the chair as I stared out of the window on a cold February evening, watching the snow silently falling outside.

Eventually, the door opened and yet another officer came into the room. 'I'm so sorry to have kept you waiting,' he said.

'What's another hour on top of the many we've already waited?' Mike replied. He too was clearly at breaking point.

The young policeman, handing me an envelope and a set of keys, said, 'We found this letter and keys in the bedroom when we arrived at your daughter's house this morning. The door was unlocked but it's secure now.'

David asked him about Allison's cat, Barney. 'We have left the cat in the house, sir,' he replied, 'but someone will need to attend to it.' There were so many questions I wanted to ask. Did she look peaceful when you found her? Where was Barney? I knew that her beloved cat would never have left her side, but the words wouldn't come out.

As I stared at the policeman who had found my child all alone in her bed, the anger that flared so quickly had now disappeared.

I just felt sorry for him; he was so young; it must have been hard to do what he had to do that morning. I thanked him for his kindness as it wouldn't have been his decision to keep us waiting so long.

I gave the keys to David, as he had offered to go to Allison's house to ask the neighbours if they could feed Barney until other arrangements could be made.

At last, we were finally free to go home. As I sat in the car on the way back to Harrogate I slumped down in my seat, once again watching the snow as it swirled about in the headlights, my mind now locked into some kind of shocked trance. There was so much more I could have written about that truly horrific day, but it's perhaps better to leave it in the past. Suffice it to say, the trauma Mike and I suffered in that little room hasn't been, nor ever will be, forgotten.

It had snowed the week before when we took Allison home from the hospital. 'Hurry home, Mum,' she had said. 'The snow's getting worse.' I didn't want to leave her there on her own, she looked so pale and defeated. Once again, I had asked if she would consider coming back with us so that I could look after her, but of course the answer was no. So, with a heavy heart, I had to leave her. She stood at the front door waving to us with snowflakes whirling all around her, and as we drove away, I frantically waved back until I could no longer see her.

On the way home, Allison's sad face haunted me. Her words, 'I will be okay, Mum,' played heavily on my mind. But she wasn't okay, yet I couldn't have known on that snowy February evening that we would never see her alive again. The memory of that day, seeing her standing at the door with the hall lamp lighting up the snow as it gently fell around her, will stay with me forever. And now I dread the winter months, because the first fall of snow will always take me back to the last time I saw my daughter's face.

Arriving home, we went into the living room where our daughter Lucy and her friend Becky were sitting on the floor, surrounded by photos. Lucy, seeing the distress on our faces, asked, 'Is Allison okay, Mum? You look upset.'

I had to tell her that her sister had passed away.

And so it began, the terrible task of telling the family our devastating news. I remember standing in the kitchen, warming some soup I didn't want but knew Mike needed. When he came into the kitchen, he was horrified. 'What are you doing, Jackie? Leave it to me.'

Sitting in the living room with mugs of soup going cold in our hands, Mike said, 'We should go to your mum's now.' So, Mike, Lucy, and I got into the car and went to see my mum and stepfather. Earlier, Mike had arranged for Dave to meet us there, and as if my heart wasn't already broken enough, to see my poor mum fall apart when she heard the news that her first beloved grandchild had died shattered it into tiny pieces. The last phone call of the evening to my sister finally brought me to my knees. Mike insisted I went to bed where, mercifully, sheer exhaustion must have knocked me out, for the next thing I heard was the phone ringing at the side of the bed the following morning.

Jackie

February to July 1996

A man's voice on the phone began to speak almost before I was awake; it was the mortuary who wanted someone to identify Allison. I was so angry to have been kept from seeing her yesterday, but now, perversely, when I had the chance to see her, I couldn't do it.

Mike, alarmed by my hysteria, rang for the doctor. When he arrived, we sat together in the living room as he listened to all I had to say. 'They want me to go to Leeds to identify her, but I'm just too scared,' I sobbed.

'What are you scared of?' he asked gently, but I honestly didn't know the answer to his question.

'Listen to your heart, Mrs. Wallis, it's clearly telling you to stay at home, you're too fragile for such an ordeal,' said the doctor. It was therefore decided that Mike, together with my stepfather Eric and son David, were to go. This decision, made at a time of extreme shock and stress, was to cost me dearly, as I never did get to say goodbye to Allison, my first-born, who arrived when I was only nineteen. The pain and guilt of that decision will remain with me for the rest of my life.

People came and went; flowers and cards began to arrive and soon every surface was covered with them. My son Iain, now living in Kent, was skiing in Austria when Allison died, so we had no way of contacting him. Mike left a message on his home answerphone asking him to ring as soon as he could, which he did immediately after he heard the message. Utterly appalled, he got into his car and drove straight to Harrogate.

The funeral director was contacted, and when he arrived, I made him tea.

To this day, I will never understand how, when faced with such grief, we can still function, wash and dress ourselves, and clean our teeth. Our daily needs routinely attended to while still managing to observe all the social niceties and rituals we have been brought up to perform, such as serving tea to a funeral director, while my body screamed at me to show him the door.

I didn't want to talk to this kind gentleman about what kind of funeral we should choose for my daughter, I just wanted her back. But a decision had to be made, and everyone looked to me to make it. 'Would you like some personal music played?' he asked just before leaving. 'If so, we will require a cassette tape the day before her funeral.'

I looked at Lucy for advice on this. 'I know exactly what she would want us to play, I will deal with it,' she said as she showed him to the door.

The letter given to me by the young policeman just a few days earlier wasn't just a farewell letter, it was a list of who should receive her possessions, and Allison had charged me with fulfilling her wishes.

Lucy was to receive, amongst other things, her extensive collection of tapes and her cassette player. We had only been given a week to clear the house that Allison had rented from Leeds City Council, so her possessions were stored in a friend's garage awaiting distribution. Smaller possessions, such as the tape player, were in my house, so out it came along with dozens of tapes.

'It has to be George Michael,' Lucy said as Allison had adored the pop star and his music. Then the search began to select the most suitable tracks, finally narrowing it down to two songs

Allison would approve of for her final goodbye. That afternoon spent with my three children as we sat listening to George Michael was a welcome pause from reality.

The day of the funeral arrived, a day that is often said to bring closure, and for some that may be so but not for me; my true grieving didn't begin until the day after. The need to organise Allison's funeral had been the only thing holding me together, and now my purpose had gone the real pain started, along with guilt, anger, and every negative emotion you could think of preying on my mind.

I have always believed my breakup from her father, which I instigated, was the starting point of her troubles. As a fourteen-year-old, she found the breakup difficult to accept, and for a while she hated both her father and me.

Rebellion followed when I remarried, and when Lucy arrived, she was horrified, a feeling made worse when her father also remarried and produced yet another child for her to try and accept. She eventually came to terms with her changed family life, but I believe she never fully got over it, which caused her all manner of problems. I loved all my children equally, but Allison was the one who gave me sleepless nights. Her brothers, David and Iain, were also affected by the breakup, and they too had many adjustments to make. I know it wasn't easy for them at eleven and nine, respectively to accept a new stepfather and stepmother, but to their credit, both boys seemed to embrace their new way of life much easier than Allison did.

When Allison died, my sons, who were grown men, had lives of their own. David was married to Carole, and they had two sons with a baby due in the summer. We were and still are very fortunate as they live close by. Iain had left Harrogate to forge a career in computer software and lived in Kent with his girlfriend, Sally. Lucy, our daughter, was in her last term at Harrogate college, studying drama and performing arts. Allison, a highly intelligent girl, had an IQ of 164 as her Mensa certificate testified, but found it difficult to settle anywhere, almost like a Romany looking for a place to belong.

At the age of twenty-one Allison got engaged, but it didn't last long due to her fiancé's violent temper, which was a relief to us all. Unfortunately, they reunited three years later. He hadn't changed but Allison still loved him and within a year they were married. We all knew this farce of a marriage had no future, but for Allison's sake we went along with it.

Within a month they separated and were divorced the following year, but to our horror she took him back. Once again his vicious temper, fuelled by alcohol, ended in another separation. This dangerous relationship continued in the same vein for ten years. She kept moving house with our help, but he always found her.

Allison's self-worth, never very good to start with, was now on the floor and so the overdoses began, clearly cries for help.

We had no choice but to watch helplessly as she sank further into depression.

Eventually, she managed to free herself from this toxic merry-go-round, but the damage had been done and we were now living with the consequences. I blamed myself, and only a month after her death guilt completely consumed me.

The next two months passed in a haze of pain and sorrow; people came and went, each day the same as the one before, all with the hope that this would be the day I came back to life.

But nothing changed for me until the day Mike's sister Glenda, a frequent visitor, called to see me. As we sat on the sofa drinking tea, where she had spent many hours listening with patience to my tale of woe, she said, 'I don't know how you get up in the morning, Jackie.'

I replied, 'What else is there to do?'

I then remember her saying, 'I'm sure if anything happened to my children I wouldn't be able to.' We had no idea that a few hours later her beautiful twenty-five-year-old daughter Helen would be involved in a fatal motorbike accident. This second family tragedy rocked us even further, two young women with their lives ahead of them lost within three months of each other. Glenda turned to me for solace. I was the only person who could possibly know how it felt to lose a child without any warning, and we clung to each other in our shared grief.

Life continued as always, but I found it impossible to move on. The years spent worrying about Allison were now replaced by an aching empty space in my heart that nothing could fill. All those years of fretting had become normal for me, and now she had gone I had no idea how to live my life.

My usual optimistic and resilient nature had gone: paints remained in the cupboard, sewing was left untouched, and my books lay unread.

Everything had become grey and bleak, my creative nature and everything I enjoyed doing now buried under a huge weight of guilt and longing for my child.

I knew Mike and the family were worried about me, but I couldn't do what Allison had done, having seen the devastation suicide brings to the ones left behind.

I wouldn't do that to my family, they had suffered enough. Grief should never be confused with depression but sadly it often is. It's a natural deep sorrow for the loss of a loved one and the grieving process is different for everyone, each dealing with it in their own way.

I was often the person to help others through their pain and had spent many hours in the past listening to friends as they talked through their problems, but now I had nothing left to give. I just felt empty.

That was until one day, my fifty-fifth birthday, when I watched the postman walk down the path and with a sigh went into the porch. *More cards*, I thought as I bent down to pick them up. As I took them into the kitchen and dropped them on the table my eyes filled with tears. I knew there would be a card missing this year.

Leaving them unopened on the kitchen table, I took a cup of tea into the living room and leant back in the sofa. As I did so, my mind went back to the day that David, Eric, and Mike brought back Allison's belongings and I couldn't bear to watch as they unloaded her precious things into Penny's garage.

Instructions had been written in her farewell letter, telling me who amongst her friends and family were to receive certain items. Her personal things, such as clothing, jewellery, and books, were left to me but had been taken into Penny's house where they remained for a couple of weeks.

It was Penny who unpacked all her clothes after the men had pushed them into bin bags and, unbeknown to me at the time, carefully ironed everything before hanging them up in her spare wardrobe until I could face seeing them again.

I can't thank Penny enough for her kindness after such a terrible time. Eventually they came back to me, but I couldn't leave them alone as they smelt of Allison, especially the coat she had worn on the day I last saw her. As I sat there lost in misery on my birthday, they were still hanging in my wardrobe.

The back door suddenly opened, diverting me from these morose thoughts, and going into the kitchen I found Mike's sister Glenda standing there with a large bunch of flowers in her hand. 'Happy birthday, Jack,' she said, 'put the kettle on, I'm parched.' Glenda had recently taken a part time job in an antiquarian bookshop as a distraction, as she too struggled with her own loss.

'Thanks, Glen, they're lovely,' I replied. With flowers in water and mugs of tea in our hands, Glenda took a tiny book out of her bag.

'What's that?' I asked.

'It's a diary,' she replied, 'and it was written in 1835.'

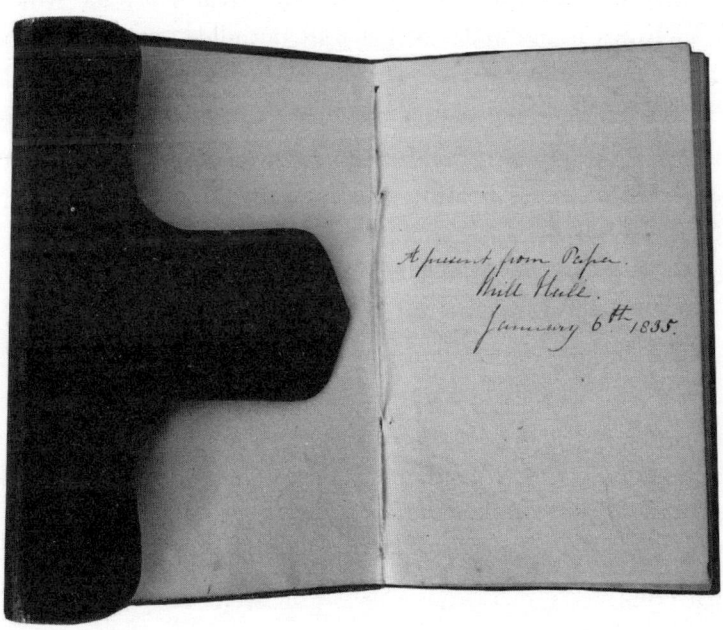

6th January 1835

A young woman sitting in her bedroom is warming her toes by a flickering fire. The candles have been lit to chase away the lengthening shadows as her room slowly darkens on a cold January afternoon, presenting a cosy scene. She is holding a small diary, a present from her papa. Her name is Rosamond, and she is twenty years old.

Her life is one of privilege as her father, a wealthy businessman, provides very well for his large family. They live in the mansion house in Mill Hall, a small hamlet outside Aylesford in Kent which she shares with her ten brothers and three sisters. It's a happy household, often chaotic but filled with much love and laughter. As she sits in the comfort of her cosy room with her new diary in her dainty hands, she is dreaming of a bright future with her beau, secure in the knowledge that all is well in her world.

She has no idea that her life is about to change, as the perceived happy life she has planned will soon be threatened as her health begins to be troublesome, leaving her in fear of losing her young man as well as her faith in the God she loves so much. All is not as it seems, which will unfold as we venture into the little diary.

| JANUARY | *Engagements, &c.* | 31 DAYS. |

January.
From JANUS, *a Roman divinity.*

1 JANUARY. Th. *Circumcision.* Christ circumcised. Holiday.
Johny Jones arrived. I went for a tooth after dinner. Mr Hamm called in the morning rather wet.

2 F. Dr. J. M. Good died, 1827 ....
Johny Jones left at 10 o'clock .... and Jeffry after tea, he went to Aylesford. Papa was very poorly.

3 S. General Monk, restorer of Charles II., died, 1670 ....
Went no where all day exceedingly dull.

4 S. Philip V. of Spain resigned his crown, 1724 ....
I went to church morning and afternoon. ... received ... from J.F. to inform us of his ... illness. we all stayed ...

5 M. His Royal Highness the Duke of York died, 1827 ....
Mamma and Henry went to ... they called on Mrs Day to see ... I stayed at home all day rather dull.

6 Tu. *Epiphany,* an appearance of light. *Twelfth Day.* Holiday.
Henry and I went to Aylesford called on Grandmama. Mr and Mrs Hobson came home from London. They left Mr Jones a little better.

7 W. Sir Thomas Lawrence died, 1830 ....
Mary, William and I called on Mr Hobson. ... Mrs Henry Pepperson ... Papa went to ... for 2 or three days.

Rosamond Spong's Diary

1st January to 19th January 1835

THURSDAY 1ST JANUARY
The Circumcision. Christ circumcised. Holiday.

John Jones and I went for a walk after dinner. Mr. Staines called in the morning, rather wet.

Although this is the first entry in Rosamond's new diary, it had been written on 6th January, the day she received it from her papa.

Sitting by the fire in her cosy bedroom with the curtains closed to keep out the cold wind, she tried to recall the first day of the New Year.

She remembered how wet and miserable it had been, but her heart had been lifted by the thought of a visit from John, her young man. The pouring rain on that day had not mattered to Rosamond as she waited for a knock on the door, and when it came, she ran into the hall before the maid appeared to answer it.

John, who lived in London with his parents, had been spending Christmas in Aylesford with Mr. and Mrs. Robson, the latter being a cousin of John's mother.

The Robsons were also very close to Rosamond's family, so this meant John and Rosamond had spent much time together during their childhood, and later as young adults, so along the way their feelings for each other had grown into an understanding that one day they would marry.

The young couple had made plans to go out walking on what

would be their last day together for a while, as John was to return to London the next day and it could be some time before he returned. However, as the rain continued to beat against the windows and howl down the chimney, they were forced to share the drawing room with Mr. Staines, vicar of their local church St. Peter and St. Paul's in Aylesford, which was just across the river from the family home in Mill Hall.

Rose, being a devout young lady, had a great deal of respect for Mr. Staines. Having enjoyed many of his rousing sermons in the past, she had to admit that on this occasion she rather wished he had stayed at home. They had little choice but to politely sit in his company as he sat in the nearest chair to the fire while Mamma served him morning tea.

And that's where he stayed until Hannah, the maid, came in to announce dinner was about to be served. Thankfully, with no mention of a seat at the table for him, Mr. Staines alighted from his chair to take his leave. There was a seat for John, however, as Mamma had previously invited him to dine with them.

As the family made their way to the dining room for a celebratory New Year's Day dinner, John whispered in Rose's ear that if she was agreeable, they should brave the weather and go on their walk as planned. Rose thought this to be a splendid idea, but on hearing of their intentions Mamma made it perfectly clear that she most certainly did not.

'Don't you think you would be better served by staying indoors, Rosamond?' she said.

Rose realised Mamma did not intend accepting any argument in this matter as she had called her 'Rosamond' rather than 'Rose,' her usual name when addressed. Mamma only ever used her given name when she was cross, so it was quite clear she did not want her daughter to disobey her.

Rose, however, not normally given to disobedience, didn't care about the rain or fear her mother's wrath, as the only thing that mattered to her was spending time with John, and there would be little chance of that if they were to stay in the drawing room. Rose was one of fourteen siblings, ten boys and four girls, and in normal circumstances she loved spending time with her family, but due to the bad weather the drawing room was full.

Two of her younger brothers, Octavius and Septimus, were fighting over their toys and three-year-old Grace with her boundless energy was pleading with Rose to join her in play.

However, when baby Elizabeth began wailing for attention Rose decided she could not stay indoors another minute. So, standing up, she said, 'Please don't worry, Mamma, we will wrap up warm against the elements.' She then ran out of the drawing room and up the stairs to her bedroom to change into warmer clothing before Mamma had a chance to respond to her boldness.

Suitably attired with stout boots, warm gloves, and a thick hooded cloak on her shoulders, Rose then stepped out of the house with John and on to the lane. They were determined to go on the walk they had planned beforehand.

At first, they tried to ignore the wind driving the heavy rain into their faces, which was making it difficult to see where they were going. This was not the gentle stroll they had imagined, and it wasn't too long before they were overcome by the deluge that poured from the heavens. Finally admitting defeat, they ran back to the house, laughing all the way.

When Mamma saw her soaking wet daughter dripping water all over the hall carpet, she said crossly, 'What did you expect,

Rosamond? I warned you it was a foolish thing to do.' Rose began to shiver in her wet clothes, so Mamma immediately sent her upstairs to change into dry ones. Warm towels were produced for John and a seat made available close to the fire, for he was as wet as Rose, and when Rose returned to the drawing room, hot tea was sent for.

Mamma, having calmed down by this time, said, 'We will say no more on the matter, Rose. I am sure no harm will come due to your foolishness.'

Rose, much relieved to hear Mamma calling her by her usual title again, said, 'I should have listened to you, Mamma, I'm very sorry.' Peace was restored, and the family spent what was left of the day in their cosy drawing room until it was time for John to return to Aylesford.

While standing in the hall, John gently kissed Rose then promised he would write to her on his return to London. Closing the door behind him she went up to her bedroom, eagerly anticipating the promised letter to add to the many in her rosewood writing box.

Climbing into bed with the wind howling down the chimney and the rain drumming against her window, she pulled the bed curtains closed and settled down to dream of a happy future with the man she loved so dearly.

FRIDAY, 2ND JANUARY
Dr. J. M. Good died, 1827.

John Jones went to London on the 3 o'clock coach. Mamma and Septimius after breakfast went to Aylesford. Grace very poorly.

Today was a sad one for Rose, as John returned home to London on the three o'clock stage. She had hoped to wave him goodbye from Aylesford as his coach departed, but at breakfast Mamma asked Rose and older sister Mary if they would stay at home with Grace as she had developed a fever during the night.

Rose's heart sank at this request; not only did it mean she would be unable to say goodbye to John, but she also worried that whatever was ailing the little sister she loved would turn out to be serious.

'Of course, Mamma,' both girls said in unison. Thanking them for their help, Mamma told the girls she intended to leave for Aylesford directly after breakfast to obtain some medicine for Grace. Seven-year-old Septimus, on hearing this exchange, began to cry, as he got most upset when Mamma went anywhere without him, so she reluctantly agreed Seppy could travel with her.

As soon as they were out of the door Rose and Mary hurried up to the nursery where Hannah the maid awaited them, eager to resume her normal duties.

On entering the nursery where the youngest children slept, Rose was alarmed to see how poorly Grace looked as she laid listlessly in her little bed.

The sisters did their upmost to cheer her up, but it was to no avail. The little girl who was usually a bundle of energy and full of mischief had disappeared, now replaced by a sullen and weepy one. 'Oh dear,' Rose said to Mary, 'she must be gravely ill indeed.'

Mary, always more optimistic than Rose, said, 'Nonsense, she will recover soon enough, I am sure it's just a head cold.'

Mary suggested to Rose that she should take Elizabeth and Octavius downstairs and leave her with little Grace until Mamma returned. The moment they arrived, Mamma left Septimus with

Mary and quickly disappeared upstairs to attend to the patient.

The weather by this time had not improved, so Rose and Mary remained confined to the house, as were Octavius and Seppy who were both less than pleased with this, as the place they preferred to be was in the garden climbing trees.

The rest of the day dragged on with nothing to brighten it up. Rose hoped they would receive some callers, but it would seem nobody wished to venture out in the unpleasant weather. Eventually, with all the little ones tucked up in their beds, the sisters escaped back to their own bedrooms.

Sitting by her fire Rose reflected on what a difficult day it had been, although she was pleased to have been able to help Mamma as she knew her mother's burden was a heavy one.

She also felt sad to have missed the opportunity to see John before he returned to London. A country girl at heart, Rose had never visited London and could only imagine what it was like. What she did know, however, was that when they married, she would certainly find out, and as much as Rose wanted to be his wife, she was not entirely sure about London being their home.

SATURDAY, 3ʳᴰ JANUARY
General Monk, restorer of Charles II, died 1670.

Went nowhere all day. Exceedingly dull.

Nothing much of interest occurred today other than the fact little Grace was now improving. Mamma had stayed with her all through the night, attempting to sleep in a chair. Rose and Mary spent the morning in the nursery, allowing Mamma to attend to the many duties she faced daily.

The rain continued to pour down with no one venturing out except Papa, who had plenty of work to do attending to his many businesses. Rose and Mary's favourite pastime was to go out walking, and much of that time was spent in Aylesford village calling on their family friends and elderly grandmamma, so neither of the sisters took kindly to being kept indoors on yet another wet day.

Rose, thinking that the day had been exceedingly dull, was in low spirits – which were not improved by developing the chill Mamma had predicted – so she was glad to climb into bed with a large mug of warm milk which Hannah had brought to her room, along with a hot brick to keep her toes warm.

SUNDAY, 4ᵀᴴ JANUARY
Phillip V of Spain resigned his crown, 1724.

I went to church, morning and afternoon. Mamma received a letter from G.N. to inform us of her Father's illness. We stayed home all evening.

As she drew back her bedroom curtains, Rose grimaced when she saw the rain pouring down her window, so heavy it bounced off the ground outside and obscured her view of their gardens across the lane.

This meant another day of being confined. 'Well, I suppose at least it's Sunday and I can attend church,' she thought as she dressed for breakfast.

One of Rose's greatest pleasures, other than walks with her adored sister Mary, was sitting in St. Peter and St. Paul's church in Aylesford listening to their vicar Mr. Staines as he stood tall in his old oak pulpit addressing his flock. His rousing sermons always made her think of all the people less fortunate than herself.

After breakfast Rose went upstairs and hastily prepared herself for today's visit to the House of God. Suitably dressed, she went back downstairs to find the family gathered in the hall deciding who should go with Mamma, Rose, and Mary in their coach.

Papa and the boys opted to brave the rain and walk, so off they went, taking the riverside path leading to the old bridge across the river Medway and into Aylesford.

When the service was concluded and seeing that the rain had stopped, Rose asked Papa if she could walk back to Mill Hall with Mary. Papa, however, did not think this a good idea, so he said,

'No, Rosamond. Mamma has informed me you have a cough, no doubt brought on by your gallivanting in the rain with John Jones on Thursday past, so I think you should avoid any risk of a further soaking.' Hearing her full title again, Rose realised it was Papa's turn to be obeyed. Even though she wasn't happy to be denied the opportunity to walk home with her sister, she had no other choice but to return home in the coach with Mamma, Seppy, and Octavius.

On arriving back at Mill Hall, Rose and Mary went upstairs to remove their cloaks and bonnets before returning to the drawing room where they discovered Papa and two of their brothers, George, now twenty-two, and John, nineteen, already ensconced in the chairs nearest the fire. Edward, who was seventeen, William, fifteen, and Henry, thirteen, having not yet returned to their school in Sevenoaks, were taking up the next best seats. John, ever the gentleman, jumped up to offer his seat to Mary while Rose sat on the fender to warm her feet. By this time Mamma had gathered the younger boys, Frederick who was eleven, Augustus, nine and Septimus, seven, and announced that dinner was served. One by one, they all reluctantly left the warmth of the drawing room and made their way across the cold hall and into the dining room, which was not much warmer than the hall as the fireplace really wasn't large enough for the room.

There were sixteen people in Rose's immediate family, most living under the same roof apart from Thomas, the eldest at twenty-five, who, having qualified as a lawyer, now kept chambers in London and was rarely at home. Little Grace, baby Elizabeth, and Octavius still took their meals in the nursery, but all the others required a seat at the large table that dominated the dining room. Papa sat at the head with Mamma at the other end, and the rest of the family took a seat wherever they could find one.

With the meal over, the family returned to the drawing room where Hannah had built the fire. Once everyone was seated, Mamma read a letter she had just received from her half-brother, George Nash, who lived in Gillingham with his sister Elizabeth and their father and Mamma's stepmother, Mrs. Nash. The letter informed them that Grandpapa Nash was unwell again, and being already frail, this was a concern to them all.

On hearing this sad news, Rose decided to attend the afternoon service to pray for him, and asked Mary if she would accompany her. But Mary had no desire to leave the fire and declined, saying, 'No thank you, Rose, it's too cold to go out again. I would rather stay by the fire with my sewing.'

Rose went upstairs again to collect her outdoor things, and when suitably attired, climbed into the coach that Wood, their coachman, had brought round to the front door and went on her way.

Sitting alone in one of the three family pews, Rose said a prayer for her grandpapa whom she adored, then joined in with the congregation singing hymns and left the church feeling quite uplifted.

She spent the rest of the afternoon reading in her bedroom with the heavy curtains drawn to keep out the cold winter draughts. With a warm fire glowing in the hearth and candles flickering on the mantlepiece, Rose fell asleep in her chair.

MONDAY, 5TH JANUARY
His Royal Highness the Duke of York died, 1827.

Mamma and Mary went to Maidstone. They called on Mrs. Day to see Emily. I stayed at home all day. Rather dull.

Rose stayed at home today because the annoying tickle in her throat had now become a troublesome cough, and to make matters worse she was feeling rather unwell. Mamma told her it was just a cold, caught from Grace no doubt, and then went on to say she planned to go to Maidstone after breakfast in order to visit Mrs. Day and her daughter Emily, and that Mary was to accompany her.

Rose, not happy to hear she was to be excluded from this excursion, asked why she couldn't go with them. 'Because you are unwell my dear,' Mamma replied. 'It is better that you stay indoors today, as we don't want your cold settling onto your chest.'

So, feeling sorry for herself, poor Rose went up to her bedroom to read her latest book, a heavy tome by Hannah More, one of her favourite writers.

The dark and gloomy day made reading difficult and it was hard to see the words as she sat by the fire, so she stood up to light the candles. Rose hated winter; she didn't like the cold and dismal days or having to stay indoors when it rained or snowed, so when spring came, it always lifted her spirits.

Putting aside her book, her thoughts turned to John and the longed-for letter he had promised to send that had so far failed to arrive.

Finding herself sinking into melancholy, she decided to join Hannah, the maid, who had been left in charge of the little ones in the nursery. Even the company of her youngest sibling did little to lift her mood, and the morning seemed to pass so slowly.

At long last dinnertime arrived, and Rose left the nursery to join the family in the dining room. Having not yet returned to his chamber in London, Thomas was seated in Papa's chair, as Papa had just left for the city during the morning. Sat at the table without her parents and Mary there, the meal was a rather sombre affair, so as soon as it was polite to do so, she made her excuses and went back to the nursery to be with the children.

It was well into the afternoon before Mamma and Mary returned. Rose was so glad to see them she rushed over to Mary, saying, 'Thank goodness you are back, Mary, I feared that I may die of boredom.'

Mamma declared that it was too cold to have their meal in the dining room and went directly into the kitchen to supervise tea with Cook, and soon they were all toasting muffins on the drawing room fire.

When tea was done and the little ones had gone to bed, Rose decided that as her cold had not improved, she would also take herself to bed. Having said goodnight to the family, she wearily climbed the stairs and went into her cosy bedroom where, thanks to Hannah, another warm fire awaited her.

Sitting down in front of it and watching the flames as they danced in the grate, her thoughts turned to John once again and she wondered why he had not written to her. Rose speculated that perhaps Mr. and Mrs. Robson, who were due to return home from London tomorrow after staying with John's parents, would bring back a letter. With this happy thought, she picked up her book and settled down to read until her eyes grew tired in the dim light.

TUESDAY, 6ᵀᴴ JANUARY
Epiphany, an appearance of light. Twelfth Day. Holiday.

Mary and I went to Aylesford, called on our Grandmamma. Mr. and Mrs. Robson came home from London. They left Mr. Jones a little better.

After many days of heavy rain, the sky finally brightened, and as Rose's cough had also eased, a walk to Aylesford with Mary was decided upon.

With breakfast over, Rose went upstairs full of excitement at the prospect of dressing for the much longed for outing.

When the sisters were suitably attired, they set out for Aylesford, taking the path by the river, the quickest but perhaps muddiest way to the village after all the rain. The ground was indeed extremely soggy, but the girls weren't deterred by the mud, although they took the greatest of care to keep their dresses from trailing in it. The cold air soon had their faces stinging, but simply being outside again with Mary was wonderful for Rose as she skipped along, chattering away to her sister.

They decided between them that today's outing would be to call on their grandmamma who lived near the church in the village. Mary was the eldest by two years. However, close in age they may be but close in nature they were certainly not, as Mary's character was a cheerful and happy one, while Rose, even though she tried to follow Mary's example, found herself fretting over things beyond her control and worrying about things that may or may not happen.

When they arrived at Grandmamma's house the maid showed them into the cosy drawing room where a warm fire blazed in the hearth.

'Sit down, girls,' Grandmamma said. 'I am so pleased to see you both, do tell me all your news.' The maid soon appeared with a tray of tea which Rose was glad of, as the walk had left her shivering with cold.

Grandmamma, also called Rosamond, was a sprightly old lady of eighty-six years with a sharp eye and quick wit. She had lost her husband John when Rose and Mary were infants, so they had little memory of him.

Over the years so many tales had been told to the grandchildren about Grandpapa and what a great character he had been that Rose had a clear picture in her mind of the personality he possessed.

She knew what he looked like due to the large portrait hanging above Grandmamma's drawing room fireplace, which Rose didn't like to look at when she was little as the stern looking man's eyes always seemed to be watching her, but now, as a young woman, she loved looking at him.

Grandmamma happened to know all the gossip in the village, and today was no exception. 'Mr. and Mrs. Robson have returned from London,' she said, 'and I believe that poor Mr. Jones is now much improved, Rose, which will be a relief for your John I should imagine.'

'I am glad to hear that,' Rose replied, as she was rather fond of John's father.

As they sat in Grandmamma's comfortable drawing room listening to all the news of Aylesford, the sisters lost track of time with the dinner hour nearly upon them. Suddenly realising the time, the girls said their goodbyes and hurried home as quickly as they could, splashing through the muddy puddles on Aylesford High Street with Rose's bonnet flying behind her as she ran.

Both girls were only too aware that Mamma and Cook frowned upon anyone who dared to be late to the dinner table, but as they ran across the bridge Rose became breathless and needed to stop awhile.

The pair arrived home at Mill Hall with minutes to spare, and with no time to attend to their untidy hair they went straight into the dining room. There, sat at the head of the table, was Papa who had just returned from London. 'There you are, girls,' said Mamma. 'I was just about to send George and John out to look for you.'

When dinner was over and the maid had cleared the table, Papa handed Rose and Mary a small package each. Rose eagerly opened hers to discover a dainty ladies' diary bound in deep maroon leather, while Mary received a similar one in deep blue.

Delighted with her gift, Rose could hardly wait to examine the present in the privacy of her bedroom, so after thanking Papa she hurried upstairs.

Alone in her room and sitting comfortably by the fire with candles lit to chase away the shadows, she opened her little treasure and found to her delight that not only did the diary have pages to write in, it contained wonderful poetry, scriptures, historical facts, views of faraway places, and fashions of the day, as well as several stories, one of which was so amusing it made her laugh out loud. Looking forward to reading more, Rose decided that the most important thing was to start recording the daily events that had occurred since the beginning of the new year.

Sitting at her table with an inkwell and pen, she began writing in her new diary all she remembered of the last few days.

Now seated comfortably by her fire with the task completed and the sky turning dark outside her window, Rose's thoughts turned to the year ahead, wondering what events it may hold in store for her and hoping that some of these would be agreeable.

WEDNESDAY, 7ᵀᴴ JANUARY
Sir Thomas Lawrence died, 1830.

Mary, William and I called on Mrs. Robson, found Mrs. Henry Peppercorn, her sister and brother there, Papa went to Sevenoaks for two or three days.

When Rose awoke today, she was relieved to find that the head cold she had suffered from for the last few days appeared to have left her, so at breakfast she suggested to Mary that they walk to Aylesford again, this time to visit Mrs. Robson in the hope she would have returned from London with a letter from John. Rose's brother Will overheard their conversation and asked if he could join them, a request to which the girls readily agreed. After finishing breakfast, they all put on their winter clothing and the three siblings set out on their walk.

The path alongside the river had dried a little since yesterday, but it was still necessary to raise their skirts to avoid the hems trailing in mud. William had no such problems as he marched along, singing as he went. Will was a handsome boy, full of mischief just like little Grace, and Rose adored him.

On reaching the bridge he wanted to stop there awhile to watch the boats and barges going up and down the river, but the girls had to urge him on as it was far too cold to stand about.

Mrs. Robson had already received callers when they arrived at her house, for Mrs. Peppercorn and her brother and sister were sitting in the drawing room. Mrs. Peppercorn lived on a farm just outside the village where Rose and her siblings spent so much of their time when they were children. Delighted to see her, they all took turns in giving Mrs. Peppercorn a warm hug. Mrs Robson's maid brought in a tray of tea and a jolly morning followed, but to Rose's bitter disappointment, there was no letter from John.

On arriving back home, Mamma told them Papa had left for Sevenoaks and would be away for a few days. Rose missed her papa when he went away on business, and she was not pleased to hear this news.

The girls spent most of the afternoon in the drawing room. Mary, an accomplished seamstress, was engrossed with her sewing while Rose had her head in a book. Mamma served tea by the roaring fire once again; a pleasant place to be on a cold blustery afternoon.

As Rose sat on the fender by the fireside, she reflected on the day and how she had enjoyed most of it but couldn't help feeling disappointed about John's lack of correspondence, causing her to worry about why he hadn't written one letter since he left for London. Another thing bothering her was the cough, which seemed to have returned.

The heat from the fire made her feel a little sleepy, so she went upstairs to her bedroom in order to write in her diary.

THURSDAY, 8ᵀᴴ JANUARY
Lucian, a Syrian, martyred, 302.

We stayed home all day. Nothing particular happened, all very dull.

Due to the inclement weather the family stayed at home today. Rose spent the morning in the nursery with the children and stayed there until she heard the dinner gong. Entering the dining room, Rose saw her elder brother Tom, who obviously had yet to return to London, sitting in Papa's chair. No doubt thinking, Rose thought to herself, that he was the temporary head of the household in his father's absence.

The afternoon saw most of the family amusing themselves in the drawing room where Rose was finding it hard to concentrate on her book. Putting it down, she went over to the window to stare at the rain pouring down the panes with a vengeance, longing to escape the confines of the house.

Freddy, Augustus, and Seppy were also not taking to their confinement too kindly, which resulted in fights breaking out until Mamma lost her temper with them and ordered them to leave the room.

Rose returned to her bedroom after tea and picked up her pen to write in her diary, but with little of interest to record she was relieved to see the end of a very dull and miserable day and hoped to see a better one tomorrow.

FRIDAY, 9TH JANUARY
Fire Insurance expire. Public Funeral of Lord Nelson, 1806.

Went nowhere all day. I saw F.G. and W.G. After dinner I went to sit in my bedroom and looked out of the window and thought of a future day until I became quite miserable.

Frederick and William Golding, who resided in Ditton, called this morning. They were friends of Rose's brothers, John and Edward. Rose spent some time talking to them before going up to the nursery to see her little sister Grace, who was much restored to her usual sunny self and played for a while.

After dinner Rose went up to her bedroom feeling in low spirits, despite having given herself a good scolding to be more cheerful. Sitting by the window and watching the rain pouring down the glass while thinking about her future soon left her feeling miserable.

Then the tears started running down her face. Rose was worried that her future may not be with John as she had believed, because his attentions towards her had been somewhat lacking just recently.

He had now been in London for more than a week and Rose would normally have received at least two letters by now, so her imagination was plaguing her with a thousand reasons for his silence. Her rational thoughts told her that most likely business was keeping his mind occupied, but different possibilities still troubled her.

Mary, 'the sensible one' of the two sisters, came up to see her. 'Rosamond, you must stop torturing yourself and remain calm. The reason he has been unable to write will reveal itself in time, so I urge you to be patient,' she advised her sister, but patience was a virtue seemingly absent from Rose's character, as she was not given to being very patient at all. How she wished to be more like Mary.

When tea was ready, Rose and Mary joined the family in the dining room, with the remainder of the evening spent together by the fire in the drawing room where Rose privately resolved to be more hopeful and cheerful. Now sitting writing by the bedroom fire, she hoped for a happier day tomorrow as Papa would be home from Sevenoaks: she had missed him today.

SATURDAY, 10TH JANUARY
Archbishop Laud beheaded, 1645.

Mamma, Mary and I went and called on Mrs. Robson. Mr. Morris, and Mr. Summerfield were there. Papa had come home from Sevenoaks.

Rose awoke this morning to find the rain had stopped at last, so during breakfast Mamma, Mary, and Rose decided to walk into Aylesford and call on Mrs. Robson. Wrapping themselves in warm cloaks, putting on gloves, and pulling on stout shoes to protect their feet against the puddles, they felt suitably attired to face the elements and set off.

Glad to be out in the fresh air again after being confined to the house for a few days, the trio walked along in high spirits all the way to Mrs. Robson's house where, to no great surprise, they found she already had callers as Mr. Morris and Mr. Summerfield were sitting in her drawing room.

More tea was sent for, and all settled down beside the warm fire. Listening to everybody's news made for a most entertaining morning, with Rose feeling quite uplifted.

The morning soon passed and, bidding farewell to their dear friends, the girls hurried home for dinner which Cook always had ready for one o'clock sharp, and like Mamma, she would not be happy if anyone failed to arrive on time. She was such a wonderful cook but could become quite cross when dinner needed to be kept warm. Fortunately, they were home before the clock struck one and dinner was saved, as were they from mutterings about spoilt food.

The girls spent the afternoon in the drawing room. Mary continued with her stitching as did Rose with her book until Mamma brought Elizabeth and Grace to join them.

Baby Elizabeth, now toddling, attempted to climb on the furniture which meant no more reading for Rose as the baby had to be watched constantly. Eventually the boys joined in the games, and it became very noisy indeed. They were all having such fun playing together when Papa arrived home, and everyone was so pleased to see him.

Tea was served in the drawing room again, always such a cosy place in which to take tea. Rose was beginning to tire, however, and her cough was starting to bother her, so she made her excuses and went upstairs to her bedroom, supposedly for a rest, but in truth it was to find some peace so that she could write in her diary.

It had been a much better day for Rose today as she had tried to be more like her sister in not brooding so much, although she suspected she would not be able to continue with this new-found hopefulness for too long, but for now it served her well.

SUNDAY, 11ᵀᴴ JANUARY
Hilary Term begins. Sir Hans Sloane died, 1753.

Went to church in the morning. Mary and I called on Mrs. Robson to enquire after Mr. Jones health. He was not well. I went to church in the afternoon. Mary and I and William went to chapel. I heard a beautiful sermon.

Today was Sunday, Rose's favourite day of the week because she loved to attend the local church, St. Peter and St. Paul's. After breakfast Rose and Mary walked to Aylesford for the morning service. The weather remained cold but thankfully dry.

Their vicar, Mr. Staines, read a most interesting sermon, speaking of the brief passing of time and how we should relish every moment and everyone we love, and not to waste our days concerned with our mortality and worrying over what cannot be changed. Extremely welcome advice, thought Rose, and as he spoke, she noticed the warm mist of his breath as it hit the cold air of the church.

Mamma and Papa took the little children there and back in the coach, whilst the older boys made their own way home. Rose suspected they would also take heed of Mr. Staines' advice and would not be seen until dinner time.

On their way home, the girls decided to call on Mrs. Robson again to see if she had any news about Mr. Jones' health. She sent for some tea as soon as the girls arrived as she could see both were suffering from the cold air.

Sitting in the church was a wonderful experience for the congregation, apart from the bone chilling cold turning breath to mist and numbed fingers and toes, so Rose and Mary were grateful for a hot drink and a warm fire. Mrs. Robson imparted the sad news to them that John's father was quite ill, and everybody was worried for him.

It was troubling news because Mr. Jones was a kind natured gentleman, and the girls were most fond of him. They had spent many hours talking together and hoped he would recover soon, drawing Rose's thoughts to Mr. Staines' sermon once again.

Thanking Mrs. Robson for her hospitality and the warming tea, they set off to walk home. On the way, Rose said to Mary she wished to return to church for the afternoon service to pray for Mr. Jones.

When they arrived home for dinner, Rose told Mamma of her intentions, who then suggested that if she wished to do so, it would be sensible to go in the coach, and instructed Wood to take her there after they had eaten.

Rose asked Mary to accompany her, but Mary declined, saying she wished to stay by a warm fire and intended not to waste time regarding her mortality by worrying over what could not be changed.

Rose did not think Mr. Staines had intended it that way in his sermon, but struggling with her cough this morning, she realised she should probably have done the same.

Yet Rose felt the need to be in the House of God as her spirits were lifted there, and her prayers seemed to prevent her from worrying about things she could not change and brought about a better resolution to any situation she may find herself in.

The service was indeed uplifting, and Rose enjoyed singing the hymns. Mr. Staines stood on the old oak pulpit looking down on his congregation, with the Spong family pews quite close to him.

Rose sometimes imagined he was speaking directly to her as he preached his sermons, but then remembered she was small and insignificant. It was fanciful of her to think she was important enough to be singled out. Rose had no qualms about attending church on her own as she usually met someone there to pass the time with as Aylesford and Mill Hall were not heavily populated, hence most of the congregation were neighbours and friends.

Rose arrived home to find the family were all in the drawing room, and she stayed with them until tea was served, during which time Mary and William talked about attending the Methodist chapel in Aylesford which was a notably different place of worship to St. Peter and St Paul's. Finding the speakers at the chapel always interesting, Rose decided to join them for what would be her third church visit of the day, and the sermon proved to be as beautiful as she had imagined.

On their return from Aylesford, Rose retired to her bedroom to read the bible. Contenting herself by reading a few pages, she closed it and put it down to write in her diary when her cough returned, making her chest hurt. As it became increasingly painful, she began to worry it may be more than the cold Mamma had suggested.

MONDAY, 12ᵀᴴ JANUARY
Plough Monday. Ploughing commenced in feudal times.

Mrs. Nash, Elizabeth, and George Nash came to dinner. Grand Mamma's birthday. Mr. and Mrs. Robson called around after dinner. XXX went into another situation.

Rose woke up feeling a little happier and calmer in her mind today; the visits to church yesterday seemed to have helped her greatly. A dinner party in honour of Grandmamma Spong's eighty-sixth birthday was held at Mill Hall today.

There were eighteen people at the table, which was quite a squeeze. Smiling at her grandmamma across the table, Rose hoped she too would achieve such a great age and remain as sprightly. Included in the gathering apart from Grandmamma and the immediate family were Mamma's stepmother Mrs. Nash and her two children, George, to whom Rose was particularly close, and Elizabeth, her half uncle and aunt, but as they were both younger than Rose and Mary, they seemed more like cousins.

Mr. and Mrs. Robson called after dinner to pay their respects. The drawing room was full of happy people who were all chattering away, making the atmosphere most lively. Then Mrs. Robson told Rose she had word of John, causing her to momentarily lose her breath and sit down. Mrs. Robson took Rose's hand and informed her that John had taken another position and was now employed by the London Waterboard. On hearing this news, Rose felt sad to think she had not received a letter from him, telling her directly of his intentions to change his employment. She could not understand why he had not written to her since his return to London, thinking she should have been the first person to be told due to their understanding. She made a vow to write a letter to him, enquiring if he was out of sorts with her in some way.

When the guests had departed, Mamma ordered tea to be served in the drawing room, after which Rose went upstairs to her bedroom. The cheerful mood she had enjoyed earlier in the day had now evaporated due to Mrs. Robson's news; also, her cough was becoming more and more tiresome, so she wanted to be alone.

When Mamma came up to see her a while later, Rose told

her of the worries she harboured about John, with Mamma suggesting all would come right in the end and that she should be patient. Rose was upset to think this did not come easy to her, knowing her life would be much happier if she could learn the art of patience.

Mary called in to see Rose before retiring to discuss today's happenings, and to tell her sister not to feel too sad about the news of John's position. 'It will only bring your engagement a little closer if he is in a more gainful employment,' she mused. Rose had not seen it that way and resolved to be more patient and trust that he would return whenever he was ready.

TUESDAY, 13TH JANUARY
Hilary, Bishop of Poictiers, 334. Cambridge Term begins.

Mrs. Hazell and Jane and Lucy Hazell called. Mary and I walked to Aylesford with the two latter. Henry's birthday. 13 today.

Mrs. Hazell came to visit today along with her two daughters, Jane and Lucy. Rose and Mary asked the two girls if they wished to accompany them on the walk to Aylesford they had planned as the day was quite a pleasant one for the time of year, although the morning frost still lingered, indicating warm clothes were still required. Jane and Lucy eagerly accepted the invitation thinking that it may be fun, so after wrapping up warm, the four girls set out.

Aylesford was a quiet village with little to see or do, but nevertheless it was considerably larger than Mill Hall, which amounted to a group of cottages, a larger house where Rose lived with her family, and the George public house, which was no place for young ladies to visit. The George was mainly frequented by Papa's labourers who worked at the rear of the house and were employed in running his businesses.

When the girls arrived in Aylesford, they gazed into all the shop windows in the hope of finding a present for Rose and Mary's brother Henry, who was celebrating his thirteenth birthday today. The girls chose a sweet little chess set which they decided would be perfect, and had it carefully wrapped.

Mary bought some pretty ribbons for her hair, which was dark and thick like her father's, in contrast to Rose's, which was fine and thin like her mamma's, causing hairpins to fall out constantly. Rose often longed to tie up her own hair in ribbons and bows so that it would stay in place like that of her sister.

Time went quickly as the four chatted away merrily, but being past noon, Mary thought it best to hurry back home as it would soon be time for dinner, so off they set post-haste to Mill Hall, with no dawdling this time.

When they arrived home, Mrs. Hazell was a little cross with her girls for staying out all morning, prompting Rose and Mary to apologise for not paying attention to the time.

Once the Hazell's had left, they all went into the dining room to enjoy a special dinner Cook had prepared in honour of Henry's birthday, after which gifts were handed to him by his assembled family, including the little chess set which he loved.

After dinner, the girls went into the gardens for a while, but soon the cold was affecting Rose's chest, causing her to cough once more, so a seat by the warm fire in the drawing room was sought. Mamma brought in a splendid cake for Henry at teatime, rounding off a rather pleasant day.

It was now almost bedtime, Rose's favourite time of day when she could sit quietly in her room and reflect on the days' events and then note them down in her diary. But the effort of doing so was making her eyes grow heavy with the need for sleep, so putting aside the pen, she retired to her bed.

WEDNESDAY, 14TH JANUARY
Oxford Term begins. Henry Mackenzie died, 1831.

Mary, I and William walked to Town Malling. Saw F.G., and W.G., but was not to speak to them until tea. They were in the laundry room with the boys.

Over breakfast this morning, Rose and Mary were discussing in which direction to go for a walk when William suggested Town Malling. 'A good idea, Will,' said Mary.

'As it is quite a distance from Mill Hall, we will have to make haste with our preparations to be home in time for dinner at one o'clock,' replied Rose. William at this point pleaded to join them, the girls only agreeing after he promised to stay alongside them and not wander off on his own. As soon as breakfast was over and all were suitably attired, they started off in the direction of Town Malling.

The girls always looked forward to visiting there as they considered it such a pretty town and enjoyed looking at the shops, which were seemingly more interesting than those Aylesford had to offer. Papa provided the sisters with a small allowance, enabling purchases to be made when out shopping. Rose bought some combs in the vain hope they would spend more time in her hair than they did on the floor.

Looking at all the shop displays had allowed time to slip through their fingers, so hastily they started the long walk home, hoping not to be late for dinner.

Fortunately, they arrived home just in time to enjoy a hearty vegetable soup with meaty chunks of fowl in a delicious warm broth, followed by Cook's special apple pudding smothered with cream, all greatly appreciated after a long walk in the cold air.

After such a substantial meal and feeling rather tired, Rose went to her bedroom for a rest, which she was having to do more frequently of late after going outside.

Having spent many hours during her life walking for miles without any ill effect, she was beginning to worry about what was recently causing her to feel so tired. Rose knew her sister would be displeased with her for letting herself fret about it and wished she could find a cure for this bad habit.

From her bedroom window Rose saw her brothers in the garden with Frederick and William Golding, who had called in the afternoon. Feeling a little refreshed she hurried downstairs when tea was announced, bumping into four mischievous looking boys as they burst from the laundry room of all places. Heaven knows what they had been up to in there, but boys will be boys, thought Rose. The guests stayed for tea, and she enjoyed their company for a little while.

Soon tiredness took its hold once more, and Rose went directly back upstairs after tea to read her book and write in her diary. Having read a little, and with the day's events duly recorded, she sat in her chair by the fire before retiring, feeling in rather low spirits as no letter had yet been received from John.

THURSDAY, 15TH JANUARY
Duke of Gloucester born.

Mary and I called on Mrs. Robson and Grand Mamma, Papa, George and John and William went to the jollification on the heath. They brought George Nash back to dinner here.

Although the morning was blustery, Rose and Mary had decided to visit Grandmamma in Aylesford despite the windy conditions, so sturdy hair pins were once again required. While walking towards the village, Mary began talking about her future and what it may hold. Rose replied, 'I am unsure about mine, as John has not yet written to me.' Mary reminded her of their previous conversation regarding John's newly found position keeping him busy.

'You told me you were going to be patient, Rosie,' she reprimanded.

'I know,' Rose sighed. 'But I cannot help but fret.' She then added to her tales of woe by confessing how worried she was about her cough. 'I have been afflicted with it for over two weeks now and fear it is becoming worse.' Possessing the calmest nature of the two, Mary reassured her it would pass in time, and her gentle approach soon had a soothing effect on her younger sister, raising her spirits once again.

Grandmamma was delighted to see them when they arrived at her home and seeing how cold they both looked, she immediately sent her maid to fetch tea and hot buttered scones to warm them. Mary and Rose came from a large family, so comprised just two of her grandchildren. What an amazing life she has had, thought Rose, wishing the same good fortune for herself.

As they left Grandmamma's they decided to visit Mrs. Robson

on their way home as she lived quite close by. Happy as ever to receive guests, particularly Mary and Rose, Mrs Robson ushered them both in and bade them take a seat by the hearth.

Mrs. Robson's house was one of the most frequently visited homes in all of Aylesford. She was an extremely kind lady who soon had everyone smiling. Well acquainted with most of the goings on in Aylesford society, she was held in high regard by friends and family alike. The morning passed quickly as she kept her two guests entertained with all the local gossip, supplemented by further cups of tea.

When the sisters finally arrived home, they found George Nash had come to join the family for dinner. He and Papa had been to the jollifications on Barnham Heath, which happened to be a gentleman's drinking festival, accompanied by brothers John, George, and William. All returned home in an extremely happy mood, so the day's dinner was a most jolly affair indeed.

The afternoon was spent in the drawing room playing with the little ones by the fire on a cold January day.

After tea, Rose went up to her bedroom to read and afterwards write in her diary, thinking it had been a most pleasant day.

FRIDAY, 16ᵀᴴ JANUARY
Battle of Corunna, 1809.

A very dull day. Went nowhere all day. In the afternoon I sat in my bedroom and read Hannah More.

Nothing of any consequence happened today, no visitors were received, and the weather was most unpleasant with heavy rain and blustery winds.

Cold draughts coming through the window frames had everyone competing for a spot nearest the fire and the children were extremely restless, especially the boys who, more so than most, did not like being confined to the house. Because of the downpour, Mamma would not let them out into the gardens despite their pleadings and whining. It all made for a long and tiresome morning.

After dinner, Rose left the family to their squabbles and went to her bedroom to enjoy some peace and quiet by sitting next to the fire and immersing herself in a book. With it being such a dark and dismal day, the maid had lit the candles due to the lack of daylight which added to the sense of cosiness, and she felt thankful to be alone in her bedroom.

All would have seemed so satisfactory had it not been for her cough which was becoming more troublesome and making her feel unwell. The book she was reading served to distract her from this irritation to some degree as it was written by Hannah More, one of her favourite authors.

When tea was called, Rose joined the family again in the drawing room and stayed with them until the time came to retire. When bedtime beckoned, Rose made her way upstairs to write a little before Mamma brought her hot milk. With little to record as it had been a rather dull day, she closed her diary and blew out the candles.

SATURDAY, 17ᵀᴴ JANUARY
Dr. Horne, bishop of Norwich, died, 1792.

Mr. Robson called in the morning. Mamma sent Mrs. Robson some relish. I went in the garden after dinner. Rather busy after tea.

A much better day than yesterday; the rain had ceased, the sun was shining, and Rose was feeling altogether a little better in herself. Mr. Robson called in the morning and drank tea with the ladies in the drawing room. He stayed for an hour or so and as he was about to leave, Mamma asked him to wait as she had something for him. Disappearing into the kitchen, she returned holding a jar of her homemade relish.

'Would you please give this to Mary,' she said, 'as I know she is quite partial to it served with cheese.' He thanked her and replied that he also found it most delicious, and after bidding them all farewell, he left. Mr. Robson was considered a true gentleman and an old family friend who was always especially kind to the children.

After dinner, Rose ventured into the walled garden, which she preferred to the larger, more open garden set out with lawns as it offered more privacy with little paths to meander down while admiring the beautiful flowers throughout the seasons.

At the end of the walled garden was a bench where Rose liked to sit and read. Although well wrapped, and despite the winter sunshine, she felt quite cold and chilled through, so the thought of her warm bedroom soon had her scurrying back indoors.

As comfortable and warm as it was inside the house compared to the bitterly cold wind outside, she soon became bored of her own company and went in search of a distraction, whereupon she found tea was being served in the drawing room. 'There you are, Rosie,' said Mamma. 'I was just about to send Mary to fetch you.'

A pleasant family evening was spent together, and once the younger children had retired to their respective beds it was not as noisy. Mamma informed Mary and Rose that the county elections were to be held in Maidstone on Monday next and asked if they wished to attend the proceedings.

Delighted at the opportunity to go, they were both happy to agree. Mamma then advised them to go straight upstairs and prepare themselves, as they would not be able to do so tomorrow, it being the Lord's Day.

The girls hurried excitedly upstairs to decide what to wear. At last, something to look forward to, thought Rose, although this caused a problem in terms of which dress to choose. Always so indecisive in such matters, she soon had her bed covered in various rejections. 'Vanity is not a good quality to have' – Mr. Staines' frequent quote during his sermons came to Rose's mind, as she confessed to being far more interested in her own appearance than she ought to be.

Eventually she chose a lovely fine wool dress in a flattering pale grey that not only seemed to suit her complexion well but would also serve to keep her warm. Her chosen dress, together with a heavy cloak and bonnet, made Rose feel satisfied she would be suitably attired to withstand the cold.

By the time she had returned the rejected garments to where they belonged Rose was feeling rather tired, so she climbed into bed to dream about their trip to Maidstone on Monday.

SUNDAY, 18TH JANUARY
Prisca, an unmarried lady of Rome, martyred, 276.

Went to church this morning and afternoon. Mary stayed at home in the morning after we called on Mrs. Robson to enquire after Mr. Jones. They have received a letter that morning to say that he was much better. No one went to chapel.

Rose walked to church this morning with five of her brothers. Elizabeth and little Grace stayed at home in the care of Mary who preferred to stay at home rather than attend church today, with Mamma and Papa taking the younger boys in the coach. The family loved their church, Rose in particular admired Mr. Staines standing tall in his pulpit, encouraging them all to be better people through their love for the Lord. It stirred her greatly and inspired her to try her utmost to be good and kind and not vain and fanciful.

When sitting in the church she sometimes imagined that being a vicar must be a wonderful profession. She thought that had she been born a boy, she would have taken the vows and then her life would have been entirely different, but the only path set out for her as she saw it would be marriage and children.

Although perfectly happy with the latter situation, she was beginning to fear that because her future with John seemed to be very much in question, with two weeks passing and still no correspondence whatsoever, she may become an elderly maiden aunt.

The only possible reason for his silence that Rose could think of was that his affection for her had grown cold. Perhaps his new position had led him to another young lady who was enjoying his attentions instead. Following the advice of the vicar regarding when your heart rules your mind was something Rose was finding rather difficult.

After the service was over, the family called on the Robsons before dinner to enquire after Mr. Jones and were informed that a letter had been received the previous morning from London, which assured them he was making a slow but sure recovery. This was excellent news, especially for John, thought Rose, as perhaps his father's illness had been a reason for his silence, and now he was recovering John may find his mind less troubled, enabling him to find the time to write. Joyful news indeed.

On the way back to Mill Hall, Mamma took three of the brothers home in the coach, leaving Henry and William to walk home with Rose, a situation she found quite vexing as they dawdled all the way, throwing sticks into the river. She was most relieved when they finally arrived home.

After dinner Rose and Mary went to the afternoon service without the distracting company of the children, allowing Rose an opportunity to chat to her sister on the way back about whatever possible reasons there could be for John's lack of communication.

Mary's comforting words and reassurances on their return journey home helped Rose to feel more positive, but due to a persistent cough she also felt extremely tired.

Thinking it was the extra journey that had caused her cough to resume, she laid on her bed for a while in the afternoon to rest and fell into a deep sleep.

When she awoke the only light came from the flickering of the fire in the hearth. Feeling slightly disorientated and having no idea of the time, or even if she had missed tea, Mary came in and gently nudged her to see if she was awake. 'Tea is being served,' she whispered. 'Gather yourself to come and join us.' Stretching her arms out wide and still feeling sleepy, she dragged herself to her feet. Mary lit the candles and together both went down to join the family in the drawing room.

With no one feeling it necessary to go the Methodist chapel they all remained in the drawing room.

It wasn't long before Rose's eyes were growing heavy again, so wishing everyone goodnight she returned to the comfort of her bedcovers, excitedly looking forward to the county elections tomorrow and hoping her sleep would not be broken with coughing, as they were to depart for Maidstone bright and early in the morning. Putting down her diary, she retired to bed.

MONDAY, 19TH JANUARY
The sun enters Aquarius, the watercarrier.

Mamma, Mary and I and Frederick went to Maidstone to see the county elections. We had a nice room at the Mitre. I saw Frederick Burgess. Mr. Robson went to Norfolk to vote.

Breakfast was had by candlelight this morning as an early departure time of eight a.m. was required in order to journey to Maidstone to witness the county elections. Because the winter months could be insufferably long and boring, confined to the house due to the weather for days on end, Rose was really looking forward to this excursion and having something interesting to do.

All wrapped up in heavy woollen cloaks to keep out the extremely cold and windy conditions prevailing today, Mamma, Mary, Rose, and Frederick waited inside the front door while Wood brought the coach to the front of the house to collect them, leaving the maid and Cook at home in charge of the younger ones. Once everyone was safely in the coach, Wood started the horses for the journey to Maidstone.

Papa had reserved a comfortable room at The Mitre Hotel so they could all watch events unfold from the window while enjoying the warmth, but they soon went outside to join the throng in the main square. Rose found it rather exciting to see so many different faces, although the crowds of townsfolk prevented her from seeing much of the proceedings. As the atmosphere was a merry one, she didn't mind too much, but she did manage to catch a glimpse of Frederick Burgess, one of the candidates for Maidstone County.

All in all, it was a most enjoyable day, with a hotel meal of buttery roast turkey and crisp duchesse potatoes. After the meal Mamma allowed Mary, Frederick, and Rose to visit the local shops nearby, while she stayed with Papa who had come to join them.

When the time came to travel homewards, they all climbed into the coach feeling tired but happy. Rose was grateful for the hearty meal enjoyed earlier at the Mitre, as it seemed to be keeping her warm on the cold and dark journey home.

It was almost seven o'clock when their coach arrived back at Mill Hall, and everyone was happy to see a warm and welcoming fire. Cook served tea and hot muffins, and they all agreed it had been a most wonderful day. Staying in the drawing room for a while chatting about their adventures, it was soon time to make their way to bed.

As Rose sat by the bedroom fire wearing her robe, remembering all the enjoyable things that had occurred today, her mood was uplifted. It occurred to Rose that making her days busier was preventing her brooding over her woes so much. Unfortunately, however, she was beginning to think that the more she tired, the more troublesome her cough was becoming. She also suspected the cold air was a reason for its persistence. With the rain pouring hard against the window and the wind causing it to rattle, she decided to retire, thinking it would not be possible to venture out tomorrow. However, as it was Mary's birthday, it would surely be a good day regardless of the weather.

Rosamond

20th January to 3rd February

TUESDAY, 20ᵀᴴ JANUARY
Fabian, bishop of Rome, put to death, 250.

Mary's birthday, 23 today. We went nowhere all day. Mr. Summerfield called after dinner. He would not stay for tea. The land water was very high.

As predicted, the heavy rain did indeed keep everyone indoors today. The River Medway at the rear of the house was alarmingly high this morning, and the fields were flooded. Mary was hoping to see an end to the incessant rain as it may deter any callers wishing to visit on her 23rd birthday. 'I do hope the rain will soon stop, or we will have to build a boat, or even an Ark like Noah's,' she said to Mamma.

Mamma and cook prepared a special dinner in her honour: a rich cream of vegetable soup followed by baked salmon with sauce hollandaise, and lashings of marbled jelly to follow. Everyone was full to bursting after the meal, and a happy time was shared by all.

After dinner Mr. Summerfield called, having decided to brave the inclement weather in order to wish Mary a happy birthday. Rose was glad of the distraction as the children were growing increasingly restless due to being kept indoors. The weather started to worsen, and the sound of thundering rain against the windows was quite alarming. The deluge causing the river to rise even higher made Mr. Summerfield declare he ought to leave sooner rather than later as his horses did not like venturing into water and he feared his chaise may get stuck in the lane, causing him to abandon it and wade through. Mamma invited him to stay for tea in the hope it may begin to subside, but he decided on the most sensible option of going before things got even worse.

Following Mr. Summerfield's departure into the storm, Rose retired to her room for a while until Mary came up and invited her to join the family in the drawing room for tea and birthday cake. Even though she felt tired, she had no wish to disappoint her sister by refusing her request on her birthday. The cake looked wonderful and tasted delicious, with icing and little pink flowers decorating the top.

Now back in her bedroom and with her cough no better, Rose felt a little feverish, but despite poor weather and the persistent cough, her day had been a most enjoyable one. As she fashioned her hair into pigtails to avoid the inevitable tangling during sleep, she thought it a most arduous task to endure every night, and that men were so lucky not to have the bother.

WEDNESDAY, 21ST JANUARY
Agnes, an early devotee to Christianity, Louis XVI, beheaded, 1793.

Mary and I took Grace to Aylesford to see her God Mamma, Mrs. Robson. Afterwards we called on Mrs. Peppercorn. She was out. I was very poorly in the evening. Papa came home.

After breakfast Rose and Mary walked to Aylesford with little sister Grace to visit her god mamma Mrs. Robson. The ground was quite wet underfoot due to yesterday's flooding, but the girls were relieved to see the rain had ceased at last.

During the walk Rose found herself becoming a little breathless, which was happening more often of late and had the effect of slowing her down. This was not what she was used to, as she was usually the first to go on long walks without feeling tired. Although quite alarmed at this situation, it was still pleasing to be out in the fresh air, although Rose was grateful for a rest when they arrived at Mrs. Robson's house, with a refreshing cup of tea in her hands. When the time came to leave, Rose felt sufficiently restored to continue.

Mary suggested taking Grace to Mrs. Peppercorn's to see her animals, so off they set towards the farm just outside Aylesford. Grace, excited at the prospect and fully recovered from her bad cold, gaily skipped along between her two big sisters. Along the way Rose wished to herself that she would recover from whatever was ailing her, as it was getting worse, causing her to become breathless again as they continued their walk.

Eventually arriving at their destination, they were disappointed to find Mrs. Peppercorn was not at home. Ushering them into the parlour, her maid bade them take a seat and said, 'I will bring some tea for you before your return home.' Mr. Peppercorn, however, had seen their arrival from the meadow and went to greet them. He asked Grace if she would like to feed the chickens with him.

'Oh yes please,' she replied, jumping up and down with excitement. Mary accompanied them to the barn while Rose stayed in the parlour, needing to take a rest. With the chickens fed, Mary and Grace returned to the parlour. It was time to start the long walk home.

On the journey back Grace was full of chatter about what she had seen and done which gave Rose a glow of satisfaction at having taken her to see the animals. Even though the walk was much harder than usual, it felt good to see Grace's little face light up, which always made her smile.

On arriving back home for dinner, an account of their adventures was given to Mamma. When Mary told her Rose had not been feeling well, Mamma insisted on Rose going straight to her bedroom after they had dined to recuperate, asking if she should send for Mr. Trested on this occasion. Rose replied, 'No, Mamma. I am just a little weary after the walk home from the Peppercorns.'

Once she was in her bedroom, she laid on the bed and fell asleep, eventually waking to realise how dark it had become. This was becoming a regular habit, and one she was finding quite a worry. Mamma came up to see her, only to be told she was still feeling poorly and wished to stay in her room, so Mamma lit the candles and told Rose the maid would be sent up with a tray as it was now time for tea, and also that Papa had arrived home. The tray was brought and placed on Rose's little table which she both wrote and took meals on. Finding she had little appetite, most of the food was left on the tray.

Feeling quite feverish as well as cold and shivery, she had just changed into her night attire and warm dressing robe to sit by the fire and write about the day's events in her diary when Papa knocked on her door and entered to bid her goodnight. He wished her a speedy recovery from whatever was affecting her chest and brought a warm and welcome drink of milk to help her sleep, placing it on her table before removing the tea things. Rose hoped the warm milk would ease her chest, as she was becoming increasingly frightened by the persistent cough which was causing her to have worrying thoughts about her health and, in turn, making it difficult to sleep. As soon as the day was recorded, she drew the bed curtains to keep out the cold draughts and retired.

THURSDAY, 22ND JANUARY
Vincent, a Spanish deacon, who was cruelly martyred.

Much better today, went nowhere all day. In the afternoon I finished the first volume of Hannah More.

Rose thought herself foolish to have walked so far yesterday, as it left her feeling rather poorly last night. She was pleasantly surprised, however, to discover she was much improved on waking. Mamma impressed upon her how important it was to stay indoors today, and she gladly agreed. Grace wanted Rose to play with her this morning in the nursery and enjoy some games when breakfast was finished. Rose was always so happy to play with her dear little sister, but she had to confess that it could be exhausting. Nevertheless, Rose stayed with her all morning until the gong rang for dinner. After a very pleasant meal with the family, Rose found it necessary to retire to her bedroom, feeling tired after a busy morning with little Grace.

Sitting in the chair by her window, she watched Mary playing with the boys in the lawned garden, at the bottom of which were some trees the boys loved to climb. As the day was cold, Rose decided to lay on her bed and continue reading her current Hannah More book, an author who wrote about various subjects. Today, she was reading the first of one of her trilogies entitled 'Practical Piety'. It explained how to keep faith in God throughout our lives, which Rose somehow managed to finish in the afternoon. Hannah More was considered by her to be an inspirational and spiritual writer who also happened to write wonderful poetry.

The family home sat by the river Medway, at the rear of which

Papa conducted his businesses on the two wharfs. Amongst other things he was a coal merchant, with his many barges going up and down the river, landing coal to be stored in the sheds at the side of the house prior to delivery elsewhere. It could be quite noisy at times, so Rose was relieved that her bedroom was situated at the front where she was able to enjoy the view across the lane into their gardens.

As the afternoon light gave way to darkness, the maid entered her room and lit the candles, also making sure her fire was not in need of coal. Mamma knocked on her door to ask how she felt about joining the family for tea, so Rose, now feeling a little better and wanting company, followed her downstairs.

Tea was being served in the cosy surroundings of the drawing room; a more comfortable place than the dining room, thought Rose. After spending a pleasant evening with her family, she returned upstairs and sat by the fire to write in her diary, hoping she would continue to improve tomorrow.

FRIDAY, 23RD JANUARY
Rt. Hon. W. Pitt died, 1806. Duke of Kent died, 1820.

Stayed at home all day. I saw FG & WG. I did not speak to them. They went into a warehouse to see John who was building a boat. I read Hannah More in the afternoon.

Another day spent indoors as the weather was still very cold and windy. The winter months were not Rose's favourite time of year, as she enjoyed walking in fresh air. With just one week to go it would soon be the end of January, which had been such a long and difficult month for her to endure.

Frederick and William Golding called this morning to see John, who was now nineteen and the same age as Frederick, and all had been good friends since they were small boys. John was building a boat in one of Papa's warehouses and the boys were interested to see how it was progressing. Rose heard them arriving, but, reluctant to leave the warmth of the drawing room to greet them, she left them to enjoy their own company.

Rose and Mary stayed by the fire most of the morning and had a long discussion. Rose confided in her sister about her feelings towards John, saying, 'My illness has distracted me from fretting over him temporarily, but I remain worried as to why he has not written to me yet. It has now been three weeks since his return to London.' As usual Mary tried to reassure her that all would be well but, in her heart, Rose believed it would not be so.

They reluctantly left the warmth of the drawing room fire when dinner was announced, knowing how much colder the dining room would be. Icy northerly winds were making it particularly cold today with draughts coming from the windows and whistling down the chimney. How Rose longed for spring – it seemed so far away.

Spending the afternoon reading the second volume of Hannah More in her bedroom, she was happy to learn that when tea was announced, it was to be served in the drawing room. When their bedtime came, Mamma took the smallest children first, following which it was the turn of Seppy and Octavius, with the older boys making their own way when tired. Mamma always visited everyone to say goodnight, which was a lengthy procedure as there were so many of them.

Mamma worked extremely hard, and with just a cook and a housemaid to do the chores she was always tired. Rose and Mary helped as much as they could with the younger children, usually by keeping them amused and taking them out when the weather allowed them to do so.

Rose was in her bedroom by the fire, writing in her diary and looking forward to getting into bed as the maid had just put a warming pan in the bed for her.

Mamma would be coming up soon with a bedtime drink to help her fall asleep and say goodnight. Before she did, Rose lay there with a sense of relief that her cough had eased a little today, giving hope that her former health would be restored, and she prayed she would soon recover from whatever had been afflicting her.

SATURDAY, 24ᵀᴴ JANUARY
Several Directors of the South Sea Bubble ordered into custody of the Serjeant at Arms, 1721.

Mamma called on Mrs. Staines in the morning. After dinner Octavius and Augustus went to Aylesford for a walk. Rather dull.

Rose spent a pleasant morning playing with Grace and Octavius while Mamma visited Mrs. Staines, the vicar's wife, leaving Mary with the younger children and baby Elizabeth.

Spending time with the little ones was something Rose enjoyed doing as it was usually so much fun. Unfortunately, today it was freezing outside with ice on the ground, so they had to remain indoors. Mamma suggested it may snow later, and the older boys hoped she was right. Rose, however, did not and tried to avoid venturing out when it was snowing as she found the hem of her dress getting wet an unpleasant experience, which was never a concern for the boys who were unaware of how fortunate they are.

Seppy and Augustus had their usual lessons at home to prepare for their schooling in Sevenoaks, where Freddy, Henry, William, and Edward were being taught. Once their studies were completed, they simply disappeared. Just where do they go? mused Rose. With so many boys in their family, fights and squabbles were a regular event. A quiet household it certainly was not.

After dinner, some of the family were sitting in the drawing room, when Mary, after looking out of the window to observe the situation with the weather, said to her sister, 'Shall we brave the cold and go for a walk, it is so dull staying inside the house all day.' As the ground was crisp with no flurries of snow so far, Rose readily agreed. Octavius and Augustus, who were listening to their conversation, asked if they could accompany them, as they too were feeling restless. Mary approved straight away but Rose was not so eager, knowing they would dally and hold them up. 'Please, Rosie,' they both cried, so she agreed on the condition they were not to keep running off.

Once outside they questioned the wisdom of braving such cold weather, as fingers and toes soon became quite numb as they walked along, despite their gloves and boots.

On arriving at the old bridge, the boys wanted to play, climbing up and throwing stones into the icy water. After enduring this for what seemed like an age, the girls started stamping their feet in a vain attempt to warm them up, eventually telling the boys it was time to go home.

Rose and Mary removed their boots in the hallway the minute they arrived home, then hurried to their bedrooms to sit by the fire and warm their toes. Rose was sorry to find her cough had returned, probably as a result of the freezing cold, so she decided to stay in her room until teatime.

After writing a few letters in her own room, Mary called in to see Rose to inform her it was time for tea, and they both went downstairs together. It had been a very dull afternoon, with the evening no great improvement and no one wanting to play games of any sort. Rose returned to her bedroom to write in the diary, feeling in low spirits once again and worrying about her future.

SUNDAY, 25TH JANUARY
Conversion of St. Paul.

Went to church in the morning and we all stayed at home in the afternoon. Papa went to London by the 3 o'clock stage. Mamma, Mary, George, and I went to chapel. Heard Mr. Bruton speak.

Sunday today, Rose's favourite day of the week. Mary, Octavius, and Mamma accompanied her to church in the coach in the morning as it was still quite icy underfoot and slippery to walk on, but Papa and the boys were all able to walk. Grace, being only three, could not sit still and remain quiet for long, so she was left at home in the maid's charge.

Rose, as usual, thought Mr. Staines gave a most interesting and informative sermon, and how wise he appeared to be. It was exceptionally cold in church, so all were grateful for the hot dinner awaiting them when they arrived back home.

No one was inclined to return to church for the afternoon service, as it was just too tempting to stay at home by the warm fire, thawing out from this morning's visit. They were all sorry for poor Papa though, who had to go out in the cold again to catch the three o'clock stagecoach to London.

Rose spent the afternoon reading a book, with Mary busy embroidering. Her work was beautiful, unlike her sister's – every time Rose picked up a needle, she managed to prick her finger.

She preferred drawing instead, though mainly as a summer pastime when the pretty wildflowers were out and the roses in the walled garden were at their best. As she looked out of her window on this dark and frosty day, she thought that when the summer, which seemed such a long way off, did finally arrive, she must fill every day with joyful things.

At the tea table, Mamma asked if anyone wished to accompany her to the Methodist chapel. Mary said she would like to go, as did Rose and George.

When the party arrived at the Chapel, Rose was pleased to find the speaker was Mr. Bruton whose sermons she always enjoyed, and tonight's was no exception.

It was dark and the ground quite slippery when they left the chapel, making it necessary for everyone to hold hands while walking down the path to avoid falling on the ice. It was a relief to see Wood standing there with the coach.

As soon as they arrived back at Mill Hall, Rose went directly to her bedroom to write in her diary, feeling a little unwell and coughing a great deal.

MONDAY, 26TH JANUARY
Dr. Jenner died, 1823. Holiday.

Mary, I and Grace went to Maidstone. I called on Mrs. Day, Emily and Martha Brenchley. We also called on aunt Brenchley of Albion Place.

There had been a slight thaw this morning and it was not quite as cold, so Mary suggested taking an excursion to Maidstone, if Rose was agreeable. She was more than happy with the idea, and Mamma asked if they could take Grace with them.

It would be a pleasure, they replied. Grace jumped up and down with delight at the thought of going out in the coach with her two big sisters. Making sure she was well wrapped in warm clothing by Mamma, they set off for Maidstone with Grace excitedly looking out of the coach window as it travelled along the country lanes.

The fields which had been covered in water a few days ago were now frozen over. The snow Mamma had forecast never materialised but may yet happen as spring was still some way off, so there was plenty of time for a heavy snowfall before then.

The girls were looking forward to visiting Maidstone, which was a much larger town than Aylesford and therefore had a greater number of shops, many of which displayed the very latest fashions and as many pretty accessories as you could ever wish to see. The first thing they planned to do on arriving was to go directly to Mrs. Day's house for morning tea, and when that social call had concluded, they left Wood with her groom in the Coach House and walked to the High Street.

Looking round the shops was so much fun; they made a few purchases of ribbons and sewing threads for Mary, books and writing materials for Rose, and a little doll for Grace.

After an hour or so with Grace beginning to tire, Rose suggested calling on cousins Emily and Martha Brenchley who lived nearby for rest and refreshment. After exchanging news and with Grace rested, they said goodbye to their cousins and left to pay their next visit, this time to Aunt Brenchley at number 10 Albion Place. It was getting rather late after all this social activity, so a dash back to Mrs. Day's house where Wood was waiting for them was necessary. The movement of the coach and the rhythm of the horse's hooves soon made Grace fall fast asleep between her two big sisters on the return to Mill Hall.

Arriving back home just in time for dinner, at the table the travellers recounted all their experiences on the excursion to Mamma, also passing on the good wishes sent from Mrs. Day and Aunt Brenchley. It had been a most enjoyable but tiring outing for the three sisters, particularly Rose and little Grace. After dinner Rose went up to her room, laid on the bed, and, inevitably, soon fell fast asleep.

While she was sleeping, the maid quietly entered to light her candles and attend the fire, which was blazing merrily away when Rose eventually awoke. Not only was she surprised at not hearing the maid go about her duties, but she had also managed to sleep until dark yet again.

With teatime now approaching, Rose got up to revive herself by splashing her face with cold water from the jug and bowl on the washstand, hoping to feel more awake before going downstairs to join the family. Happy to see tea was being served in the drawing room again, she stayed with the family and spent the remainder of the evening conversing with them. One of the subjects mentioned was Papa having to travel home from London in the bitterly cold weather, but Mamma hoped he would return tomorrow.

TUESDAY, 27TH JANUARY
Duke of Sussex's Birthday.

Papa came home from London. Mary and I went to Aylesford to see Grandmamma.

Hopefully, with January soon at an end and spring not too far away, the meadows would eventually be bursting with wildflowers, but Rose fully expected to endure a lot more unpleasant weather before then.

At breakfast, Mary suggested to her sister the possibility of a gentle walk to visit Grandmamma in Aylesford. As the morning air was quite pleasant with a hint of sunshine she agreed, hoping that the milder fresh air would be good for her lungs which had troubled her greatly for many weeks now.

Setting off to enjoy their walk when suitably attired, they chattered away merrily along the way. As they crossed over the medieval bridge into Aylesford, Rose suggested visiting the churchyard before calling on Grandmamma, to pay their respects to Grandpapa who died when she was only a year old. With no memory of him but having heard so many stories of his deeds and achievements, she felt he had always been a part of her life.

Grandpapa was buried in the Spong family vault which was just inside the church gate and surrounded by an iron railing underneath the ancient Yew tree. Nearby and closer to the church with their own memorials lay four tiny infants who were lost to him and Grandmamma. It must have been terribly sad for them to lose so many little ones. If I am ever blessed with children, Rose thought, I hope God will not take them away from me.

Once their prayers had been said, they went to call on Grandmamma who was surprised and delighted to see them. 'Sit down, girls, and make yourselves comfortable, I will send for a pot of tea to warm you both.' When told about the respects they had paid to Grandpapa and the babies they had lost, she exclaimed, 'Oh, you are good girls, your mother must be very proud of you.'

With the pot of tea having arrived and been duly poured, she told them all the news of who had called, and whom she had called upon in return to share the local gossip. A truly active and busy lady considering her age of eighty-six – quite remarkable, thought Rose. After enjoying their morning with her, which passed all too quickly, they said goodbye and set off to Mill Hall for dinner.

The girls arrived back home to find Papa had returned from London. Even though they saw little of him during the day, as he was either in his study or on the wharf attending to his business, it was good to see him at home safely returned from his travels at dinnertime.

After dinner, as the afternoon was quite pleasant, Rose played with Grace and Octavius in the garden. The children just loved running around on the grass playing ball games.

When Mary joined in the fun, Rose felt good to be out in the fresh air with them all and seemed more like her old self again. She began to hope for a full recovery from the lung complaint she had suffered for most of January. When Mamma came to take charge of the children, Rose went up to her bedroom and read until tea was ready. After tea, with her happy mood continuing, she stayed in the drawing room playing cards with William. It had been a very encouraging day for her; if only word could be had from John, she would feel so much happier.

WEDNESDAY, 28TH JANUARY
Admiral Byng tried and condemned at Portsmouth, 1757.

Mary and I went to Aylesford directly after breakfast and called on Mrs. Robson. Papa went to 7Oaks. I read Hannah More in the afternoon.

Once again, the cold weather was back, so Mary and Rose needed to wrap up warm for their walk to Aylesford this morning. 'At least it is not raining,' said Rose as they walked along by the river. On arriving in the village, they decided to call on Mrs. Robson who made them most welcome. Having no children of her own, she delighted in receiving visitors and enjoyed the company of others. Rose found it sad that Mr. and Mrs. Robson were unable to have a family and, probably as a welcome diversion, spent a great deal of their time helping others with their problems. Their house seemed to have more callers than most and was privy to all the latest gossip and goings on in the village, which always made for an interesting visit. Being Mamma's dearest friend, Mrs. Robson was chosen to be Grace's god mamma, a position she took most seriously and was always so kind and generous to them all, particularly Grace whom she adored.

Having realised the time after chatting for an hour or so with the morning all but passed, they said their fond farewells and departed for home. Hurrying back along the path by the river to avoid being late, they arrived in plenty of time for dinner.

After the meal, Rose and Mary went to warm themselves by the fire in the drawing room. Eventually they were joined by Seppy, Octavius, and Augustus, all of whom wanted a place by the fire after playing in the garden and getting chilled through. It was hard to believe how mild and sunny it had been only yesterday.

Because Rose was beginning to feel unwell again today with her cough returning, it occurred to her that the cold weather may be affecting her chest, as she hardly coughed at all yesterday when the air was so mild. These thoughts gave her hope that she would surely return to good health when spring arrived. Mamma suggested she should go to her room to rest, so Rose made her way wearily upstairs. Papa called in to see her before going to Sevenoaks to say he would be home in time for tea.

Finding her bedroom so cosy, Rose laid on the bed and settled down to continue reading Hannah More.

After a while Mamma went to see if she was feeling any better. Rose replied she was, and with her cough subsiding somewhat, hoped to join the family for tea. Although Rose usually found it peaceful and calming to read and enjoy her own company for a while, she would soon need to find someone to talk to. However, today was not one of those days as her mood was a little low, and she wished to be alone with her thoughts.

When tea was being served in the drawing room, Mary went to tell Rose and they went down together. While sitting with the family and chatting after tea about the visit to Mrs. Robson's this morning, Rose began to feel unwell again, so Mamma helped her upstairs and to prepare for bed.

Sitting by the fire and wrapped in her warm dressing robe with cosy slippers on her feet, she thought she should be happy living in a nice home with a loving family around her when so many do not enjoy the privileges that she had. But the truth was all she could think about was what would become of her, and what would her future be? Eventually, after a few tears, she closed her eyes and fell fast asleep.

THURSDAY, 29TH JANUARY
King George III. died, 1820. First meeting of the Reformed Parliament, 1833.

Stayed at home all day. Mary went for a walk by herself. Mrs. Peppercorn called. A beautiful day. Mr. Robson came home.

Rose slept reasonably well last night considering her preoccupations about her future and went downstairs for breakfast. Mary asked her if she felt well enough to go for a walk around Mill Hall as the weather was quite springlike this morning. She was inclined to go, but still felt a little poorly and with her cough still troubling her, she decided to stay at home. Reluctantly, Mary put on her coat and went on her own.

She had only been gone a few minutes when Mrs. Peppercorn called. Mamma and Rose entertained her in the drawing room and served tea, so a very pleasant hour was spent chatting and learning about all the doings of farm life, and how sorry she was to have missed Mary, Rose, and Grace's visit last week. Mrs. Peppercorn also informed them that Mr. Robson had returned from his visit to Mr. and Mrs. Jones in London, something she had just learnt from her earlier call on the Robsons, so the news was fresh this morning.

Shortly after Mrs. Peppercorn's departure, Mary returned with her news. Apparently, the snowdrops were now flowering beneath the trees, and she had picked a bunch for Mamma. They looked so pretty on the dining table for all to enjoy while dinner was served.

When dinner was concluded, Rose went upstairs for a rest. After reclining on her bed with her eyes closed for a while, she read some of the short stories in her little diary which she found most interesting.

One was particularly funny; it was a story about a Marquis whose cabriolet broke its shaft after his horse had reared up when a stray donkey crossed its path. As it was pouring with rain, he had no choice but to stop a local omnibus that happened to be passing.

The Marquis, being a haughty man, was horrified to think that he may have to continue his journey sitting alongside the type of ordinary people he had never had to mix with in all his life.

When he stepped into the omnibus the coach jerked suddenly, sending the Marquis sprawling across the lap of the fattest woman ever seen outside of a caravan at a fair. She was, unfortunately for him, carrying a jar of pickled onions on her knee which was upset by his tumble, saturating the front of his waistcoat with its fragrant juice. Suffice it to say, the poor Marquis was stuck between various characters the like of which he had never encountered before, plus a basket of live hens that were constantly escaping.

As they rolled along, they picked up more passengers and soon there were rabbits sitting beside the hens. Upon arriving in Piccadilly, the omnibus stopped abruptly, causing it to crash, thereby scattering all its occupants on to the ground. The poor Marquis lost his hat, and instead was wearing a fine bantam cock upon his head complemented by a hen on each shoulder. His humiliation was complete when his contemporaries, who happened to be waiting outside the bank, witnessed his sorry state, thereby prompting his fall from a position of high regard. This is perhaps a reminder to us all that it is unwise to think too highly of oneself. With so many more amusing events in the story, the reading of it had Rose laughing heartily, lifting her spirits.

Mary called into her room to be told of this amusing story, which she resolved to read for herself. They went down to tea together and as Rose's cough was a little better, her mood was much lifted.

She remained in the drawing room for the evening and played cards with Mary and William.

FRIDAY, 30TH JANUARY
King Charles I. martyred, 1649. Holiday.

Mary and I went to Aylesford, called on Mrs. Robson. Mary received a pencil from Mr. Rixon that Mr. Robson brought down from London. I read Hannah More in the afternoon in my bedroom.

Mary suggested a walk this morning as the weather was still dry, albeit somewhat cooler than yesterday. 'Some fresh air is all you require to bring some colour back to your cheeks,' she said to Rose. Wrapping up warmly, they set off for Aylesford and enjoyed a pleasant walk, stopping at the spot where Mary had found the snowdrops she picked.

Rose declared, 'They are so beautiful, and their little white flowers are the first sign that spring is on its way.'

The first thing to do when arriving in Aylesford was to visit the shops. With that soon done, as there were only a few, Mary suggested calling on Mrs. Robson who lived on the high street. Knocking on her door promptly brought an answer from the maid, who ushered them into the drawing room where Mrs. Robson was sitting taking tea.

Jumping up to greet them with arms outstretched, she said, 'How good it is to see you girls. I have something for you, Mary,' and went to fetch whatever it was. The girls were most intrigued by this and on her return, she was holding a small parcel in her hand, which she said Mr. Robson had brought back from London.

He had been entrusted to give it to Mary by Henry Rixon. 'I was going to bring it to you the next time I called, but now you are here it will save me the journey.' Mary delightedly opened the parcel to discover a very pretty Mother of Pearl covered propelling pencil. She would be sure to write and thank him straight after dinner, no doubt using her new pencil.

They stayed for a while, taking tea and discussing the weather. As usual, time passes quickly when you are thus occupied so, saying their goodbyes, they hurried away home for dinner.

After dinner, with the tiredness affecting her once more, Rose went up to her bedroom for a rest. Finding her mind troubled again while sitting in front of the fire, she stared into the flames.

She was deeply concerned that whatever ailed her may become a threat to her health, and she was also finding it difficult not to worry about John. She then considered writing to him, but her pride prevented her from doing so. With her mind in such turmoil, she remembered her sister's advice and tried to occupy herself by concentrating on something positive, so taking out her book she sat by the window to read.

However, Rose's concentration was soon interrupted by the view from her window, as the lane between the house and garden was always bustling with carts, carriers, and people going this way and that, until she became bored with that and returned to her book, hoping to finish the second volume of Hannah More.

The sky had darkened by this time, so she joined the family in the drawing room for tea and stayed there until she became sleepy. Saying goodnight to everyone, Rose made her way upstairs. Unfortunately, while doing so her cough returned, but luckily Mamma was in the hallway and heard her distress. Going quickly to her aid, she helped her to the bedroom.

When Rose was finally alone, dark thoughts returned to haunt her and finding it difficult to stop them becoming all consuming, she had another cry. Her greatest fear was that the cough she was troubled by was caused by something which may prove to be her undoing, despite everyone constantly saying, 'It will get better in time'. No sooner did she think her condition was improving then her cough returned, and with it the fear in her mind once again.

SATURDAY, 31ST JANUARY
Hilary Term ends. Pheasant and partridge shooting ends.

Sat in the garden with little Grace before dinner. After dinner I set my diary to rights. Missed my watch hook that J.J. gave me, which made me very uncomfortable.

It was quite sunny this morning and pleasant enough for Rose to take Grace into the garden. They played their favourite game called 'walk the wall' just outside the house, something Grace always wanted to do when leaving by the front door.

When she tired of this game, they went across the road and into the walled garden. Another game Grace really enjoyed was running up and down the paths separating the flower beds. Grace's exuberance soon found Rose struggling to keep up, so she sat on the bench for a minute to catch her breath.

After that exercise, they went for a more restful walk round the lawned garden where the boys were usually found, climbing trees at the bottom whatever the weather. As a result of spending the entire morning playing outside in the fresh air, Grace had a very rosy complexion by the time Mamma called them in for dinner.

Rose had been feeling out of sorts recently and not inclined to write anything in her diary for the last two days, so, after their meal she went to her bedroom to bring it up to date. Once recent events had been recorded, she went down to join the family in the drawing room, taking a book to read, but as the children were making so much noise, she abandoned it to join them in their games.

While playing with the little ones she realised the watch hook was missing from her waist belt. Rose was most upset to find it had gone as it was a present from John, and very precious to her.

Everyone joined in the search, looking in the gardens, dining room, drawing room, everywhere she had been and could possibly think of all to no avail, leaving her heartbroken to think it may be lost forever.

Rose joined the family for tea with an even heavier heart, afterwards going directly to her bedroom as she wanted to be on her own and wrote today's entry with great sadness.

SUNDAY, 1ST FEBRUARY
York Cathedral burnt down, 1829.

Went to church in the morning, also in the afternoon. Mary stayed at home. Mamma, Papa, Augustus, and Mary went to chapel. I stayed at home and read my scripture stories.

Today was Sunday, and with the weather so cold and wintry, Rose was relieved to travel in the coach to and from the church service as her cough was being troublesome again. The cold air inside St. Peter and St Paul's made Rose shiver, but Mr. Staines' rousing sermon helped to take her mind off this discomfort and the list of worries growing in her head. She accepted there were many who had far bigger problems, as Mr. Staines kept reminding the congregation on a regular basis in his sermons every week.

With that in mind, Rose decided to go to the afternoon service to pray for these poor souls, whoever they may be.

Returning home for dinner, they all hurried into the drawing room, hoping to be the first to reach the chairs nearest the fire as their fingers and toes were numb with cold. Usually too slow to claim such a seat, today even more so as running made her cough even worse, Rose was resigned to a place furthest from the hearth.

When cook called them in to dinner, Rose found she had little appetite so, excusing herself, she made her way upstairs to sit by her bedroom fire and wait until it was time for the afternoon service at church. Before going upstairs, she asked Mary to accompany her, but Mary, as usual, declined, saying she wished to remain in the drawing room and continue with her embroidery.

When Rose arrived home, she joined the family gathered in the drawing room and stayed with them until tea was served. During tea, Mamma suggested to Rose that they go to the evening service at the chapel. As a child, Mamma always attended the Methodist Chapel and continued to do so. Rose usually accompanied her, but today she declined, having already attended two services. However, Mary, Papa, and Augustus said they wished to go and left with her.

Rose heard the coach returning as she was preparing to retire, followed by Mamma's footsteps making her way up the stairs to her bedroom to see if she had improved. Rose confided to her that she felt quite fretful of what her future may hold. Mamma tried to assure her that when winter had left and spring had arrived, she would begin to improve as the weather became warmer, a sentiment Rose hoped was correct.

Comforted to see the maid had put a warming pan in her bed,

Rose sat at her little table to write in the diary when Mamma brought her some warm milk. With events recorded and the milk drunk, Rose removed the warming pan and slipped into a nice warm bed.

MONDAY, 2ND FEBRUARY
Purification of Candlemas, a festival in honour of the Virgin, kept with many lights. Hol. at the Exchequer.

Tom and William Golding called in the morning, whilst Mamma and Mary were at Aylesford. I had a long chat with the former. Went in the garden after dinner. I gave T.G. the views he lent me. I wrote to Hannah Spong.

Rose awoke feeling much improved this morning, so after dressing she went to join the family for breakfast. Although trying hard not to worry too much, her cough still troubled her and Mamma's fussing was making it obvious that she too was concerned about her condition, which made it more difficult for Rose to keep her resolve. With Mamma constantly telling her there was no cause for worry and that things would soon improve, Rose wondered if in her heart of hearts, she was of the same mind and really thought her daughter was in mortal peril, or she was only reacting as a mother does when one of her children is poorly.

Tom and William Golding called this morning whilst Mamma and Mary were visiting Aylesford. Tom had lent Rose some pretty scenes to view on his last visit which she retrieved from her bedroom to return to him.

They stayed for quite some time, and during the conversation

Tom informed her he would soon be going to study in Cambridge. *He seems such a clever young man now,* thought Rose. She could hardly believe it was the same boy who used to run around the garden with her brothers getting into all kinds of scrapes, but now, being nineteen, he must apply himself and prepare for the future as every young man should. When Tom and William left it was time for dinner.

As soon as Mamma and Mary returned, the girls went into the dining room to hear all about their visit to Aylesford and who they had seen there. After their conversation, Rose, wrapping up well, went for a walk in the garden to enjoy some fresh air as the day was cold but dry. Soon finding herself becoming chilled, she made a hasty retreat, and returned to the drawing room fire.

A new maid began her duties today, and because Mamma needed an extra pair of hands with the little ones, she was employed in the nursery. Her name was Ann and being younger than Hannah it would be easier for her to run around after the children, allowing Hannah more time for other duties. Ann was previously employed in a smaller household by a Mrs. Perfect who resided in Town Malling, so would probably find the Spong family more of a challenge. The family had taken to her already, especially the young ones, as she was blessed with a kindly manner.

After sitting awhile with the family in the drawing room, Rose decided to write a letter to her cousin Hannah Spong at the table in her room, resolving to correct her recent tardiness through correspondence. Once that overdue task had been completed, Rose enjoyed a pleasant evening after joining the family for tea and was able to record in her diary how improved and positive her mood had been today.

TUESDAY, 3ᴿᴰ FEBRUARY
Blaise, bishop of Sebastia and a patron of wool combers.

Mamma and I went to East Malling to see Ann's mother. Expecting to see my watch hook but could see nothing of it. Afterwards we went to Town Malling and called on Mrs. Perfect for Ann's character reference; she gave her a good one. Mr. Shepherd called in the morning.

As Rose was feeling a little better this morning and her cough had settled, she accepted Mamma's proposal to accompany her to visit Ann's mother in East Malling after breakfast to introduce herself. Although the weather was quite fair, Mamma decided to take the coach, not wishing to walk in view of Rose's recent delicate situation. Rose was anxious to retrace her steps in the hope of discovering the watch hook, but Mamma firmly insisted on riding there.

Arriving outside Ann's mother's house they were most interested to see where she lived as well as meet her mother, who appeared to be such a friendly soul, saying how happy she was that her daughter had been offered a position in their household.

Mamma replied, 'We are pleased to have her with us, and you may be assured we will take great care of your daughter.'

Upon leaving Ann's house it was time to go to Town Malling, as Mamma wished to call upon Mrs. Perfect, whose home in which Ann had previously been employed, to enquire whether she would be kind enough to write a letter informing them of Ann's character.

'I will be most happy to oblige you,' she replied. And when it was done, she had given high praise indeed, which satisfied

Mamma that the correct decision had been made in taking Ann into their home.

It was important to secure some extra help with the children and essential to have the right person, and it would seem Mamma had found this in Ann. Rose was disappointed not to be reunited with her watch hook but had a pleasant morning, nonetheless.

Upon arriving home for dinner, they learnt Mr. Summerfield had called. Rose suspected he had called to see Mary who had entertained him in the drawing room in their absence, as she thought he was quite sweet on her. After dinner Rose went into the garden with Grace, but the cold soon had them scurrying back inside to continue their games in the nursery until teatime came.

With her spirits somewhat lifted, Rose reflected on a most enjoyable day, thinking that no matter how sad she sometimes felt, what a blessing it was to have such a loving family around her, with someone always there to make her smile.

Jackie

July and August 1996

Glancing at the little book on the table, I asked Glenda if she had brought it from the bookshop.

'Yes,' Glenda replied, 'I saw it in the window when I arrived at work this morning and wondered if you would like to see it as you are into anything historical.'

'How fascinating,' I said, picking it up.

'It's on loan, so you can only keep it for a couple of days,' she warned.

'Don't you want to keep it yourself?' I asked.

'I have spent all morning looking at it,' she replied. 'And I agree, it is very interesting, but it's more your kind of thing than mine and the tiny writing is difficult to read.'

Opening the diary and reading the handwritten script on the first page, *A present from Papa, Mill Hall, 6th January 1835*, something stirred in my heart. 'I wonder who the writer was?' I remarked.

'I don't suppose we'll ever know the answer to that,' Glenda replied. 'You may find some clues if only we could read her writing, but remember, you haven't got long, so you had better get on with it.'

Squinting at the tiny writing, I could make out the odd word here and there. 'This isn't going to be easy,' although I knew as I said this that I really wanted to take on the challenge I had been presented with.

As she got up to leave, Glenda reminded me again that I only had two days in which to do it. 'Unless you want to buy it, Jack,' she said.

'I would love to buy it,' I said. 'But it's thirty pounds, Glen, which is a luxury I can't afford as I'm not working at the moment.' So, with that, she kissed me goodbye and left.

Once on my own I took the diary into the sitting room. I need a magnifying glass, I thought, and luckily, at the back of a drawer, I found a small silver handled one, not big enough for the task but it would have to do. So, settling down in a comfy chair with a notepad and pen at my side, I began the arduous but rewarding task of trying to decipher the words that had been written so long ago.

Losing all track of time, I didn't hear Mike come in. 'What's that you have there?' he said, making me jump at hearing his voice.

'I didn't hear you come in,' I replied. 'I've been so engrossed in this little diary Glenda brought at lunchtime.'

Mike, who spent his working days surrounded by antiques, picked up the little book. 'Oh wow,' he said. 'What a lovely little thing, we have a similar one at work in black leather only it's a gentlemen's diary for the following year, 1836. I'll bring it home tomorrow, but it hasn't been written in though.'

'But that's the fascinating thing about this one,' I said. 'It's the words that bring it to life.'

'Well, you had better find out what the words say,' he chuckled, clearly pleased to see that something had sparked an interest in me at last.

I spent the evening reading the diary until my eyes began to water. 'Put it down, Jack, and give your eyes a rest, it's time for bed,' said Mike. Reluctantly closing the book, I headed upstairs with my head full of the things I had managed to read so far, and how much Allison would have loved to see it.

The next morning found me poring over the diary once again. I didn't want to waste a second, as I knew I only had a day to spend with such a special thing. Looking at the inscription again, I wondered where Mill Hall could be? I had certainly never heard of it. So, I went in search of a map as we didn't have a computer, but even if we had, the amount of information on historic research engines was not as detailed as it is today.

Feeling quite frustrated, I began to flick through the diary looking for clues. And there, within the back pages, I came across a list of children who had been christened at St. Peter and St. Paul's church in Aylesford. Out came the map again, and to my delight I discovered that Aylesford happened to be in Kent, where my son Iain and his fiancée Sally currently lived.

Earlier in the year, a holiday had been booked at the insistence of the family, but I didn't want to go. 'You need to get away,' my mother had said, so against my better judgement a week on the Norfolk Broads had been arranged, then Iain invited us to spend the following week with them in Kent. The Norfolk trip was to include my mum, stepfather Eric, and my sister Dian. What an opportunity to visit Aylesford I thought, with excitement rising in my heart. Unfortunately, the diary was due back in the shop the next day, which saddened me. I knew that buying it would be an indulgence, as thirty pounds was not a small sum to us then, and because I wasn't working due to a back injury, my own personal funds were somewhat depleted. 'Oh well, never mind,' I tried to tell myself, 'At least we can visit Aylesford.'

When Mike came home that evening, I told him of my discovery. 'Guess what, the writer lived near Iain,' I said. 'We'll be able to go to Aylesford, but sadly we won't have the diary to take with us,' I lamented, as I was now completely captivated by this wonderful little book. Nothing I had tried previously could lift the heavy grief engulfing my every waking moment, but in the last two days a voice from the past had been taking me to another place, and I didn't want to give it up.

The next morning, Mike offered to return the diary back to the shop, so with a heavy heart I reluctantly handed it to him, saying, 'See you at lunchtime.' The morning passed slowly, and I tried hard not to think about the diary, but it was impossible. Having had a glimpse into the young woman's life, I desperately wanted to know more. I'll clean out the fridge, I thought, but that didn't work, and the morning dragged slowly on.

Lunchtime came round, but Mike, normally home at the same time every day, was late. 'Where on earth is he?' I wondered, but at last I heard his car coming down the drive. 'Sorry I'm late, love,' he said. 'I've been to the bookshop to return the diary, but I decided to buy it instead.' And with that he pulled the diary out of his pocket, and with a flourish said, 'Happy birthday, Jack, I bought it because I can see this little book has put a smile on your face when nothing else could, so it's yours now to spend as much time with as you want.'

Lost for words, and with tears streaming down my face, I hugged him tightly. 'Thank you so much,' I sobbed. We embraced like that for some time with my tears soaking his jacket, but tears of sorrow were now tears of joy – what a wonderful present I had just been given! I couldn't help wondering if Allison had in some way helped to bring it to me; after all, it had been my birthday the day before. Many people would think, 'how silly, it's just the grief talking,' but whatever the reason, I wanted to believe that this diary had been meant to come to me, and now twenty years later, I still do.

What a wonderful feeling it was to be the new custodian of this young woman's diary, although at this stage I had no clue as to who the first owner had been, but I intended to do all I could to find out, and now I had as much time as I needed to do so.

This new venture I was about to embark on didn't stop the grief I felt for Allison, but now I had a reason to get up in the morning and I couldn't wait to get started.

This I did with renewed vigour, and as I read on, I began to feel a connection to the woman whose diary I had in my hand. What did she look like? I wondered. Was she tall or short? What colour were her eyes and hair? So many questions without answers, so I let my imagination take over. It wasn't long before she became real. In my mind's eye I could see her clearly, a young woman whose large blue eyes dominated her delicate features, with her hair a light brown and styled in ringlets. The lady I had conjured up in my mind stood about 5 feet 3 inches, and I sensed she was rather shy and a little unsure of herself. Imagination is a wonderful thing, as I now had an image of her sitting in her bedroom by her fire, writing down all that had happened in her day. If I ever find a portrait of her, she will always look like the young woman I conjured up in my head.

At this point I didn't know her age, but I solved this mystery when I read her entry for March 19th where she had proudly written, 'My birthday today, twenty-one years old'. Yet another clue, for I now knew she had been born in the year 1814; surely, I thought, this will help when we go down to Kent. By coincidence, our daughter Lucy celebrated her own twenty-first birthday two days before I had read about the diary author's special day. Also, on that day of 31st July, my third grandchild Emma Allison arrived. It was a new life for our grieving family to focus upon, and another grandchild for me to cherish. Packing our suitcases for the trip to Norfolk and then to Kent, it occurred to me that I was about to take the diary back to the place where it had been written, another reason for me to believe that this diary had been meant for me. Stranger things have happened, I thought, as I tucked it into my handbag.

On the day of our departure, the early morning sun greeted us as we set out on our journey, with my sister Dian sitting in the back of the car. 'All strapped in?' Mike asked as he reversed out of the driveway. 'Norfolk, here we come.' Arrangements had been made to meet my mother and Eric in Norwich, as they had travelled down the day before.

Sitting in the front passenger seat watching the fields and towns pass by, I thought about the holiday we were going on. I didn't like boats, they made me feel sick, so being stuck on a longboat for a week with four other people worried me.

Would this holiday be a repeat of our ill-advised trip to Scotland just a month after losing Allison? It had been suggested I should get away somewhere, but despite Scotland being my favourite place in the world (my mum, a staunch Scot, had taken Dian and I every year during our childhood to stay with relatives), it proved to be a disaster. My cousin Mabel, who sadly is no longer with us, sent me home again the moment she realised I wasn't ready to face the world, so I knew that once on the boat, I would be trapped.

'Not far now, Jack,' Dian said from the back seat. My sister, forteen months older than me, was my rock; we were extremely close and always supported each other through the good and the bad times in our lives.

Sitting in the car as the miles disappeared, I started to think of the bond between sisters, my own with Dian, Allison's with Lucy, and now the sisters in the diary. It was clear to me that the writer had a close bond with her sister Mary and thinking about the diary tucked away in my bag lifted my spirits. What will be will be, I thought to myself. If I struggle during this river trip, I can always lose myself with my little treasure. Then there was the visit to Iain and Sally's to look forward to, and I couldn't wait to start the search for the writer's identity.

With the long journey finally at an end, we pulled into the hotel car park where we had arranged to meet Mum and Eric, and after a quick cup of tea we made our way to the boatyard. Having seen the brochure I thought I knew what to expect, but when we arrived at our allocated boat, I couldn't believe how long it was. It would seem my sister had the same thought as she was horrified. Dian, who was a born worrier, hadn't wanted to come on this trip in the first place, she was only doing it for my sake, but the visit to Iain and Sally's afterwards had helped her make the decision to join us.

We all climbed aboard the boat, each with our own expectations and what this holiday meant. Mike and Eric were both excited, Mum not so sure, and Dian and I, for different reasons, dreading it. We both watched as the boatman gave our men a lesson on how to pilot the boat, 'It's all in the manual,' he said, 'It will tell you everything you need to know about sailing on the Broads.' And with that, he left us to it.

'Are you sure you know what you are doing, Eric?' Dian asked nervously.

'Of course,' was the answer. 'Stop worrying, Di, Mike and I will be fine.' And true to his word, excluding a few minor bumps against the wharf as they tried to navigate our way out of the boatyard, we were indeed doing fine, in fact both men were now in their element with a captain's hat perched proudly on Eric's head as he steered the boat out on to the Broads.

With cabins allocated, and the provisions bought from the boatyard shop stored away in the galley kitchen, Di, Mum, and

I went to sit at the front of the boat. The peace and tranquillity as we gently made our way at a sedate pace of four miles an hour while listening to the gentle sound of water lapping against the side of the boat was so soothing, I could feel myself beginning to unwind at last. As I watched a mother duck swim towards the bank with a line of little ducklings in her wake, I began to think that perhaps Mum had been right to suggest this holiday after all.

With the sun beginning to set, Eric, expertly mooring the boat for the night, said, 'Time to get the dinner on girls, Mike and I are starving.' The holiday I had dreaded proved to be the best thing for me.

The slow meandering along the Broads with people I loved while watching the abundant wildlife that inhabited its banks was healing. It felt as though I had stepped out of my life and into a safe place. Ever since we had lost Allison, I had found it difficult to sleep, but every night in our tiny cabin I slept soundly as the gentle rocking of the boat was better than any sleeping pill. I never liked sailing and still don't, but the pace of life on a narrowboat is so gentle and calming it doesn't seem like sailing at all. Dian, however, didn't agree with me; she could not relax.

Every docking became something to endure. 'Watch what you're doing, Eric, we might crash,' was her constant cry. Di saw danger everywhere, and only relaxed when back on dry land.

Feeling sorry for her, I involved her in the diary, and we spent many pleasant hours together poring over the tiny writing. Dian, a teacher living in Cheshire, hadn't seen the diary until this holiday, and when she held it in her hands for the first time she became just as enchanted with it as I had.

We talked about what may be awaiting us in Kent, but without any more clues I couldn't help thinking it may be impossible to discover who had written this little book. The author had, however, mentioned the names of her siblings: her elder sister Mary whose 23rd birthday was recorded in January, appeared in nearly every diary entry, as the girls seemed to do most things together. Also appearing on a regular basis were her two little sisters, Grace and baby Elizabeth. As for her brothers, Thomas, John, George, Henry, Edward, William, Frederick, Septimius, Augustus, and Octavius were also mentioned frequently. A large family indeed, and as she wrote about each one fondly, it wasn't difficult to see they were all extremely close. This, however, did not give me the writer's name, but I hoped all her sibling's names may be the key to discovering it. Not much to go on but it was a start.

When our boating holiday finally came to an end, we took the barge back to the Marina with everyone apart from Dian agreeing it had been a wonderful experience. Now it was time to say goodbye to Mum and Eric who were returning home to Harrogate. Hugging Mum tightly, I said, 'Thank you for insisting we came on this holiday. You were right all along; it has been good for me.'

'Mothers always know best,' she replied, hugging me back. 'Now go and enjoy your visit to Iain and Sally and give them our love.'

After waving until they had disappeared, I turned to Mike and said, 'At last, it's time for our second adventure.' As we left the car park, I looked at Dian who had perked up considerably now we had left the boat for good and said, 'Do you think we will have any luck in our search, Di?'

'I don't know, Jack,' she replied. 'But I for one can't wait to find out.'

Rosamond

4th February to 10th February

WEDNESDAY, 4ᵀᴴ FEBRUARY
Richard I. released from captivity, 1191.

Grandpapa and George came to dinner. Mamma and Mary went to Maidstone. I went to Aylesford after dinner on my own, called on Grandmamma. Octavius spent the day at Mrs. Robson's.

After breakfast Mary and Mamma went to purchase some items in Maidstone that were not readily available in Aylesford, leaving Octavius at Mrs. Robson's to spend the day there. Rose was left to entertain Grandpapa and George, who were expected to arrive at Mill Hall sometime in the morning having been invited to dine with them today, so Mamma and Mary could not afford to dally. Fortunately, they arrived in time for dinner. They did not enjoy Grandpapa's company as often as they would wish due to his poor health, so they were quite looking forward to his visit today. He was in good spirits despite his illness, and a jolly dinner was had by all.

Afterwards, they all retired to the drawing room where Mamma gave Grandpapa the comfiest chair by the fire, which allowed him a rest before returning to Gillingham. Rose had an enjoyable chat with George, until the sunshine streaming into the drawing room had her fidgeting. Unable to resist the urge to venture outside, she asked to be excused as she needed some fresh air. Aware of his granddaughter's recent issues, Grandpapa suggested Rose should take the opportunity while the sun was still shining, as he would be leaving shortly anyway. So, kissing Grandpapa goodbye, Rose dressed in warm clothes and went out on her own, deciding to walk into Aylesford and look for signs of spring along the way.

How pretty the snowdrops looked underneath the trees, she thought, slowly walking by, but on reaching the bridge and finding herself tiring, she decided to call on her grandmother in order to rest and have some refreshment before returning home.

Rose received a warm welcome from her grandmother who always delighted in seeing her, and she immediately arranged tea to drink as they sat by the fire to have a long chat. Rose enjoyed their conversations which she found most interesting. Grandmamma had been widowed since the year 1815 and was an old lady now, but still quite active considering her age, and she loved to tell stories of her childhood, which usually led her into memories of her marriage to Grandpapa. Together they were blessed with ten children, sadly losing four in infancy, and she always shed a tear or two when speaking of them. But her mood soon lightened to laughter when the conversation changed to all the mischief the little ones got up to.

They spent so much time conversing that Rose failed to notice the light was fading until the maid came into the room to light the candles, and she was quite surprised at how dark it had become. Now late afternoon, she needed to hurry home before night fall. 'I must make haste and go directly home, as they will be worried about me,' she exclaimed. Grandmamma then offered Rose her coach, saying she would be home in no time, but Rose foolishly declined the gesture, and assured her she would soon be home by walking apace, so after kissing her goodbye, Rose set off to run across the bridge.

Although she was able to see the towpath at this stage, she soon became distressed on realising how quickly the afternoon was turning to darkness around her with still some distance to go. As she ran along, the once familiar trees suddenly started appearing as ghosts with their branches reaching down to grab her. Trying hard to reassure herself it was all in her imagination and not to be so fanciful, she vowed to stop reading stories designed to scare the reader, but her heart still hammered in her breast.

Seeing a light shining ahead Rose started to run towards it, hoping she was not running straight into the path of a villain, but to her great relief she heard Papa's voice calling her name. Catching sight of him she ran into his arms sobbing, saying how sorry she was to have been so tardy in not realising the time.

Safely arriving back home, they found the family waiting for them in the hall. Mamma was standing by the door with her arms folded and looking very cross. 'Where have you been, Rosamond?' was the first thing she said. 'I thought you were going for a short walk and would soon return; we were all so worried for your safety when it became dark.'

Rose answered timidly, 'I did not intend to stay out so long,' and explained she had been to visit Grandmamma.

Papa then said, 'She should have offered her coach to you.'

Rose replied that, 'She had indeed suggested it, but in my foolishness, I declined her kind gesture.'

'You were a very silly girl to refuse her offer,' Mamma scolded. 'But thankfully no harm seems to have been done, so let us all go into the dining room for tea.'

Rose was so upset she could not eat a thing, and once again apologising for her thoughtlessness, she asked to be excused and went to her bedroom.

Feeling quite miserable and tired by this time, she sat by her fire thinking about the day's events and vowed never to go out unaccompanied again until the spring came. Rose believed it was all the running she had done today that made her lungs painful once again, as her chest was hurting and causing her to cough as she attempted to write. Mamma brought a cup of hot milk before helping her into bed.

THURSDAY, 5ᵀᴴ FEBRUARY
Agatha, a Sicilian lady, who suffered for Christianity.

Mrs. Peppercorn and Mrs. Humphrey called in the morning. Went nowhere all day, very busy preparing for the party. Mr. and Mrs. Jones and Mr. Patchett came down from London to stay with Mrs. Robson. Mr. Jones very ill still.

Rose went downstairs for breakfast this morning, feeling a little nervous that Mamma and Papa would still be cross with her after yesterday's drama and was relieved to hear the talk around the table concerned the dinner party being held at Mrs. Robson's tomorrow, to which Mamma, Papa, Rose and Mary were invited.

When breakfast was finished, the girls went excitedly upstairs to help each other choose a dress to wear for the occasion. The decision in Mary's room was soon made– she had chosen a dark blue woollen dress with a pink lace collar which suited her well. It was a far more difficult process in Rose's room, however, as she could never make up her mind on what to wear.

Mary and Rose were quite different in appearance, Rose considered her sibling to be quite handsome with beautiful dark hair and brown eyes, while she on the other hand was smaller in height with blue eyes like Mamma's, and her hair a lighter brown shade which she found difficult to tame. Unlike Mary, Rose's complexion was pale, made worse she felt by the mystery illness which seemed to be plaguing her.

As a result of her indecision, all the winter dresses she owned were soon covering her bed until Mary entered to help with the confusion, holding a pale blue woollen dress up to Rose and saying, 'This colour suits your eyes, Rosie, it will also serve to keep you warm,' so thankfully the decision was made for her. A soft woollen shawl was included to cover her shoulders as an extra layer as lately she seemed to be more sensitive to the cold.

With their outfits decided, the girls returned to the drawing room to find they had visitors. Mrs. Peppercorn and Mrs. Humphrey had called to discuss tomorrow's party at Mrs. Robson's, informing them of Mr. and Mrs. Jones' arrival from London together with Mr. Patchett, and that Mr. Jones was still unwell.

Rose was looking forward to it greatly and was quite excited at the prospect, although she would have been even happier if John had been accompanying his mamma and papa to the Robsons'.

After dinner, she went to tidy away the dresses on her bed and having done so, began to feel rather tired. Laying on the bed for a rest, intending to read a book, she fell asleep. When Rose's eyes eventually opened, she saw Mary smiling at her from the foot of her bed, saying tea was about to be served. Rose would have preferred to take it at her little table by the fire, but instead reluctantly arose and made her way downstairs to join the family.

Going into the drawing room after tea, she unfortunately found herself starting to feel quite unwell again and coughing quite alarmingly. Readily agreeing to Mamma's advice, she said goodnight to everyone and went upstairs to her bedroom. Ann had been in earlier to tend the fire, so on opening the door Rose was greeted by the cosy glow from the hearth and the softly flickering candles, a sight she found most welcoming especially when feeling so tired, so she settled herself down in the comfy chair beside the fireplace. Although compact, it was a very pleasing room, with enough space for her bed with its floral drapes that drew together to keep out the draughts, her washstand, the fireside chair, and a little table for writing letters and taking meals on when required.

Sitting at her table wrapped in a warm robe with cosy slippers on her feet, she began to write in her diary about the day's events, occasionally glancing around to think how fortunate she was in having such a loving family and a comfortable home.

Mr. Staines' sermons, about how we should be humble and kind to those less fortunate than ourselves and to remember those in need, came to her mind. As the hour was late and her eyes were tired, Rose closed the diary and laid down the pen just as Mamma brought her hot milk. Finishing the drink, she thought about the dinner party tomorrow, sincerely hoping she would be well enough to attend, before preparing to sleep.

FRIDAY, 6ᵀᴴ FEBRUARY
Dr. Priestley died in America, 1804.

Very much frightened today. I broke a small blood vessel in my lungs. Mary and I called on Mrs. Robson to see Mr. and Mrs. Jones. They had a dinner party. Mr. and Mrs. Robson, Mrs. Humphrey, Mrs. Peppercorn and her son John, Mr. Maurice, and Richard Summerfield.

Today started well enough, and even though Rose's cough was a little troublesome it did not stop her from looking forward to the dinner party at Mrs. Robson's house. Mary suggested it would be a good idea to set out early to the party as soon as they were ready, enabling them to spend some time with Mr. and Mrs. Jones before the other guests arrived. Rose readily agreed to the idea, and both made haste upstairs to prepare for the occasion.

After putting on the dress she had chosen, Rose gave her hair a thorough brushing before curling it up into ringlets, although not expecting them to stay in as they usually dropped out after a short while, but she told herself that for now she looked most presentable.

Satisfied all had been done in her preparations, Rose went downstairs to join Mary who had been waiting in the hall. They had a pleasant walk into Aylesford, but it did make her a little breathless nonetheless, and on arriving at Mrs. Robson's house she had to sit down in the chair as she suddenly felt overcome with tiredness.

The guests began to arrive dressed in their finest clothes with Mamma and Papa first to enter, followed by Mrs. Peppercorn and her son John, then Mrs. Humphrey and Mr. Maurice, and finally Richard Summerfield. The dining room looked quite splendid; the table was laid with a crisp white linen cloth and at its centre stood a magnificent silver centrepiece filled to overflowing with fruit and greenery from the garden. With crystal glasses sparkling in the candlelight from two large candelabras, it was indeed an impressive sight. Everyone was in a jolly humour but unfortunately Rose was beginning to feel quite unwell again. The food served was of the finest quality and looked quite delicious, but because her cough was troubling her, she was unable to eat a morsel. When Mamma saw her distress, she immediately asked their hosts if they could be excused as Rose was feeling ill.

Once in the hall, Mamma instructed Mrs. Robson's parlour maid to inform Papa they were leaving for home immediately. Having looked forward to attending the dinner party so much, Rose was most upset at leaving it so soon but accepted that her condition was worsening. Her cough became more violent in the coach, and she was greatly relieved to arrive back home.

Going directly to her bedroom she started shivering and feeling very cold, so Mamma sent for a warming pan and a hot drink for her, but as she sat by the fire her cough returned even more violently than before. After holding a handkerchief to her mouth, Rose soon realised it was covered in blood which had begun pouring out then, attempting to cry out in distress, she started to choke. As nothing so severe had occurred to her before, she became hysterical and frightened. The blood was all over her hands and had soaked her beautiful dress.

When the bleeding finally ceased, Mamma called for a jug of hot water and a bowl to clean up the terrible mess the distressing episode had caused. The shock of what had just transpired made Rose shake violently. Mamma tried to soothe her, saying she believed it had been a burst blood vessel caused by persistent and violent coughing, and nothing to be concerned about. When Ann arrived with welcome supplies of hot water and cloths, Mamma gently washed her stricken daughter then helped her into a clean nightgown.

As soon as the trauma subsided, Rose sat quietly on her own by the fireside feeling vulnerable and terrified at the prospect of her health worsening, and she recorded the terrible episode in her diary before closing it and attempting to sleep.

SATURDAY, 7ᵀᴴ FEBRUARY
Mary Queen of Scotland beheaded, 1587.

The vessel in my lung bled again, Mamma sent for Mr. Trested. He gave me some physic to take. Mrs. Robson, Mrs. Jones, and Mr. Powell called in the morning. I felt poorly all day. In very bad spirits. Mr. Powell went to London in the afternoon. Brought up more blood in the afternoon.

Mamma went to see Rose in her bedroom first thing this morning, hoping to find her much improved but was disappointed. In response to Mamma's enquiries, Rose said if anything she felt even worse than yesterday, admitting she was frightened.

When her breakfast arrived, she could not face it, even the smell of it made her feel sick. She eventually got out of bed hoping to feel a little better but found her legs were weak, and she still felt nauseous. It occurred to Rose that she may have a fever, and then to her horror another blood vessel burst as she started coughing. Mamma immediately summoned the maid using the bell pull, and as soon as Ann arrived, she was despatched to the coach house with a note for Wood to take to their physician Mr. Trested, requesting his earliest attention. The bleeding ceased after a while, but Rose started shaking violently so Mamma tried to calm her down, but Rose was not to be consoled and was truly terrified of what may become of her.

On Mr. Trested's arrival, he could see for himself what had occurred earlier. Mamma had changed Rose's nightgown, but the soiled one along with several blood-stained handkerchiefs had not been removed and remained on the floor. When Mr. Trested's examination was complete, his assessment was that, as far as he was concerned, severe bouts of coughing had caused a blood vessel in Rose's lung to be compromised but was nothing to be concerned about. He prescribed a physic and left a small bottle of it, assuring her that by treating the cough in this way, her health would return to normal. As soon as he left, Rose went back to bed hoping to rest, but the distress and fear of bleeding again made it impossible for her to settle.

Mary came to sit by her side and spoke of who she had seen on her walk by way of distraction. Mrs. Robson and Mrs. Jones had called earlier to enquire after her health, having been worried by the hasty departure from the dinner party yesterday. They were accompanied by Mr. Powell, who came to say goodbye to Papa as he had to leave on the three o'clock coach to London. Mamma informed them of Rose's circumstances and what had transpired since yesterday, after which they sent their best wishes for a speedy recovery before returning to Aylesford.

Rose was hopeful that Mr. Trested's diagnosis was correct. She wanted to believe him, but her mind was filled with the fear that her illness was something far more serious which she may die from or become an invalid, and she would never be able to venture out walking with Mary or feel the sun on her face again.

Mamma went to her bedroom carrying a bowl of Cook's soup on a tray, saying to her, 'Now, Rosamond, will you please try some soup, you need it to get your strength back, which will then help to make you better.'

But once again the smell made her feel sick. 'I'm so sorry, Mamma, for all this worry and bother I am causing you, but I just cannot eat anything at the moment.'

Mamma replied, 'I understand you have lost your appetite for the time being, Rose, so I will leave you to rest for now.'

Once on her own, thoughts of what the future may hold were

running wildly through her mind, until she became so agitated her dreaded cough returned. So frightened of causing another blood vessel to burst, she tried to suppress the urge to cough but it just became more violent, resulting in her handkerchief being covered in blood once again. Rose rang the bell for Ann who answered promptly and, realising what was happening, ran downstairs to fetch Mamma. As before, poor Rose needed a change of nightwear, only this time her bedsheets also needed changing.

When these issues were attended to and the invalid settled and made comfortable, Mamma promised to send Mary to sit with her as she needed to attend the little ones. 'Please send her directly, Mamma, as I fear being on my own now,' Rose pleaded and was relieved moments later when Mary appeared. She was often calmed just by the presence of her sister, probably due in the most part to her happy and cheerful nature, as no one could remain in a low mood when in her company. Mary read some of the short stories in Rose's diary to her, and they were soon laughing together at the antics of the Marquis and his ride on the local omnibus.

Mary stayed until her dear sister had fallen asleep. On waking, Rose found Mamma sitting by her bed asking if she could manage some tea as she was worried about her having barely eaten anything since yesterday. Rose declared she could not face any food tonight but agreed to try a cup of warm milk, which the maid brought directly. As it was now teatime, Mamma returned downstairs to supervise and Rose laid back on her pillows, utterly exhausted.

The terrible events of the last two days had left her feeling tearful, especially when thinking about how much she was missing John. In these thoughts she resolved to write to him as soon as she felt a little better. Mary returned to her side after tea and stayed for a while, but there was little conversation as Rose was too tired to speak. When she was alone, she eventually wrote in her diary to record yet another dreadful day, then prayed to her Lord for a better one tomorrow.

SUNDAY, 8ᵀᴴ FEBRUARY
R. Pendrill, the preserver of Charles II. Died, 1671.

I stayed at home all day. Mr. Trested came to see me in the morning, the vessel in my lungs bled twice today. Mamma, Mary, George, and John went to chapel. In very bad spirits, had a good cry.

The prayers Rose had said last night went unheard, as there was no improvement in her condition this morning. She attempted to eat some of the breakfast Mamma had brought to her room, but she had no appetite for it. Not being able to attend church today was a cause of sadness to her as she really wanted to talk to Mr. Staines the vicar, hoping for some words of comfort and solace.

Mr. Trested called in the morning to enquire into her present situation, Rose told him of the bleed she had yesterday afternoon and of the two endured this morning. When he left, she stayed in her bedroom trying to read, but found it too difficult to concentrate as her eyes were tired through lack of sleep, not to mention all the crying during the night which added to her discomfort.

Mary went to Rose's bedside to comfort her again after hearing her crying. After consoling her sister, Mary left the room and Rose tried to read once more, but it was impossible. All she could think was, 'What is to become of me?' She knew she was making it more difficult for herself by constantly brooding on her woes but felt it impossible not to do so. Mary returned to her room with a tea tray, but Rose sent it back downstairs untouched, as she had also done for her breakfast and dinner.

To care for Rose, Mamma did not attend church this morning, deciding instead to attend the Methodist Chapel this evening and taking George, John, and Mary with her.

Laying down in bed trying to read her bible, which failed to give her any comfort, Rose fell fast asleep, eventually waking to find Mamma sitting by her bed. Holding Rose's hand, she asked what was troubling her so much. After a long talk, during which Rose spoke about her fears of dying from her terrible affliction, Mamma, trying to reassure her, said she would return to good health in the fullness of time, but she must remain patient and accept with good grace that which the good Lord had sent to try her, at which Rose made a vow to try and pray even more. Mamma suggested that when she did recover, it could possibly leave a weakness in her lungs, meaning great care should be taken when going out, particularly avoiding damp weather.

Rose answered she would be willing to do anything if she were well enough to venture outside again, providing God grants her the chance.

After Mamma brought her some hot milk, Rose sat by the fire for a while to write in her diary. Sorry to record yet another terrifying day and feeling so very unhappy, she knelt by her bed in prayer hoping that God would grant a better day tomorrow, before climbing into bed and closing the drapes.

MONDAY, 9TH FEBRUARY
The peace of Luneville concluded, 1801.

Went nowhere all day. I felt very ill this morning, brought up a good deal of blood before I got up. Mr. Trested came to see me in the morning. Mr. Staines called. Mamma went to Aylesford to see Mr. and Mrs. Jones. T.G. went to Cambridge.

Yet another trying day for Rose, who awoke this morning feeling just as ill as she did yesterday and suffering more frightening bleeds, giving her no inclination to rise.

Mr. Trested made his morning call, but Rose did not believe he had any idea how to stop the attacks of bleeding, nor indeed did she have any confidence in his ability to cure her of this sudden terrible illness she was having to endure. Another struggle ensued at dinnertime, as Rose was aware that Mamma wanted her to eat something to gain back the strength she had lost in the last few days, but even contemplating it just made her feel sick.

Rose was happy to receive Mr. Staines when he called in the afternoon. He stayed for quite some time, offering encouragement and reading scriptures to her. Then, before he left, they prayed together, and doing so helped stop her heart hammering in her chest for a while. Rose resolved to read the bible and pray more in the hope, as Mamma had said, that God would give her the strength to endure with good grace whatever she must.

Mamma went to visit Mr. and Mrs. Jones in Aylesford with Mary, which left Rose on her own for a while and, feeling quite vulnerable in her solitude, she soon became afflicted with bad thoughts crowding her mind again, so she prayed to the Lord once more for help.

On their return, Mamma and Mary informed Rose that Tom Golding, a family friend, had left to study in Cambridge this morning. All agreed he would be greatly missed and looked forward to seeing him again during the holidays.

Mary joined her sister for tea in her room which delighted Rose, as it seemed such a long time since Mr. Staines had left earlier in the day. Rose spent the evening reading the bible and a little book of psalms, which always gave her pleasure.

Eventually Mamma brought some hot milk, which was the only thing Rose could manage in her present circumstances as it served to soothe her chest. Carefully sipping the warm liquid, she wondered if tomorrow could be the day her condition began to improve. She would just have to wait and see.

TUESDAY, 10ᵀᴴ FEBRUARY
Darnley, husband to Mary Q. of Scotland, murdered, 1567.

A day of great confusion, Mamma went to Maidstone to fetch William home, who was ill, whilst she was gone Mr. Jones and Mr. Robson came to enquire after me. Mary went to Aylesford. George Nash came to dinner. Mr. Trested came to see me. Bled again. William was poorly in the afternoon.

Rose was relieved to find herself a little improved on waking this morning as the fever seemed to have left her, which helped raise her spirits a degree. Leaving the bed to walk a few paces, she appeared to have slightly more energy than in the last few days. Mamma entered her room with breakfast in an agitated state having just received word that William had been taken ill at his school, therefore she needed to leave in the coach immediately to bring him home.

Almost before the dust had settled from Mamma's hurried departure, Mary ran up the stairs to tell her sister they had visitors waiting in the drawing room. Rose asked her to serve them tea while she dressed, sending word she would join them shortly. The maid had brought up hot water earlier, so she quickly washed, dressed, and was ready to help Mary entertain the callers.

When Rose entered the drawing room, their guests were delighted to see her up and about. Mr. Robson took her hand and said, 'You are still looking a little pale, my dear, please take care not to overdo things too soon.' While talking to Mr. Jones, Rose asked if he would pass on her best wishes to John on his return home. What she really wanted to say was, 'Please ask him why he has not written to me since he left on New Year's Day' but felt it improper to do so.

When the visit was concluded and the guests were ready to leave, Mary asked to join them in their coach on the short journey to Aylesford, and happy to oblige they all, apart from Rose, left together.

The moment William arrived home with Mamma, he was taken straight upstairs, with Hannah receiving instructions to bring plenty of cold water and cloths in order to cool him down and reduce his fever. He appeared to Rose to be quite poorly indeed when she entered his bedroom to see him, but Mamma promptly sent her out saying, 'Do not get too close, as you are still not well.'

They were all quite concerned at William having to be brought home from school in such a condition. Mamma sent Wood to inform Mr. Trested that William was ill, and could he please attend him as soon as possible. No sooner was that arranged then Hannah announced they had another caller – George Nash had come to visit. Apologising to Mamma for arriving so unexpectedly, he said how sorry he was to find them in such turmoil. After promising to return on a more suitable day, he bade goodbye to afford them some peace, but Mamma would not hear of it. 'No, George, you have come all the way from Gillingham, I insist you stay for dinner.' Rose, despite feeling tired after such a hectic morning, joined them in the dining room, but with her appetite not yet returned, she left most of her meal on the plate.

As soon as dinner was over, Mamma went directly to see how William was and Papa invited George into his study. As Ann was looking after the little ones, Rose wearily made her way back upstairs in need of a rest. Sitting in her chair by the window, dreaming of being well enough to go out walking again in the spring, she saw Mr. Trested arrive in his chaise. Hannah answered his call and took him straight up to see William.

Once William had been attended to, he entered Rose's room with Mamma, unfortunately this was just as she began to cough which led to another frightening bleed. Rose, having allowed herself to think she was improving, found the episode extremely upsetting. Mr. Trested, appearing not to be too troubled with her distress, said, 'It is only the damp weather that has settled on your chest. As soon as the warmth of spring arrives, you will be much restored.' Rose wished she could believe him, but her earlier raised spirits had evaporated completely, and all she could see now was her imminent demise.

After Mr. Trested's consultation with Rose, Mary went to her bedside where they spoke of William's heavy cold, until Rose told her what Mr. Trested had said and what her thoughts were on his diagnosis of her affliction. At this, Mary scolded her and suggested morose and morbid thinking would not help at all, but only serve to make her more unhappy and certainly delay any healing. Mary continued her scolding by saying, 'You should spend your time thinking about our spring walks that will surely happen in time, you will just have to keep saying your prayers.' She looked so serious that Rose could not help but smile, and it wasn't long before they were both laughing and hugging each other.

It was nearly teatime when Mary left, saying to her sister before doing so that Mamma or the maid would bring a tray. Poor Mamma, thought Rose, what a difficult day it had been for her, with William being so poorly and the return of her bleeding, she must get very tired running after all the family. How fortunate we now have Ann, as her help with the younger children is invaluable.

Apart from not expecting tomorrow to be any different regarding her health, all Rose could add to her diary was how disappointing it was to awake each morning hoping today would be the day she improved, only to find nothing had changed. She thought bitterly that she must learn not to hope too much.

Rosamond

11th February to 18th February

WEDNESDAY, 11TH FEBRUARY
Stanislaus, King of Poland, died, 1798.

I bled twice today, felt poorly all day. Mr. Trested came to see me in the morning, he found William much better. I kept to my bedroom all day. Mr. Robson and Mrs. Jones called. Mrs. Jones came up to see me. Mary went to Aylesford after dinner. I have found my watch hook.

Rose awoke this morning with the same feeling of dread that refused to leave her. Mamma entered the room with the news that William was much improved today and would soon be able to return to school.

This news came as a great relief to Rose, especially when Mamma assured her it was just a head cold, as it had occurred to her that he may have been suffering from whatever was ailing her. When Mamma enquired how she was feeling today, Rose could only pour out her worries again about not surviving her illness. At that Mamma became quite cross and, in much the same tone as Mary's response, said, 'You must stop this feeling sorry for yourself, Rosie and put away these thoughts of your death being imminent. We have been assured by Mr. Trested that you will recover when spring comes, and I know it must be difficult for you to endure all the bleeding, but it will end in good time.'

Shocked by her harsh words, Rose began weeping which caused her cough to return, and that soon resulted in another blood vessel bursting, spoiling her nightgown once again. Rose, amidst her distress, felt sorry for Ann and all the extra laundry she was having to do.

Feeling cold and miserable she started to sob. Mamma hugged her and stroked her hair and tried to reassure her stricken daughter by saying, 'All will be well, Rosie, you will get through this terrible time, just wait and see.' A sentiment she did so want to believe.

Ann knocked on her door to say that Mr. Trested was waiting downstairs. 'Show him into Miss Rosamond's room first, he can attend to William later,' Mamma replied.

When Mr Trested entered and saw Rose's tears, he asked what all the tears were for, and when she told him of her fears his reply was, 'Stuff and nonsense, you will soon be back to your old self again,' and gave her some more of his unpleasant physic. Rose wasn't sure just how effective it was or even if it was helping in any way but resigned herself to the hope that what he said was true.

After attending to her, he and Mamma went across the landing to see William. Rose was so overcome with tiredness she fell asleep, eventually waking to discover Mamma by her bed with another unrequested bowl of Cook's soup. Rose's scowl at the offering provoked a terse reply from Mamma. 'Don't look at me like that, young lady. Mr. Trested expressly told me you are lacking in nourishment, which is not helping you to regain your health, so will you please sip a little of this broth.' Rose did try a few sips, but it had the usual unfortunate result of making her feel sick, so reluctantly Mamma took it back downstairs again. It distressed Rose to give Mamma so much trouble when she knew she was just looking after her best interests.

A short while later Rose had another visitor. It was Mrs. Jones who was directed to her bedroom by Mamma. Rose was glad to see her and soon enquired as to how John was. 'He is doing very well in his new position thank you, Rosamond,' was her reply.

Rose longed to ask if she knew the reason why he had not written to her for weeks, but again resisted the temptation, feeling it would be unseemly to do so. 'I am sorry to find you so poorly, Rosamond, it must be a terrible trial for you.' Rose admitted it was and spoke of her difficulties in accepting her illness with good grace. Mrs. Jones suggested her mamma should ask Mr. Staines to return so they could pray together. Wishing Rose a speedy recovery she returned downstairs. After she left Rose went to sit by her window and saw Mary leaving the house wearing a pretty bonnet, which made her weep at seeing her go out without her.

However, something good did happen for Rose today – she found her watch hoop hiding behind the bed curtain which brought her to the conclusion that it had fallen off her belt and been kicked under the curtain accidentally. This lifted her spirits a little because it was quite special to her, having been a present from John. But her joy was short lived as another bad coughing fit came on, quickly followed by more bleeding and a further change of nightgown and washing for Ann to deal with.

Mamma came in with a fresh bowl of broth for Rose which she was also unable to drink, so it just sat there growing cold and even less inviting. Apart from finding her watch hook, she was relieved to see an end to such a terrible day. Laying down her pen, Rose retired to bed in the hope of being able to sleep.

THURSDAY, 12ᵀᴴ FEBRUARY
Lady Jane Grey and her husband beheaded, 1554.

Bled 3 times today, Mr. Trested came to see me this morning, I stayed in my bedroom until after dinner, then I went into the drawing room. Had tea in my bedroom, remained there. A wet day. Mary stayed at home. Mr. Trested came back to see me.

Another frightening day for Rose who awoke this morning continuing to feel ill and fretful. When Mamma brought her breakfast, she was determined to eat as much as she could, because of Mr. Trested's insistence on building up her strength. All these good intentions were to no avail, as the smell of poached fish soon had her retching, and the effect of this was to bring about a violent coughing fit, causing the first bleed Rose had that day. The fact she was on her own at that moment made her more frightened and ringing the bell in panic soon had Ann scurrying into her room. Seeing what had just occurred, Ann cried, 'I will fetch your Mamma, Miss Rosamond.' Before running back downstairs. Although the bleeding had stopped by this time, Rose was in a dreadful mess and in need of assistance, but thankfully, much to her relief, Mamma went quickly to her aid.

As a result of this latest episode yet another change was required with Ann's help, who returned holding a clean and freshly ironed nightgown. Just as well she knows my requirements, Rose now thought, extremely worried that the re-occurring attacks of bleeding meant she was gravely ill, and in her distressed state she thought she had never felt so wretched.

No sooner had Mr. Trested arrived, and having only been in the room a few minutes, to her horror the bleeding and coughing started again. More panic ensued with Mamma ringing for more cloths whilst all poor Rose could do was become hysterical. Once the situation was under control, Mr. Trested looked quite concerned. Rose sensed he was struggling to know how to treat her illness. 'I will leave you to rest,' he said and promised to return later. Rose, who was feeling extremely tired by this time, fell asleep. When she awoke, Mamma was watching over her holding a bowl of Cook's broth. Having no appetite Rose sipped a little anyway, fearful that if she did not take some nourishment, starvation may prove to be the cause of her demise.

Feeling isolated and alone when Mamma left, Rose put on her dressing robe and slippers to make her way downstairs, much to the surprise of everyone in the drawing room. Mamma rushed over to the door, saying, 'Go back to bed, Rosamond, you are really too ill to be downstairs.'

Papa went over to her and taking Rose's hand he led her over to his chair and said to Mamma, 'Let her stay here for a while, Eliza, the girl needs a change of scenery, it may do her some good.' He then sat Rose in his chair by the fire: she was so grateful to him for that kind gesture.

Staying for a while amongst the constant chatter and excitement of the little ones made Rose wonder if venturing downstairs had been somewhat foolhardy. Mamma, observing her constantly, saw she was becoming distressed. 'Come with us, Rose, let Mary and I help you back upstairs, I can see you are tiring.' She was more than happy to comply but climbing the stairs proved to be quite difficult for her and becoming breathless, she leant on Mary for support. Once in her room, Rose had another coughing fit which led to the third bleed of the day, causing tears to well up in her eyes which were already red and puffy through crying so much in the last few days.

When Mr. Trested returned, Mamma mentioned her daughter's latest attack. Turning to Rose, he said, 'I am sorry to hear that, Miss Spong, but after some deliberation I have decided the time has come for me to seek a consultation with my colleague, as your condition is a most interesting case.' Rose was pleased to hear this, as her faith in his skills as a physician had been sorely tested of late. As it was teatime when he left, Mamma rang the bell to summon the maid to fetch a tray. When the tray appeared, Mamma returned to supervise the children in the dining room, leaving Rose alone with the fear of coughing blood again, but she was relieved to eat a little food without it reoccurring. Being aware of the family's concern regarding her health only served to convince Rose her demise was nigh.

Now nearly bedtime, she sat at her table to record all the terrible things she had to endure today. Seemingly unable to have any control over her thoughts, Rose's mind kept returning to a very dark place where she imagined all manner of frightening things coming to pass, also fearing that if she did not learn to control her thoughts, she may soon descend into madness. Kneeling by her bed in prayer, she begged God for the strength to overcome the melancholy overwhelming her.

FRIDAY, 13ᵀᴴ FEBRUARY
Duc de Berri assassinated, 1820.

Better today, Mr. and Mrs. Jones called. Mrs. Jones came up to see me in my bedroom. I remained there until teatime, then I went down in the dining room. Mary Nash and George dined at Mrs. Robson's. They met Mr. and Mrs. Smith, Papa and Mrs. Lucas, Mr. Trested came to see me.

On waking this morning, Rose was happy to find God must have heard her prayers as the fever had left, and she felt much improved.

When Mamma brought her breakfast, she was delighted to see Rose sitting in her chair by the fire. 'You must be feeling a little better this morning, Rosie,' she said with a smile. Rose answered that she was and seeing the sun shining through her window, expressed a wish to go into the garden for some fresh air, only to be disappointed when Mamma replied, 'No, Rose, it is not sensible for you to go out just yet, even though the sun is shining it has no warmth to it. If you continue to improve it may be possible, but not today.' However anxious she was to escape the confines of her bedroom; Rose reluctantly accepted her advice.

The morning passed by reasonably quickly, thanks to a visit from Mrs. Jones who stayed with Rose for over an hour. Whilst enjoying the company and listening to Mrs. Jones' news, Rose enquired about John in the hope of hearing a reason as to why he hadn't written to her for six weeks now, but all Mrs. Jones said was that her son was well, and that his new position was keeping him extremely busy. 'I am sure this is so.'

Rose replied, thinking to herself surely, that he could have found the time to write at least one letter since he returned home in early January; why he couldn't even find the time to send just a note was a puzzle to her. Rose was aware she could write and ask him for an explanation but in truth, she was scared to hear what his answer may be. She then asked Mrs. Jones if John had any plans to visit Aylesford soon, to which Mrs. Jones replied, 'I do not think so.'

Following Mrs. Jones departure, Rose's next visitor was Mary delivering her dinner on a tray. She managed to eat a little of it and feeling satisfied with herself, she sat by the fire to read her bible. The sound of rainfall, however, made her glance up and seeing the sunshine had been replaced by grey clouds, she drew up her chair to the window and watched the raindrops as they trickled down the panes. As she did so, tears began trickling down Rose's face as she fretted over John's neglect. What could have happened. Had he found another to love? Her mind was in turmoil as to the reason for his silence.

Rose was more than happy to see Mary enter the room. She often seemed to appear when her sister's spirits were low, just how she knew when her presence was needed was both a blessing and a mystery to Rose, who was most grateful to receive it. The two sisters spent the afternoon chatting away until the evening shadows fell, prompting Ann to light their bedroom candles.

Mary persuaded Rose to take her tea in the dining room, so they descended the stairs together. Papa was there to greet them with tales of a dinner he had attended at Mr. and Mrs. Robson's house, accompanied by George, their cousin Mary Nash, Mr. and Mrs. Smith, and Mrs. Lucas. Mamma had declined the invitation, wishing to remain at home with Rose should she suffer another bleeding episode. Rose was happy to report in her diary that she had not been troubled at all today; a cause for celebration, she thought.

Papa continued to keep them amused with tales of gossip from the dinner party he had attended earlier in the day, much to Rose's enjoyment. Just being downstairs amongst the family and so pleased with her spirits made her feel all the better in their company.

A knock at the door was answered by the maid, who announced Mr. Trested had arrived. As directed, she duly ushered him into the drawing room where he was delighted to find Rose dressed and looking much improved since his previous visit.

Eventually, after Mr. Trested's earlier departure and with the hour now late, Rose was once again sitting by her bedroom fire, happy to be recording how much better in her mind she seemed and feeling certain she would indeed make a full recovery. With spring just weeks away now, she was determined to put her mind to all the pleasurable things she would soon be able to enjoy. Although concerns about John still troubled her, she hoped everything would be resolved in the fullness of time.

With tiredness beginning to overtake her, Rose put down her pen and crept into bed where her thoughts turned to hope of seeing a further improvement in her health tomorrow, before falling fast asleep.

SATURDAY, 14ᵀᴴ FEBRUARY
Valentine, a Roman Bishop, beheaded, 285. Hol. At Exch.

A little better today. William Golding called in the morning. Mr. Trested came to see me. George Nash came after dinner to enquire after me. I write to Mrs. Robson to thank her for the books she sent to me to read. She sent me some Jelly.

Rose felt even better today. Taking breakfast by the fire in her bedroom, she was greatly encouraged to discover her appetite had returned.

After dressing she went downstairs to the drawing room, and while she was there Mr. Trested called again to see her. He was most relieved to find his medical administrations seemed to be having an effect, and his patient was starting to recover. 'We will soon have you back to full health, my dear,' he said.

'I do hope so,' Rose replied, 'as I must own that for the past week I have been worried for my life.' The prospect of further doses of his dreadful 'physic' were also a worry.

Rose received another visitor shortly after Mr. Trested had left; it was William Golding whom she was delighted to see. Mamma brought them tea while they spent a very pleasant hour talking together. When William left, Rose went in to have dinner with the family who were all as happy to see her as she was to see them.

It had been quite a busy day for visitors with George Nash also calling to see her and they spent a pleasant afternoon talking together by the fire. He told Rose how pleased he was to see an improvement since his last visit. 'I have been quite worried about you,' and kissing her on the cheek he said, 'I will return to see you soon, Rosie.' She was disappointed when he had to go but knew that Grandpapa was expecting him back home for tea, so off he went to Gillingham. Although Rose was extremely fond of George as he was always so kind to her, she had to admit that all the visitors today had left her a little weary so, in need of a rest, she went upstairs.

After a short nap she wrote a letter to Mrs. Robson, thanking her for the parcel of books sent with Mrs. Jones yesterday together with some of her homemade jelly, informing her how much she had enjoyed it at breakfast time, finding it quite delicious. After joining the family for tea, it wasn't very long before tiredness began to overcome her and wishing to write in the diary, she retired to her bedroom. Today was the first day for over a week that Rose had something other than her illness to write about. Two days had now passed since her last bleed, an experience she hoped never to repeat.

SUNDAY, 15ᵀᴴ FEBRUARY
Rome declared a Republic by France, 1798.

I stayed at home all day. Mary stayed at home with me in the morning and Mamma in the afternoon. Mamma, Mary and William went to chapel, they left William at school. I sat in the drawing room all evening and read.

Hoping she would be able to attend church this morning, when Mamma brought her breakfast Rose asked her if she could go with her, but unfortunately Mamma wouldn't hear of it and told her that sitting in a cold church so soon after her illness would be a risk not worth taking. Rose knew Mamma was worried that she may have another episode of bleeding because she had asked Mary to stay with her whilst she attended the morning service with Papa and the children. Rose was glad of her sister's company as they sat by the bedroom fire, chatting together. Although feeling a little better, her cough still troubled her, causing her to worry another attack may happen. Rose realised it was prudent of Mamma to insist she stayed at home today, and foolish of her to ask in the first place knowing she was not yet fully recovered.

Mary helped Rose to dress, and when the time came for dinner, they went down to the dining room to join the rest of the family.

When Mary went to church for the afternoon service it was Mamma's turn to stay with Rose. Awareness of her mother's ever watchful gaze for any sign of a relapse made Rose anxious. Mamma, sensing this, went to find little Grace and Elizabeth, both of whom were in the nursery with Ann, as she knew her daughter could not be miserable when in company with the little ones. Rose was soon distracted from her gloom through the joy of playing with them. However, tiredness soon overcame her, so asking to be excused she retreated to her bedroom for a rest.

Having slept until teatime, Rose was pleased to learn on waking that tea was to be served in the cosy surroundings of the drawing room with its welcoming hearth, as she felt so cold when not near a fire. Brother William, now fully recovered, was due back at school that evening in readiness for his morning lessons. Mamma and Mary decided to take him to the Methodist chapel prior to his return to school.

When they left, Rose stayed in the drawing room with the younger children and Papa, the older boys having disappeared by this time. Thomas, who was four years Rose's senior, ventured out with brother George. She didn't bother to ask where they were going, presuming their destination was The George public house close by. Ann came in for the children and returned them to the nursery in readiness for bedtime while Rose stayed with Papa in the drawing room to read a book and wait for Mamma and Mary's return from chapel.

Not wanting to be without company regardless of the tiredness overtaking her, Rose had no desire to go to her room just then, having felt so lonely there of late. This was the time of day when dark thoughts plagued her mind and she found her fear difficult to control when no one was there to distract her. Ultimately unable to resist her eyes closing, Rose said goodnight and returned to her room.

Sitting by the fire in her night attire and writing in her diary, she hoped tomorrow would find her even more improved.

MONDAY, 16ᵀᴴ FEBRUARY
Dr. Mead, an enlightened physician, died, 1754.

Mr. Trested came to see me in the morning. Much better today. Mary called on Mrs. Staines and Mrs. Robson. Mr. Jones was not well today. Papa went to 7 Oaks after dinner. I was not in very good spirits all day.

Feeling much recovered after sleeping soundly, Rose washed and dressed to join the family in the dining room for breakfast, all of whom were most pleasantly surprised to see her up and ready for the day.

Mamma fussed over her, checking whether she was warm enough, asking her if she would like this or that, and asking Thomas to give up his chair so she could be closer to the fire. As the weather was so pleasant this morning Rose asked Mamma whether she could have a walk in the garden. Happy to approve, Mamma thought it would be good for her, but only if she agreed not to tarry too long outside. Rose returned to her room excitedly to put on some warm clothes, and once warmly attired she ventured out to the walled garden.

Free from the confines of her bedroom, it was wonderful to feel the fresh air on her face. The crocuses were all coming out and looked so pretty, with everything so marvellous and the promise of spring seeming closer making Rose feel momentarily elated.

She was soon brought back to reality, however, by becoming a little breathless and beginning to tire, with her legs feeling weak and needing to sit down on the bench for a rest.

Realising it was time to go back indoors and not being able

to walk any further was deeply disappointing for Rose. Being in the garden had not lifted her spirits after all, it had only served to make her even more aware of just how poorly she had been.

Spending the rest of the morning in the drawing room, Rose read one of the books sent by Mrs. Robson until she was interrupted by another visit from Mr. Trested. On entering the room and seeing her, he remarked, 'You look much improved, my dear. I can see you will be enjoying walks with your sister before long.'

Rose would have preferred to be reassured by his words, but she could not accept that the terrible affliction had actually left her.

Mary stayed to keep her sister company on her return from Aylesford until the time came for dinner. They talked of all she had done on the morning's excursion, first calling on the Vicar's dear wife Mrs. Staines, then going on to see Mrs. Robson, taking morning tea there and hearing all the gossip, including the news that Mr. Jones wasn't well today. Rose told of her walk in the garden, and what Mr. Trested had said. Mary's response was, 'What he tells you is correct, Rosie, you will indeed accompany me again in time.' She explained how much she missed their walks and looked forward to the day they would continue once more. Having forgotten the hour in their conversation, Mamma came to remind them dinner was being served so they should make haste.

After dinner Papa left for Sevenoaks on business and Rose stayed in the drawing room to play with the children, but despite their games and ensuing laughter her spirits remained low. Mamma noticed her unhappy face and tried to reassure her all would be well. Rose's mind, however, would not give up its melancholy thoughts.

Tea was announced and then taken, after which Rose gave in to her misery and returned to her room for solitude. Mary often told her she brooded and fretted about her troubles to excess; knowing this to be true, Rose was still unable to help herself. She thought that if only a week could pass without further episodes of bleeding, perhaps then would she feel more confident of her future and being free of her affliction. She read her bible for encouragement until it was time to retire, finally writing about the day's events in her diary before going to bed.

TUESDAY, 17ᵀᴴ FEBRUARY
American frigate, President, captured, 1815.

Mr. and Mrs. Jones called to see me in the morning. Mr. Trested came also, after he was gone the bleeding came on and the cough. Mr. Stevens sent a fish down from London.

Rose's worst fears came to pass this morning, as she knew they would. After breakfast Mr. and Mrs. Jones called with Rose dressed and in the drawing room when they arrived. She was happy to see Mr. Jones was feeling better and they passed a pleasant hour chatting.

Rose enjoyed being able to join Mamma and Mary again to entertain callers. Mr. and Mrs. Jones had only just left when Mr. Trested arrived to see her. Remarking how satisfied he was with Rose's improvement, he suggested she would soon have no need of his services. When Rose spoke of her fears, he tried to reassure her by saying that in his opinion the danger had passed, and if she resumed eating nourishing foods and taking the air, she would be restored to good health in time for spring.

Rose did not believe this, and as soon as he left, she was unfortunately proved correct by suffering a bad coughing fit and bleeding again while still in the drawing room. This was a terrifying episode for Rose who could not be soothed despite Mamma and Mary's best efforts, so she was now resigned to having no hope of a cure and the certainty that she would die from this terrible illness.

Mamma, with a heavy heart, slowly helped her stricken daughter upstairs to the sanctuary of her room, where Rose sat down in her chair and wept. Mary stayed with her as Mamma had to oversee the serving of dinner, sending up a tray for them both. With Rose's appetite gone she could not eat a morsel, leaving the meal untouched.

She was inconsolable and could not stop crying. Mary was so upset at her sister's plight, holding her hand as gently as she could while trying to calm her down. Rose managed to stop crying after a while, and Mary, such a comfort to her, made her smile when she mentioned they had received a fish from Mr. Stevens who lived in London, delivered by the Wallace coach. He had sent it in the hope it would aid her recovery, but Rose thought it would take more than a fish to cure her ills.

Mary stayed until it was time for tea and then Mamma took her place at Rose's bedside. She became upset at seeing her daughter so unhappy with nothing she could say or do to stop her tears from falling. It wasn't long before Rose's eyes were red and swollen again.

Putting on her nightgown, she sat by the fire after Mamma had left to tend the little ones. Her mind was in a turmoil as she stared into the flames, thinking her worst fears had now been realised and there was no further hope. Writing her deepest thoughts into the little diary which she cherished gave Rose some comfort. She was delighted when Papa had presented her with it, blissfully unaware of the terrifying thoughts and events she would be recording in its pages just a few weeks later.

WEDNESDAY, 18ᵀᴴ FEBRUARY
Martin Luther, the reformer, died, 1546.

My chest very hurtful all day. Mamma went to Aylesford to see Mrs. Jones. After breakfast Mr. Trested came to see me. After tea I brought up a great deal of blood. Very low spirited.

Another bad day. The pains in Rose's chest were hurting so much they made her feel quite ill, and she nervously anticipated a further bout of bleeding. Mamma sent for Mr. Trested, and on his arrival he was shocked to see how much Rose had deteriorated since his visit yesterday, prompting him to leave another bottle of his truly unpleasant physic which Rose suspected was doing little or nothing to help at all.

Mamma went directly to Aylesford in the chaise after he left to inform Mrs. Jones and Mrs. Robson of her daughter's illness returning. Not having the will to dress, Rose sat up in bed in her nightgown. Mary sat at the bedside wanting to spend some time with her, knowing how upset her sister was as well as wanting to keep a vigil. She may as well not have been there, as Rose was too occupied with her inner turmoil to notice her company.

After Mary left, Rose sat by the fire in fear of suffering yet another episode until Mamma came in with news regarding John. She had heard during her visit to Mrs. Robson this morning that Mrs. Jones had received word that her son John was coming down from London on Saturday and intended to visit. Rose's mood lightened a little at this news but wished she had received a letter from him to inform her of his intentions, as it remained a mystery to her as to why he had ceased all correspondence. This latest information, although welcome, made her fretful as she had no wish to receive him in her bedroom. She wanted to look her best for their meeting.

Rose spent most of the afternoon lying on her bed worrying about these coming problems until Mamma came in with her tea tray. She climbed out of bed and sat at her table by the fire in order to eat, but the sight and smell of food turned her stomach. When Mamma returned, hoping to see a clean plate she was disappointed to find it had not been touched. Just then, Rose began to cough and the bleeding reoccurred, fortunately this time Mamma was present, so she helped her into a clean nightgown.

Now in total despair with her life seemingly in ruins, Rose wondered where it was all going to end. At the conclusion of another terrible day which was recorded as such in her diary, Rose hoped her prayers to see John on the coming Saturday would be answered but feared even God had deserted her.

Jackie

1996 – 1997

The journey from Norfolk to Kent took quite some time as we decided to explore the county of Suffolk – having never been there before – which resulted in several stops along the way. In Saxmundham, I bought a pretty silver locket to hold Allison's photo. We had photographs of her all round our home, but this locket meant I could carry my daughter next to my heart wherever I went.

As we drove nearer to Kent, my thoughts turned back to last year when Allison had arranged a trip to London for us both. When we boarded the train, I had no clue that at the end of the journey, Iain and Sally would be waiting at Kings Cross station ready to whisk us away to their new house in Kent.

Allison loved surprising her family and friends, and trips arranged during the school holidays to take Lucy away were a regular thing. They went everywhere together, and I know Lucy has never forgotten being taken to Wham's farewell concert at Wembley. A trip to Egypt had also been planned, Allison's present for her little sister's twenty-first birthday. This trip, booked for July 1996, never happened, as Allison's depression worsened so much it had to be cancelled. Allison, only fifteen when her half-sister Lucy was born, found it difficult to accept a new sibling, but as time went by a bond began to grow, which soon developed into a deep love for each other. Lucy adored her big sister and loved spending time with her. I was not the only one grieving her loss, we all were.

Back in the present, we finally arrived at Iain and Sally's house where we were soon sitting with glasses of wine in our hands and a delicious aroma of food drifting from the kitchen made us feel quite hungry. After dinner, I placed the diary on the coffee table.

This was the first time Iain and Sally had seen it. 'I didn't realise it was so tiny,' Iain said, 'How on earth are you managing to read it?' I admitted to finding it difficult at first, but her style of writing had become much easier once I had became used to it and I couldn't wait to find out what else she had to say.

Iain had taken a week's holiday so he could help with our search, and he told us an appointment had been made for the following day with the verger and the curate of St. Peter and St. Paul's church in Aylesford. 'That's fantastic,' I replied, 'I wonder if they will be able to help us?'

I woke up early the next morning eager to get the day started. I could hear Iain moving about in the kitchen so, leaving Mike asleep, I slipped on my dressing gown and went to join him.

'Cup of tea, Mum?' he asked as soon as he saw me.

'Yes please, love,' I replied. We then took our tea out into the garden and sat down on a bench. Having not seen me for a while, Iain enquired as to how I was feeling as he knew how hard I had struggled to accept Allison's death. 'A little better,' I said. 'The week in Norfolk has helped and being given the little diary has provided me with something to focus on other than my misery.'

Mike appeared in the garden, quickly followed by Dian, with both looking for a cuppa.

'Time to start breakfast,' Iain said. 'And then we'll get started on our search for the mystery diary writer.'

Getting into Iain's car an hour later with the diary and notepad safely tucked away in my bag, I couldn't help feeling excited about the day ahead. 'I wonder what Aylesford will look like?'

I said to Mike. Iain had told us as we set off that Aylesford was only fifteen miles away from their house in West Kingsdown, so the journey didn't take long.

Never having seen a photo of Aylesford, I didn't quite know what to expect so when we arrived, I was delighted to see how pretty it was. It clearly hadn't changed much since the diary was written. Mediaeval and Georgian houses sit comfortably alongside each other, and an ancient bridge, also mediaeval, spanning the river Medway captivated me, the only nod to the modern age being the odd parked car, traffic lights, and so on. As we walked along the High Street, my head was full of questions: 'Which one of these beautiful old houses had been Grandma's?' 'Where had Mr. and Mrs. Robson lived,' and 'What is St. Peter and St. Paul's church going to be like?'

Climbing up the hill towards the church, it wasn't hard to imagine the two sisters walking arm in arm on their way to attend a Sunday service. Entering the churchyard, we paused to admire the view overlooking the village and the river. This view will have changed little since our mystery writer wrote the diary, and the thought that I was looking at the same scene she had all those years ago absolutely thrilled me.

The verger and curate were waiting for us as we entered the church. After introducing ourselves I showed the diary to them before explaining how it had come into my possession. I hoped, as it had been written locally, that they may be able to help in identifying the writer. 'We will certainly try our best,' the verger said. He then asked where my sister-in-law had found the diary.

'In an old antiquarian bookshop in Harrogate,' I replied. 'The owner had found it amongst a box of old books he had bought in a house sale in Knaresborough.'

'How intriguing,' the curate said, 'that it should end up in

Yorkshire. I wonder how it ended up there?'

'That's what I'd like to know,' I said. 'But I fear we'll never get an answer to that question.' When they asked if we had any more clues to go on, I replied, 'The only facts I am aware of is that the young woman who wrote the diary lived in Mill Hall with her large family, and they all worshipped at this church in the days when a Reverend Staines was the vicar.' I asked if there were any parish records, we could look at.

'I'm afraid not,' the verger said, shaking his head. 'They were all taken to Maidstone County Hall to be put onto microfilm, but you will need to make an appointment.' I then asked if they knew where Mill Hall was. 'It's located on the other side of the river, but most of it has gone,' said the verger. 'Now replaced by several ugly industrial units, only a handful of old cottages remain there now.'

After thanking them for their time, we made our way back down the hill. Once in the car, I couldn't help feeling sorry about the fate of Mill Hall, but at least I knew what Aylesford looked like, I thought as we drove away.

Arriving at the County Hall in Maidstone, we parked in the carpark opposite and trooped inside hoping to get an appointment before our holiday ended. To our delight we were told to come back at three o'clock that afternoon. Result! With over an hour to spare, we went looking for somewhere to have lunch on Maidstone High Street.

With lunch over, and now back in County Hall sitting in the records room, I stared at the rows of machines and filing cabinets. I didn't know where to begin; there were hundreds of boxes all containing parish records from Maidstone, Aylesford, and surrounding villages to wade through.

But it would seem my mystery diary writer wanted to be

found, for as soon as I had loaded a file picked at random from a box labelled 'Aylesford,' I came across a record of all the children who had been christened at St. Peter and St. Paul's church since the beginning of the 19th century. Scrolling down the list I found a family with fourteen children, all the offspring of a Thomas Spong and his wife Mary Eliza; their address – The Mansion House, Mill Hall. My heart skipped a beat when I read those words. Could this be the family I was looking for? I read all the names of their children, firstly Thomas, quickly followed by Mary, George, and Rosamond, their dates of birth being 1810, 1812, and 1814.

I had already discovered our mystery writer had been born on March 19th, 1814. How exciting, I thought, was this her? But ever cautious, I looked at my sister who was sharing the screen with me. 'Another positive clue, Di, but we need more proof,' I said, and we continued reading down the lengthy list of names. Then, there it was, all the proof we needed. John's name appeared after Rosamond, followed by Edward, William, Henry, and Frederick, all mentioned in the diary. But the names that utterly convinced us we had found her family were Augustus, Septimius, and Octavius, plus the two little girls, Grace, and Elizabeth.

All the children had been given the middle name of Nash, so I presumed it was their mother's maiden name, thereby explaining the frequent visits of a George Nash from Gillingham and Mary Nash of Dover, the young lady who came to stay for several weeks. I didn't, however, get to know the true nature of the Nash connection until a much later date. 'What do you think, Di?' I asked.

'We have struck gold, Jack,' she replied excitedly. 'We have found her, and it only took half an hour.' Turning to Mike and

Iain who were using the machine next to us, we showed them our discovery. This revelation had us jumping up and down with excitement, but other researchers sitting nearby were clearly not amused by our obvious joy as much tutting and shushing followed. After making apologies for our poor behaviour, we tiptoed out.

I could not believe how easy it had been to find her. My original flights of fancy that fate had brought the diary to me were a little half-hearted. I wanted to believe it had been meant for me, but my sensible side told me that it could not possibly be true. Yet the number of coincidences suggested it could be so, as the trip to Kent had been organised before the diary had been discovered, and then finding that the village Rosamond had written it in was only a short distance away from Iain and Sally's house and discovering her identity so quickly with hardly any clues to guide us, convinced me it really was meant to be mine.

Feeling elated we returned to Iain's, and I could not wait for Sally to come home to tell her our news. When she did, we all sat in the living room and Sally asked, 'Well, have you discovered anything yet?'

'You won't believe this,' I replied. 'We have found her!'

'That's amazing,' Sally said. 'What is her name and who was she?'

I said excitedly, 'Her full name was Rosamond Nash Spong, and she had thirteen brothers and sisters. Her father was a merchant in coal, whatever that is, and that is all I know now, but now we have her name I hope to do more research on the family.'

The very next day, armed with our latest information, we went back to Aylesford Church and its graveyard to search for family graves. As we went through the gates, the first thing

Mike noticed was a stone memorial. 'Look at that, Jack.' he said, pointing to a large stone monument surrounded by iron railings. 'And look at the name.' To my delight, I was able to read the inscription which said, 'Here lies the remains of John Spong of Mill Hall.' This impressive monument surmounted with a classical urn was engraved on all four sides. Sadly, most of the inscriptions had been eroded by time but we could just make out the name 'Rosamond' on one side although not the date.

At the time I believed this was 'our' Rosamond, but I found out later that the inscription referred to John Spong's sister and not 'ours.' The name William Spong was written on another side, which I eventually discovered was Rosamond's uncle. Situated just inside the churchyard gate underneath an ancient Yew tree, this monument was clearly the family vault.

Turning left on the path outside the church door we found four small graves, each marked as an infant child of John Spong and his wife Rosamond. How sad, I thought, knowing how hard it is to lose a child, and this poor family had lost four in infancy. Compared to yesterday's visit when we knew so little, everything had changed now; names began to leap out at us.

Going into the church, we began to scrutinise all the plaques around the walls and to my surprise I noticed a stone plaque dedicated to Rosamond's grandparents. Calling to the others, I excitedly said, 'Look what I've found,' and we all stood gazing at the plaque placed high up in a quiet corner. I remembered seeing it the day before, but it had no meaning then. Rosamond's grandfather died in 1815, the year following her birth, but her grandmother, Rosamond, lived until 1840. By strange coincidence, she passed away twenty-five years later, on the same day of the year as her late husband. This lady was clearly the grandmother frequently mentioned in the diary.

Leaving the church, we decided to look for the location of Mill Hall, this however turned out to be as the curate had said, a great disappointment. There was no sign of a large house, just a few cottages opposite, all surrounded by several untidy industrial units. We saw nothing to tempt us out of the car. 'Let's head home now,' Iain said. 'I've got the phone number of a local historian. I will give him a call, and with a bit of luck you can see him before you go back home to Harrogate.'

We spent another pleasant evening discussing our latest findings and I could not wait to meet the historian as the need to find out more was already consuming me. Next morning, John Vigar rang Iain to say he could see us in two days' time which seemed ages away, and as there did not seem to be much more we could do to further our research, we spent the next day sightseeing around the beautiful Kent countryside.

The following morning Iain suggested that Mike and I should go on our own to visit Mr. Vigar so, with instructions on how to find his house, we set off. I felt quite apprehensive when we found ourselves standing outside his front door, but I need not have worried because we were greeted by a friendly faced gentleman who smiled and said, 'Please, do come in,' and then ushered us into the hallway.

Sitting in his office with a tray of tea and biscuits on his desk, I thanked Mr. Vigar for seeing us and hoped he wasn't too busy. Mr. Vigar replied, 'Not at all, my dear, and please call me John.' Taking the diary out of my bag I explained it had been found in Yorkshire, and how I had come into possession of it. He said, 'How fascinating, I wonder how it ended up there?' and then asked, 'What have you discovered so far?'

So, I told him what we had found in Maidstone. 'Her name was Rosamond Nash Spong and she was twenty-one years old.

Her home was Mill Hall where she lived with her parents and thirteen siblings.' I then told him about the plaque in Aylesford church that was dedicated to her grandparents, John, and Rosamond Spong.

'I know it well,' he said. 'As ecclesiastical history is one of my interests, and the Spongs were quite an interesting family.' With that he pushed his chair back and stood up. 'I believe I have a photograph somewhere of the Mill Hall Mansion House, give me a minute to find it.'

When he left the room, I whispered to Mike, 'I didn't expect that, how exciting is this?' Mike said he could not believe the change in me; he could see that this little diary had begun to work some kind of magic. He had feared that on that terrible February day in the hospital I would never recover from the trauma, but as we sat in John Vigar's office awaiting his return, he knew the road to recovery had begun.

John came back in holding a black and white photograph. 'This is the photo of Mill Hall Mansion House,' he said. 'It must have been taken in the early twentieth century because this lamppost in the lane certainly wouldn't have been there in young Rosamond's day.' I asked him if he knew when it had been demolished but he wasn't sure, and guessed it was around the 1950s. 'It was probably knocked down round about that time to make way for those ugly industrial units. More's the pity,' he added.

Carefully putting away the precious photo in my bag, I asked him what he knew about the Spong family. 'I do know that at the time this diary was written, they were quite a prominent and wealthy family,' he answered. 'Well respected and liked, but where they all went to, I can't say, as there are no more Spongs left in this area now.'

I couldn't help but feel sad on hearing this, as I imagined we would find some family members to speak to. According to John, Kent had been full of Spongs in the 19th century with branches in Frindsbury and Rochester, but even they had disappeared, another mystery to be solved.

Mike then asked him what he meant when he said the Spongs were quite an 'interesting' family. 'Well,' he said, 'Mr. William Spong, Rosamond's uncle, lived at Cobtree Manor not far from Aylesford, and it's well documented that Charles Dickens used him for the character of Mr Wardle in the Pickwick Papers.'

'How wonderful!' I said. 'I will see if I can find out any more about that story when I get home.'

'That's not all my dear,' he said. 'It is also well documented that Rosamond Walters, grandmother of our Rosamond, is descended from Charles II.'

'Oh, my goodness, but how?' I exclaimed.

'Well, apparently,' he went on to say, 'King Charles II had fivechildren with his mistress, Barbara Villiers. Another thing for you to research when you go home.' With these revelations, we stood up and thanked him again for sparing the time to talk to us. 'It has been my pleasure. I intend to do some digging on your behalf and I will be in touch,' he said as we shook hands.

Eager to share the photo of Mill Hall, we left to go back to Iain's, and all too soon it was time to go back to Yorkshire. I usually didn't like leaving Iain behind in Kent, but this time I couldn't wait to continue with the transcription and find out what else Miss Rosamond Nash Spong had to tell me in her tiny burgundy leather diary.

Back home in Harrogate again, I took out the diary plus the latest information we had discovered in Kent to begin the transcription with even greater enthusiasm. My days were now spent poring over her tiny writing with the help of a larger magnifying glass, and then carefully copying each daily entry into a large notebook. It was extremely laborious, but I loved every minute of it. The writer I now knew as Rosamond had become a real person, and with every entry I became more involved in her world. It wasn't difficult for me to imagine Rosamond sitting by her fire on a cold winter's evening with candles casting shadows around a cosy bedroom as she wrote down all her cares and woes in the little book.

Our first Christmas without Allison was a setback for me, I didn't feel as if we had anything to celebrate. But Lucy insisted we should try to carry on as normal for the family's sake as David and Carole were coming to visit us on Christmas day with our three grandchildren. So, putting on a brave face, I got through the day as best as I could, feeling sorry for myself as well as nursing a bad cold.

At last, 1996 finally ended, and as the clock struck midnight to herald in a brand-new year, I raised my glass to the heavens to toast whatever or whoever brought Rosamond to me. 'I cannot thank you enough,' I said to myself. There was no doubt in my mind that finding Rosamond while in my darkest moments had given me a reason to continue and to be there for the rest of my family.

With Christmas and New Year now over, I took down the tree and packed away the decorations festooning the house, feeling relieved it was over. 1997, a new beginning, I thought as I took out Rosamond's diary. The transcription was nearly finished, and it felt good to be back in a world I felt safe in. The weeks flew by until there were no more diary entries to transcribe, so the next question was what do I do with it now?

There had been plenty of interest from family and friends

who were eager to read Rosamond's words, so I decided my hand-written transcription needed to be typed. This, however, would not be easy as my typing skills were non-existent. Not to be put off, I bought a second-hand typewriter from a junk shop. The machine was placed on my kitchen table where I taught myself the rudiments of typing, albeit with copious amounts of wasted paper and swearing. I would like to say this was an easy task, but I cannot lie, it was a nightmare. As an artist, I have no interest in mechanical things, but the need to see Rosamond's words in print was enough to make me persevere.

A few months later when the typing was completed, I photocopied each page of the diary so the reader could see her original hand-written entries, and on the opposite page, my transcriptions. I then put them all into an A4 binder so that everyone could read them. This was another labour of love, and the whole process took forever. There was no click of a button on a computer in those days, not in my house anyway.

With that done, I typed a brief introduction explaining where such a wonderful piece of social history had been found, followed by an epilogue which included photographs of the family vault, the Mansion House, and Aylesford with its wonderful bridge.

Finally, after eighteen months of hard work I was ready to pass it on to my friend Penny who had offered to bind it for me at her place of work. When I held the finished article in my hand, I must admit to feeling a sense of pride in what I had achieved, but I only had one copy and the list of names waiting to read it had become rather long.

Iain came up with the solution of taking the original book home to Kent, where he printed several copies and posted them to me. Such was the demand, it became difficult to keep track of who had taken a copy to read, so unfortunately most have disappeared. As a result, I have only one copy and the original left in my possession. Eventually, when the fuss died down, I put Rosamond's diary and my research notes away.

Spending so many months with my nose in someone else's troubles had truly helped to get my life back, a different life without Allison but one I could now cope with. You cannot recover from the loss of a child completely, the grief merely goes underground, only to return when ill or over tired. But my time with Rosamond and her wonderful little diary had given me another chance to at least try to live a normal life again, and for that I feel truly grateful.

With my journey now seemingly over, I couldn't help but wonder what had happened to the rest of her large family. So, to find out, Mike and I returned to Kent to revisit the Maidstone archives, hoping to discover what had become of her siblings. All we were able to find on that occasion was a reference to the sale of Mill Hall in the year 1852. Where did they all go?

This lack of information frustrated me, but, as nothing more could be found, I reluctantly said goodbye to Rosamond and her brothers and sisters and put the diary away in a drawer again. Leaving it languishing there was so difficult as I missed her being in my life, and I often took the diary out of its hiding place and talked to her. It had been suggested I write a book about Rosamond, but with no further information, what could I write about? As time went by, I looked at the diary less frequently, and eventually left it in the drawer to get on with my life.

Soon, my desire to paint returned – I had always appreciated the beauty in the world around me with its brilliant seasonal colours. The soft greens of spring, followed by summer in its full-blown glory, vibrant autumn with its gold and yellow leaves falling to the ground in a multitude of beautiful hues, and winter with its skeletal trees covered in frost or snow, would have me reaching for my paint brushes. My world had become grey, but thanks to a young lady from long ago I began to see the colours around me once more and I couldn't wait to get started.

Like Allison, Rosamond will always be with me, and her diary is something I will forever cherish and keep safe, but now it was time to pick up my life. As I put it away and closed the drawer, I had no idea that a time would come when I needed Rosamond's help even more.

Rosamond

19th February to 23rd February

THURSDAY, 19ᵀᴴ FEBRUARY
The sun enters Pisces, the fish.

Had a very bad night, in great pain. I got up at 2 o'clock. Very ill all day, also in very bad spirits. Mr. Jones called after breakfast. Mary walked back to Aylesford with him. Capt. Lucas called with Mrs. Robson and Mrs. Jones, did see them.

Another day of pain and illness for Rose to endure, dejectedly thinking that this was to be her life from now on. A restless night was suffered, with her cough causing a great deal of chest pain. All she could do was lay there praying for sleep before the morning came. Mamma had asked Rose if she wanted her to stay during the night, but foolishly Rose had said no.

Ann made sure her fire would stay lit overnight and left a few candles burning. Not even this cosy scene was enough to chase away the demons in Rose's head, as the bad thoughts crowding her mind always seemed worse in the midnight hours, regardless of her comfortable surroundings. Feeling alone and scared, Rose got out of bed at two o'clock in the morning to sit by the fire, trying hard not to cry.

Mamma made an early appearance to check on Rose and found her suffering with severe pains in her chest and back, which made it difficult for her to take a deep breath. Ann entered the room with the breakfast things and was immediately asked to take them away again before the sight of them had the usual effect.

As Ann departed with the tray, Mary went in to say Mr. Jones was in the drawing room. Mamma went downstairs to receive him, and Mary stayed for a while before mentioning she intended to walk back into Aylesford with Mr. Jones when he was ready to leave. Rose was afraid to be left on her own, and really wished Mary had stayed.

The morning passed slowly. In the afternoon Rose sat by her window watching the carts go to and from Papa's coal yards. Eventually her sister arrived back and went directly to Rose to share her news and observations of her walk to Aylesford this morning. She had called on Mrs. Robson to inform her of Rose's current situation, which prompted a call from her in the afternoon. The sisters observed Mrs. Robson arrive with Mrs. Jones and Captain Lucas from Rose's window.

As the afternoon turned to early evening, Mary stayed and took her tea in Rose's room. Her company was much appreciated by her sister who was fearful of the coming night and of being alone again.

FRIDAY, 20TH FEBRUARY
Sir Nicholas Bacon died, 1579.

> *Very poorly all day. Remained in bed. Had a blister on. Mr. Trested came to see me in my bedroom. Mary wrote to Henry Rixon to invite him down next Tuesday.*

Mamma stayed by Rose's bed until the early hours for her own peace of mind. Her presence was reassuring for Rose who was able to relax and fall asleep knowing her mamma was watching over her.

The shadows did not seem as dark as when she was alone with a head full of dark thoughts. Rose slept for quite a while, eventually waking to discover she was alone with the soft light of morning beginning to appear behind the curtains to herald yet another difficult day. When Mamma returned with her breakfast, Rose again had no appetite for food.

Mr. Trested called quite early, and during his visit he applied a blister to Rose's chest. 'To draw out the impurities in your lungs,' he said. She rather hoped this method would prove to be more successful than previous attempts. Mr. Trested was still in attendance when Rose suffered another attack of coughing, followed by copious amounts of bleeding. Shortly after he left, the episode was repeated with poor Rose certain she would not live to see the sunset and she spoke of her fears to Mamma.

Mamma admonished her again for thinking that way, saying, 'It is nonsense to have such dark thoughts, you must put them from your mind, Rose, as it will only serve to prolong your recovery.'

Ann appeared in her room to inform her that Mr. and Mrs. Jones were downstairs and had asked to see her. Rose was prepared to receive them in her room if Mamma could entertain them downstairs whilst she prepared herself for visitors.

Getting out of bed, she immediately put on her dressing robe and slippers, feeling a little uncomfortable to be entertaining Mr. Jones in her bedroom while still wearing her night attire. After a few minutes Mamma reappeared with the visitors, and during their conversation Rose mentioned how much she was looking forward to seeing their son John tomorrow. She also enquired as to when they may be returning home to London 'We have no immediate plans at the moment,' they replied. After twenty minutes or so, Mr. and Mrs. Jones realised Rose was becoming tired as the effort of polite conversation can be quite exhausting, so after wishing her a quick recovery they retreated downstairs for a while before leaving.

Tired out after talking to her visitors, Rose returned to bed. Ann brought her a bowl of soup on a tray along with a small piece of bread. Drinking half of the soup and finishing the bread, she resolved to continue her attempts at trying to eat something, even if only a little, at every meal.

Mary came up to show her a letter she had written to Henry Rixon inviting him to come down from London next Tuesday. Rose wondered if her sister was rather sweet on him. Mary stayed with Rose for some time to calm her simply through her presence. When another tray arrived at teatime with dainty sandwiches and two small cakes, Rose managed to eat some. Although this had the unfortunate effect of making her feel quite bilious, she felt proud at the achievement.

After a long and lonely evening, Mamma brought a cup of hot milk and asked Rose if she wanted her to stay again tonight. Rose could see she was very tired and declined the offer. 'I am pleased to see you sitting in your chair and writing in your diary, Rosie,' Mamma said. 'You must be feeling a little better.'

'In truth, Mamma, I am not, but I cannot write in bed as I will surely spill ink on my sheets.' Mamma laughed and kissed her goodnight.

Left in solitude the melancholy soon returned. Rose felt sad that her illness now prevented her from entertaining John in the drawing room, and she was horrified at the prospect of Mamma inviting him upstairs to her bedroom, as her appearance was not how she would wish it to be when receiving a gentleman caller, especially John. Her predominant fear was that if he saw how ill she was, he may not wish to continue with their understanding any longer.

SATURDAY, 21ST FEBRUARY
Despard executed, 1803.

I felt very ill and remained in bed all day. Brought up blood three times. Mr. Trested came in the morning. Expected JJ down by Wallace coach but he did not come. I suppose the Robsons told him I was ill. After dinner Mary called on Mrs. Robson. George Nash came to enquire after me, the boys came home from school. I felt very bad all day.

Rose knew when she woke up feeling poorly that it would be another day spent in bed. Mr. Trested called to see her in the morning and during his visit she had a fit of coughing, causing more bleeding. Occasionally the bleeding was light, but mostly the attacks came on quickly and continued for quite a while which understandably was distressing for Rose who tried hard not to become hysterical but found it difficult to control her fear, thinking each time it happened she was about to die.

When this latest attack was over, Rose asked Mr. Trested bluntly if he knew just what was causing her terrible affliction. As he was unable to give a satisfactory answer to this question, he simply repeated that she would recover in time. She continued to believe he either had no clue as to what was ailing her, or he already knew she was suffering from a terrible disease and was hiding it from her.

As the morning slowly passed, Rose laid in bed feeling more and more fretful about what John was going to think when he came to see her today. She had decided to get out of bed and attend to her toilette but when she put her feet on the floor with the intention of standing, she found her legs too weak to support her weight, which surely was not excessive considering how little she had eaten, she thought. Rose came to realise that if she were to receive John at all, it would have to be from her bed, a situation she really did not want. Mary happened to pass her door, and seeing the distress Rose was in, went in to help tidy her appearance a little by brushing her hair and drying her eyes. Rose felt a little calmer after Mary had done all she could to make her presentable.

Dinner arrived on a tray but, as usual, was sent back downstairs untouched. Mary went to tell her sister she was going to call on Mrs. Robson in Aylesford to see if J.J. had arrived, hoping to speak to him on her behalf. Rose waited anxiously for news as she laid in bed waiting to hear if he was going to call.

When Mary returned, she had to tell Rose that John had decided not to come down this weekend after all, which made Rose wonder if someone had informed him of her illness. She was most upset at this news as she hoped that if he had heard about her condition, he would have wished to see her even more. If the situation was reversed and John was ill, Rose knew her need to help and comfort him was unquestionable, so why do men find it difficult to understand a lady's feelings?

Mary left her sister alone with her own thoughts which were, as usual, very dark. Rose did not like the person she had become through this illness, acknowledging the fact her character had never been as happy and sunny as Mary's, but she had been quite contented with her life as it was and now felt sad to have lost the cheerfulness and spirit she had taken for granted.

With the afternoon passing even more slowly than the morning, Rose was glad when Mamma opened her door to say how sorry she was to have taken so long in coming up to see her after entertaining her half-brother George Nash, who had called to enquire after Rose's situation.

Thinking it better not to disturb her, he passed on his wishes for a speedy recovery and took his leave. Rose was disappointed not to have seen him as his cheerful company would have been a welcome distraction from her woes. Mamma also mentioned that Edward, William, and Henry had returned home from school for the weekend and all three paid a visit to her room shortly after Mamma had left; however, realising their sister was feeling unwell, they went to fetch Mamma again.

On Mamma's reappearance, Rose had two more attacks of bleeding which meant her nightgown had been changed three times so far today. Poor Ann had such a pile of laundry to do.

The attacks seemingly over and Mamma having retreated downstairs, Rose sat up in bed, quite resolved to get out and record all the terrible events of today in her diary. Feeling quite unsteady on her feet, she took her place in front of the fire and put all her thoughts into the little diary.

SUNDAY, 22ND FEBRUARY
Great eruptions of Mount Vesuvius, 1822.

A little better, got up for dinner but stayed in my room all day. Mr. Trested came to see me in the morning. Mary stayed at home all day. Mamma went to Church in the morning. Bled 4 times.

Mamma brought a sweetened bowl of oats and milk for Rose this morning, who was feeling a little better. 'To give you some strength,' she said. 'And I will ask Cook to make a nourishing broth later in the day for you to sip.' Longing to be well again, Rose promised to drink it.

Sitting in her chair by the window, admiring the spring crocuses in the garden which looked so pretty, Rose prayed for full recovery before summer arrived. Feeling the warm sun on my face again will be wonderful, she thought, as will wearing of one of my summer dresses again after such a long and hard winter. Her spirits were uplifted a little this morning with these thoughts. Her Mamma had said that if she drank some of the broth Cook made especially for her, it would help to put the flesh back on her body as she had become rather thin these last few weeks.

Rose went back to her chair by the window and sat down, gazing out to watch the children playing in the garden as the weather was quite pleasant. She watched little Grace running around on the lawn and Mary carrying baby Elizabeth, who was struggling to be put down on the grass. Watching them having fun without her and not being able to join in their games made Rose feel so isolated from the rest of the family. Mr. Trested drew up in his chaise to see her as she watched the children playing, and was shown upstairs to her bedroom by Ann, as Mamma had already left for church in Aylesford. After checking her over, Mr. Trested remarked how pleased he was to find her in better spirits than yesterday.

When she returned from church, Mamma took the bowl of broth to Rose which she found delicious. Mary went to sit with her sister for a while after dinner, during which time the coughing resumed as did Rose's fear of bleeding which inevitably followed. It was worse than ever this time as four attacks were to be endured. No sooner had it seemed to settle, then another one occurred, causing Mary to run downstairs in alarm and inform Mamma. When the bleeding had subsided, Rose was able to get back into bed and read her bible, at the same time praying to God for help in accepting with good grace whatever may happen. Mamma produced some more broth at teatime, but this time Rose declined it.

Sitting in her chair by the fire to write once again before retiring, she felt so very unhappy and dejected.

MONDAY, 23ʳᴰ FEBRUARY
Sir Joshua Reynolds died, 1792.

Not so well, remained in bed all day. Mr. Trested came to see me in the morning. Mary went to Aylesford, called on Mrs. Robson and Grandmamma. Miss Baines came to enquire after me, I bled once.

Rose's spirits were low this morning and she did not want to get out of bed. Making matters worse, she could sense Mamma was worried about the situation, making her even more afraid. Rose could not even look at the breakfast Mamma had brought for her, so it was taken away.

Mr. Trested called again; he was obviously finding it difficult to decide which medicine to use to treat her condition. Rose was not disappointed that the regular doses of physic had stopped as the taste had been dreadful and clearly hadn't helped at all. During his visit, Rose had another bleed which made her cry in anguish again. Mary went to Aylesford to inform Mrs. Robson and Grandmamma that her sister was still very poorly. On her leaving, Mamma entered Rose's room to say Miss Baines had arrived downstairs to enquire after her, and to ask if she wanted her to come up and visit, to which she replied, 'No thank you, Mamma, I am too poorly to see anyone today, but will you please thank her for her enquiry.'

Once on her own, Rose laid on the bed to read her bible for the rest of the morning. Mary, now returned from Aylesford, went directly to see her sister with the intention of cheering her up, but Rose was not to be consoled and only wanted to be left alone to cry. Shortly after her request was granted, she began to feel sorry for being so unkind to Mary.

Mary returned with Mamma at dinnertime with a small bowl of jelly. Rose ate a little for the trouble they had gone to, but in truth did not want anything to eat. Apologising to Mary for her mean behaviour earlier brought a hug from her sister, who told Rose not to worry as she understood just how she must be feeling.

Rose spent the afternoon much like the morning, quietly laying on the bed watching the flames as they flickered in the grate. Her bedroom had always been a warm and cosy place, somewhere to escape to when she wished to be alone, but unfortunately it had now become a place of frightening shadows, especially in the darkness of night when her thoughts ran wild with terrible fears and loneliness. How she longed for things to be like they were. She feared God had not given her the strength to accept her fate with ease, and knew she was not helping Mamma by being so difficult.

Teatime saw Mamma trying to tempt Rose's appetite once again, this time with some pastries, but she just turned away from them. As soon as Rose was alone, she got up to sit by the fire to write in her diary. When Mamma brought some warm milk, she sat with her for a while as they talked about her illness, saying she was certain that a return to good health would occur, but she must trust in the Lord to take care of her. Rose was desperate to believe this was so and promised to try even harder.

Rosamond

24th February to 28th February

TUESDAY, 24ᵀᴴ FEBRUARY
St. Matthias. Duke of Cambridge b. Queen's Birthday. Hol. at Bank. Exchange. Cust. Excise and S. Sea Ho.

Mrs. Jones and Mrs. Robson called to see me in the morning. I remained in bed until teatime. Mr. Trested came, I felt very poorly. George Nash came to enquire after me. Henry Rixon came down to stay here. He gave me an unkind letter from JJ.

As Rose's mood was extremely low yesterday due to feeling certain she would not survive the night, it was a great relief when she awoke to find another day had dawned for her. In gratitude, she was determined to at least try not to be so morose, thinking her sister was quite correct when she said it would only serve to make her situation more difficult. When Mamma entered Rose's room with breakfast, she was delighted to see her eat most of it and was also happy at seeing the change of mood in her daughter.

Mr. Trested called and was shown to Rose's bedroom, who told him that although she still felt very poorly, she would bear it with good grace as she had upset Mamma and Mary with her ill humour. He replied by saying, 'I am pleased to hear that, young lady. We will soon have you better and out and about with your daily business.'

As Mamma was bidding him good day she received two more

visitors, Mrs. Jones and Mrs. Robson, who were also shown to Rose's bedroom to see her as Mary had informed them about her sister's health not improving, but their visit was not a long one.

Dinnertime found Rose still in bed, so Mamma took her some hot soup to drink. George Nash called after dinner as Grandpapa had sent him to enquire after Rose's health. It would seem everyone was concerned for her except John, as no enquiry had yet been received from him regarding Rose's illness, which she found most upsetting.

Henry Rixon arrived from London in the afternoon, having come to stay with them for a few days on Mary's invitation. Mary entered her bedroom with the letter Rose had yearned for, delivered at John's request by Henry. Rose waited until she was alone to open it, her hands shaking as she did so due to the many long hours spent worrying as to why she had not received word from him during her terrible trials.

When Rose read his missive she burst into tears, her worst fears had indeed come true. He had written in his letter that he wished to be released from their private understanding. She did not understand how the man who had declared his love for her and expressed a wish to be married when the time was right could be so unkind. They were never formally engaged but she hoped that one day they would be. There was never any doubt in Rose's mind that they would marry eventually, but now it would seem her illness had changed his way of thinking, and obvious to her that his new position in London would require a robust wife to support him. Even if she were to survive her affliction, she realised it would leave her with a weak chest, and he may have realised this too. Nothing of this had been mentioned in his letter, just that the time for them was not now, as he was extremely busy with his work and could not devote the time needed to make frequent trips down from London to visit her. He also mentioned coming down on Saturday to talk to Rose in person, with the hopes of discussing their situation in more detail. This news made Rose's spirits drop considerably, despite her earlier resolve to be more cheerful. When Mary arrived with a tea tray to find her sister distraught, she held her close while she wept uncontrollably.

Eventually calmed and sitting on her own, Rose took up her pen to write in her diary about how John's letter had been such a terrible shock, and once again she was in despair. How could he have been so cruel?

WEDNESDAY, 25ᵀᴴ FEBRUARY
Cambridge Term din. m. Earl of Essex beheaded, 1601.

I was very poorly. Mr. Trested came. I saw Henry Rixon before I was up. I got up for dinner. Mary and Henry went to Aylesford to call on Mrs. Robson to see Mrs. Jones. Mamma, Mary and Mrs. Robson sat with me in my bedroom after dinner.

It was difficult for Rose to remain in good spirits after her promise to do so yesterday, having just endured another restless night of pain and illness, not to mention the lack of sleep. All the family were worried about her situation and tried to disguise their feelings with endless happy chatter, but she knew what they were really thinking.

Mr. Trested called to see her in the morning. Rose believed he was of the same mind as Mamma and Mary in always trying to cheer her up, but in her heart, she knew she would never be completely well again, even if she did survive the terrible attacks of bleeding. She was convinced this was the true reason John had abandoned her and it explained why he wrote that unkind letter. Rose resolved to ask him for a proper explanation when he called on Saturday.

Dinner was served on a tray in her bedroom by Mamma, who at the same time informed her that Mary and Henry had called on Mrs. Robson as they wished to see Mrs. Jones who happened to be staying there. A half-hearted effort was made to eat a few morsels, but most of her meal was returned to the kitchen uneaten.

Mrs. Robson, whose arrival by coach was observed by Rose from her window, paid a visit after dinner. Mamma led her upstairs to Rose's room accompanied by Mary. With only three chairs present, Mary went to find another so they could all sit around the fire together.

It was a most pleasant visit which served to distract Rose's attention from her problems a little with all the chatter about what had been occurring whilst she had been ill, and it would seem a great deal had been missed by her.

As Mr. and Mrs. Robson were the most congenial of hosts, it comes as no surprise that their home was constantly full of people, all wishing to sample the hospitality that was readily available to all. Mrs. Robson, a cheerful and kindly lady, was quite short but stout. She sat in her chair by the fire with a lace cap on her white hair, being motherly to everyone. Mr. Robson was equally kind and jolly. He too was rotund and small, giving them both the appearance of a pair of matching bookends. His hair was now a little sparse, but the grey whiskery beard on his chin made up for it. Rose missed the visits to their home intensely.

The shadows were lengthening by the time they left, so Mamma sent Ann up to light her candles and build up the fire. Rose stayed in her chair to take tea and write in her diary, awaiting John's arrival on Saturday with great trepidation.

THURSDAY, 26ᵀᴴ FEBRUARY
J. F. Kemble died, 1823.

Much better, Mr. Trested came to see me. Papa went to London. Mrs. Jones called to see me in the morning. Mamma drank tea at Mrs. Robson's.

Rose felt much improved today and managed to eat some breakfast, making Mamma feel extremely relieved and pleased her advice was being heeded. Having had no episodes for three days, Rose's mood was so much brighter, but the fear of them returning was never far from her mind as they could easily do so.

When Mr. Trested called, she confessed her fears to him, but as usual he tried to reassure her that all would be well in time, and she must put her trust in God. Although wishing his words to be true, she found it difficult to trust what he said. Moments later, Papa called into her room to say goodbye and tell her how pleased he was to see her so improved before leaving for London on business. Mary kept Rose company for a while during Mamma's visit to Mrs. Robson in Aylesford.

Rose was visited by Mrs. Jones while Mamma was out and found it a little uncomfortable to see her so soon after receiving John's letter. She wondered if John had told his mother about his changed feelings towards her, but giving no reason to believe she knew of his decision, Rose felt she couldn't ask her. She was very fond of Mr. and Mrs. Jones; they were, along with Mr.

and Mrs. Robson, Mamma and Papa's greatest friends and had always been in her life. Rose felt they would be most unhappy if John did not marry her. As children they were always close, and each visit was anticipated with great excitement. She believed that both families expected that one day they would marry, and dearly hoped it could still be so. Shortly after Mrs. Jones had left, Mamma brought Rose's dinner on a tray, a portion of which she did manage to eat.

After her meal, she sat by the window to watch the daily activities in the lane. Two gardens were owned by the Spong family, one of which was a large lawned area where Septimus and Octavius were happily playing a ball game. Rose was longing to join in their games and could only hope it would soon be possible. Going back to her chair by the fire she tried to read but soon fell asleep. Waking with a start an hour or so later with an aching back and stiff legs prompted her to walk unsteadily round the bedroom, trying to get some strength back in her legs after sleeping for so long in the chair.

With the daylight long since faded, Mamma brought tea and stayed with Rose for a while, until Rose asked her if she had told Mrs. Jones about the unkind letter she had received from John. Mamma replied she had not.

'Let's just see what happens on Saturday,' she said. 'There's no need to worry until we know for certain what he meant in his letter which he may be regretting writing. If not now, he may when he sees you again, I think it best to keep it to ourselves for a while and let us just hope there will be nothing to say on the matter after all.' Rose felt greatly cheered by her words of wisdom, thinking Mamma may be correct in thinking he could change his mind when she saw him face to face.

Mary called in to say she was sorry for leaving her alone for so long, having had to entertain Henry in the afternoon. Henry not only happened to be a friend of Rose's older brother Tom; he was also Mary's friend. Rose believed she was quite fond of him. She mused that if they were to marry, and she were to marry John, they would both be required to live in London and that would be truly exciting. Now she feared it would not be happening for her, and if she had to stay in Mill Hall and Mary went to London, she would find it unbearable and would miss her greatly.

Rose spent the evening alone with her thoughts, eventually writing in her diary before retiring to bed and hoping Mamma would soon bring her milk as she began to feel overcome with tiredness.

FRIDAY, 27ᵀᴴ FEBRUARY
The senate-house, Dublin, burnt, 1797.

A little better today, got up for dinner. Mr. Trested came to see me in the morning. Mary and Henry Rixon drank tea at Mrs. Robson's. I was not in good spirits.

Rubbing the sleep from her eyes, Rose woke up feeling a little better in health today but unfortunately unable to enjoy good spirits for most of the day as her heart was heavy with the constant worry of having yet another serious episode of bleeding, as well as the nervous apprehension of seeing John tomorrow. She did not know which issue was the worst.

Mr. Trested made his usual call and was her only visitor apart from Mamma, who brought her breakfast. She mentioned to Rose that Mary and Henry were going to Aylesford to see Mrs. Robson, making her realise she would not see her sister for a while.

It was a lonely and drawn-out morning with too much time for negative thoughts to torment her mind. She was therefore extremely relieved and grateful to see Mamma when she brought her dinner tray, even though her presence was brief as she needed to oversee the meal elsewhere.

Rose tried eating, but not being hungry put aside the tray to choose a gown to wear tomorrow when John called to see her, as she was determined to be dressed and in the drawing room when he arrived. She also thought she would ask Mary to wash her hair in the morning. After selecting what she considered to be her most flattering gown, Rose read her book for a while before going to sit by the window again to pass the time.

Mary eventually appeared, saying how sorry she was to have neglected her again today. Rose said she did not mind as she realised Henry had to be entertained, but in truth she did mind. However, she could not tell her this as it would have been mean spirited of her to say so. As her dear sister was good to her in so many ways, she had no intention of upsetting her. Rose then asked Mary if she could wash her hair in the morning to prepare for John's visit and, delighted to be asked, Mary said, 'Of course I will, we will have you looking your very best when you receive John tomorrow.' Rose explained how important it was for her to receive him in the drawing room appropriately dressed when he called, but uncertain as to what time that might be, they had better make her preparations early in case he arrived later in the morning rather than after dinner.

'I will come to your room directly after breakfast,' Mary assured her. It made Rose feel a little calmer knowing her sister was willing to help, as she had no desire to receive John wearing her night attire and looking like a pale invalid, which indeed she was.

With those arrangements settled, Mary returned to Henry and Rose attempted to read another chapter of her book, but it was impossible for her to concentrate as her mind kept wandering with thoughts of what she should say to John tomorrow.

She was hoping to find the right words in order to change his mind, but feared this would not be the case. If so, what else could she say to make him love her again? Confused with all these thoughts, Rose put down the book and sat in front of her fire staring into the flames, and very soon the tears began to fall again.

All she could tell her diary that night was how unhappy she had been today with the prospect of tomorrow not being any better, and possibly a whole lot worse.

SATURDAY, 28TH FEBRUARY
Hare hunting ends.

Came downstairs for the first time. Mr. Trested came. Mrs. Jones and William Goulding called in the morning. Mrs. Jones took Grace back with her. John Jones came down from London just before dinner. He dined at Aylesford and had tea there, had a long talk with him myself. He gave me a bottle of Attar of Roses. He came again after tea.

Rose's nerves about what lay ahead this morning had a detrimental effect on her newly found appetite as she sat up in bed reluctant to face the day, resulting in a repeat of her breakfast tray being returned downstairs untouched. It seemed an age before Mary appeared to help wash her hair, and when she did, she apologised profusely for her lateness, blaming the conversation she had just had with Henry about how he intended spending the morning with Thomas, their brother.

As Rose had no idea when John was likely to arrive, they had no time to spare in her preparations. She had hoped that Mamma would let her use the slipper bath, but as she may catch a chill so soon after her illness, the request was refused. Rose understood her reasoning but could not help thinking how pleasurable it would have been to recline in lovely warm water.

Mary reassured her she would do whatever necessary to make her sister presentable, starting with her hair. Ann brought up a large jug of hot water and Mary soon set about the task of brushing and washing the unruly tangle. The process took quite a while, and once completed Rose sat in front of the fire willing it to dry. The moment it had, Mary curled it into ringlets and put in the two recently purchased combs for the first time.

With her hair satisfactorily prepared, Rose put on the gown she had selected yesterday, which unfortunately now seemed a trifle big due to her lack of appetite. Standing in front of her looking glass, she was surprised to see she looked quite presentable and somewhat like her old self.

After viewing the effect from different angles, she hoped John would be reassured by her appearance. Once they were confident everything had been done to make her appear in good health, they went downstairs. However, although Rose may have looked in good health, the truth was she felt far from being restored to her former self as her legs began to wobble when she descended the stairs, so it became necessary to hold on to Mary in case she should fall. Entering the drawing room, they found Mamma entertaining Mrs. Jones who remarked how pretty Rose looked.

She then went on to say that John was due to arrive at Mrs. Robson's before dinner.

Making his daily visit, Mr. Trested was pleased to see Rose in the drawing room dressed for the day and looking greatly improved. After pronouncing her well on the way to recovery, he advised her to take great care to avoid catching a chill, as her illness would have left her quite weakened. Rose knew this was true and expected it always would be. She accepted her constitution was never going to be a robust one, nor had it ever been so. She was the child who caught the first cold which lingered longer than it did with her siblings, especially Mary, who had always been strong and healthy. It was Mary's fortitude that had helped to heal Rose when her own was lacking.

Mr. Trested left as everyone was gathering for dinner, and when Rose appeared, the family made such a fuss as they were so pleased to see her among them again. Cook had made a wonderful dinner, and Rose managed to eat a little of each course.

After dinner she went into the drawing room to await the arrival of John. Having heard from Mrs. Jones earlier that John's plans were to visit directly after he had dined and with the moment now approaching, her recent meal started churning in her stomach so alarmingly she feared she was going to be sick. Sitting nervously on the edge of her chair, the front door knocker suddenly clattered, giving Rose such a start. Hannah then came in to announce that Mr. John Jones was here, asking to see Miss Rosamond, so Mamma said to show him in. Rose quickly pinched her cheeks in order to make herself appear healthy rather than pale and sickly.

When John entered the room Rose's heart was bursting in her chest; she had not set eyes on him since the first day of the year. How handsome he looked, but she could tell he was nervous.

Mamma invited him to take a seat, asking if he was well and enjoying his new position and various other polite enquiries. It seemed to take forever for the social order of things to pass, but eventually Mamma stood up, nodded to Mary and said, 'Come, Mary, we will leave these two young people to talk to each other alone.'

Rose had begun to think they would never be alone together, but perversely the minute they we were, neither of them could say a word to each other and her mouth had gone quite dry. She had rehearsed in her mind just what she wished to say, but now could not say anything at all.

Eventually finding the courage to speak, she asked him to explain what he had meant in his very hurtful letter. He tried to explain how things were for him, with his new position proving to be far more demanding than he had expected it to be, and he found it difficult to come and see her during her illness. 'I have been very worried for you,' he said as he took her hand in his.

Rose replied, 'Surely if that was so, why have you not written to tell me all this? I would have understood your difficulties and taken great comfort from knowing you still cared for me even though you could not visit for a while.'

John did not answer this question immediately, but after a long awkward silence, he replied, 'As your health has been poor of late and may continue to be so in the future, I decided it would be prudent for us to make no further plans for a future together, as I am clearly needed in London on a regular basis to help support the company I am employed by.'

Rose, so upset by this, could not stop the tears from falling down her face. John, appalled to see how much pain and anguish he had caused, tried to embrace her, but she shrugged him off.

A terrible silence followed her outburst, and all they could hear was the ticking of the mantle clock. John was the first to speak, repeating how sorry he was, and could they just remain friends as they were when children. 'How can we do that?' cried Rose. 'After all our plans and dreams have now gone. I do not believe I can ever see a time when we can just be friends, John, we cannot simply turn the clock back.'

At this point Ann came in with a tray of tea and doing her best to be the hostess by observing the necessary social etiquette, gave Rose time to think as she poured the tea. After handing John his cup, she spoke about understanding the position he was in, but regarding his request to remain friends, Rose told him she needed to think about this, knowing their paths would cross many times in the future because their families were lifelong friends. 'We will not be able to avoid each other forever, but for now I need time to think it over.'

'I still care for you, Rosie,' John said. 'It's very upsetting for me as I do not want to lose your friendship.' He then produced from his pocket a bottle of 'Attar of Roses' which he told her had come from Persia. Rose thanked him for such an expensive gift. A costly farewell present indeed, she thought, and one that would give her no pleasure.

He stood up and kissed her on the cheek, saying he was expected back at Mrs. Robson's for tea but would not be returning to London until tomorrow, so he hoped she would allow him to call again before his departure. Rose replied that he may do so if he so wished and with nothing else to be said, she saw him to the door.

After watching John walk away down the lane, she sat in the drawing room on her own to cry. When Mamma and Mary eventually went in to console her, they were shocked and surprised to hear what had occurred, and as Rose recounted the events, Ann appeared, asking if she should bring the younger children down for their tea. Rose realised there would be no more time for tears with Grace and Elizabeth running round, and said to Mamma, 'Let them come in, it will help me compose myself.' Elizabeth had just started to toddle and kept tumbling down, much to everyone's great amusement, which proved to be a welcome distraction.

The family were still in the drawing room after tea when Ann went in to announce Mr. John Jones was in the hall once again asking to see Miss Rosamond. Rose went into the hall to ask why he had returned so soon. His answer was, 'I have been worrying about how much I hurt you and I just wanted to say sorry again.' He obviously did not wish her to think badly of him, and still wished to remain a part of her life as a friend. She told him he was asking too much in the present circumstances, considering he had just taken away all her hopes and dreams of their future together, and asked him to leave.

As Rose closed the door on John, sadness overwhelmed her, and feeling so upset she went straight up to her bedroom, seeking solitude. Sometime later Mamma sent Mary to comfort her, where she found Rose crying on her bed.

'Everything is changing,' she sobbed. 'I am facing a terrible illness which may prove to be my undoing and it has already taken John from me. I cannot deal with any more of this pain.' Sitting together on the edge of the bed, Mary tried to calm her distraught sister. Mamma joined them as Rose was explaining her actions in sending John away as being due to her finding it too difficult to talk to him. John's mother was Mamma's dearest friend, so it would be difficult for everyone in both families.

After a while Rose asked if they would leave her alone with her thoughts. Mamma and Mary left the bedroom, closing the door quietly behind them. Rose feared the night may be a long and lonely one.

Jackie

1997 – 2015

The decision to leave Rosamond's diary in its hiding place wasn't an easy one, as there were times during the following year when I felt the need to take it out again. The connection I had made with a young woman who had been dead for over 160 years felt remarkable to me. I missed her, but with my life so busy there wasn't time to start a new venture, and even if there had been I didn't know what I could do with it, so Rosamond stayed in the drawer, and I got on with my life.

Many things happened to Mike and I over the next twenty years. Life was never dull, and like everyone else we had our share of good times and bad. Lucy moved to Edinburgh in 1997 with her boyfriend Brendan, where they rented a flat together. Brendan had arranged to study music at Edinburgh University, and Lucy, having already completed three years at Harrogate college studying drama and performing arts, wanted to continue her studies at a college in the city. This arrangement went on for four years and although we missed her greatly, we had many happy visits to Scotland, my favourite place in the world.

Iain and Sally were married in 1998 in Dover, followed by a reception in Calais. What an adventure, it was great fun but poignant also, as Iain and David's father had died the year before, so he wasn't able to share it with his sons, and neither was their sister.

In the year 2000 my stepfather Eric suffered a stroke, a situation Mum found very difficult to accept, and that brought on depression quickly followed by dementia, so Mike and I were needed to help with their care.

A year later Iain and Sally moved to the States, a blow for me as I feared we may never see them again. I needn't have worried though, for within three months of them leaving, Mike, Dian, and I were on a plane to visit them.

Having never ventured further than Europe, it was an exciting experience, and when we landed at Philadelphia airport enroute to Atlanta, it seemed as if we had stepped into a film set. Very different to the U.K. but somehow quite familiar, that first trip to America had been a thrill. Iain and Sally lived in Georgia when they first moved to the States – *Gone with the Wind* country, which I fell in love with. As the nature of Iain's work meant they had to move frequently we got to visit many wonderful states, but Georgia remains my favourite.

It was during that first trip, while sitting in Iain and Sally's garden one evening with mosquito candles lit, listening to the crickets, and watching the fireflies dancing in the trees, that Iain began to talk about his brother David. At the age of seventeen, his brother had fathered a baby girl with his girlfriend, also seventeen, both too young for the responsibility of parenthood. His girlfriend took the baby girl away without any warning, saying she wished to put her up for adoption – a heart-breaking situation for us all, especially David as he had no choice in the matter. As a result, I never had the opportunity to bond with my first grandchild. 'She must be twenty, I wonder where she is now?' Iain said.

'I have no idea, Iain, but I wish we did,' I replied. Donna Marie had often been in my thoughts, and I always hoped a day would come when we would be able to meet her. Usually nobody spoke about her, so I was surprised Iain had. I asked, 'What made you think of her now?'

'I don't know, Mum,' he replied. 'She just popped into my

head.' We were totally unaware while having this conversation that Donna Marie had already contacted her birth father.

Shortly after returning from America, David came to see us with something obviously on his mind and told us he had been seeing Donna Marie, now named Anna. I was utterly thrilled, my first words being, 'When can I see her?' David warned me that I should prepare myself.

'Anna bears a strong resemblance to Allison,' he said. I wasn't sure how I felt about this news, would it be a blessing or a painful reminder of what I had lost? And when I did finally get the chance to hug my first grandchild, now a woman, I saw that she did indeed resemble Allison, both in looks and mannerisms. So much so, I needed to look away on many occasions to hide my tears, but as time went by, I began to accept Anna for who she was. Her similarity to her aunt, who she never got to meet, now comforts me, and it is wonderful to have her back in our family with, of course, the greatest respect to her adopted parents who rescued her and gave her a loving home when we were unable to do so. As far as we are all concerned, they will always be her mum and dad.

The next four years went by, during which time I got to know Anna better, and she soon became a frequent visitor to our home. Much of my time within those years was spent looking after Mum and Eric. With Mum's dementia now worsening and trying to keep them in their own home, life became much more difficult for Mike and I. Dian helped when she could but living and working as a teacher on the other side of the Pennines meant it was only practical for her to come over at mid and end of term.

It was wonderful having David and Carole living around the corner coming to the rescue when needed, but with their young family and full-time jobs they couldn't be there all the time, so most of the day-to-day care burden fell on my shoulders, with a great deal of help from my long-suffering husband. All of this came to a head in 2005 when Eric had to go into hospital, and with Mum's deterioration because of dementia now so bad, her needs were more than we could cope with, so the authorities insisted she go into care.

There was, however, a happier family event in that year. Lucy and her fiancé Dan were married on a beautiful sunny day in July 2005, a much needed and uplifting occasion in a difficult year.

Sadly, Eric passed away in November, and as Mum had no memory of him, we decided it best not to mention he had gone. The following year brought us another beautiful granddaughter, Ella Rebecca, Lucy and Dan's first born. Their second and equally beautiful daughter Lily Charlotte arrived three years later. Once again, my life became extremely busy as I juggled childcare with daily visits to Mum in her nursing home, and of course my painting.

It was about this time that a well-known and highly talented local artist and his equally talented wife invited me to exhibit my paintings in their twice-yearly art exhibitions. I felt honoured by this invitation but terrified in equal measure. Nevertheless, I accepted the challenge and committed myself to producing several pieces of work for each exhibition, and this commitment was to last for ten years.

During that time, I met some wonderful people, one couple have now become dear friends. Mike, also a talented artist, was invited to join in the venture, which now comprised four artists with completely different styles showing their work together, making what I am told was an interesting exhibition.

My family commitments and painting workload meant there was never enough time to think about poor Rosamond, who remained hidden in a drawer. Whenever she did come to mind, I resolved that one day I would have the time to tell her story. When and how I would find this time, I had no idea. I am an avid reader of all genres of books, from the classics to popular fiction, but I realised this did not qualify me to write one, so I accepted it was just a pipe dream and got on with my life.

In 2008 we visited America again, this time to Colorado and what a fabulous state it is, true cowboy country. Iain and Sally had bought a house in Eagle close to several popular ski resorts and are still keen skiers. It may have been breath-taking scenery, but you couldn't pay me to put on a pair of skis, far too dangerous. A people carrier was hired so we could explore further down the state and into Utah in comfort. Mesa Verde, the ancient site of the native American cliff dwellers, was our main destination, but many other iconic views were seen on the way. Like most holidays it was over too quickly, and we soon found ourselves back in the routine of life.

In the year that followed tragedy struck again: my sister Dian was diagnosed with lung cancer despite being a lifelong non-smoker. This was an immense shock which had us all reeling as she had no symptoms other than a slight cough and the diagnosis was stage four because it had spread to her other lung. A prognosis of four to five years was given, sending us all into panic and despair, a terrible blow and, as you can imagine, I tried so hard not to show how devastated and shocked I felt for her, but inside I wanted to scream and shout at the unfairness of it all. A new drug trial was suggested that gave us a ray of hope and something to cling on to. Many rounds of gruelling chemotherapy followed, and at first it did seem to be working but unfortunately the cancer began spreading to her brain and bones. Just over four years since her initial diagnosis Dian went into a hospice in November 2013.

For Mike and me, all normal activities were put on hold as we travelled to and from our home in Harrogate to St. Anne's Hospice in Cheshire. I needed to be with her as much as possible as we had no idea how long she had left. Her two sons Stuart and Andrew also put their lives on hold. Andy travelled from his home in Devon, and Stuart from Cumbria, both now occupying their mum's house where we stayed whenever possible, but my ongoing commitment to my ninety-five-year-old frail mother in her Harrogate nursing home meant I needed to keep returning home to see her. I will never forget how torn I was by this as I needed to be with both. It was a very difficult time for us all, especially witnessing the ravages of cancer on poor Dian.

She did, however, bravely manage to keep her spirits alive, literally! On her bedside locker stood a large bottle of gin, and at six o'clock every evening the nurse would pour her a glass before the evening meal.

The time spent at my sister's bedside with my nephews, and sometimes Stuart's partner Kath, were precious. Dave and Lucy came when they were able. Dian loved it when her room was full of her family; she sat up in her bed like a queen with her face fully made up by the nurse, and any trace of her illness masked by her favourite perfume. It is painful to recall those weeks spent by Dian's bedside as she rapidly faded before our eyes. Her mind, once so razor-sharp, began to fail, the multiple tumours in her brain now making it difficult to have a coherent conversation with her.

There were many upsetting things about this terrible time I will never be able to forget, but the hardest thing to bear was having to leave her to return home for two or three days to be with Mum. Dian, inexplicably, was still able to use her phone, and would ring me at six o'clock every evening, with her gin at her side. My heart would lurch every time I answered, as I knew what she was going to say at the end of each call. 'I'm not going to die tonight am I, Jack? Please tell me I won't,' was her pitiful cry.

It broke my heart as I knew there was a good chance that she would, so I had no choice but to tell her gently, 'No darling, I promise you are not going to die tonight, I will see you very soon.' Fortunately, a nurse would take the phone from her at that moment, leaving me in floods of tears eighty miles away.

Stuart and Andy spent Christmas Day with her. Mike, Lucy, Dan, their two girls, and I shared Boxing Day with her at the hospice, where we were given the day room for our little party. Dian was wheeled in by a nurse who then transferred her into a large comfortable chair. I have a treasured photo from that day of her sitting there propped up by cushions with a gin and tonic in one hand and the other holding mine. Lucy is kneeling on the other side of her beloved Auntie Di, and Ella and Lily are sitting at her feet. A poignant and sad picture but very precious to me, making me smile and sad in equal measure.

The next harrowing thing we had to face was the hospice needing her bed as she had exceeded their expectations of life. Therefore, we had no choice but to make alternative arrangements. On the day she moved into the chosen nursing home, the light went out of her eyes and her spirit, the only thing she had left, was now gone.

Two weeks later, on 26th January 2014, she passed away, her troubles now over, but our grief was just beginning as we struggled to come to terms with her loss.

After the shock of her passing, we all said our individual goodbyes and left that miserable little room to go back to Dian's house where we shut ourselves away. Lighting Dian's many candles we held our own wake, drinking wine and recalling her life through tales of what an amazing woman she had been to every one of us. Even though the last few weeks had been tremendously harrowing, we agreed it had also been a privilege to have had so much time with her as she went on her final journey. Heart breaking but bittersweet, I will never forget the time spent at her bedside with her two boys.

The very next day I received a call from Mum's nursing home in Harrogate to inform me she had been taken ill, so we set off for home. Another bedside vigil, as the next few days were spent sitting at my mother's side as she slipped into a coma, finally passing away just five days after Dian on 31st January.

I tried to come to terms with the overwhelming events of the last few weeks. I accepted that Mum's passing at the age of ninety-five was only to be expected, and even though I was grieving for her I understood it was her time to go, but the grief at the loss of my sister was almost as severe as losing Allison. She had been there for me all my life, as a child defending me against bullies and other troubles, and as adults we propped each other up no matter what life threw at us.

Losing Mum and Dian together made me feel like an orphan, all alone with no family, and the fact that I had a wonderful one did not seem to compensate for the loss of my own birth family, all now gone with just me left. I carried on with my life, trying to be strong for everyone, and apart from a period following the loss of Allison, it is what I have always done, but inside I was a mess.

We got through both funerals somehow, but the phrase 'life goes on' didn't seem to work for me, as I had no idea how to live it without my sister to share it with me.

As an adolescent Dian was quite a tomboy, but this changed

dramatically as she became a teenager. The girl who played rough with the boys had been replaced by a lady who looked down her nose at her ragamuffin sister. When walking out with her posh grammar school friends at the age of fourteen, she would cross the street if she saw me approaching. I, however, thought this hilarious and would tease her mercilessly. Fortunately, this phase passed but her ladylike ways did not, remaining that way right to the end with her eventual nickname of Lady Di suiting her well.

Eighteen years had passed since finding Rosamond, years filled with numerous wonderful moments, great holidays in America, Italy, and Scotland, as well as many in our own beautiful country. The enjoyment I had in these new experiences were helped in no small measure by the little diary that came into my life when I had needed it most, but the death of my sister had shaken me so much I began to struggle again.

Rosamond

1st March to 11th March

SUNDAY, 1ST MARCH
St. David, tutelar patron of Wales.

Mamma and Papa went to chapel. I felt better today. I wrote to June Gill. Mary, and H. Rixon went nowhere all day. J.J. came to see me again the morning after church. He came after dinner again; he and I sat in the Drawing Room all afternoon by yourselves. After tea he went to London.

To Rose's surprise, John called again in the morning. When Hannah announced his visit saying that he was asking to see her, Rose went into the hall to receive him. Taking her hand, he told Rose how sorry he was to see how distressed she had become during their last meeting, and could she please reconsider his request to remain as friends.

'I do not know what to think,' was her reply to his outburst. 'It is far too soon to consider if we could ever be friends again, John, as my heart is truly broken.' She then asked him to leave, to which he agreed and, saying his goodbyes, set off for dinner at the Robsons.

With a heavy heart she joined the family for dinner in the dining room. Too upset to eat, she excused herself from the table and retired to the drawing room intending to read a book but, to her astonishment, John made another call. He clearly did not want to leave for London without the assurance Rose would speak to him again. It was difficult for her not to hope that he was regretting his decision on this further visit, so she invited him into the drawing room to take a seat. Mamma came to see who the visitor was, and on seeing it was John, greeted him with good grace out of politeness. Having fulfilled these duties, she left to attend the younger children, leaving Rose grateful to her for keeping everyone out of the drawing room for the entire afternoon.

Sitting in silence alone together and waiting for John to speak, she realised he still held her in high regard, but clearly not enough for him to change his mind about committing to her. When he eventually broke the silence with another plea to Rose for her not to think badly of him, she replied by repeating how difficult it was for her to accept his change of affection based purely on her recent health, as they had no way of knowing its duration, or what the outcome would be.

John tried to reassure her that his decision was not motivated by her illness alone, it was also due to being so involved with his new position in London which required him to be free whilst giving his career a chance to develop, plus the intensive training he was undergoing accounted for much of his time. Rose had already begun to understand how he felt and knew he was sincere in wishing to keep her friendship but had to tell him she did not know if it could ever be possible and would need more time to come to terms with their changed circumstances.

Taking her hand, he said, 'Oh Rosie, not only have you had to cope with your terrible lung condition, I have also added to those troubles with my change of heart for which I am truly sorry. Please explain just what has transpired since my last visit.' Rose gave him a full account of the bleedings she had suffered which frightened her so, and of longing for a letter from him to give her some comfort when it was most needed. John was upset to hear how awful things had been for her, with no certainty as to their conclusion.

Rose had calmed down a little by the time Mamma came into the room and noticed they were holding hands; she clearly assumed they had resolved their differences as she immediately asked him to stay for tea. John, gladly accepting the invitation, said he would be delighted, which left Rose without an opportunity to inform Mamma of the true situation between them. The time soon came for John to depart for London, leaving their differences unresolved.

As he left, Rose gave him a hug, and with a smile, wished him a safe journey home, but inwardly her heart was breaking at the loss of all her hopes and dreams. It had been a most difficult afternoon, and even though she had a better understanding of his problems, she still couldn't forgive him for betraying all the plans they had made for their future happiness together.

Mamma followed Rose to her room wanting to know what had transpired between them, as it was obvious by her tears that all was not well. Rose explained to her the outcome of their discussion, and how she felt about it. Having unburdened herself, Mamma told her she would eventually accept the change of circumstances and her heart would heal with time.

After Mamma left, Rose sat at the desk writing to her friend June Gill with information regarding the situation between herself and John. She thought June would be sorry to hear this news, then tried to imagine a future that did not include John.

MONDAY, 2ND MARCH
The pacha of Egypt revolted, 1824. Hol. at Exchequer.

Mr. Trested came to see me, He brought me some more Physic. George Nash came to dinner, Mr Summerfield and Mr. Robson drank tea here. Mr. Robson took him back to Aylesford to see Mr. Jones.

This morning, Rose got dressed despite her sorrows and went down to breakfast. At the table, Mamma enquired if she was feeling any better after her upset yesterday to which she replied, 'In truth, Mamma, I am devastated. It will take a long time before I can recover from John's decision and how it has affected me, but I know I must accept it, regardless of my anger as to why he felt he had to make it.' Mamma gave her a hug and reminded her that time was a great healer, then encouraged her to concentrate on restoring herself to full health and follow all Mr. Trested's instructions, whatever they may be.

Rose had only been in the drawing room for two minutes after breakfast when Mr. Trested arrived with some of his dreadful physic, but with Mamma's words fresh in her mind she drank it all down, knowing she would never grow to like it.

As Mary had ventured out for a walk, Rose spent a quiet morning on her own, reading. On Mary's return they chatted for a while until George Nash, who had been invited to dine with them, duly arrived. George was most sympathetic to hear her news when she told him what had occurred yesterday between herself and John. 'I am so sorry to hear that, Rosie,' he said.

After dinner they all retired to the drawing room, where they were soon joined by Mr. Robson and Mr. Summerfield. Mamma served tea to all their visitors who stayed for most of the afternoon, which helped to divert Rose from her troubles. Rose wondered if John had told his parents about their situation, feeling certain he would have done so, while also believing that most of their friends and acquaintances would soon find out. It was most unsettling to think that in due course she would be the subject of much gossip in the drawing rooms of Aylesford.

Nothing much else happened during the day for Rose to record in her diary.

TUESDAY, 3RD MARCH
Shrove Tuesday. Hol. at the Exchequer.

Henry Rixon went to London on the 3 o'clock stage. Mary and he went to Aylesford. Called on Mrs. Robson to see Mrs. Jones. I do not feel quite so well. In bad spirits all day.

It was Mary's turn to be in a low mood today, as Henry was going back to London. After dinner they both went to see Mrs. Jones and remained there until it was time for Henry to depart on the daily three o'clock stage to London.

On her return home, it fell upon Rose to do the consoling this time, as Mary's affection for Henry was obvious. However, Mary was unsure of his feelings toward her. Rose believed he felt the same way but had so far not declared as much; maybe one day soon he would ask for her hand.

Rose was feeling quite poorly again today and once again fearful for her future. It seemed to her that she was never to be rid of this problem with her health. Feeling defeated, she returned to her bedroom and cried. Having nothing further to say to her diary tonight, she climbed into bed and attempted to sleep.

WEDNESDAY, 4TH MARCH
Ash Wednesday. Hol. at the Exchequer.

Capt. Lucas called, Mamma and Mary went to church in the morning. They called on Mrs. Robson and Grandmamma after church. I stayed at home all day. Took Physic. Mary heard from Emily.

It was another difficult day for Rose, who had neither the inclination nor the heart to venture outside. Mamma and Mary invited her to accompany them to church, but as her cough was troublesome, she declined the invitation as it was making her feel unwell and she decided to remain at home in the warmth instead.

Rose was tempted to speak to Mamma about the unhappiness she was feeling with the traumas in her life, but she had second thoughts as it may have caused Mamma to worry about her state of mind as well as her lungs. Another concern was the possibility that everyone had heard about her situation with John, making her the subject of pitying looks in church, which she would not be able to bear. Mamma and Mary returned home before dinner with the latest gossip following their visits to Mrs. Robson and Grandmamma.

After dinner, Rose went up to her bedroom accompanied by Mary until they were informed that Captain Lucas was in the drawing room and would they care to join him, as Mamma was serving afternoon tea. Once again Rose declined, choosing to be alone with her misery. Mary was displeased with this self-pity and scolded Rose severely, but it made no difference to her decision, so Mary left her alone. As Rose's heart was truly broken, she could not countenance being among people who were happy and jolly for the time being.

Rose had no words for the diary again today and feared neglecting it, but in truth it was too painful to write of her feelings.

THURSDAY, 5TH MARCH
Battle of Barossa, 1811.

Mary Nash came from Dover to stay with us. Mary went in the chaise to Maidstone to fetch her. Called on Mrs. Day. I was not very well. In bed in the afternoon.

With her fever and cough persisting this morning, Rose's illness was showing no signs of improvement, although mercifully the bleeding had stopped. Feeling no inclination to dress and go down for breakfast, she stayed in her bedroom.

As soon as the morning meal was finished, Mary took their chaise into Maidstone to collect Mary Nash from the coach stand on the High Street, using the opportunity to call on Mrs. Day whilst there. Mary Nash lived in Dover and was to stay at Mill Hall with the family for a few weeks. It was usual for Mary and Rose to go out on walks with her during her visits, often to places quite a distance away, so for Rose to see them setting off without her this time was very hard for her indeed. Feeling so poorly after making the effort to venture downstairs for dinner, of which little was eaten, she had to return to her bed.

After the chaise arrived back at the house later in the afternoon, Mary Nash went directly up to see Rose to say how sorry she was to hear of her illness, also expressing her sadness at hearing about John's desertion. She suggested that perhaps when he had finished his training and Rose was well again, he may reconsider his decision. Rose's response to this was, 'If he cannot love me during my illness, how could we expect a happy marriage, even if he were to change his mind. I am therefore resolved to decline any proposals of marriage should he now do so.' Mary agreed it would be better to set her mind to getting well again.

'Then you can cast your eye on finding another beau,' she said.

To which Rose replied, 'I have spent so long planning my future with John, I have never learnt the art of flirtation and would not know what to do.'

Mary laughed and remarked, 'When a handsome young man sets his cap at you, you will soon learn.' Rose felt much cheered by her visit and had a little more hope that the future may bring about changes for the good.

Mary Nash returned downstairs for her tea, leaving Rose to attempt hers in her room. With the hour growing late, she left her bed to sit by the fire and write in the diary.

FRIDAY, 6ᵀᴴ MARCH
Dr. Samuel Parr died, 1825.

Felt very poorly all day. Mr. Trested came to see me in the morning. Mary and Mary Nash called on Mrs. Robson. In bad spirits all day. A very windy day.

The same routine was observed by Mr. Trested on his daily visit to see Rose in her bedroom this morning. She was sure he had no notion of how to treat her as he seemed to repeat the same medical phrases on every visit. The only medicine he prescribed was his dreadful physic together with a blister plaster on her chest. He often implied he was consulting with other doctors about her case, but up until now Rose had neither seen anyone else nor any different form of treatment, which brought her to the conclusion he had not done so.

After his visit Rose went to sit by her window to watch the north easterly wind blowing in the treetops across the lane. She was just in time to see the two well-wrapped Marys leaving the house to enjoy a walk together; it made her feel sad, left out, and lonely. Rose's spirits were so low seeing this, and she feared that this was how her life was to be, forever confined to her room like an ailing maiden aunt, watching others go about their daily lives from a window. She had often noted in her diary how miserable she was becoming, but her spirits just keep getting lower and lower and she could not see any way out of her unhappiness.

Sister Mary went straight to Rose's room on their return to assure her of their intentions to join her as soon as dinner was concluded with an account of their adventures and to keep her company. Feeling a little cheered by this, she managed to eat a small portion of her dinner when it arrived. It was good for Rose to spend some time with Mary Nash when the girls eventually joined her, and they heard all about her life in Dover. The conversation turned to Rose's various problems until Mary changed the subject by speaking of their walk this morning.

An agreeably pleasant afternoon was spent together which helped still Rose's negative thoughts for a while. Now late evening, she was to be found in her usual position sitting alone in her bedroom making notes in the diary by the fire. As she sat back in the chair waiting for Mamma to bring her bedtime drink and to kiss her goodnight, the dark thoughts began to return, making her fear it was going to be another long and lonely night.

SATURDAY, 7ᵀᴴ MARCH
Perpetua, a Roman lady, martyred.

We all stayed at home all day. Extremely windy. Did not feel well. Had pains in my stomach and head. Tom received a parcel from Henry Rixon on business.

No improvement again for Rose today; her stomach and head were hurting, and not being able to face any breakfast she stayed in her room while the rest of the family were in the dining room. Rose was rather hoping she would receive callers to keep her company, but nobody appeared.

Fearing previous visitors to her bedroom would have grown tired of seeing a miserable face to greet them, she was quite resolved to cheer herself up. The March winds gusting strongly down the lane made the windows rattle which gave her a headache, so she sought a distraction by venturing downstairs in her night attire to find someone to talk to.

Most of the family were in the drawing room, which was full of life and joy – just what she needed to aid her new resolve. When Rose noticed little Grace was absent, Mamma went to collect her from the nursery where she was playing with Ann, as she knew about Grace's ability to make her big sister's heart swell. And sure enough, within a short space of time little Grace had Rose laughing at her tricks, but inevitably, as tiredness took its toll, the company Rose had craved proved to be too exhausting, so Mamma helped her back upstairs to take dinner alone at her table by the fire.

After a rest following her meal, Rose was happy to see the two Marys appearing at her door. The fierce March winds had kept them inside, thereby affording Rose the benefit of their company for most of the afternoon. The girls constant chatter, however, soon tired her, and she felt relieved when the time came for them to leave. It had been a difficult but satisfying day, and she could only hope to continue her resolve tomorrow.

SUNDAY, 8TH MARCH
Sir W. Chambers, architect of Somerset-house, died, 1796.

I stayed at home morning and afternoon. Mrs. Robson and Mrs. Jones called before tea. Mary Nash and Mary and I went to chapel, Wood drove us there.

Rose was a little better this morning, but Mamma did not think she should accompany them to church as she felt the cold air would not be good for her cough and advised her to stay by the warmth of the fire instead. As this seemed the most sensible option, Rose spent most of the morning reading with her feet up on the hearth, sitting in Papa's armchair.

When dinner time drew near, she went upstairs to dress and tidy herself in order to join the family when the gong sounded. Feeling better for being dressed, Rose realised that spending too much time in night attire was not having a good effect on her.

The family adjourned to the drawing room after dinner where they spent most of the afternoon, eventually being joined by Mrs. Robson and Mrs. Jones. Mrs. Jones spoke to Rose about her son John's decision in asking to be released from their attachment.

Rose tried to reassure her that she understood it was probably for the best given her poor state of health. Mrs. Jones was most sympathetic and sorry to learn how the attacks were so frightening for Rose. She advised her to trust in God, as it would surely help her to bear the suffering she was experiencing.

Rose thanked her for the concern, but in her heart, she still did not understand how John could have declared his love then changed his mind when things became difficult. She would never have sought to abandon him if it had been the other way around, but she could not voice her true feelings to his mother as she had always been so kind. How could she ever wish to hurt her? She was already sad at the knowledge she would not have her as a daughter-in-law, and being Mamma's greatest friend, Rose felt she had a duty to keep her true feelings to herself.

Asking Mamma if she could go to chapel after tea, Rose was pleasantly surprised to be allowed, especially when Mary and Mary Nash offered to accompany her. Once tea was over and the party appropriately dressed, Mamma had the coach brought round to the front door for Wood to drive them there.

Rose enjoyed being in a house of God again; it seemed a long time since she had last attended. The Methodist Chapel's order of service was different to the one at the Parish Church, but an enjoyable experience nonetheless with the speaker's sermons usually most interesting. Highly satisfied with their devotions, particularly Rose, the girls were returned home.

Safely back at Mill Hall, Rose went directly to her bedroom and attended to the diary before she became too tired to write.

MONDAY, 9ᵀᴴ MARCH
General Blucher defeated Buonaparte at Laon, 1814.

Mamma and I went to Gillingham directly after breakfast. Mr. Trested came to see me, but I was gone. Got home at 9 o'clock in the evening.

Rather a busy day today. On the return from Chapel yesterday Mamma had asked Rose if she wished to accompany her to Gillingham in the morning to see Grandpapa who was in poor health. She thought that as Rose seemed much improved, an excursion would be a good way of distracting her from her recent struggles. Delighted at her suggestion, she said, 'Yes please, Mamma, that would be wonderful.'

With the visit to see Grandpapa a real prospect, Rose woke this morning feeling happy to have something to look forward to, and to escape the confines of the house and her bedroom. She hurriedly dressed in warm clothes to avoid catching a chill on the journey as the weather was still quite cold – spring had not yet arrived despite the pretty crocuses in their garden.

As Grandpapa's house was quite some distance away from Mill Hall, Mamma and Rose set off in the coach as soon as breakfast was over. Although the hedgerows were still awaiting new growth the journey was a pleasant one. Not having been anywhere for such a long time, it was a tonic for Rose to see the fields and villages once again. It gave her fresh hopes of a recovery after all the sickness she had endured, but as Mamma kept reminding her, she may be delicate for some time. Chatting away as they rode along, Mamma told her Grandpapa had been most concerned about her, so it would please him greatly to see the progress she was making to improve her health.

The journey took nearly two hours, and they arrived feeling quite chilled, so the pot of hot tea that was promptly organised felt most welcoming. The rest of the morning was spent talking to Grandpapa, unfortunately now frail and needing the assistance of a cane to help him walk. At least, thought Rose, he had not yet succumbed to using a bath chair.

While speaking to him of her illness, she told him of her daily prayers to not see the return of the dreadful bleeding attacks which were so frightening. 'I am so sorry to hear about your troubles, Rosie, including how upset you are with John's change of heart.' She was surprised he knew about this and could only suppose Mamma had written to tell him of it. He went on to say that John was a very foolish young man to have ended their understanding. 'I hope he will come to regret such a rash decision.'

Rose said in return, 'Even if he did, I am sure I would not have the ability to forgive him. I must use all my efforts in getting well again now, so I have no room in my life for affairs of the heart at the moment.'

He chuckled while taking her by the hand, and with his kindly eyes glinting, said, 'Given time your heart will heal again, my dear. You have your whole lifetime to live, and I am sure another handsome young swain will help you to live it.' Rose was greatly cheered by his remarks and hoped his words would come true.

When dinner was announced by the maid, they all went into the dining room. A pleasant afternoon was spent catching up on everyone's news until teatime. The time passed quickly, and it soon became quite late, so, putting on their coats and scarves, Mamma and Rose said their affectionate goodbyes to Grandpapa and his wife. It was time to enter the coach to begin the journey home. Once seated, Wood secured the door and climbed up to his perch where he shook the reins to start the horses. It was a dark, damp, and cold night so the warming rugs on their knees were most appreciated.

A good while later, becoming quite weary, Rose and Mamma were relieved to hear from Wood that the lights of Mill Hall were approaching. As the hour was well past nine o'clock, the family had become quite concerned of their whereabouts, and were waiting in the drawing room to welcome the weary travellers' safe arrival home. With tea now sent for, the family gathered round to hear the story of the excursion and the reassurance that Grandpapa's condition had not worsened since his last visit to see them.

It had been a long but most enjoyable day for Rose, and saying goodnight to everyone, she went upstairs to prepare for bed. Sitting by the fire wearing her nightgown, robe, and warm slippers, she felt a little more hopeful for her future than she had done of late.

TUESDAY, 10TH MARCH
Don John VI., King of Portugal, died, 1826.

Mamma and Mary both went to Maidstone. After breakfast the other Mary and I dined at Mrs. Robson's. Mr. Jones very ill all day. Mr. Abbot and Mr. Summerfield came in the evening. We rode home.

The day started in a positive mood for Rose. Her first thoughts on waking were of the invitation to dine at the Robsons' house with Mary Nash, an exciting prospect to look forward to, one that marked a welcome change from her usual unhappy disposition.

Mamma and Mary left for Maidstone in the coach directly after breakfast, as a trip had been arranged there to make various purchases, while Rose and Mary Nash spent the morning preparing for the dinner invitation in Aylesford. When she was ready to leave, Rose considered taking the chaise now the coach was unavailable, and had it not been for her lack of confidence in handling the horses she would have done so. After dismissing that idea, she suggested setting off on foot by taking the path alongside the Medway. 'The exercise and a probable improvement in my complexion would be most beneficial,' she declared.

The walk into Aylesford alongside the river was an enjoyable one, with both girls looking for signs of spring along the way. Many brightly coloured crocuses were to be seen under the trees, with the daffodils beginning to make an appearance also.

Rose found it gratifying to see winter starting to lose its grip, but accepted it was still too early to be sure it was over, as just when they thought it was time to cast off heavy winter clothes, many a spring sees an unwelcome return of snow and frost to make them shiver again.

They arrived at Mrs. Robson's to hear Mr. Jones had taken another bad turn and was confined to his bedroom. He was not in good health, a worrying situation for his family, and for Rose too, so Mrs. Jones was requested to send their best wishes to him when she next attended to his needs.

Dinner was an enjoyable affair with only five at the table, not what Rose was used to at home with her large family. The afternoon was spent chatting in Mrs. Robson's comfortable drawing room. During the conversation, Mrs. Jones spoke of her worries concerning the health of her husband as he appeared to be showing no signs of improvement. She considered it may be prudent to return to London and seek a second opinion from another doctor.

Rose asked her if John was well, to which Mrs. Jones replied he was, but offered no further information as to his wellbeing. Rose quickly realised her question had made Mrs. Jones uncomfortable, as it had been her son who had caused her unhappiness. Holding Mrs. Jones in high regard and with no wish to upset her, or lay any blame for John's decision upon her, Rose vowed not to ask about him again.

The rest of the afternoon passed pleasantly until the lengthening shadows prompted the maid to light the candles. Mrs. Robson's cook entered to announce tea was ready to be served and all were invited to partake, so word was sent to inform Mamma of their delay. Enjoying the day thus far, they were further delighted when Mr. Abbott and Mr. Summerfield called, which made the girls' evening even more enjoyable. However, Rose was beginning to tire when eight o'clock chimed, so it was time to return home. Mrs. Robson's coach was sent for, and they were soon under way.

Grateful to be home at Mill Hall, Rose thought she may be asking a little too much of herself, especially after yesterday's lengthy visit to Gillingham. After greeting her daughter with a fuss, Mamma took her straight upstairs to her room with a mug of hot chocolate, which Rose then sat by the hearth in her night attire to enjoy.

WEDNESDAY, 11ᵀᴴ MARCH
John Pinkerton died, 1826.

A wet day went nowhere all day. Papa came home from London. He sent a parcel to Mrs. Walsh in India.

The darkened skies and non-stop pouring rain confined all to the house today. It was a depressing sight to behold for Rose when she drew back the curtains to be greeted by dark skies and rain running down the windowpanes. When the inclement weather kept the family cooped up in the house it could become rather noisy, and so it was today. Mamma told the younger boys, who were particularly boisterous, to go and play in their own room, while Rose took Elizabeth and Grace up to the nursery, allowing Ann, the maid, to go about her other duties. Shortly after, the two Marys joined in the games in the nursery, creating lots of fun and laughter, and the conditions outside were soon forgotten.

After dinner, Mary Nash went upstairs to write letters and Rose sat in the drawing room with her sister Mary to enjoy her singular company. Amongst other things discussed was the relief of seeing how much improvement she had made after all the trauma the last few months had brought. Rose explained, 'Indeed, I do feel much improved in my health, but I'm still most unhappy about John. I have not changed my mind about rejecting his offer of friendship, because I am so angry about the promises he made and so easily broke. It is impossible for me to remain friends with him now.'

'You will forgive him in time,' said Mary.

Mamma entered the drawing room along with the rest of the family as tea was about to be served. Papa returned from London before tea was over, making his family happy to see him safely back home. With nothing more of interest to tell the diary tonight, Rose closed its pages and retired to her bed.

Rosamond

12th March to 20th March

THURSDAY, 12ᵀᴴ MARCH
Gregory, Martyr, the first bishop of Rome, elected 590.

Very wet today. I wrote to Mathilda Knott in the afternoon. Mary and Mary Nash went in the garden between the showers.

Another wet day kept the family at home again. Rose became increasingly restless at being confined to the house against her will, finding it most tiresome.

The morning seemed to be a long one, with the announcement of dinner when it came a welcome distraction. The two Marys were also restless and decided to go out into the garden if the rain ceased. Mamma thought this plan to be foolhardy and advised Rose that if they were to do so, she was not to join them because the heavy downpours experienced yesterday, and this morning would have left the ground muddy and waterlogged.

Occupying themselves with various pastimes the girls made frequent visits to the windows to watch for signs of the rain abating. As soon as it became clear the rain had stopped, the two Marys rushed to the hall for their outdoor clothes and an umbrella each before going out into the garden. Rose went up to her bedroom for a better view of them splashing about in the puddles like children, laughing loudly as they did so. Although Rose accepted Mamma's advice not to venture out into the wet due to the strong possibility of catching a chill, it did not cushion the blow of envy at seeing the two Marys having so much fun and not being able to join them.

Returning to the house after their games, they dripped water all over the hall floor, making Mamma quite cross. She sent them both upstairs immediately to change into dry clothes to avoid falling ill with a cold. As both girls were in robust health there seemed little chance of that happening, but Mamma's concern over Rose made her overly cautious.

They then returned to the drawing room with their various pursuits. To keep dullness at bay, Rose sought a corner to write to her friend Mathilda Knott to tell her of the recent upset with John. She was certain Mathilda would be sympathetic at hearing of her many problems with illness while at the same time having to deal with a broken heart Unfortunately, writing down all her woes brought them to the fore again which reminded her of what she had lost. Upset at this, she began to sob.

The two Marys went directly to her side, and upon receiving their comforting words she was soon laughing with them.

When things had settled, Rose gazed out of the window lost in thought over how difficult it would be and how long it would take, if ever, to forgive John's betrayal. Mamma advised her not to dwell on her troubles, so she drew in a deep breath and tried to cheer herself up, but she could not solemnly promise she would be able to keep up a false cheerfulness, especially during the night.

Retiring to her room after tea with little to write of in her diary, or the will to do so for that matter, Rose prepared for sleep and prayed to wake refreshed.

FRIDAY, 13ᵀᴴ MARCH
Buonaparte outlawed by the Allies, 1815.

Mary Nash, Mary, and I went to church. After church we called on Mrs. Robson. I remained there while they went to the Friars. Mrs. Peppercorn and Mr. Shepherd came in. I came home in Mr. Robson's chaise. Mrs. Jones walked here with the two Marys. Mr. and Mrs. Jones came to say goodbye. I never expect to see Mr Jones again.

The rain had stopped at last. As there was a church service this morning that Rose and the two Marys wished to attend, they decided to walk into Aylesford together. The ground was awash with puddles, but with stout shoes and careful sidestepping they managed to keep their feet dry. When the service had concluded they called on Mrs. Robson who was delighted to see them, providing morning tea and biscuits for her impromptu guests.

Now the weather had settled, the girls wished to take full advantage of it by visiting the Friary, a medieval monastery visible from the rear of Mill Hall on the opposite side of the Medway towards Aylesford and the old bridge. It was a place they often delighted in visiting. The chapel and cloisters were so peaceful; an ideal venue for those in need of solace and comfort.

Had Rose felt strong enough she would have loved to accompany them but decided it would be prudent to stay in the warmth of Mrs. Robson's drawing room. Had she gone, a visit from Mrs. Peppercorn and Mr. Shepherd would have been missed. Both happened to call while she was there, helping her to pass the time most agreeably by catching up on all their news and recent activities. Being a part of this social interaction in the heart of the local community had been sorely missed by Rose after the lengthy confinement to her bedroom.

A knock on the door signalled the return of the girls from the Friary and time to leave the Robsons'. Mr. Robson offered to take Rose back to Mill Hall together with Mr. Jones, as he and Mrs. Jones were returning to London the next day and wished to say their goodbyes to her Mamma and Papa. As Mr. Jones was still unwell the walk would be too difficult, so Rose decided to accompany him in Mr. Robson's chaise for the same reason, arriving home in next to no time.

Meanwhile, Mary, Mary Nash, and Mrs. Jones walked back to Mill Hall together along Friary View, enjoying each other's company as they did so.

With Mr. Jones being so ill, the family feared the possibility that it would be the last time they saw him in Aylesford due to his condition gradually declining. They hoped this would not be so, as he was so dear to them.

Another dreary afternoon spent in the drawing room with no callers to entertain was a distinct contrast to the events earlier in the day. Rose read for a time, then resorted to playing with Grace. However, Grace soon tired of her big sister's company, preferring that of her brother Octavius instead. At just two years her senior, he was deemed to be the better option.

The afternoon passed slowly by until the clock indicated it was time to have tea, served by Mamma in the dining room. Although Rose's preference was to take tea in the drawing room by a warm fireplace, she did not seem to mind today, and following the meal, sought out her bedroom in order to read in peace. Having read what she could, her diary received the day's occurrences before being blotted and closed.

Lying on the bed with her eyes closed, Rose knew her strength was not what it should be, but the fact she was able to go visiting and share the company of those she held so dear pleased her greatly. Stepping out into the world took her mind off her troubles and woes for a while. The fear of her attacks returning as before, or even worse if that were possible, would not leave her and she wondered if she could bear it should they do so.

SATURDAY, 14TH MARCH
Lepanto taken by the Greeks, 1824.

Mr. and Mrs. Jones went home by the 3 o'clock coach. In the afternoon I and Mary Nash went in the garden after dinner.

A largely uneventful day at Mill Hall today, slowly passing with no great traumas or delights to dwell upon. At least Rose's fearful cough was not so troublesome. Mr. and Mrs. Jones were returning home this afternoon on the three o'clock stage to London following their lengthy and popular stay at the Robsons' residence where their company had been enjoyed by all, and they would be sorely missed. The Spongs were quite concerned about Mr. Jones' state of health; although he was not as elderly as Grandpapa Nash in Gillingham, it was likely they both suffered from a similar heart condition.

Mary Nash asked Rose to accompany her in the garden after dinner. Pleased to have been asked she gladly agreed, though Sister Mary declined as she wished to continue with her sewing. Warm clothes were sought and when suitably attired, they crossed the lane to the garden together.

The girls were delighted to see an assortment of spring flowers poking their heads up as if to greet them on entering the walled garden. Such a welcome sight and a promise of things to come. After walking back and forth along the paths for a while, they sat on a bench beneath an old pear tree to rest.

In answer to Rose's question as to whether she was enjoying her stay with them, Mary said, 'Oh yes, and I'm in no hurry to return home, but not wishing to take advantage of your Mamma's kind hospitality, I surely must return to Dover soon.' Rose told her that she also enjoyed her company and did not wish for her to leave just yet.

It was usual for Mary Nash to share Rose's bedroom when visiting, but on this occasion, because she was not fully recovered, it was thought more appropriate to share with her sister instead. Rose sincerely hoped to be sufficiently recovered on her next visit so that they could resume the usual sleeping arrangements with late night talks behind the bed curtains they both enjoyed so much.

After a pleasant hour or so, the girls returned to the house to discover the children were making far too much noise for Rose's comfort, so, seeking some peace and quiet, she went up to her bedroom. Her solitude ended when Mary entered to say tea was being served, after which she spent the rest of the evening in the drawing room conversing with the family while the two Marys played cards in the corner together. It was all rather dull.

Eventually saying goodnight, Rose went back upstairs to tell her diary of yet another boring day. How she longed for the day when she was able to set out on an adventure with her sister again, not knowing where they may end up on one of their frequent walks. Mamma had assured her she was getting a little stronger every day, so with hope and good fortune it may not be too long before they could continue. With this in mind, she closed her eyes and prayed for their swift return.

SUNDAY, 15ᵀᴴ MARCH
Julius Caesar assassinated, B.C. 44.

We stayed at home in the morning on account of the rain. We all went in the afternoon, except Mamma. She and I went to chapel to hear Mr. Jenkins beautiful sermon.

With a wet and dismal morning to start the day, it came as no great surprise that when Mamma enquired during breakfast if anyone wished to attend church, there seemed a distinct lack of enthusiasm to do so as the rain was quite heavy. It was therefore decided that the afternoon service would be attended if the weather improved.

An uneventful morning saw Octavius and Seppy becoming increasingly restless, which in turn led to another quarrel, giving Rose a headache. The winter was dragging its heels, she thought, making us all the worse for it.

The rain eventually stopped falling and the skies gradually cleared after dinner. Gazing through the windows they observed how waterlogged the lane and fields were but, undeterred, they put on suitable clothes and set off walking to church, leaving Mamma at home with baby Elizabeth, Grace, and Octavius.

Papa left the house first with Thomas, George, and John, followed by Rose and the two Marys, Seppy, Augustus, and Freddie – quite an addition to swell the congregation. The younger boys enjoyed splashing about in the puddles along the lane, getting all wet and muddy as a result, though Rose suspected Mamma would not join in their pleasure on seeing their muddy clothes.

Walking along the path by the river, they were alarmed to see how high and fast flowing it was, almost up to the top of the bank. If the rain continued to fall there was a distinct possibility of Mill Hall being flooded.

Fascinated with the intensity of the river, the boys dawdled all the way to the bridge, eventually catching up with Papa and the older boys. When Papa saw their muddy shoes and trousers, he was very cross, saying, 'Have you not spared a thought for the person responsible for laundering your clothes?'

The boys' self-imposed punishment was to endure a lengthy church service followed by what seemed to be an equally lengthy tramp home in their cold and wet garments and shoes before finding comfort in warm and dry replacements. It would be satisfying to know the experience had taught them a lesson, but as most small boys are irresistibly drawn to puddles, as Papa probably was before them, it was highly unlikely that it would. Rose chuckled to think what Mamma would say when they arrived back home.

Reflecting on the service during the walk home, Rose thought how enjoyable it had been, and how happy she was at seeing Mr. Staines their vicar again after missing his company so much of late. She had hoped he would call more frequently while she was ill, but as he only managed to visit the once, she decided his Parish work must be keeping him fully occupied. Rose found his sermon as uplifting as ever and felt lighter in spirit through singing the hymns.

Just as she had foreseen, Mamma was not amused to see the sorry state of the boys' attire when they arrived home, taking them both straight upstairs to wash and change.

The rest of the afternoon passed quietly enough, with tea served in the drawing room much to Rose's satisfaction. Afterwards she went with Mamma to attend chapel for the evening meeting.

Mr. Jenkin's speech made the service as enjoyable as the afternoon one for Rose, who went directly to her room on returning home, feeling tired but content. It was good to write in the diary about spending a happy day doing things with the family again, and she hoped this would remain the case.

MONDAY, 16ᵀᴴ MARCH
The King of Sweden shot, 1792.

Mamma, Mary Nash, Tom, and Mary went to Maidstone. Mary and Tom called on Mrs. Hollingsworth and Mrs. Day, Mrs. McKenzie, Mrs. Brenchley, and Mary McKenzie called. Felt poorly all day. Mr. Trested called.

Rose awoke feeling poorly again this morning. It would seem, she thought, that being in poor health for the rest of her life was to be her fate. Mamma, having been told how she felt, said yesterday's damp air settling on her chest was the most likely cause, and did not appear too concerned. But feeling ill once again put Rose in fear of it becoming worse, including further attacks of bleeding which would be more than she could possibly bear.

Mamma, the two Marys, and Tom went to Maidstone, with Rose feeling miserable as she looked down into the lane from her bedroom window, longing to be with them as they climbed into the coach and departed.

While Rose was reading a book Ann knocked on her door to announce that Mr. Trested had arrived and was asking to see her. He said Mamma had stopped by to request a visit, as her illness had returned. After his examination, he declared that in his opinion it was nothing much to worry about and echoed Mamma's words about the damp weather being sent to try us all. When the warm and dry weather returned, she would be much restored. Rose hoped to be reassured by his visit, but as he seemed to be repeating Mamma's words, it was obvious he had borrowed them as he had no new ideas of his own.

As soon as the party returned home, Mary went to break Rose's solitude to tell her of their excursion, starting with their initial arrival in Maidstone. Alighting in the main square, she and Mamma had gone directly to the shops to make the necessary purchases Mamma needed, while their cousin Mary made some of her own. After completing these, they went to visit Mrs. Hollingsworth and Mrs. Day with Tom. While they were there Mrs. Brenchley called, along with Mrs. McKenzie and her daughter Mary.

'It made for a very jolly morning for them,' Mary said. Then, holding Rose's hand, she added, 'I am sorry you were unable to go with us, Rosie, I really missed your company.' Rose tried to hide how upset she was to have been left out of the excursion, for she knew it wasn't Mary's fault, and of course Mamma had been correct in saying she would be far better staying at home today as the air was still quite damp.

Rose had dinner on her own in her bedroom and felt very lonely doing so. Unhappy at this, she vowed that when dinner was over, she would go downstairs and join the family. Resting for a while by reading a book, she dressed and went down to the drawing room. It was quite noisy in there, as it usually was when the weather prevented the boys from playing in the garden, but Rose didn't mind as her own company did not help her spirits. However, the noise soon gave her a headache, causing her to seek sanctuary in her room straight after tea for a bit of peace and quiet. After reporting of a not so happy day in her diary, it was time to sleep and hope of a better one tomorrow.

TUESDAY, 17ᵀᴴ MARCH
St. Patrick, a Scotch missionary, patron of Ireland, d. 493.

Went nowhere all day, rather dull, it rained in the morning. Augustus's birthday, 9 today. Mr. Trested called.

The persistent rain this morning made Rose decide to stay in the house as a precaution, even though she was feeling a little better today. The two Marys braved the elements, however, to walk around Mill Hall checking for signs of flooding. On their return, they reported seeing the fields were extremely waterlogged and that the River Medway directly behind the house was rising. Papa was quite concerned as his business would be at risk if the river burst its banks and flooded the wharf. All eyes anxiously watched the weather from the windows, hoping to see a sign it was abating.

A welcome distraction from the weather was the fact that today was Augustus's ninth birthday, so dinner was a jolly one. A special meal was always prepared and served by Cook on Mamma's instructions whenever one of the family had a birthday, and a celebratory cake was baked and decorated to enjoy at teatime.

The girls whiled away the afternoon indulging in a variety of minor occupations in the drawing room, with the only visitor being Mr. Trested who called to attend Rose. Pleased to see her dressed and in the drawing room, he immediately said how much improved she looked to which Rose replied by asking,

'Why have I relapsed for the second time then?' He answered in his usual way by blaming her setback on the weather.

Not convinced with his observation, she told him as much, suggesting it may not be the cause at all, as something was telling her there was another reason why she was so afflicted. None too pleased with Rose's self-diagnosis, he replied quite forcibly, 'Poppycock, my dear! You must not let your imagination get the better of you.' She was sorry to make him angry, but at the same time believed that her thoughts were correct.

Mamma served tea in the drawing room again, and when cook brought in Augustus's cake, they all enjoyed a slice. Sadly, this little ceremony did not serve to improve Rose's mood, and not wishing to make everyone else as miserable, she returned upstairs and once again hoped for a better day tomorrow.

WEDNESDAY, 18ᵀᴴ MARCH
The American Stamp Act repealed, 1766.

A wet morning. It cleared up in the afternoon. Mary went and called on Mrs. Robson and I and Mary Nash went to church after tea, heard Mr. Staines preach. Martha B's birthday 22 today.

Another wet morning did not bode well for a better day than yesterday, as all were confined indoors again. Most of the family were bored and restless, trying to pass the time with a variety of games and such like. Seppy and Augustus were the most difficult to amuse as their preferred form of entertainment, running around outside and climbing trees, was not possible. Dinner hour finally arrived to everyone's relief, as it offered a break from the tedium.

When the meal was over, looking through the dining room window suggested that the rain had finally ceased. Fortunately, the river had kept at a low enough level so as not to cause a flood, but everywhere was dripping wet.

Rose decided to stay indoors as did Mary Nash, as she wished to write a letter to her Mamma and Papa in Dover, but Mary, who could not stay indoors for long, decided to walk into Aylesford to call on Mrs. Robson.

The boys, along with Frederick, disappeared to who knows where, much to Rose's relief. They were none too pleased when Mamma asked them to include Octavius in their games, but Mamma insisted upon it, so they had to obey. Rose felt sorry for Octavius as he was a little too young to play with his older brothers, but his only alternative would be the nursery with his equally little sisters. The older boys might not have been happy with the situation, but Octavius's little face beamed.

It was Rose's cousin Martha Brenchley's birthday today, now twenty-two years of age, and as some time had passed since their last meeting, she resolved to write a letter soon.

During dinner, Mamma mentioned a service was being held in Aylesford church that evening, so Mary Nash and Rose decided to attend, taking the coach to the village after tea. Rose enjoyed being inside St. Peter and St. Paul's church on dark evenings, with the flickering candlelight on the stained-glass windows and carvings casting shadows everywhere.

She thought how beautiful it looked. Rose found the service enhanced by these surroundings, and so humbled was she by Mr. Staines' inspired preaching, she once again vowed to be a better person. To her delight, Mr. Staines approached them as they were leaving to enquire after her health.

'I am so pleased to see that you appear to be much improved,

Miss Rosamond,' he said. 'But please take care to keep warm and dry in this very unpleasant weather that we have all had to endure.' Rose thanked him for the wonderful sermon, then after saying goodnight, she went to find Wood who was waiting outside with the coach to take them home.

The girls joined the family in the drawing room on their arrival, but soon Rose was ready to retire, so after saying goodnight to everyone, she ascended the stairs. A blazing fire greeted her on entering the room which pleased her. After changing into night attire, she took a place at her table to write a little before climbing into bed and thinking about tomorrow, hoping for a happy day and better weather.

THURSDAY, 19ᵀᴴ MARCH
Charles of Spain resig. his crown to his son Ferdinand, 1808.

Mrs. Day called, George Nash came after dinner; he brought me some oysters. Mamma gave me a handsome dressing robe. Mary Nash gave me a pair of white kid gloves. Mary and Mary Nash went to call on Mrs. Peppercorn, Mrs. Staines, and Mrs. Robson. My birthday, 21 today

The first thing that came into Rose's mind when she awoke this morning was the joyful thought that today was her birthday. She was now twenty-one years old. During the darkness of her recent illness, she feared not reaching this milestone and thanked God to have done so. Now she could share her delight with the family by celebrating her coming of age with them all. Not wishing to dawdle in her bedroom, which had been her want of late, she set about the task of dressing and making herself presentable for the day ahead. Once satisfied with her appearance, it was time to go downstairs and present herself to the family who were already gathered in the dining room.

With various happy birthdays and good wishes extolled, Rose saw several packages arranged on the dresser, but Mamma insisted on breakfast being served first as Cook would be cross if it was spoilt. The ceremony of opening presents after breakfast took place on everyone's birthday, not just Rose's. As a child she would fidget with anticipation. wishing the repast to finish quickly in order to open her many presents, and now at twenty-one years old, the frustration seemed no different to when she was ten.

At last, with breakfast over and the dishes cleared away, Mamma brought the parcels and placed them in front of her. Opening the first gift, from Mary, Rose found two new books inside that she had long wished for. They were written by her favourite writer Hannah More, so she thanked her sister for her thoughtfulness.

The next parcel from her eldest brother, Tom, contained a large drawing pad with an assortment of watercolour paints. Her old ones were almost finished, so this was a welcome gift indeed.

Brother George's present to her was a selection of prettily coloured ribbons and two hair combs. Rose, surprised at his choice, laughingly asked if had visited the ladies' fashion emporium in Maidstone, or had he asked Mamma to assist in his purchases perhaps? He chuckled and replied he had indeed asked Mamma for help, she was quite correct in her assumption; he had been 'found out'. There was much laughter around the table at this exchange. Rose thanked him for his gift, saying the combs may just help control her fine hair.

John's gift was next. Inside the wrapping she found a large

box of sweetmeats as he knew his sister's fondness for anything sweet, and he too received her thanks.

The next parcel, from cousin Mary, had a pretty pair of white kid gloves nestled inside it. Rose was delighted with such a beautiful gift and promised to cherish them.

The largest parcel of all was from Mamma and Papa. She smiled broadly when she discovered it contained a handsome dark green dressing robe with a fur trim around the neck. It looked so soft and luxuriant compared to her old one, which had become rather worn and limp having been laundered so frequently due to the frightening bleeding episodes.

Feeling truly blessed in the company of her loving family, Rose thanked everyone for their wonderful gifts before they all went into the drawing room where Ann had built up the fire.

The two Marys decided on a walk into Aylesford, where they were to call on Mrs. Peppercorn, Mrs. Robson, and Mrs. Staines. Rose declined the offer of joining them as she was eagerly anticipating reading one of the new books that Mary had bought her.

After the girls had left for the village, Rose settled by the drawing room fire and ventured into the first volume of *Hannah More*, a book of poetry by a writer she found inspired her to be a better person, and to be more mindful of others who had so little in life. Rose felt she had so many things to be thankful for, being truly blessed with a good home and a loving family. While she was absorbed in her new book a visitor called to see Mamma; it was Mrs. Day whose company was always so entertaining. Putting the book aside, Rose joined them, and the morning passed most pleasantly.

The girls arrived home just in time for the birthday dinner. As usual, Cook didn't disappoint. Every course was carefully chosen as being a favourite of Rose's, especially the pudding of burnt cream, a sort of custard with demerara sugar sprinkled on which Cook toasted in some way, making the top go a dark brown colour. After eating a large plateful of this delicious confection, Rose declared herself full to bursting and sought out Cook to thank her for preparing such a special meal for her birthday, to which Cook cheerfully replied, 'It was my pleasure, Miss Rosamond, it is good to see some colour in your cheeks at last.'

The family were resting in the drawing room after dinner when a chaise pulled up outside. George Nash had come from Gillingham to see Rose on her birthday, bringing a gift of oysters, a delicacy he knew she enjoyed. He also had a gift from Grandpapa, a packet of pretty writing paper so she could write to him. She happily wrote a thank you note there and then and handed it to George to deliver on his return.

The rest of the afternoon passed so quickly it was soon time for tea. Cook entered the dining room where they had all reassembled, holding Rose's birthday cake aloft which she carefully sliced and shared around the table.

The time eventually came for George to make the long journey home, so thanking him once again for the oysters, Rose kissed him on the cheek and asked for her love, as well as the note for his kind gift, to be given to Grandpapa before he set off down the lane.

Rose stayed with the family for a while in the evening, but having enjoyed such a wonderful and uplifting day, it had also been a tiring one. Saying goodnight to all, she went upstairs to her bedroom to write in the diary about all the wonderful things that had occurred today, before climbing into bed and falling fast asleep.

FRIDAY, 20TH MARCH
Duch. of Cumberland's Birthday. Vernal equinox begins.

Mrs. Peppercorn called; Mamma went to Maidstone by coach. Mary took Grace to church. George Nash sent me Peter Simple to read. I went in the garden to read the first volume.

Straight after breakfast, Mamma was taken to Maidstone in the coach by Wood.

Mary attended the Friday morning service in Aylesford Church, taking Grace with her as she was being rather troublesome, and Mary thought Rose would still be quite exhausted after the celebrations yesterday. This would afford her the chance to recuperate. Rose, however, was more concerned that Grace may continue her naughtiness inside church.

Half an hour or so after their departure, Mrs. Peppercorn called. With her sister and Mamma absent, it fell upon Rose and Mary Nash to entertain their guest, so Rose sent for tea, and they settled down by the fire to spend a pleasant hour learning Mrs. Peppercorn's news before imparting their own. When she was ready to depart, Mrs Peppercorn said, 'I am so glad to see that you are recovering from your recent illness, Rosamond, and will you convey to your dear Mamma when she returns that I was sorry to have missed her today.'

Just as their guest was leaving, a parcel arrived from Gillingham addressed to Rose. After waving goodbye to Mrs. Peppercorn, the parcel was taken into the drawing room to be opened, where she discovered that George had sent her three volumes in the series titled 'Peter Simple'. Rose had previously intimated to him how much she wished to read them. What a lovely surprise it was. She wondered why he had not presented them to her yesterday, maybe he thought she would be feeling a little flat after her birthday and it would serve to lift her spirits. Whatever the reason, she was delighted with his gift and looked forward to being alone to enjoy reading them.

When Mary returned from church with Grace, Rose enquired if she had misbehaved, as they all knew it was not Grace's habit to remain still for long.

'On the contrary,' said Mary, 'I think she was quite in awe of the proceedings and sat very still beside me but reverted to her usual self later by running away on the walk home. It was quite exhausting keeping up with her.'

Mamma arrived home in time for dinner and was told of Mrs. Peppercorn's visit and how sorry she had been to have called during her absence. Thanking Rose for entertaining their guest, they sat down for dinner.

At the first opportunity following dinner, Rose crossed over the lane into the walled garden to sit on the bench underneath the pear tree, eager to start reading the books she had just received from George. Even though the weather was quite pleasant, it was still necessary to put on a warm shawl for protection against the chill wind as she settled down to read.

Opening the first volume of Peter Simple was delightful, but to think there were two more volumes to read felt truly wonderful. The author of this enjoyable tale was Captain Frederick Marryat, and the hero of the story was a young man considered to be the fool of his highborn family. He was sent by his father to train as an officer in King George's Navy, as no useful purpose could be found for him at home. Thus, young Peter Simple went to war at the age of fifteen. Rose found reading about his escapades most enjoyable, but alas the early spring chill was beginning to make her shiver, forcing her to leave the tranquillity of the garden to go back into the house where it was anything but peaceful.

The idea of going to her bedroom to continue the absorbing tale of Peter Simple was dashed when Mamma insisted that she took charge of Grace and Elizabeth as the two Marys had gone for a walk together, so, putting the book aside, she went up to the nursery to play with her little sisters until teatime.

After tea, Rose went straight upstairs to spend the rest of the evening immersed in Peter Simple's world, a place she found most amusing to behold. Eventually realising it was time to bring her diary up to date, and with Mamma's presence expected at any moment with her night-time drink, Peter Simple was put to one side.

Jackie

2015 – 2016

Mike and I raised a glass to happier days as Big Ben chimed in a New Year: 2015 had arrived.

Our hopeful optimism was short lived when Geoff's (Mike's stepfather) cancer worsened, as did his eighty-seven-year-old mother's ability to cope with the worry of it all.

It was now Mike's turn to witness the unravelling of his parents, something many of us must face at a point in their lives when they turn to us for help and support. We tried our best to keep them in their home, but his mum no longer wanted to do so, and asked me to arrange accommodation for them at the nursing home my mother had lived in for nine years. So, after a long discussion with Glenda and Geoff, we agreed this was the best solution. After pulling a few strings with my long association, they moved into the nursing home within two weeks.

The daily visits, however, proved difficult for me, as my own mother's room had been on the same floor as my in-laws. This meant that every time I walked down the corridor, all the memories of my mum's terrible dementia came flooding back. Eventually I did get used to it, and to be amongst the nurses who had cared for her proved to be comforting.

It was now Mike's turn to manage his parents' affairs, including selling their house and disposing of all their furniture and effects. I handled this unpleasant task for my own mum and stepfather, so I knew the emotional impact it would have, both on him and his sister.

Mike and I had just settled into this routine when the next

trauma shook our world. I received a phone call from my daughter-in-law, Sally in Florida, to tell me that Iain had been admitted to hospital for a quadruple heart bypass. At first, I couldn't get my head round what she was saying to me.

'How can this be?' I said. 'We were only talking to you both on Skype three days ago, and he didn't seem ill in any way, just the opposite in fact as he was climbing a twelve-foot ladder over the pool!'

'We had no idea then,' she said. 'But the next morning he complained of chest pains and admitted to having had them for a while.' On hearing this, Sally persuaded him to go to their doctor for advice, who immediately sent them to the main hospital in Orlando.

After a thorough check-up, Iain's main arteries were found to be almost completely blocked, so a quadruple heart bypass was promptly arranged for the following morning.

My first reaction as his mother was to get on a flight to Orlando but I understood later that Iain didn't want that. At the time I just wanted to be there with him. Sally was incredible, I will never forget her kindness to me during a time of great stress as she took it upon herself via Skype to share her anxiety as we waited for him to come out of the operating theatre. We stayed connected throughout the long hours of his operation, only stopping for necessary breaks and refreshments.

At long last, when the wait was finally over, Sally took her laptop into the intensive care unit so I could see him and talk to him myself. I saw him propped up in bed smiling at me. 'Hello, Mum,' he said. 'Do you want to see my stitches?' and there it was, running the entire length of his chest, the sight of which brought tears to my eyes. Trying hard not to cry, I told him I loved him, but he must rest now, and as soon as the screen went blank, I gave in to the tears I had managed to suppress during the length of our call. I had been reassured he would be fine with my own eyes, which would not have been possible without Sally's kindness, and there are no words to express how grateful I am for her thoughtfulness in involving me.

I will also never forget the closeness we shared as we sat waiting for news, Sally in Florida and me in Harrogate, thousands of miles apart but together in the love we shared for the same man. I am relieved to say Iain made a full recovery and soon resumed his extremely busy life as if nothing had happened.

With this drama behind us life returned to normal, until three months after Iain's major surgery when another crisis arose, this time involving me. I woke up one morning with a severe pain in my side unlike anything I had experienced before.

Mike, rather concerned, rang the surgery who advised him to take me there to see the doctor, which proved to be rather difficult as I was becoming feverish. Getting out of bed to wash and dress seemed like a mountain to climb but climb it I did. Once inside the doctor's surgery, I was diagnosed with an abdominal infection, source unknown.

With the antibiotics I was prescribed we made our way home again and I crawled back into bed where, over the next couple of hours, I quickly deteriorated. Alarmed by my rapidly worsening condition, Mike rang the doctor again, and when she heard of my sudden decline she rang for an ambulance. This action on her part probably saved my life, as my body which had been fine a few hours ago, was now in septic shock.

My memories of that day are rather hazy. I remember seeing paramedics in the bedroom at which point I must have passed out, as the next thing I remember was finding myself in hospital with several doctors and nurses surrounding me. Looking back on that day I don't remember feeling anxious or fearful, just strangely detached with my mind not connecting to the surroundings or danger I was in. That was to come later, when I learned how ill I had been, and it is with grateful thanks to our wonderful NHS who came to my aid so quickly and efficiently that I survived to tell my story.

After a lengthy stay in hospital, I was sent home armed with more antibiotics and a box of hypodermic needles to treat a blood clot found in my stomach, plus lots of advice to rest. The sepsis had left me as weak as a baby, so there was little chance of doing anything else as the simplest of tasks such as showering were beyond me. So poor Mike became my carer; a situation I found rather difficult and prayed it wouldn't go on too long. As the weeks passed, I gradually took back some control of my personal care, but the weakness and exhaustion took longer to recover from, and it was at least two years before I could say things were relatively back to normal.

My mental health concerned me most as I constantly fretted about my rapid near-demise returning and what to look for if it did. Sepsis seemed to have magnified everything; I found myself living in constant fear with my usual optimistic character all but disappeared. All I could feel was doom and gloom, and into this mix I found myself reliving over and over the year Allison had died, and the feelings of guilt that I had tried so hard to suppress began to overwhelm me again. Sepsis had not only taken away my physical health; I began to fear I was also losing my mind. I will never forget the vulnerability I felt at that time. Where had my stoic nature gone? How I wanted my sister to hold me. I could hear her voice in my head saying, 'it will pass, Jack, you will get better in time,' but she had died the year before and she was the only one I wanted to talk to.

I couldn't burden my children with my pain, and I kept much of it away from Mike and my friends. For years I had buried the pain of my daughter's death deep inside me – it was the only way I could cope and finding Rosamond's diary had helped to keep it there. But now, as I tried to recover from a serious illness, I couldn't stop thinking about Allison, and the death of my sister and mother the previous year, so once again I became overwhelmed by grief for the three of them.

At this difficult time Mike's stepfather's health rapidly deteriorated: his prostate cancer had started spreading. As Mike's mother couldn't deal with the fact that nothing more could be done, it was time for me to put my own worries aside to help Mike. He had been there for me, now it was my turn to support him.

Most of our spare time for the rest of that year was spent in their room in the nursing home. Although my mother-in-law was frail, mainly through lack of appetite at Geoff's suffering and the thought of not being able to cope without him, she had no other significant health issues. Her refusal to eat led to dizzy spells, and just two days before Christmas Mum had another fall. A doctor was called for, and by eleven o'clock that evening she was rushed to York Hospital where she passed away on Christmas Eve. Sepsis had struck our family again with no warning.

I had been lucky, but Mum's inability to eat through stress had weakened her so much she stood no chance against such a deadly infection. Shocked by this sudden turn of events, our Christmas passed in a blur.

I don't know how Mike managed to smile as the grandchildren opened their presents while his mother lay in the mortuary at York Hospital. He is a truly remarkable man. Geoff's reaction at learning the love of his life had passed away was heart breaking, and after three long months of pain and agony they were reunited.

Throughout all these setbacks, which affect most of us at times, it must be said we had many happy moments with the family and grandchildren, but the past year had been almost as terrible as 1996. Yet remarkably, just when I thought things couldn't get worse, something truly positive happened.

With most of our time taken up caring for Mike's parents as well as my own health problems, Mike and I had been unable to produce any new paintings for the next art exhibition in May. Mike's help was requested for setting up and dealing with clients, so I went along with him as we knew most of the clients well.

Included among these were the highly regarded art collectors Trisha and Brendan Robinson, who had purchased quite a few of our paintings over the last ten years and we looked forward to seeing them again. Apart from polite conversation we knew little about each other's personal lives, and as they live in Hertfordshire, there wasn't much chance of changing that.

Having been told earlier in the year that Trisha had been ill, I sent her a get-well card, and when she heard I had also been ill, she sent me one. Trish spotted me sitting at the desk when they arrived at the exhibition and came straight over. 'I'm so glad to see you, Jackie,' she said. 'We hoped you would be better now as we missed you at the last exhibition. Heather told us you had been in hospital; I do hope it wasn't serious.'

'Yes, I'm afraid it was,' I replied. 'But what about you? You have also been in hospital; I hope that wasn't serious.'

Trish replied, 'Yes, it was also serious. I was rushed into hospital with sepsis caused by an abscess from a fall down the stairs. It was touch and go for a while and I am still struggling with the aftereffects.'

'Oh my God!' I spluttered. 'That's exactly what I had, and I'm still struggling with it too.'

This revelation shocked us both and we were soon sitting in a corner exchanging our experiences, which was when I discovered that all the strange and unpleasant things I had been going through had also happened to Trish. Apart from the cause of the sepsis, our stories were almost identical, all the fears and worries I continued to fret about a year later she also found hard to cope with. I no longer felt alone, and this was to be the start of a deep and lasting friendship as we took comfort from each other. We may have started out as sepsis buddies, but it didn't take long before we discovered we had much more in common than a near fatal illness. We have connected and bonded over the years in such a remarkable way. I feel blessed to have found such an amazing friend at my time of life, the bonus being that her wonderful husband Brendan has also bonded with Mike. The only difficulty is the distance between us, but thanks to modern technology we keep in regular touch via Skype, telephone calls, and messages.

During our many conversations I talked about losing Allison, and how finding Rosamond's diary had helped me to come to terms with it, but now, since having sepsis, I find my mind focusing on the day she died with all the guilt over her passing haunting me again. '

Oh dear,' she said, 'I am so sorry to hear that, have you thought about writing your feelings down?'

'No,' I replied. 'I have never thought to write about myself, and I wouldn't know where to start.'

'That's a shame, because I believe that's what you need to do.' I realised by now that Trish had a wise head on her shoulders, so I agreed to give it a go.

To my surprise, I found that once the pen was in my hand the words came tumbling out of my head and I didn't even pay attention to the tears that kept falling onto the notebook as I did so. With the last word written, I felt drained but surprisingly calm. Trish's prediction had worked. When I rang to tell her, I had finished my journal she suggested we visit them in Harpenden. 'And when you do,' she added, 'bring that 1835 diary with you.'

Rosamond

21st March to 31st March

SATURDAY, 21ˢᵀ MARCH
Benedict, founder of that order of monks.

Went nowhere all day. Rather dull. I finished the volume of Peter Simple. In bad spirits all day. Had a pain in my side.

Rose woke this morning with a pain in her side, and once again feared the dark days were returning to plague her.

The weather today was cold and wet, so a stroll by the river by way of distraction was not advisable. With no option other than to stay indoors, it fell to the contents of a book to occupy her mind; not an entirely disagreeable option, she thought, and certainly the safest.

Rose confided in Mary at breakfast about her further concerns regarding her health. Mary tried to allay her fears by telling her not to fret and have faith it would not be so. As Rose had seemingly recovered after previous attacks only to be struck down again, she found it very difficult not to be fretful.

Losing herself in a book, she finished reading the first volume of Peter Simple while sitting in a comfortable chair in the drawing room. It did serve to help her mood for a while as she found the story to be most entertaining, following as it did the fortunes and adventures of a young man in the Royal Navy. Apart from this the rest of the day was mostly uneventful, and with no callers to distract her from the dark thoughts, she had little to tell her diary at the end of the day, apart from how low her spirits were becoming again.

SUNDAY, 22ND MARCH
Porto Bello taken, 1740.

I went to church in the morning and called on Grandmamma before dinner. Whilst I was there my old cough came on and I spat a great deal of blood. I stayed at home in the afternoon. Felt poorly. Mary, Mamma, George, and I went to chapel.

After spending a fitful night with irritations in her chest, Rose reluctantly got out of bed, dressed, and went down to the dining room for breakfast. During breakfast, Mamma asked if she felt well enough to attend morning service with the rest of the family. Although feeling a little unwell, Rose thought it may be good for her chest to get some fresh air as the day seemed a fine one, so she decided to join them. Considering her daughter's delicate situation, Mamma insisted on taking the coach to Aylesford rather than walking. Leaving shortly after breakfast they were soon inside the church.

Once seated in the family pew, Rose knelt in prayer. With her eyes tightly closed, she silently beseeched the Lord to be spared from any more of her frightening bleeding attacks. Only she found that her prayers were either unheard or unheeded, for while at Grandmamma's house her cough returned. Rose was in great despair when she couldn't control the bleeding that followed, so Mamma had to hurriedly organise a return to Mill Hall in the coach. Soon back at home, Rose went straight to her room, trying hard not to cry whilst being aided by Mamma. But when she was eventually left alone with her worst fears coming to pass, she wept uncontrollably for some time.

An hour or so later, Mamma took her some dinner on a tray, of which she ate very little. Her sister Mary went to keep her company after dinner, shortly joined by Mary Nash. The girls tried hard to make Rose smile with tales related to them by Mrs. Robson during their visit after the church service, but despite their best efforts, they failed to raise her spirits. Eventually giving in to a lost cause, the two Marys left Rose to her misery.

After a while and still feeling unwell, she decided to break her solitude and seek company downstairs by joining the family in the drawing room for tea.

Mamma, who had planned to attend evening service at the chapel, enquired if anyone would like to accompany her. Mary and George said they would; Rose also wanted to go, but Mamma did not think it wise for her to go out in the evening air. After pleading with her mother of her spiritual need to be in the house of God to pray for her own salvation, Mamma eventually agreed, and the foursome left in the coach for Chapel. Rose was fearful the bleeding would reoccur during the expedition, but thankfully it did not.

In the sanctity of the chapel, she repeated her prayers to the Lord, firmly believing in his ability to hear all prayers no matter where they are conducted, in church or chapel. Rose felt a sense of calm on returning home as she had prayed for the strength to accept her fate. However, fears of her illness resulting in a life spent in the drawing room, languishing on the chaise longue with a blanket upon her knees whilst watching everyone going about their lives and not being able to join them, truly terrified her. She began to think it would be better to be in the arms of the Lord, if that was to be her fate.

MONDAY, 23ʳᴰ MARCH
A. Weber died, 1829.

Felt very poorly all day. Mr. Trested saw me in the morning, he gave me some physic. Mamma, Mary Nash, Seppy, and Octavius went to Gillingham. Mary Nash and Octavius came back in the evening and left Mamma and Seppy there. Mr. and Mrs. Robson came to see me in the morning. I finished the third volume of Peter Simple. Tom went to Gillingham. Alfred Nash came back with him.

A very troublesome day began to unfold, with a letter arriving in the morning addressed to Mamma. She had received word from her papa's housekeeper to say he had taken a bad turn, so her presence was required in Gillingham as soon as possible as Mrs. Nash suffered from poor eyesight. This urgent communication threw the Spong household into great disarray. As he had suffered with poor health for some time, the family were naturally worried at this latest turn of events.

Mamma hurried upstairs to pack some clothes for herself, and as Seppy was prone to anxiety on her absence, he was to go too, Mamma informing Ann of this arrangement as her duties usually involved minding the little ones. With Octavius also wanting to see his grandpapa, Mary Nash joined the party to bring him home again in the evening. With all due preparations made and bags stowed, they boarded the coach and left for Gillingham post-haste. On the journey, Mamma's thoughts turned to Rose whose illness had returned. The fact that her daughter Mary had promised to take great care of her stricken sister did not stop her fretting.

Back at Mill Hall, Rose felt flustered and worried about Grandpapa, hoping this latest setback would not prove to be the undoing of him and prayed for his swift recovery.

While Rose and Mary were sitting in the drawing room discussing poor Grandpapa's situation, Mr. Trested arrived. When told of their traumatic experiences that morning, he expressed his sorrow at hearing of it, and that Mrs. Spong seemed to have so many troubles happening all at once. After these sympathies he enquired after Rose's health, who replied that in truth she was feeling very poorly. Producing some of his unpopular physic from his valise, he handed it to her with the usual instructions for its usage and took his leave.

Mr. and Mrs. Robson were the next to visit: they had called to enquire after Rose. Mary sent for tea and during the taking of it, they were also told of the morning's occurrences. Eldest brother Thomas entered the drawing room to say he intended going to Gillingham to see Grandpapa. With the girls fearing his condition may be quite serious, Rose suggested that perhaps she and Mary should accompany him, but Thomas would not agree to this, stating that due to her own poor health, putting herself in danger would serve no useful purpose. Rose agreed that it would be more sensible to stay at home considering her own condition. Moreover, Ann and Hannah would appreciate help with the little ones.

It was a very unsettled morning, making dinner a most sombre occasion. Ann had decided to give the little ones their dinner in the nursery, so even their lively chatter was missing to cheer her up.

After dinner Rose went to her room and sat by the fire to read the last volume of Peter Simple. A most interesting story, which nonetheless failed to lift her spirits today.

Mary entered her room at teatime to say Mary Nash had just returned with Octavius. They had left Mamma and Seppy at Grandpapa's house for Mamma to nurse him, as he was indeed very ill.

While taking tea in the dining room, they were joined by their brothers and Papa. Ann had taken the little ones up to the nursery again for tea. At the table, Mary Nash told them of the day's events in Gillingham. The doctor had been sent for, who had, not surprisingly, declared Grandpapa to be very ill due to his heart. This meant Mamma would have to stay with him until he recovered or whatever else fate dictated. Before leaving the table, the family joined together in prayer for Grandpapa's swift recovery.

Tom returned home in the evening, bringing Mamma's half-brother Alfred Nash back with him. Rose returned to her bedroom to write in the diary about how anxious and sad she was feeling tonight.

TUESDAY, 24TH MARCH
Queen Elizabeth died, 1603.

I received a letter from J. Jones by post to enquire after my health. I wrote him a letter in the morning and sent it. The two Marys went to Aylesford after dinner. Felt poorly all day.

Despite feeling unwell again this morning, Rose got herself dressed and went into the nursery across the landing to ask Ann if she wanted her to take Grace and Octavius downstairs for breakfast. She replied, 'That would be a great help, Miss Rosamond, thank you.' Mary was already in the dining room with Papa, Freddie, and Augustus, then Tom, John, and George came in with Alfred. Breakfast too was a sombre affair without Mamma sitting at the end of the table watching over her children like a shepherdess with her sheep. Her presence at the morning meal was sorely missed by all. The house seemed incomplete without her at the helm, with everyone silently hoping she would return home soon.

The postman delivered a letter addressed to Rose this morning. It had been sent by John who had written to enquire after her health, but its true purpose was to enquire if she had thought about his request for them to remain friends.

Rose went straight to her bedroom to reply to his letter, and in it she said that, yes indeed, she had spent much time thinking of his request and now having considered everything, in her heart she did not feel it would be possible to be just friends. The reason she gave for this decision was that, as her illness had now returned, she truly could not deal with both the pain of seeing him again and that caused by ill health. She concluded her letter by wishing him well in his new position, and to accentuate her anguish, she signed it with her full title of Miss Rosamond Nash Spong.

After sealing the envelope, she stood up from her chair, feeling quite resolute in her written words and vowing never to have her head turned again by false promises. Going downstairs with the letter clutched in her hand, she gave it to Mary, asking her to post it when next in Aylesford.

The rest of the day was a sad one and passed very slowly.

WEDNESDAY, 25TH MARCH
LADY DAY. Holiday at the Exchequer.

Mr. Trested came to see me, Mary Nash, Mary, and Alfred Nash walked to Town Malling. They called on Mrs. Lucas. A. Nash went home, took back the books George Nash had lent me. I wrote to him. Mary went to Aylesford, called on Mrs. Robson.

Today was another day of worrying about Grandpapa. Rose was finding it difficult without Mamma's support but knew she was needed elsewhere, so she accepted the situation with good grace.

Mr. Trested called again, and as usual Rose feared he would be unable to find a cure for her illness. It had become clear that he had no way of making this happen, as she still had nothing more than his physic, a blister plaster, and meaningless words, none of which had worked. He spoke again of asking another physician to attend her, but when this was to happen, he did not, or rather would not, say.

Mary Nash and Mary walked to Town Malling after breakfast with Alfred Nash, taking Rose's letter with them. It was just before dinner when they arrived back at Mill Hall. Mary told her sister they had called on Mrs. Lucas whilst they were there, which made Rose wish she could have gone with them had she been well enough to walk that far.

After dinner, Alfred was to return home to Gillingham, so Rose asked him to take back the books George had lent her. She also included a letter to George, asking him to assure Mamma that all was well at home and not to worry about them.

Mary went to Aylesford to see Mrs. Robson in the afternoon,

while Rose stayed in the drawing room with cousin Mary. They played with Grace and Octavius, but Rose, soon tiring, asked to be excused, seeking her bedroom to rest on the bed where she fell asleep for a while.

When Mary returned, she crept into her sister's bedroom to gently wake her, stroking her hair whilst asking how she was feeling, and then to say that tea was being served. When Rose was sufficiently awake, they both went downstairs arm in arm to the drawing room.

Mary, as the eldest daughter, had assumed Mamma's role in her absence and was doing an admirable job taking charge of the household. This was especially true as far as Rose was concerned, who hoped there would be no frightening episodes of bleeding for them to deal with whilst Mamma was attending the sick elsewhere.

Rose stayed in her bedroom to read for most of the evening, frequently pausing with a heavy heart at the situation and waiting for news from Gillingham.

THURSDAY, 26ᵀᴴ MARCH
Sir A. Boswell killed in a duel by Mr. Stuart, 1822.

Mr. Trested came to see me, brought some more physic. We all stayed at home all day. Felt rather ill. After dinner Papa went to market. In bad spirits.

Rose felt rather poorly all day and missed her mother greatly. Word had been sent to say that although Grandpapa continued to be unwell, there were signs of a slight improvement. Until he had fully recovered, Mamma would be required to stay in Gillingham to nurse him. Rose was also missing her seven-year-old brother Seppy and would be more than happy to have him home causing mischief once again.

Everyone stayed at home as the weather, being cold and dull, tempted no one to venture out, until after dinner when Papa went to the weekly market in Aylesford. Had Rose been in better health she would have accompanied him, as she enjoyed seeing the colourful market stalls with all their local produce, often helping Mamma to purchase vegetables and fruit. With these melancholy thoughts she confessed to her diary about being in very low spirits all day.

Mr. Trested called earlier with more of his delightful physic for her to drink, the partaking of which did not serve to lift her mood in any way.

Feeling overcome with sadness and nothing more of interest to write about today, she sought solace in sleep.

FRIDAY, 27ᵀᴴ MARCH
James I. died, 1625. Peace of Amiens, 1802.

Mrs. Robson called in the morning. Papa, George, and Mary went to tea at Mrs. Robson's. Papa went to a meeting with Mr. Robson. I received a letter from XXX by Wallace coach. Mr. Trested called.

Mrs. Robson called this morning to enquire after Rose's health and for news of Grandpapa. Mary, fully aware of her duties as the eldest daughter in the absence of Mamma, served her tea.

In the afternoon Papa went to a meeting with Mr. Robson, and as Mary and brother George had been invited to take tea with Mrs. Robson at their home, they went with him. Rose, sorry to be excluded from this excursion, knew a walk to Aylesford would be too difficult for her to undertake so she reluctantly accepted she couldn't go with them.

A letter arrived by Wallace coach addressed to Rose from John. He had written again imploring her to reconsider her decision not to remain friends. It was obvious he still held her in high regard and still wished to have her in his life, even if only as a friend. Reading this, she began to think that perhaps she had been rather hasty cutting him out of her life completely, and she may have to reconsider what was said in her previous letter. Since he ended their understanding, she had truly missed him, and this had made her realise that having a friendship with John must surely be better than never seeing him again. She decided to write a letter to tell him of her feelings after deliberating further as to whether a friendship was enough.

'Are you taking your medicine regularly, Miss Rosamond?' was the first thing Mr. Trested asked on his afternoon's visit.

'Yes indeed,' was her reply, making a mental note to ask God for forgiveness as she was not being completely honest with him. In truth, as it was such a trial to swallow the dreadful draught, and with Mamma trusting Mary to administer the medicine herself, she managed to avoid as many doses as she possibly could.

The afternoon's task of helping Ann with the little ones proved to be quite tiring, so at the first opportunity Rose went to her bedroom for a short rest until the time came to supervise tea in the dining room for the rest of the family in Mary's absence.

Papa returned home with Mary and George after tea. Rose was relieved to see them. After welcoming them all home she took herself straight back to her bedroom to read John's letter once more. Poring over his words again and again until her tears made it too difficult to read, she knew a lot of thinking was required about their future relationship together in whatever guise it may be. With her mind in turmoil, she suspected her sleep would be much disturbed tonight.

FRIDAY, 28ᵀᴴ MARCH
General Abercromby died, 1801.

Mary Nash and Mary went and called on Mrs. Staines. After dinner Mr. Trested called to see me. Felt the pain in my side after tea. Aunt Brenchley came down by Wallace coach.

Mamma had been in Gillingham for six days now and they were all missing her greatly, none more so than the little ones. Grace cried for her every night, and when she couldn't settle, Mary had to take her into her own bed until she fell asleep before carefully returning her.

Word was received today that Grandpapa was slowly improving, but with Mamma reluctant to leave him, the family were resigned to continue without her as best they could until she felt able to return home.

Aunt Brenchley called this morning, following a request from Mamma asking her to visit Mill Hall to enquire after Rose's health, and to see how she and Mary were managing the household in her absence. Rose was delighted to see her, but with the two Marys in Aylesford visiting Mrs. Staines, the wife of their dear vicar, it fell upon Rose to receive and entertain her. Replying to Aunt Brenchley's enquiry about her health, she told her that indeed she remained unwell, but with Mary and Mary Nash's help she was able to manage her duties to the family.

Rose then spoke of cousin Mary being a great source of comfort, and how grateful she was for her extended visit, adding how much she would be missed on her return to Dover. Satisfied with this reply, her aunt then enquired if Mary took charge of ordering the meals with Cook. Rose replied that yes indeed, Mary met with Cook every morning to discuss whatever needed to be purchased for the daily menus and oversaw the household. Also, she informed her that Mary held the key to the tea caddy. Rose assured her they were managing well in Mamma's absence but missed her terribly.

'I am so glad to hear that,' she said. 'But nevertheless, I will return to visit you in due course, as your dear Mamma has charged me to do so.'

Aunt Brenchley stayed for dinner, making notes, until Wood took her to Aylesford where she could board the Wallace coach back to Camberwell. Mr. Trested was the next caller. Rose could not understand why he bothered calling every day as he never seemed to do anything to ease her discomfort, and his bill for attending her would, she feared, be rather a large one.

After a quiet and unremarkable afternoon, Mary ordered tea to be served in the dining room. As the tea things were being cleared, Rose felt the dreadful and familiar pain in her side again, making her fearful another attack of bleeding would follow as it had in the recent past. Mary advised her sister to spend the evening in her bedroom resting. Feeling very tired and anxious, Rose knew her sister was aware of how difficult she was finding her illness without Mamma there to comfort her.

'I will bring you some hot milk soon, Rosie,' said Mary, before putting the little ones to bed.

Dressed in her nightgown and robe, Rose began writing of today's events in her diary whilst waiting for the hot drink to arrive.

SUNDAY, 29ᵀᴴ MARCH
Capt. Coram, projector of the Found. Hospital, died, 1751.

We all went to church in the morning. We called on Mrs. Peppercorn after church. I stayed at home in the afternoon. No one went to chapel in the evening. Mary Nash went to church in the evening.

Fortunately, the sharp pain Rose had experienced yesterday had not led to anything worse during the night, and she managed to sleep. Fortified by this, she attended the morning church service, travelling there in the coach with Octavius, Mary, and cousin Mary. Papa, who preferred walking there when the weather permitted, did so with the rest of her brothers. Rose, as ever, enjoyed Mr. Staines' sermon and felt greatly comforted by it. It was very chilly in the church as the weather had been extremely blustery and cold.

While they were standing outside waiting to speak to Mr. Staines, Mary suggested that they call on Mrs. Peppercorn for morning tea. So, on leaving the churchyard, Wood took them in the coach to Cossington Farm where he stayed in her warm kitchen to enjoy a hot drink while waiting for further instructions. Mrs. Peppercorn and Mamma were dear friends. Rose held her in high regard. She was an extremely kind and jolly soul in whose company many happy hours were spent playing on her farm when they were children, which included helping them to feed the animals. Even now the younger boys often went there to play.

A happy and convivial hour was enjoyed exchanging news. Mrs. Peppercorn asked after Grandpapa's health and said she hoped Mamma would return home to them soon. When it was time to go home for dinner, Mr. Peppercorn brought Octavius in. He had spent his time looking at the animals and helping to feed them, much more fun for a five-year-old boy than sitting amongst ladies gossiping.

After dinner, Rose stayed by the fire in the drawing room reading a book as the busy but enjoyable morning had left her feeling rather weary. The tranquillity ended, however, when Ann brought little Grace in to play with Octavius, at which point it all became rather noisy. As a result, Mary soon abandoned her sewing, as did Rose her book. Mary Nash, meanwhile, was upstairs writing letters to her family, and remained oblivious to all the mayhem.

Mary ordered tea to be served in the warm drawing room once again. Such fun was had toasting muffins on the fire. Papa, on hearing the happy voices, went in to join them after spending the afternoon in his study, seeking his favourite chair close to the hearth. All agreed, however, that even though they were enjoying this time together, it was not the same without Mamma.

When the time came for Grace and Octavius to go upstairs to bed, Grace demanded that Mary should be the one to take her. Under normal circumstances Mamma was charged with this task, now Grace had decided that no one apart from Mary was allowed to take her place in the nursery. Rose supposed that at least when the time came for Mary to become a mother, she would know just what was required of her.

As the children were taken upstairs Rose also decided to retire, as by this time she was feeling rather unwell, so, saying goodnight to the family, she went up to her own room. Before sleep overtook her, she reflected on a most pleasant day. Even feeling poorly had not spoilt it.

MONDAY, 30ᵀᴴ MARCH
Bonaparte repulsed at Acre, 1799.

I went nowhere all day. Mary and Mary Nash went to Aylesford. They called on Mrs. Staines and Grandmamma. Papa went to Sevenoaks.

After breakfast, the two Marys made plans to walk into Aylesford. Rose, like her sister, found confinement indoors hard to bear, but her illness was making it impossible to live a normal life. Mary Nash offered to stay at home to keep Rose company, but Rose declined her gesture, insisting she should accompany her sister and assuring her she would do very well on her own with her books. When they had left, however, Rose began to feel envious of how healthy they were compared to her sorry state, and the fact they had the freedom to enjoy it while she had to stay at home and fret about her future, or indeed whether she even had one. Yesterday's happy mood had left her, and she was once again deep in despair.

There were no callers to lift her mood and with everyone else going about their business, she felt lonely and isolated. Determined to shrug off her problems, she decided to go in search of Ann who was overseeing the little ones and found them in the walled garden. Grace and Octavius were running down the paths chasing each other, Ann followed with Elizabeth, who was wriggling in her arms trying to get down to follow Grace and Octavius. It was such a happy sight to see the children having so much fun. Rose could feel her spirits lifting at their games, and once again resolved to spend less time worrying about her plight and more time with the little ones. To that end, she stayed in the garden with them until the two Marys returned. Mary

Nash came into the garden to join in the merriment, while Mary went to supervise the dinner with Cook.

During dinner, the two Marys spoke about their morning walk to the village. First, they called on Mrs. Staines at the vicarage, then made their way to Grandmamma's house. Both Mrs. Staines and Grandmamma were happy to hear news of Grandpapa's recovery and were confident Mamma would return home soon.

The afternoon was occupied much like yesterdays, except this time Papa went in the coach to Sevenoaks on business. On the journey, he thought of his wife and how much he was missing her. Surely if Grandpapa was much improved, he would have her back at Mill Hall soon.

Today had been a dreary one for Rose, apart from the brief interlude in the garden, so, with little to record, she blew out the candle and climbed into bed.

TUESDAY, 31ST MARCH
The Allies enter Paris, 1814.

Algernon Brenchley came to say Martha Brenchley was not able to come today. Aunt Brenchley came to spend the day here. Mary went to Aylesford to see Grandmamma, Aunt Brenchley slept here

A visit from Martha Brenchley, the girl's cousin, was expected today. She had sent a letter to that effect a week or so ago. Rose had been eagerly anticipating spending some time with her but was to be disappointed after Hannah showed Martha's brother Algernon into the drawing room with news. He had arrived with his mother, Aunt Brenchley, in their chaise to inform them that his sister Martha was ill and unable to visit them today. Rose was sorry to hear her cousin was ill and sorry not to have her company in equal measure, saying, 'Please tell her I hope she gets better soon and give her my very best wishes.' Algernon stayed to take morning tea before returning on his own to Camberwell.

Aunt Brenchley's re-appearance came as no surprise, as she had suggested on her recent visit that she would keep her eye on things during Mamma's absence.

Mary ventured out on her usual walk to Aylesford, calling in to see Grandmamma again. The day was pleasant enough for Rose, who rather enjoyed Aunt Brenchley's company. When Mary politely accepted Aunt's assistance in supervising the meals, Rose thought her sister was more than capable of managing them herself, but then again, Aunt Brenchley was only carrying out Mamma's wishes to watch over them.

After a tea organised through a joint effort, they all stayed in the drawing room until it was time to retire. As Rose sat by the fireside in her bedroom making notes in the diary, dressed in her night attire and ready for bed, Mary came in with a cup of hot milk and stayed awhile to talk. Aunt Brenchley, she confided, was quite satisfied they were not in want, and would be returning home directly after breakfast to inform Mamma that all was well, with no further need to worry about them.

Rosamond

1st April to 10th April

WEDNESDAY, 1ST APRIL
Napoleon married to Maria Louisa, Archduchess of Austria, 1810.

Aunt B went home after breakfast. Mary Nash and I called on Mrs. Haines. Mr. Trested came. Mr. B brought Martha B to stay with us. The two Marys went to church morning and evening.

It was the first day of April, and Rose's heart was gladdened to see spring had arrived at last. Aunt Brenchley left after breakfast, pleased with the knowledge they were able to manage the household on their own, but certain Mamma would be home with them very soon.

After saying goodbye to Aunt Brenchley, Mary Nash asked Rose to accompany her on a walk to Aylesford if she felt able enough to do so, as the sun was shining, and the air was mild. Rose readily agreed that fresh air and sunshine would be good for her health, particularly as the day was warmer than of late. The girls enjoyed a most pleasant walk and delighted in seeing the wild daffodils just starting to flower beneath the budding trees, with their yellow heads turned towards the sun. They stooped to pick a bunch as a gift to Mrs. Haines as they intended to call on her for morning tea.

Two church services were held today, with Mary and Mary Nash attending the first together. With dinnertime fast approaching, Mary wasted no time in returning home after the service to supervise the meal with Cook.

Entering the house, she removed her cloak and bonnet and went to the kitchen. Rose had seen her sister arrive from the drawing room where she was reading and thought how relieved Mary would be to hand over the responsibility of running a household back to Mamma when she returned home, hoping it would be soon as everyone was missing her terribly.

Mr. Trested called after dinner, followed shortly by Mr. Brenchley who had brought his now recovered daughter, Martha, to stay for a while, much to Rose's delight. After a happy reunion, Rose showed the visitor to her room before taking her and Mary Nash to the walled garden across the lane for a stroll down the paths where they all enjoyed a happy conversation and heard of Martha's news.

Rose and Mary were delighted to have house guests, as it was usually just the two of them, apart from their much younger siblings whom they adored, Grace who was three and Elizabeth now eighteen months. In a household that included eleven men, it made a refreshing change and enormous fun. All this was a particularly welcome distraction for Rose, serving to ease her mind from all its worries, and with the weather so pleasant and mild, Rose was able to exchange her thick cloak for a warm shawl.

Eventually the three girls returned to the house for tea, after which the two Marys decided to attend Aylesford church for the evening service, with Martha and Rose staying at home to enjoy each other's company.

Rose was happy to report in her diary tonight that the day had been a most pleasant one for a change. Her diary this year had been mostly filled with misery and sadness, so it was gratifying to note that she had enjoyed herself so much today, and her spirits had been greatly lifted because of it. She could only hope her situation would continue to improve as time goes by.

THURSDAY, 2ND APRIL
Lord Nelson's victory off Copenhagen, 1801.

Aunt B came in the morning. Mrs. Day called after dinner. Mary Nash and I went to Aylesford, called on Grandmamma. Mrs. McKenzie and her two girls were there. Mrs. M and her two girls returned with us and drank tea here.

Aunt Brenchley paid another visit this morning with news they had all been waiting for – she had received word from Mamma that Grandpapa was much improved and eating well, therefore she could return home tomorrow with Seppy. They were all delighted to hear Mamma and Septimus were coming home at last.

As Rose was feeling improved and the weather still pleasant, she decided to walk into Aylesford to visit Grandmamma. Considering her recent illness, she asked Mary Nash if she wouldn't mind walking with her. 'It will be my pleasure,' Mary replied. Suitably attired, they set off together, leaving sister Mary at home with Aunt Brenchley.

When the girls arrived at Grandmamma's they found she already had callers, as Mrs. McKenzie and her two daughters were there. Rose had not seen Mrs. McKenzie for a while, so they had many things to talk about, particularly her recent dreadful illness. Mrs. McKenzie, having only recently learnt of this, expressed her relief at seeing how much better she appeared to be.

When the subject of Mamma's imminent return came up,

Rose replied that she had been sorely missed and yes indeed, they would be all the better for having her amongst them again. She told her that Grace had been fractious without Mamma and had attached herself to Mary by wanting to sleep in her bed. But as Mary was already sharing her bed with Mary Nash, she could imagine the difficulties they both faced with a wriggling Grace between them all through the night. With Mamma home, both Marys would be glad to have some peace at last, to which cousin Mary laughed and admitted they would indeed, much to the amusement of Mrs. McKenzie and Grandmamma.

The girls enjoyed their visit, and when it was time to return home Mrs. McKenzie said she would accompany the girls back to Mill Hall in order to visit Mary and Aunt Brenchley and be served yet more tea.

Rose had enjoyed today and was praying that nothing would occur to delay Mamma's return tomorrow. Before retiring, she reported another happy day to her dairy and hoped tomorrow would be an even happier one with Mamma returning.

FRIDAY, 3ʀᴅ APRIL
Richard, Bishop of Chichester, a learned and pious prelate.

Mary and Martha went to church in the morning. I went in the garden before dinner and read Hannah More. Old Aunt and Uncle B came to tea. Papa went to Gillingham to fetch Mamma and Seppy home.

There was much excitement this morning as Mamma was coming home. She had been at Grandpapa's for twelve days and it had seemed like an age. Grandpapa was still frail but well enough to be left in the care of Mrs. Nash and his housekeeper, a kindly lady who served him well.

The morning went very slowly. Rose sat in the garden to immerse herself in a book hoping time would go the quicker for it. Mary and Martha Brenchley went to the morning service but Rose, intent on carrying on reading, declined their request to walk into Aylesford with them. After dinner, Papa left for Gillingham to collect Mamma and Seppy and bring them home.

Old Aunt and Uncle Brenchley, who were the parents of Aunt Brenchley's husband Charles, called this afternoon. Their home was in Albion Place, Maidstone. They were received in the drawing room, and once comfortable Mary served everyone tea. Having callers helped to pass the afternoon, but during their animated conversation it was difficult to listen for the coach returning. It seemed to Rose that the clock on the mantle was ticking more slowly than usual, and the hands had ceased to move, as her longing to see Mamma was playing tricks with her eyes.

When old Aunt and Uncle Brenchley left for home, the family returned to the drawing room to wait quietly with ears pricked. Grace became more and more fractious with each passing minute after being told of Mamma's imminent arrival. At last, they heard the coach arriving and everyone rushed to the door in order to be the first to greet Mamma and Seppy. Rose carried Grace out and Mary held baby Elizabeth in her arms. Once in the hall there was so much hugging and jostling that Rose was certain poor Mamma would be quite overwhelmed by the noise. The elder members of the family tried to restrain themselves, allowing the younger ones to greet her first. Rose, however, was desperate for Mamma's attention needing it as much or more so than they, but she knew she had to wait her turn.

After the joyous welcome had subsided a little, they returned to the drawing room to hear of Mamma's news about her stay with Grandpapa. She explained that although he was indeed much improved, given his age and frailty his heart could not be expected to last much longer. They must prepare themselves for what will surely come to pass.

They were all quite sombre at this news, but Mamma soon had them chattering as she asked for all the news that had occurred whilst she had been away. Turning to Martha Brenchley, she said how pleased she was to welcome her into their home and that she could stay, if she wished to do so, for as long as she desired. Then Mamma looked at Rose, and said, 'And you, Rosie, just how well are you? I can see that you seem a little better than when I left for Grandpapa's, and your complexion is a little pinker than of late. You can tell me all your news later when we are alone.' Rose assured her that she had fared well enough during her absence thanks to much help from Mary, cousin Mary, and their maids Hannah and Ann.

Cook brought tea into the drawing room to be served around the fire, and at last order was restored to the household when Mamma was charged with pouring the tea for her large family.

It was quite late with Rose in her bedroom prepared for bed before Mamma was able to go and talk to her. There had been so many demands on her attention, not least from Grace who had no wish to go to bed in case Mamma left again. Eventually, when sleep overtook her, Mamma was able to leave her in the care of their nursery maid, Ann.

Sitting by the fire, Rose opened her heart to Mamma about all the trials she was having to endure, her fear of the bleeding returning, and her thoughts of what she should do regarding John Jones. With the relief and pleasure of having Mamma home at last, Rose was confident she would sleep soundly tonight.

SATURDAY, 4ᵀᴴ APRIL
Lord Kenyon died, 1802.

Stayed at home all day, not in good spirits. Aunt Brenchley came to tea.

The high spirits Rose had enjoyed yesterday had all but disappeared and the pain in her side had returned, making her fretful she was about to be overwhelmed by illness again.

She consoled herself with the fact that whatever may happen, at least she now had Mamma to help should the bleeding occur again, which was a great source of comfort to her. Because of the pain in her side, she stayed indoors all day, not wanting to make it worse by moving about.

The two Marys took the little ones across the lane to amuse them in the garden. Rose made herself as comfortable as she could in the drawing room to read, and Mamma joined her for a while. She reassured Rose, after hearing of her woes once again, that all would be well in the end and how wise it was to rest.

While the family were sitting in the drawing room after dinner, they had another visit from Aunt Brenchley who stayed for tea. It was a dull day for Rose, with little happening apart from the pain in her side and Aunt Brenchley's visit. Had Mr. and Mrs. Robson not been in London visiting Mr. and Mrs. Jones, she felt certain the latter would have called on Mamma to hear all her news and give her the latest news of Aylesford in return.

When Rose started to feel unwell again after tea, she excused herself and went directly to her bedroom. Low in spirits, she wrote as much in her diary. Despite the resolve to improve her mood yesterday, she found her state of mind changed every day and always seemed beyond her control no matter how hard she tried.

SUNDAY, 5ᵀᴴ APRIL
John Stow died, 1605.

We all went to church in the morning. I stayed at home in the afternoon. Martha, Mary Nash, and Mary went. Mamma Papa, I and Mary Nash went to chapel.

Thank goodness, thought Rose, having woken up feeling refreshed and without pain. After rubbing the sleep from her eyes, she drew back the curtains and decided that as it was Sunday, she would go to church for the morning service. Ann looked after the two little girls at home, while Rose, Mamma, Seppy, and Octavius went in the coach, leaving the rest of the family to walk there. It was a splendid service as usual, and Mr. Staines did not disappoint with his sermon.

After dinner in the drawing room, Mamma asked if anyone wished to return to church. Rose decided to stay at home, but Mary, Martha, and Mary Nash wanted to walk back to St. Peter and St. Paul's for the afternoon service, with the rest of the family staying at home by the fire.

Mill Hall mansion house was a picture of domestic bliss; Mamma busy mending, the little ones playing with their toys, Rose engrossed in a book, and Papa in his study.

Frederick, Augustus, and Seppy had disappeared off somewhere to climb trees or throw sticks into the Medway. Wherever they may be, thought Rose, they were bound to make a magical re-appearance just as tea was being served.

John and George had also disappeared, while Edward, William, and Henry were away at school until the weekend. The Spongs were a large family, so their two extra guests created quite a tussle to get near the fire, and the ritual of tea was a long process. Mary and Rose helped Mamma serve the tea as several pots were needed to satisfy everyone, and the tea table was crammed full of cakes and fancies

When tea was finished, Mamma enquired if anyone wished to accompany her to chapel for the evening service. Papa said yes, as did cousin Mary, and as they were to go in the coach, Rose decided to join them. Mamma looked forward to attending chapel again; it always reminded her of her childhood. Unfortunately, on the journey home Rose began to feel unwell again. Upon their arrival, she went straight to her bedroom after saying goodnight to the family. It seemed to her that when she went out and about, it made her tired and breathless. As well as being very concerned about her future once more, she decided to write a letter to John tomorrow, with her answer.

MONDAY, 6TH APRIL
Badajoz taken by storm, 1812.

Mr. Trested called to see me. The Hull girls went for a walk to Holt Woods. Mamma and I went in the garden. Mary and Martha drank tea at Grandmamma's. Mrs. Peppercorn and Miss. Peppercorn called. Mr and Mrs. Robson came home.

With a fine day in prospect, Mary and Martha decided to walk alongside the river to the village and visit Grandmamma. Rose declined the invitation to accompany them as she still felt a little unwell.

Mr. Trested called mid-morning to see if she was improving. Rose replied, 'In truth, I am still afflicted with breathlessness and fatigue. I also have a cough which has no desire to leave me despite an improvement in the weather.'

'You will be better when the summer comes, my dear,' he said. Rose, however, did not share his optimism.

When Mr. Trested left, Mamma and Rose went for a walk in the walled garden, resting for a while on the bench. While sitting there in the sunshine, Mamma said how pleased she was to learn how well they had managed the household in her absence.

'Mary had a much bigger responsibility than I,' Rose replied. 'I merely assisted her.' Mamma then asked what her feelings were for John, now that some time had passed. 'I truly do not know Mamma, but I must own, I am finding it difficult to forgive his lack of care when I needed it most, so I am sure that being just a friend would be too painful for me.'

Holding her hand, Mamma said, 'You must listen to what your heart tells you, my dear, it will never serve you wrong.'

As the dinner hour approached, mother and daughter retired to the house where they found Mary and Martha in the drawing room. They spoke of their morning and how Grandmamma was today. On the way home from Aylesford, they had encountered the Hull sisters returning from a walk to Holt Woods, a favourite place to visit in the summer for Rose and Mary. At the top of Holt Hill was a quaint little summerhouse hidden in the wood where Rose suggested they took Mary Nash before she left for home.

Mr. and Mrs. Peppercorn called after dinner. Hannah showed them into the drawing room where the family were resting, whereupon Mamma instructed her to serve tea for them all. The Peppercorns informed them of Mr. and Mrs. Robson's return home following their visit to the Jones's in London.

When the visitors had left, Rose went up to her bedroom to write the letter she had been dreading to John. She recalled what Mamma had said that morning about listening to her heart as it would always tell her the truth. With pen and paper ready, she knew just what her heart was telling her to do, namely, to let him go from her mind and stop hoping that whatever they had enjoyed before would return. Fretting about it was not helping her mood or health. So, with relief, the letter she had been reluctant to write was now written. Within it were words to the effect that she had no wish to indulge in a correspondence based on friendship, but if he came to visit Mr. and Mrs. Robson in the future, she would receive him as a guest. On receipt of the letter, she would have freed him to seek another association when he felt the time was right. Similarly, he was to free her to do the same should the occasion ever arise. Rose concluded the letter by wishing him much success with his chosen profession and to have a happy life, signing it, 'Regards, Miss Rosamond Nash Spong'.

She had left him in no doubt as to what her feelings were as Mamma had helped with the wisdom of knowing just what her heart had told her. Sealing it quickly, Rose went in search of Mamma to tell her what she had done. She was relieved her daughter had finally come to a decision and acted upon it. Rose hoped not to doubt her course of action and resolved to post it in the morning before having any more regrets.

Greatly relieved this difficult task was now behind her, she sat by the fire to write in her diary. Mamma was taking her to Maidstone tomorrow. Excited at the prospect of this excursion, she snuggled into bed ready for sleep.

TUESDAY, 7ᵀᴴ APRIL
Miss Ray shot, 1779.

Mamma, I and Grace went to Maidstone, met Ellen Brenchley, we brought her home. I put a letter in the post for XXX. Mary and Martha went to Aylesford, called on Mrs. Peppercorn, Aunt B. Spent the day here and slept. Mr. and Mrs. Bishop called. Papa went to London.

It was an extremely busy day today. After breakfast Mamma and Rose went to Maidstone, taking Grace with them. The first thing they did was to call at old Aunt Brenchley's house, as Aunt Brenchley from Camberwell was visiting her mother-in-law. After helping the family out of the coach and into the house, Wood made his way to Aunt B's kitchen where he usually waited with her cook and housemaid, both of whom treated him well, and the cook made sure he was given refreshment.

After enjoying their hospitality and drinking his tea, Wood crossed the yard to the coach house where the Brenchley's coachman, a kindly man who also made him most welcome, was to be found, staying with him until his own services were further required.

Mamma, meanwhile, had many purchases to make in the town, leaving Rose to find her own amusement, who in turn had left little Grace in Aunt Brenchley's care. Rose was most excited to be outside in Maidstone, as her recent illness had confined her for so long. After putting John's letter in the post without delay in case she changed her mind, she went directly to the haberdashers in the hope of finding some pretty articles to buy. Having been unable to spend her allowance up to now, she was eagerly anticipating making a few purchases of her own.

Whilst in the haberdashers, Rose happened to see Cousin Ellen Brenchley looking at some cotton gloves and waved to her. Ellen and Rose were delighted to encounter each other and had much to talk about, as quite some time had elapsed since their last meeting. When Rose brought her situation with John and her decision into the conversation, Ellen sympathised with her dilemma and reassured her it was the correct thing to do and that her heart would mend in time. Thanking Ellen for her kind words and good counsel, Rose confided she had helped settle her mind. 'Good,' she replied.

Resuming their interest in the cotton gloves, they both decided to buy a pair. Then Rose's gaze settled on a pretty bonnet which she carefully picked up for closer inspection, Ellen urged her to try it on to see if it suited her. Complying with this suggestion, Rose put on the bonnet and looked in a mirror. Delighted at the exquisite floral trimming as well as her appearance wearing it, she considered how perfectly it would complement her muslin dresses in the summer. With enough money to buy it, another decision was made. Having paid for their purchases they set off for the booksellers, Rose's favourite shop which she considered an emporium of delight. She had spent many long hours browsing along its dusty shelves hoping to find a treasure, and today did not disappoint as she discovered a tiny leather-bound book of psalms.

While enjoying themselves in this occupation they failed to notice the time slipping away and had to hurry back to old Aunt

Brenchley's house where Mamma and Wood were waiting for them. Aunt B and Ellen got into the Spong's coach assisted by Wood, as they were going back with them to Mill Hall to stay the night before going on to Grandmamma's.

Rose had enjoyed the morning greatly and was starting to feel a little more like her old self. She was also glad Ellen was staying, as she would be sharing a bedroom with her. They could hide behind the bed curtains to talk for as long as they wished. As she had been so unwell of late, Rose had missed having one of her cousins to stay in her bedroom; that had been sister Mary's pleasure instead. Mary Nash and Martha Brenchley were sharing her bedroom now, and as Rose was finally beginning to feel much improved, Mamma decided she could share with Ellen who would be good company for her.

At the dinner table, Mary mentioned that she and Martha had visited Aylesford while Rose and Ellen were in Maidstone. They had called on Mrs. Peppercorn, and during their visit two other callers were welcomed, namely Mr. and Mrs. Bishop who had arrived to take tea with them.

Papa left for London before dinner, so Rose did not see him leave or even know how long he would be away, and she missed not seeing him go.

Late evening found Ellen and Rose comfortably dressed in night attire in Rose's bedroom, with Ellen wearing one of her cousins' nightgowns. Climbing into bed with a mug of hot milk she expected their chattering to continue well into the night.

WEDNESDAY, 8ᵀᴴ APRIL
Lorenzo de Medicis died, 1492.

Mary, Ellen, and Martha went to Aylesford.
Mary and Martha called on Mrs. Robson, she sent
Mary and I over very handsome muslin dresses.
Ellen left us after dinner. Aunt spent the day here.

Rose and Ellen were reluctant to open their eyes this morning and face the day due to their animated conversation late into the night, which happened regardless of Rose's fear of waking the household with much whispering and giggling. Rose had been much happier to have Ellen's company and wished she could stay longer, but accepted she was to return to Maidstone after dinner.

Mary and Martha took Ellen to Aylesford in the morning. Rose declined the invitation to join them, preferring to stay at home as she felt very tired after her late night. Mamma also advised that she should rest at home to ensure her cough would not return. Mary took Martha and Ellen to Grandmamma's before calling on Mrs. Robson. Mrs. Robson produced a parcel which she handed to Mary, telling her it was a surprise for her and Rose. She then gave strict instructions not to open it until she returned home.

Because dinner hour was drawing near, the girls went back to Grandmamma's to collect Ellen before returning home to Mill Hall for dinner. Rose was quite excited when Mary showed her the brown paper parcel from Mrs. Robson, which was hurriedly opened before dinner was announced, and both were most pleasantly surprised to find inside two very handsome muslin dresses, one for each of them. Mary and Rose being of similar stature meant that both dresses were the same size, but the delicate patterns were quite different. Although created from the same white muslin, one had sprigs of little yellow flowers scattered all over it while the other was decorated with little pink roses. It was evident which dress was meant for whom, as Mary preferred the colour pink and Rose favoured the yellow spring flowers. Mrs. Robson knew which of the pretty dresses each girl would choose, having known them for as long as she had.

Delighted with their gifts, they vowed to thank Mrs. Robson as soon as they next met. Rose remarked to her sister how fortuitous it was that the new bonnet she purchased yesterday in Maidstone was trimmed with yellow flowers; it would complement her new dress very well.

The sisters went into dinner in high spirits, but all too soon the time came for Ellen to leave. Wood brought the chaise to the front door while the girls, sad at leaving each other's company, hugged warmly before Ellen climbed aboard. Standing in the lane watching her leave, they hoped she would return soon.

Aunt Brenchley stayed for the rest of the day until Wood took her back to Grandmamma's after tea. Rose, eager to try on her new dress and bonnet, went up to her bedroom. Standing in front of the mirror she declared how handsome she looked in her new outfit and how well it would serve her in the summer months, eagerly anticipating the time when she could go outside wearing them. It had been another pleasant day, her health was much improved, and she was not so fearful for her future.

THURSDAY, 9ᵀᴴ APRIL
Fire Insurances expire. Lord Bacon died, 1626.

Mr. Shepherd called. Mary went with Aunt to call on Mrs. Robson. George Nash came after dinner. After dinner Martha and I called on Mrs. Robson.

A knock on the door after breakfast revealed Mr. Shepherd standing on the front step. He was shown into the drawing room by the maid, joining those of the family present for morning tea. Mary was out visiting Grandmamma, following which she called on Mrs. Robson with Aunt Brenchley, while her daughter Martha remained at Mill Hall with Rose. Rose believed Mr. Shepherd was another of Mary's admirers, and he would have been quite disappointed to find she was not at home. Mary, whilst flattered by his attentions, was not inclined to share his affections. Thus, he was obliged to accept her polite conversation only.

Mary returned home just in time for dinner and told Rose she had thanked Mrs. Robson for her generous gift of the dress. Rose, on hearing this, said she wished to thank Mrs. Robson herself for her dress and asked Martha if she wanted to go with her. Martha readily agreed and said she would enjoy the spring air at the same time.

The two girls set off down the lane to the path by the river which led to the old bridge. On the way Rose felt uplifted to be out in the fresh air and reflected on her improved circumstances. Her health seemed a lot better, and she did not feel as heartbroken as she imagined she would be following John's withdrawal of his affections. She could now accept her future would not be with him, and perhaps someone else may come along who made her smile and enjoyed her company. She hoped it would be so.

The girls arrived at Mrs. Robson's house in time for afternoon tea. Rose thanked her for the gift of such a beautiful dress, in response to which Mrs. Robson enquired as to which colour dress she chose.

'The yellow one,' Rose answered.

'Oh, I am so glad,' she replied, 'as I had you in mind when I first saw it in the shop window in London.' Rose then told her of her purchase in Maidstone the previous day of the pretty bonnet in the haberdashery emporium that she had had the good fortune to notice, and which complemented the new dress perfectly.

'What a happy coincidence, Rosamond, it must have been waiting there just for you to purchase it,' said Mrs. Robson. After enjoying tea and hot buttered crumpets it was time to return home.

Back at Mill Hall, George Nash was in the drawing room having arrived shortly after dinner. The purpose of his visit was to give news of Grandpapa. It transpired he was quite well considering his circumstances, so they had no reason to be worried about him just now. Mamma was especially pleased with this information. George stayed to have tea with them in the dining room before saying his goodbyes, then returned to Gillingham in his chaise. Rose spent the evening in the drawing room with the family and guests, cousins Mary Nash and Martha Brenchley. Mary Nash was from Mamma's side of the family and Martha from Papa's. They had been good company for Rose and would be greatly missed when they returned home.

Now in her bedroom, Rose began to think that maybe she was going to recover from her affliction after all.

FRIDAY, 10ᵀᴴ APRIL
Cambridge Term ends.

Mr. Trested called to see me. Mary and Martha went for a walk in the morning. I went in the garden for half an hour. Felt poorly all day. They all went out after tea.

Hope of recovering from her illness was dashed again for Rose this morning. She had been awoken in the early hours by the return of her cough and the accompanying nausea. Putting on her dressing robe, she made her way slowly downstairs for breakfast. With tears in her eyes, Rose told Mamma how frightened she felt.

'Calm yourself, Rose,' Mamma reassured her. 'I believe you have a head cold as you were sneezing yesterday and you said your eyes were troubling you, so I think if you stay indoors and rest, you will soon begin to feel better. I am sure it is not your illness returning, but as your lungs are weak, you must make sure you always keep your chest warm and keep yourself safe from this cold.' Her words calmed Rose a little, who then promised to keep her chest well covered with a shawl.

Having received word of Rose's setback, Mr. Trested called in the morning to attend to her. After making his observations, he concluded that she did indeed have a head cold, but unlike Mamma, he prescribed a dose of fresh air, saying, 'As the weather is fair, a walk in the garden is highly recommended to help you breathe, my dear.'

Mamma frowned at this suggestion, but said if Rose dressed in warm clothing, a walk around the walled garden for half an hour might be agreeable. Rose did so and enjoyed looking at the flowers poking their heads above ground to seek out the sunshine. The gardener was busy working on one of the flowerbeds, so she stopped to speak to him. He said how pleased he was she had recovered from her illness and Rose told him of her cold. 'You will not have to suffer that for too long, Miss Spong, a few days at most,' he replied. Thanking him for his concern, she continued down the path and left him to his digging.

When Rose returned to the house, she learned from the maid that her sister Mary and Martha had gone for a walk together, so she stayed in the drawing room until Mary Nash joined her. Mary's love of children saw her spending many hours in the nursery helping Mamma, so Rose was glad of her company on this occasion. Mary and Martha, whose walk had taken them up Holt Hill to the summer house in the woods, returned before dinner.

During the after-dinner conversation, Mary remarked how good it was to see the trees in the wood sprouting their cloak of leaves, and the many daffodils growing underneath them looking so lovely. This information prompted Rose to declare that when she had recovered from her cold, she would go and see them for herself.

In the afternoon Rose rested on the chaise in the drawing room. Mamma, ever attentive, put a blanket over her but it soon made her feel too hot, so it ended up on the floor. While Rose was reading some poetry inside her little diary, she fell fast asleep. The next thing she knew, her sister Mary was at her side gently nudging her arm and asking her to make haste, as tea was being served in the dining room.

After tea, Rose went directly to her room feeling poorly and in rather low spirits, then climbing into bed she hoped sleep would quickly follow.

Aylesford 1835

Aylesford bridge today

The Spong family mausoleum

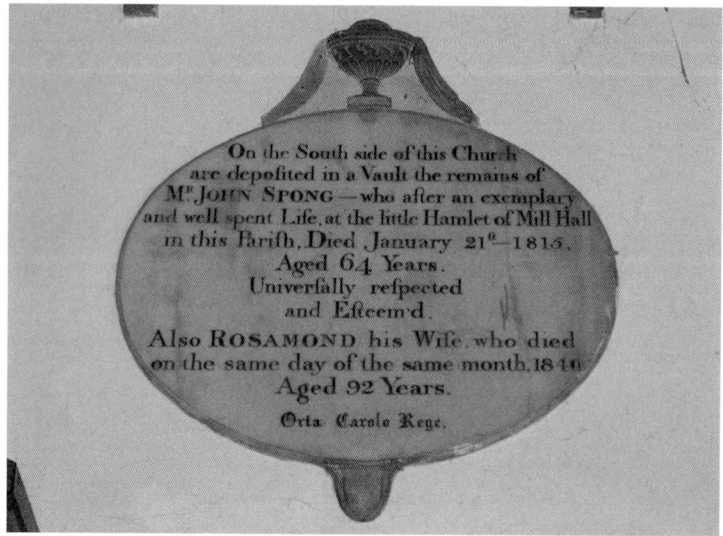

A plaque dedicated to the Spong family in Aylesford church

Aylesford today

Aylesford in the early 1800s

The Mansion House, Mill Hall. Rosamond's home

The same location today

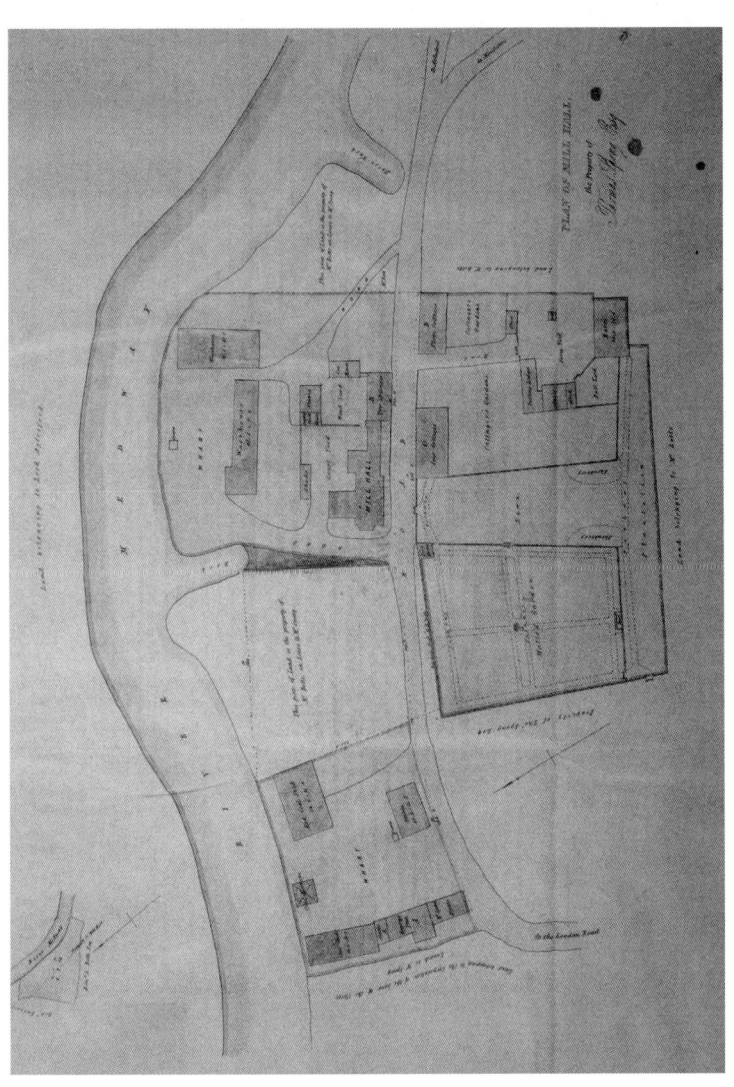

Map of Mill Hall - 1835

Rob and Trish in 2022 walking the river path
that Rosamond walked daily

Jackie standing on Aylesford bridge - 2017

Jackie standing on the lawn outside Frindsbury Manor - 2022
(It was known as Frindsbury Manor Farm in 1835)

*A present from Papa.
Bull Place.
January 6th 1835.*

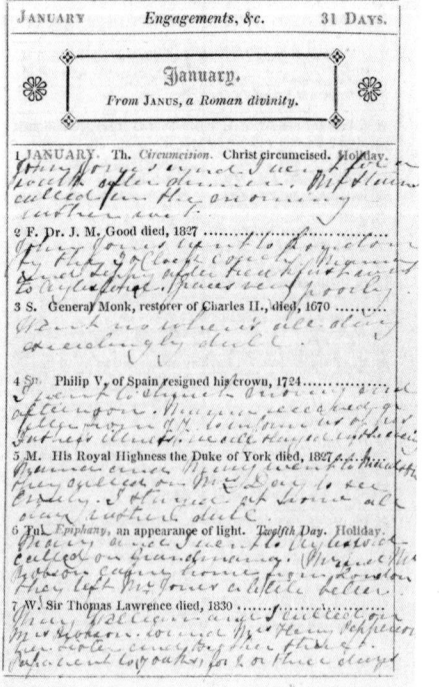

| JANUARY | Engagements, &c. | 31 DAYS. |

January.
From JANUS, *a Roman divinity.*

1 JANUARY. Th. *Circumcision.* Christ circumcised. Holiday.

2 F. Dr. J. M. Good died, 1827

3 S. General Monk, restorer of Charles II., died, 1670

4 Su. Philip V. of Spain resigned his crown, 1724

5 M. His Royal Highness the Duke of York died, 1827

6 Tu. *Epiphany,* an appearance of light. *Twelfth* Day. Holiday.

7 W. Sir Thomas Lawrence died, 1830

JACKIE

2017

With everything packed we set off for Hertfordshire with Rosamond's diary out of its hiding place and safely tucked into my handbag. Also included was a copy of the original transcription, plus the story I had written regarding my own personal journey as an aid to move forward which had been suggested by Trish. I had made the decision to let her read it if she wished. Mike had been the only person to read it other than myself, and when he did the memories came flooding back and we both cried.

Once in Harpenden, I asked Trish if she wished to read my journal.

'I certainly would, Jackie,' she said, 'and I'm honoured you have asked me, but would you mind leaving it with me so I can read it alone?'

'Not at all,' I replied. 'Take as long as you need.' That settled, I then produced Rosamond's little diary, and she was enchanted with it as I suspected she would be, as everyone who has held it has felt the same way. We left the transcription and my journal for her to read at a quieter time, but the diary stayed with me for safekeeping. I have never parted with it in case it was damaged or lost in the post; my transcriptions are replaceable, but Rosamond's precious little diary is not.

A week passed without hearing anything from Trish, but eventually a parcel arrived containing my journal, the transcription, and a lengthy letter which brought tears to my eyes. Within its pages, Trish explained she had taken a great deal of time in composing her letter, as she needed to say so much about various passages in my journal that had touched her deeply. 'I feel you have written a personal letter to Allison,' she wrote. This hadn't been my intention, but I could see now that it was. Carefully placing the journal with Trish's letter into Allison's special box, I picked up the phone to thank her.

During the conversation we spoke of her thoughts on the journal until she said, 'Having read the transcription of the diary, I feel that you should do more with it than just a legible copy of her words.'

'I have thought about it,' I replied, 'but I have no idea what to do with it.' Trish suggested that perhaps I wasn't ready then, but maybe I am now.

'Rosamond couldn't document everything in her daily life due to the tiny space in her diary. She clearly wanted to say more as she resorted to writing in the margins.'

'That's very true, those entries were particularly hard to decipher,' I replied. Trish then reiterated my own belief, saying she also thought the diary had come to me for a reason, and believed I was the one chosen to write about Rosamond's life as she herself experienced it, based on her actual entries. I wasn't so sure. 'I don't think I am a writer, Trish,' I lamented. 'And even if I wanted to be, I wouldn't know where to start.'

'At the beginning, Jackie,' she replied. 'I know you can do it. I read your journal remember, and I believe you should at least give it a try.'

Flattered as I was by her confidence in me, my first instinct was terror. How could I presume to be capable of taking on such an enormous project?

So, I said, 'I'm a painter not a writer, Trish. I'm delighted you think me capable, but I assure you I couldn't do it justice.'

'Rubbish, Jackie,' she replied. 'You should believe in yourself'.

'That's the trouble, Trish, I don't.'

Determined to change my mind, she asked me to remember the effect the diary had on me when I lost Allison. 'You believed that Rosamond's little diary was sent to you for a reason, is that correct?' she asked.

'Yes,' I said, 'and it did help me come to terms with the trauma of Allison's tragic death, for which I will always be grateful.'

'Well, if she helped you then, let her help you now, as you are clearly in need of it.' She reminded me that we had both been through an horrendous experience that had affected us in similar ways, but for me it had reawakened so many bad memories which upset me greatly. 'The past is haunting you again, Jackie, it's time to let Rosamond back into your life.'

'Do you really think I can do this?' I asked.

'Yes,' she said emphatically, 'I do believe that the person meant to tell her story is you, so please give it some thought.' I agreed to think about it, and we left it at that.

Returning home to continue with our lives, it soon became evident that since my conversation with Trish a seed had been planted in my mind which started to grow, until it was difficult to think of anything else. All sorts of ideas began forming in my head, mainly about how to approach the project in the first place. It was obvious I was ready to take on the task. So, I rang Trish to tell her. 'I will be picking your brains, as you are the one who keeps a diary.'

'Happy to be of service anytime you need me,' she said with a laugh.

Now the die was cast, and having made the decision to write it, I found myself becoming quite excited, something I hadn't felt for quite a while even though I had no clue at this stage of how to achieve it. Before I could put pen to paper, however, there were more pressing things taking my attention, so Rosamond and her diary would have to wait a little longer.

The next big occasion on the calendar was Becky's wedding, one of Lucy's dearest friends and someone we considered a surrogate daughter, and what a wonderful wedding it was.

Just three days after arriving back home from that celebration, we were packing again, this time for a three-week holiday in America to see Iain and Sally. During our visit, Iain had arranged to take us to Miami, and from there to the Caribbean. He had rented a villa in Guadeloupe, where *Death in Paradise* is filmed, a series we all followed. Iain had learnt that the cast and crew would be there during our visit, so we could witness it being filmed.

Guadeloupe is a beautiful island, and our stay was memorable, but in quieter moments my mind kept drifting back to the task awaiting me on my return home. It was merely a dream at that time, the reality of what I would be taking on hadn't really hit me.

All too soon it was time to say goodbye to Iain and Sally, the holiday at an end. From the Sunshine State of Florida, we returned to a rainy Yorkshire – time to face up to the challenge ahead. The first objective was to discover as much of Rosamond's life as I possibly could through research, so I spent the next three months glued to the PC.

Twenty-one years after my first encounter with the diary, things had greatly improved in the world of research; far more information was available if you knew where to look. Google had arrived and what a marvellous tool it proved to be. This time I was able to discover so much more about the Spong family.

Three months went by, and I still hadn't written a word. 'Let's go back to Aylesford,' Mike said. 'Make a note of all the places you want to see, and we'll visit them.'

'What a great idea,' I replied. I am glad to say my physical health was improving by this time, and thanks to Trish's suggestion to involve myself in Rosamond's life again, my deeply unhappy thoughts were now receding, and my usual optimistic frame of mind had returned.

After booking three nights at a Premier Inn close to Aylesford village, we set off for Kent on a sunny September morning and I felt quite excited to be visiting Rosamond's birthplace again. On arrival, we found our accommodation situated in a delightful position next to the river Medway at Adlington lock, and less than two miles from Aylesford. As we stood gazing at the scene with colourful boats and barges sparkling in the afternoon sun, it seemed more like a holiday than a research trip.

The first place on my list to visit was Snodland Museum, located in an old fire station and only a short drive away. Once inside we were warmly greeted by an amiable gentleman who proceeded to explain the contents of the establishment. We then told him the purpose of our visit and showed him the diary.

'How interesting,' he said, 'but the man you need to speak to is the curator, I will call him for you.'

While waiting for him to arrive, we had a good look round the museum, the walls of which were completely covered in old black and white photographs. The curator arrived twenty minutes or so later and, shaking our hands, introduced himself as Andrew Ashbee and enquired as to how he could help.

Having been shown the diary, he was fascinated by the explanation of how I had acquired it and asked us if we knew how it made its way to Yorkshire. 'Unfortunately, I don't think we will ever know the answer to that question,' I replied. After explaining what we had managed to discover so far, I asked if he knew of a historian in the area we could speak to as Mr. John Vigar, who helped us previously, had moved away.

'You are looking at him,' he said, smiling at me. I could feel my face burning with embarrassment as I apologised.

'I am so sorry; I had no idea.'

'No reason why you should, my dear,' he said, clearly amused by my red face. I then asked if he knew of any Spong family members living in the area, and just as John Vigar had told me twenty-one years ago, he replied they had all disappeared.

Andrew produced a booklet he had written about Snodland and its paper mill, which had been owned by Rosamond's grandfather, John Spong. Apparently, when he died in 1815 the mill was left to his son William, the man who had pulled Charles Dickens out of a frozen pond, and sure enough a paragraph referred to this in the booklet. The remainder of grandfather's estate had been left to Rosamond's father, Thomas.

Before we left the museum, we exchanged email addresses and telephone numbers so we could keep in touch. Once outside we set off on foot to find the paper mill, and after a short walk we found it by the side of the Medway. No longer used for its original purpose, it now houses a number of diverse businesses within its less than elegant structure.

Our first day had been interesting but we were beginning to feel the effects of our long journey, so we headed back to our hotel in Adlington for a rest and a meal. Luckily, a restaurant sits adjacent to the hotel with delightful views of the river, so we were able to enjoy the view while we ate.

Darkness soon fell, and the lights at either side of the river and on the boats came on, casting a myriad of brightly coloured reflections in the water. What a brilliant day it had been, and we still had two more days to look forward to.

'Cheers, Jack,' Mike said, clinking his glass of wine against mine. 'Here's to Rosamond, her wonderful diary, and the quest we're on to discover more about her fascinating family.'

Rosamond

11th April to 20th April

SATURDAY, 11ᵀᴴ APRIL
Oxford Term ends.

Martha Brenchley left us. Aunt B spent the day here. Mr. Trested came to see me. Felt poorly, had a bad cough. Poor Mr. Jones sent me a dress by Wallace coach, but I was not to open it until Monday.

Rose was still poorly with a cold today and her cough was continuing to trouble her. Once again, Mr. Trested's attentions were required, and he called in the morning to see her. Rose's worry and concern did not end with her health. She also feared the bills for Mr. Trested's attendances would too be large for Papa to pay as she had received many visits from him over the last few months.

Martha Brenchley went home today; Rose and Mary were bound to miss her company. Aunt Brenchley called this morning and stayed for the rest of the day, having both dinner and tea with them until Wood took her back to Grandmamma's in the chaise.

A parcel arrived by Wallace coach for Rose later in the afternoon from Mr. Jones, who was still quite unwell. Rose was sure the parcel contained a dress, but being confined to her bed and feeling ill she had no desire to get up and open it.

There was little to say in her diary and being unwell again made her feel downhearted and low in spirit.

SUNDAY, 12ᵀᴴ APRIL
Palm Sunday, Christ's entry into Jerusalem.

I stayed at home all day. I was about the same. Mr. Trested came in the morning. They all went to church. The two Marys called on Mrs. Robson. They went to church in the afternoon. Papa and the two Marys went to chapel.

Still unwell with her cold, Rose decided to stay at home today while the family went to church for the morning service.

When Mr. Trested called, he found her reading a bible in the drawing room. Rose asked if Mamma had sent for him as his attendance upon her was daily now. He replied, 'I am aware, Miss Spong, that your lung condition is much improved but as you have recently contracted a cold, it is incumbent upon me to ensure that your chest remains free of any infection. So, I am prescribing some more physic which will help to achieve this end.'

Rose wasn't pleased with these directions as she had rather hoped to have seen the last of it. However, seeing the sense in what he was saying, agreed to take it, grimacing as she swallowed down the foul mixture. 'That's a good girl, my dear,' he said. 'I will call again tomorrow to see if you are improving.'

After he left, Rose went to look out of the window. The lovely spring weather they had been enjoying had disappeared to be replaced by grey skies and icy gusts. Watching the trees at the bottom of the lawned garden blowing wildly about in the icy cold wind, she considered the possibility of it bringing snow. Her younger brothers were very fond of snow, but she wasn't, as it made the hems of her dresses wet when walking in it. Boys didn't have this problem as trousers are easily tucked into boots, keeping their legs dry, with ladies not afforded this convenience.

Leaving this dull scene by turning away from the window, Rose went to sit in front of the fire and propped her feet up on the hearth. Sitting alone in the cosy warmth on her favourite day of the week, she began to miss going to church until the sound of the wind outside made her glad to be at home by the fire rather than sitting in the cold church.

She had thought winter had lost its grip, but it would appear to have returned to taunt them once more. The family arrived home shivering. After discarding their outdoor clothes, each one of them tried to get close to the fire. Rose gave her seat up to Papa.

'Thank you, Rosie,' he said, smiling at her.

When dinner was announced they all went into the dining room, apart from Mary and Mary Nash who had been late coming home from Aylesford. After dinner the boys went about their business. Mamma, Papa, and the rest of them went back into the drawing room to get warm as the wind continued to whistle through gaps in the windows and doors.

Mary, feeling restless, asked Mary Nash if she cared to walk back to the village and attend the afternoon service with her. Rose suggested they wrap up well as the weather was becoming increasingly wild. Mary was never fond of staying indoors, even in bad weather, so they both set off for Aylesford. Rose felt grateful to be staying by the fire, as she was beginning to feel even more unwell.

Making her way slowly upstairs to rest, Rose was pleased to see Ann had built up her fire. At least the room was warm. She then remembered the parcel received from Mr. Jones yesterday but didn't feel well enough to go back downstairs, so when Mamma brought her tea, she asked if Ann could be sent up with it.

As she sat by the fire in her night clothes, writing in her diary was made difficult because her painful cough hurt her chest and she began to worry that Mr. Trested's fears about her cold settling on her lungs had come to pass. Mary went up with the parcel, but Rose was so tired she decided to open it in the morning.

Retiring to bed feeling exhausted, her fears of being in peril once more had returned.

MONDAY, 13TH APRIL
Roman Catholic Relief Bill passed, 1829.

I opened the parcel Mr. Jones sent me before I got up. It was a handsome muslin dress. Mr. Trested called to see me. Felt poorly with a cough and cold. Mamma dined at Mrs. Robson's. Mrs. Robson came home with Mamma and had tea and crumpets here, also Aunt B.

There was no improvement in Rose's condition this morning. Her cough had kept her awake and her eyes and nose were both sore from her dreadful cold. As she got out of bed to put on her dressing robe, Ann came into the room to tend the fire. She had built it up just before Rose retired to bed last night in case her cold kept her awake, which indeed it did. It had been very comforting to see the flickering fire from her bed as well as being glad of the warmth.

While waiting for breakfast, Rose decided to open the parcel from Mr. Jones. As she had thought, it was a dress; far prettier than she imagined. It was pale blue muslin with pleats all down the bodice with many flowers scattered over it, a delightful present for which she also had a bonnet that would complement it. Rose now had two new dresses to wear when summer came, but the pleasure in her gifts was marred by the fear she may not be well enough to wear them when it arrived.

When Mary brought breakfast, she noticed her sister had opened the parcel. 'Oh, what a beautiful dress, Rosie,' she said.

Rose replied, 'Indeed, it is a lovely dress.' But she confessed to Mary that she worried her old illness would return, and that she would be too poorly to go out walking with her.

Mary gave her a cross look and said, 'Please do not start with your fretting again, Rosamond, I had thought you to be better of late and were feeling much restored. So please put all such bad thoughts out of your head, as you only have a head cold from which you will soon recover.'

Rose promised her she would try. Mamma entered the room looking for Mary with the intention of asking her to supervise today's dinner, as she intended to dine at Mrs. Robson's house. Mary said she would be happy taking charge in her absence.

Mr. Trested arrived and was shown into Rose's bedroom. Seeing her sorry state, he said, 'I can see you are not yet recovered, my dear, you must stay indoors until you do, as the weather outside is too harsh.' Rose agreed she would not be so foolish as to go outside on such a terrible day.

After eating her dinner from a tray, she lay resting in bed to read when her eyes grew heavy and fell asleep. The next thing she knew was Mary gently waking her while holding a tray of tea and crumpets. She told Rose that Mrs. Robson had come home with Mamma and was in the drawing room, also partaking of tea and crumpets. After passing on Mrs. Robson's best wishes, Mary returned downstairs, leaving Rose deep in thought about her sister's reply to the bad thoughts to which she had confessed and the promise she had made to try and avoid them. It was a promise she was already finding difficult to keep.

TUESDAY, 14ᵀᴴ APRIL
Bishop Porteus died, 1809.

Very ill all day with my cold and cough very troublesome. My nose bled 7 times. After dinner I wrote to Mr. Jones to thank him for the dress. Mrs. Brown was here all day working. The boys came home from school, they brought the two little [indecipherable] home with them. In the afternoon we had a heavy fall of snow.

Another day of feeling poorly with her cough even worse caused more fretting from Rose that the cold had settled on her chest, which Mr. Trested had feared may happen.

She had hoped to have left her fears behind her, but it appeared she was not to be spared more worry and pain and must suffer instead. She prayed to the Lord for his intervention and to prevent her old illness from returning, knowing that if it did, she would not be able to bear it.

Her nose had bled many times today due to the constant blowing, and several handkerchiefs had been used, adding to the laundry for Hannah or Ann to deal with.

Mrs. Brown from Aylesford arrived to help Hannah and Mamma with the spring cleaning, a chore that would take them many days, causing great upheaval in the household. Rose had no love for this annual event which caused dust to fly everywhere, making her sneeze.

Mary and Rose usually left the house to seek comfort elsewhere during this annual upheaval, but as Rose was indisposed, there was nothing for it but to accept her fate. Mary, quite sensibly, had left to call on anyone who would give her refuge from Mrs. Brown's carpet beater, and was not expected to return home for quite some time.

Edward, William, and Henry returned home from school for Easter. Once they had greeted the family, they too disappeared on finding the house in such disarray. Returning in time for dinner, which was a meagre affair indeed as Cook had to help with the cleaning of the house, even Wood was seen to play his part by cleaning the lamps and candlesticks sent to the coach house for his attention.

A heavy fall of snow fell in the afternoon covering the ground. While the boys were putting on their outdoor clothes to enjoy the snow, little Grace asked if she could go out with them. So, after wrapping her up in warm clothes and gloves, Mamma told Edward, the eldest at seventeen years, that he was charged with her care and they were not, under any circumstances, to go anywhere near the river.

Rose watched them going out from the drawing room window. Grace was so excited to be outside with her big brothers, but Rose felt a little concerned for her welfare. She looked tiny by comparison walking down the lane holding Edward's hand, looking up at him with such a smile on her face. Rose stepped away from the window, admonishing herself for having such silly thoughts as she knew her brother would take excellent care of her.

Mamma had instructed them to go to the back of the house on their return and enter through the kitchen door as she had no wish to see her freshly cleaned hall covered in snowy footprints.

Rose hoped they would remember as Mamma could be quite fearsome when cross; however, the boys got away with much more mischief than she or Mary ever could.

While they were out, Rose went up to her bedroom and wrote a letter to Mr. Jones to thank him for her beautiful dress. Watching the snow as it continued to fall, she knew it would be quite some time before she was able to wear it as summertime seemed a long way off, with winter reminding them it was not about to leave just yet.

The boys and their charge returned home soaking wet but happy, and by entering the house via the rear door, Mamma's anger was averted. Mary also came in that way as the hem of her dress was completely sodden. Not being able to change it in the kitchen, she had no choice but to go through the hall and up the stairs in her wet dress in order to change into a dry one. The good news was Mrs. Brown had left with peace restored, while the bad news was that she would return in the morning to finish the job if she could get through the snow.

The family huddled together in the drawing room for tea as it was still very cold. Cook brought in a great plate of crumpets to toast on the fire, together with generous portions of her lovely, churned butter and homemade jam. Behind her came Ann and Hannah with several pots of hot tea to warm them all up.

It had been quite an eventful day, as Rose recorded in her diary while sitting in front of her bedroom fire before getting into bed.

WEDNESDAY, 15TH APRIL
Easter Term begins. Dr. A. Murray died, 1813.

Still very poorly, remained in bed until teatime, then I got up for a little while. Mr. Trested came, Aunt Brenchley left Aylesford. George Nash brought me some oysters in his pocket. Tom Golding came from Cambridge.

Rose wondered if the snow had melted during the night when she awoke. Getting out of bed and crossing over to the window to look, she discovered it was still there glistening in the weak sunshine. In fact, another fall had occurred during the night as all the footprints and cart tracks from the previous day had disappeared. The boys would be eager for breakfast to be over quickly this morning, thought Rose, so they could run around in the snow getting cold and wet again, making yet more work for Hannah and Ann who would have to dry a growing pile of outdoor clothes.

Rose did not venture out herself today, as unfortunately she was becoming more unwell with her chest. Seeking warmth, she climbed back into bed and stayed there until teatime taking both her breakfast and dinner there, although having little appetite she left most of both meals on her plate.

The two Marys sat with Rose after dinner and told her Mamma had received word from Mrs. Brown's son to say she would not be returning today as the weather was still bad but would continue her work when the snow had left. This news meant the house would not be disrupted today, so Mamma ceased all work until the boys had stopped their comings and goings with wet clothes that needed drying quickly.

Mary decided to stay at home, not wishing to get her dress wet again in the snow. Rose was pleased to hear this, especially when Mary told her she would return later to keep her company.

Mr. Trested called in the morning and was disappointed with Rose's progress, or rather lack of it, and prescribed her more of his dreadful physic. But she vowed to drink it this time, knowing Mamma would be watching to make sure she did.

The boys went off to see William and Frederick Golding after dinner, and Rose had a visitor. It was George Nash who arrived in Grandpapa's coach, having driven through the snow to do so. Rose said it was very brave of him, but George replied it was not a difficult journey as he had brought the large coach driven by their own coachman, who was now sitting in their kitchen with his feet on the fender drinking tea while listening to Cook's gossip.

Rose laughed at that remark and told him how delighted she was to see him. Asking with all sincerity, he enquired about her present state of health. Rose answered him honestly, saying she was once again most unwell, and fears for her safety had returned. 'I am so sorry to hear of your suffering, Rosie,' he said. 'But I have something for you that may cheer you up, I have brought you some oysters as I know you have a taste for them.' With that, he put his hand in his pocket and produced a small parcel containing six large oysters.

Thanking him for his gift, she said, 'You are so kind to me, George.' They talked for a while until he went downstairs to see Mamma before returning home to Gillingham.

When the boys arrived home from Ditton, they went straight upstairs to tell Rose that Tom Golding had returned from Cambridge and would call to see her in a few days. Rose was happy to hear this news as there existed a strong bond of friendship between them and she had missed him greatly during his absence.

Mamma entered her room to administer another dose of Mr. Trested's medicine. She also informed Rose that Grandmamma had sent a message to say she had provided Aunt Brenchley with her coach to return home due to the snow, but she would return when the weather improved.

Rose got out of bed for a while and sat at her little table to have tea, but once again her appetite had deserted her. Mamma put her oysters in the cold store to enjoy at breakfast. Writing in her diary before returning to bed, Rose offered her prayers to the Lord for an improvement in her situation in the morning.

THURSDAY, 16TH APRIL
Battle of Culloden, 1746.

T. Golding called in the morning. I did not see him as I kept to my bedroom all day. Mr. Trested came. The two Marys went to Aylesford. Bad spirits.

It was a difficult day to endure for poor Rose; feeling as ill as she did with no desire or strength to join the rest of the family, she stayed in her bedroom all day. Mamma went up to see her before breakfast and asked if she would like the oysters George Nash kindly brought yesterday. Rose had no appetite, particularly for oysters, so she asked her to offer them to Papa, or indeed anyone else who had a fancy for them, not wanting them to spoil for the want of eating.

Mr. Trested called again and went up to her room to see her. Rose knew he worried about her condition as it appeared to be worsening daily. She shared his concern, as she feared that the illness she had to endure throughout the winter months was now upon her again. This thought also brought another fear, which was that she may not be well enough to go out walking whilst wearing her new dresses with her sister when summer arrived. All these 'what's and ifs' were having a bad effect on Rose, filling her head with dark thoughts.

Mary called in to her room to enquire how she was and made a vain attempt to cheer her up. Rose could see she was also worrying about her: as the deep concern etched on Mary's sad face made Rose feel quite frightened for her future. With tears in her eyes Rose opened her heart.

'Am I to live the life of an invalid now? Languishing in the drawing room on the chaise, just like a sick heroine in one of my books. I just cannot bear the thought of it, Mary, the future life I had planned and longed for is no more, if this is to be my fate, I do not know how I will stand it.'

After these outpourings, her sister held her tightly as she wept. When Rose had done with crying, Mary said, 'If this is to be your fate, then God will give you the strength to bear it Rosie, but I still have great hope you will recover from it, and you will be walking out with me again soon." Dearly wanting to believe her words, Rose said no more on the matter.

When Tom Golding called in the morning to see her brother John, Rose was a little disappointed he did not venture upstairs to see her.

With Rose retired to bed, Mamma brought her a cup of tea and placed it on the nightstand. Alone and with her curtains closed against the night, a warm glow in her room emanating from the fire and the candles did nothing to lift Rose's dark thoughts. In very low spirits, she prayed to God before closing her eyes.

FRIDAY, 17ᵀᴴ APRIL
Good Friday, kept as the crucifixion of our Lord. Holiday.

Mary Nash went to church with the boys. I remained in my bedroom all day. Mr. Trested came to see me in the morning. Felt the pain in my chest much today. I saw Mrs. Robson and Mrs. Jennings, they had tea here.

Today was Good Friday. Unfortunately, it wasn't a good one for Rose who suffered another unhappy day, sadly missing the service at church in the morning with the rest of the family who had to go without her. Rose watched Mary Nash and the boys walking down the lane together in the sunshine from her window; it made her feel rather sad as the snow had melted.

Rose prayed she would have improved enough to attend the Sunday service, one of her favourite services. On Easter Sundays, the church was full of wild daffodils, their golden glow made more beautiful in the sunlight that streamed through the stained-glass windows, as well as the multitude of candles illuminating the darkest corners. A wonderful sight indeed, thought Rose, praying she would be well enough to attend to see it once more.

As Rose sat by her fire feeling quite lonely and dejected, Mary suddenly appeared in her bedroom. Rose thought her sister would be with the family at church and was surprised and delighted to see her.

'I decided to stay at home to keep you company today, Rosie, Mamma told me you were unable to go.'

'How thoughtful, Mary, I am so lucky to have such a caring sister,' she replied.

When Ann knocked on the bedroom door to say Mr. Trested

was in the hall, the girls looked at each other with amusement as they both knew he had no notion of how to treat her condition. He used the same words and phrases on every visit, which included, 'Now, my dear Miss Spong, we will soon have you better, just drink the medicine I have prescribed for you, and keep warm and rested.' Which is exactly what he did after Ann had shown him into her room, along with his comments on what a fine day it was today. He had visited numerous times during the last few months and still not suggested what he thought was ailing her. After he left, the girls decided it was now surely time to consult another physician in the hope of finding a cure.

Mamma took Rose's dinner up to her bedroom and she did try to eat some, but the severe pains in her chest made it difficult to swallow and take a breath at the same time, which she found quite frightening.

Sitting by her window, Rose was watching people going up and down the lane when she saw Mrs. Robson and Mrs. Jennings arrive. She rather hoped they might go upstairs to visit her, but she was to be disappointed. As soon as they left, Mamma went up to tell her about their visit and what they had talked about. She had served them afternoon tea in the drawing room, along with Mary and cousin Mary. As their visitors, Mrs. Robson and Mrs. Jennings were due to leave, they asked Mamma to convey their best wishes. Rose said, 'I wish I could have joined you all downstairs, it's so lonely when I'm confined to my bedroom.'

Mamma replied, 'You will recover completely in time, Rosie. I'm sure you just need to be patient.' Rose then told her mother about the conversation she had with Mary regarding Mr. Trested, and their thoughts of another physician attending her. Mamma promised to talk it over with Papa, and if he agreed they would make enquiries as to whom else they could consult about her illness.

The rest of the day passed slowly with Rose's mood still low at bedtime as she wrote in her diary before blowing out her candle.

SATURDAY, 18TH APRIL
J. Abernethy died, 1831.

Mr. Robson called with Mr. Jennings. I did not see them. I kept to my room all day. Mary went to Mrs. Robson's after dinner. She was in bed with the face ache. My side was painful.

It was another long and lonely day confined to her bedroom for Rose. Feeling too poorly to dress and go downstairs she tried to divert her mind from her troubles by reading but soon gave up, preferring instead to watch the world going about its business from her window. She longed to be outside as the sun was shining, and across the lane she saw her brothers playing in the garden, with Mary Nash running after Grace on the lawn. They all looked so happy to Rose who, by comparison, felt quite the opposite and left out.

It was true to say that her character had never been as sunny as her sister's inasmuch as being quite fretful and taking things too much to heart, but she had imagined herself to be a better person than the one she now seemed to have become. Consequently, she did not like herself very much. Scolding herself for being so mean spirited, she turned away from the window, vowing to try harder to be of a more positive state of mind, but fearing she would fail as usual.

Mamma brought her dinner on a tray, but once again she could eat little of it. It occurred to Rose as she pushed the plate away that eating so little may mean the pretty new dresses would be too big for her, and she must make up for this lack of appetite in future.

The afternoon seemed as long as the morning, interrupted only when Mary went up to tell her that after walking into Aylesford to call on Mrs. Robson and finding her in bed with a severe toothache, she called on Grandmamma instead. The pain in Rose's side became so bad she had to stop writing and retire to bed much earlier than usual.

SUNDAY, 19ᵀᴴ APRIL
Easter Day, Resurrection of our Lord. Alphege, Bishop of Canterbury, murdered by the Danes.

Remained in my bedroom all day. Mr. Trested came to see me. They all went to church in the morning, except Mamma. Mary Nash went in the afternoon with the boys. No one went to chapel.

The family went to church without Rose or Mamma this morning, Rose was still too poorly in bed to attend, and Mamma had stayed behind to care for her. Rose's spirits were as low as they could be, even Ann taking little Grace in to see her failed to improve her mood. After dining alone, Mary called in to keep her company for a half hour or so before returning downstairs.

Seated at her window a while later, Rose saw Mr. Trested arrive in his chaise and got back into bed. He had called to discuss engaging another physician with Papa and left without attending her. After his departure, Rose watched Mary Nash and the boys set out for Aylesford to attend the afternoon service, then spent the rest of the afternoon reading her bible and little book of psalms which gave her some comfort. Reclining on her bed and closing her eyes, she said a silent prayer to the Lord to give her the strength to bear what she must with good grace, as she felt such a burden to all those who cared for her. She had been a difficult patient and must now improve her mood for their sakes.

Mary brought her tea tray and stayed awhile. Rose was so grateful to have her company. With nothing of interest to record in her diary she climbed into bed, hoping as she did so that sleep would come to offer a respite from her troubled mind.

MONDAY, 20ᵀᴴ APRIL
Hol. at Excheq. Spanish fleet destroyed by Blake, 1657.

Mr. Trested came. I came downstairs for the first time. George Nash of Dover called. He stayed all night. Aylesford Fair. The two Marys and George Nash took the children.

Rose managed to escape from her bedroom today; Mamma suggested it would help her mood by going downstairs for a while. 'You can rest on the chaise longue, Rosie, as your recent confinement has only served to make you most miserable.'

Rose readily agreed and confessed to feeling isolated and lonely as a result of being confined to her room for so long. Slowly getting out of bed to put on her warm dressing robe, she felt quite dizzy and lightheaded when she stood up to put her slippers on. As Rose's legs had weakened through inactivity, she feared falling and needed to hold on to Mamma when descending the stairs in case she stumbled.

Making their way into the drawing room Rose was greeted by the two Marys who both expressed their delight at seeing her downstairs. Mamma placed a blanket over her as she laid on the chaise, then went off to make sure the little ones were kept upstairs in case their noisy games disturbed Rose, causing her to return to her bedroom to seek peace and quiet. Rose told Mamma it was good to be amongst the family again as her own company had been difficult to bear of late.

Her older brothers were preoccupied with their own business somewhere and were not seen until the dinner gong sounded. Mamma insisted that Rose had her dinner on a tray in the drawing room. Rose would have preferred to join them in the dining room, but not being dressed and still an invalid, she accepted the situation for what it was. She tried hard not to think about her prophecy too much, as languishing on the chaise for the rest of her days like an ailing maiden aunt was her biggest fear. If God spared her, was the drawing room the only thing she had to look forward to?

George, Mary Nash's brother, came from Dover to see them. He was planning to stay the night, it being quite a distance to travel from the coast.

It was Aylesford Fair today, so the two Marys along with George took the children. Rose had attended the local fair held in Aylesford town square since childhood, and she felt sad not to be with them. Mamma assured her she would make a full recovery before the next one came. The children were eager and excited to be going, and Rose remembered feeling just the same when she was a child. The weather was warm and sunny and helped to further their enjoyment. Grace was so full of chatter on returning, telling her sister of all the wondrous things she had seen there.

Rose stayed with the family and guests until well after the tea Mamma had served in the drawing room was over, allowing her to join in the conversation. Having been downstairs all day Rose began to tire, so Mamma helped her back upstairs to the bedroom. Being amongst her family had raised her spirits so much, she vowed to repeat the experience again tomorrow, regardless of her health.

ROSAMOND

21st April to 30th April

TUESDAY, 21ST APRIL
Hol. at Exch. Large spots on the sun seen, 1760.

Ambrose Spong called. Also Mrs. Robson to enquire after me. Mr. Trested came to see me after dinner. Mamma took the boys back to school. George Nash left us after tea. Tom Golding came. I had a long chat with him.

Relieved to feel a little better when she awoke this morning, Rose dressed and went downstairs for her breakfast.

Ambrose Spong called this morning, having travelled from his home, Manor Farm, in Frindsbury. The purpose of his visit was to ask after Rose's health, and to invite her to stay at the farm when she felt well enough to travel. As the farm was close to the coast, he had thought the sea air would be beneficial for her chest. Rose and Mary had stayed there on many happy occasions, so she was quite excited at this invitation and thanked him for his kind gesture. During Ambrose's visit Mrs. Robson called; she was so pleased to see Rose dressed and downstairs in the drawing room. Their third and last visitor in the morning was Mr. Trested, who for professional reasons was also pleased to see an improvement in Rose's condition at last. Her faith in his administrations had been restored somewhat as he was always adamant she would improve in time, and she now felt sorry for questioning his skills as a doctor. Ambrose stayed for dinner before returning to Frindsbury in his chaise.

With the Easter school holidays now at an end, it fell on Mamma to pack Edward, William, and Henry's trunks for the new term. Having done so, she summoned Wood to load them on to the coach in readiness for their departure accompanied by Mamma. The remaining household gathered in the lane and waved their handkerchiefs in a fond farewell. As the coach disappeared into the distance, Rose turned towards the front door, thinking she would miss them greatly.

The dust had hardly settled before they received another visitor. Tom Golding, still at home from Cambridge, called to ask after Rose's health. She was quite relieved to be in the drawing room on his arrival and not upstairs; it would not have been comfortable for her to receive him in her bedroom dressed only in a nightgown. They enjoyed a long conversation together. Tom told her about Cambridge, and the problems he had faced having to learn about the college itself as well as making new friends. Rose was glad to hear he had managed to overcome these adversities, and thankfully he now enjoyed college life.

After tea, Mary Nash's brother George returned to Dover. It had been a busy but enjoyable day for Rose who returned to her bedroom feeling very tired, but happily looking forward to the next day.

WEDNESDAY, 22ND APRIL
Hol. at Exch. Royal Society chartered, 1665.

Mr. Trested came in the morning. After dinner Aunt Brenchley and Mrs. Sowerby called. Aunt brought a letter from Emily and Ellen. Mary went to Mrs. Robson's after tea. I saw FG twice, morning and afternoon, but did not speak to him either time.

Rose stayed in her bedroom all morning as the activities from the previous two days had left her rather tired. When Mr. Trested called, he was concerned to find she was back in her room. Rose explained it was purely exhaustion keeping her there due to a busy two days and therefore she was better served by resting this morning, but she intended to join the rest of the family in the dining room later. He agreed she was being sensible under the circumstances, and how good it had been to see her up and about recently. 'It won't be long before you are walking out with your sister again,' he added.

After he left, Rose went to sit by her window and saw Frederick Golding arrive. He had apparently walked over from Ditton. Rose took advantage of a quiet morning by catching up on her reading until Mamma appeared to inform her that dinner would soon be served. More than ready to re-join the family, she quickly dressed and went downstairs, hoping she could finally put the last few months behind her and enjoy good health again.

After dinner, Aunt Brenchley and Mrs. Sowerby called to see them. Aunt Brenchley had brought two letters for Rose, one from each of her daughters Ellen and Emily. Rose promised to reply to them both soon. Frederick Golding returned in the afternoon and left soon after with Rose's brother Frederick. It had been his second visit today and she had not been able to see him. The Golding brothers lived in the nearby village of Ditton, less than two miles south of Mill Hall.

Mary decided to go to Aylesford to see Mrs. Robson after tea and Rose returned to her bedroom, hoping she wouldn't tarry too long in the village as she feared for Mary's safety walking home alone after dark. Anxiously watching and waiting for her safe return from the bedroom window, she was much relieved when Mary did finally appear and arrived safely home. Rose sat down by the fire, reflecting on the pleasant day she had just enjoyed and feeling certain that the terrible illness that had plagued her since February had finally left her.

THURSDAY, 23ʳᴰ APRIL
St. George, tutelar Saint of England. Hol. at the Excheq.

Mr. Trested came. Mr. Stevens called on business. I wrote to Emily Brenchley. Mary Nash and I after dinner went to Frindsbury in the chaise to call on Mrs. A Spong

It had been another good day. After breakfast Mamma asked Rose if she would enjoy a ride to Frindsbury to visit Mrs. Spong at Manor House Farm. With Rose's quick reply that she would indeed enjoy the excursion, it was duly arranged. Mary Nash was to accompany her there, and they were to leave directly after dinner. Rose was so excited and hoped the morning would pass quickly.

Mr. Trested called and when told of her trip, said he was glad to see that not only had the colour returned to her cheeks, her melancholy had faded also. During his visit, Mr. Stevens called to see Papa and was shown to his study by Ann. Rose passed the time writing a letter to her cousin Emily Brenchley, informing her she was at last feeling much restored to her old self. Once that was done, she went upstairs to select a pretty bonnet to wear for her ride in the chaise, finally choosing one with wide ribbons as she didn't want it to end up on the road should a stray wind suddenly appear. With the trip to Frindsbury in prospect, the morning seemed to pass very slowly, but at last dinner was finished and Wood was at the door with the chaise.

It gave Rose immense pleasure to be going outside again in a smart dress and bonnet, as well as proudly wearing the new kid gloves she had received from cousin Mary for her birthday. The journey to Frindsbury was as enjoyable as she had anticipated. At last, all the trees were now covered in fresh green buds just waiting to burst into leaf, and the fields were full of pretty spring flowers of white and yellow, looking radiant in the April sunshine. Rose, closing her eyes and lifting her face to the sun, smiled to herself contentedly. Eventually Mary noticed Rose's eyes were closed and nudged her to enquire how she was. Rose reassured her by saying how improved she felt. Fully aware she was still a little frail and perhaps not quite her old self again, she was determined to enjoy the afternoon and not spoil it by thinking her usual unhappy thoughts.

She really enjoyed her visit to Frindsbury, especially spending the afternoon with her cousin Fanny, of whom she was so fond. Sadly, all too soon it was time to return home. So, after much hugging, Rose said goodbye to her hosts and climbed into the chaise, and with Mary taking the reins they set off for Mill Hall. On their safe return, Mamma welcomed Rose back and was immensely relieved to find Rose had not suffered from the journey. She remarked how pleased she was to see her cheeks glowing at last.

After such a full day, and as pleasurable as it was, Rose was beginning to feel overwhelmed by tiredness, so she went to her bedroom soon after arriving home. Sitting at her table to write in her diary, she was pleased to report within its pages of a delightful day again, as it seemed that in recent times her writings had been far from happy.

FRIDAY, 24th APRIL
Mary, Q. of Scotland, married to the Dauphin of France, 1558.

Tom Golding called. He brought me some fish. Mr. Trested came in the morning. Mamma, Mary and Mary Nash and I went for a walk in the fields. Unhappy.

Not such a good day today. Rose had her usual visit from Mr. Trested who had nothing different to say.

One thing she did enjoy was a visit from Tom Golding, who had been out fishing and brought her some of the fish he had caught. He enjoyed sitting on the riverbank, dangling a line in the water. Rose thought it must be a dreary occupation spending one's time staring at the river and told him so. He laughed at her and said, 'I expect you would, Rosie. It is not a sport for ladies of a delicate nature.' They spent a very pleasant hour talking together and it helped lift her spirits a little.

At the dinner table, Mary was talking about going for a walk in the fields with Mary Nash and Mamma, and asked Rose if she would like to join them. Rose readily accepted this invitation as it was a pleasant day, and she felt the need for fresh air. The walk was most enjoyable, but she soon began to tire, and when her cough started Mamma took her home without delay. Arriving back at Mill Hall, Rose went directly to her bedroom, feeling unhappy that the walk had been spoiled by the condition she thought was behind her. Staying in her bedroom in a bad humour until teatime, she eventually went downstairs to join the family for tea.

SATURDAY, 25ᵀᴴ APRIL
St. Mark. Duch. of Gloucester's Birthday. Hol. at Exch.

Mrs. Robson and Mr. Jennings called in the chaise to take me for a ride, but I was going to Town Malling in our chaise, therefore did not go with them. Tom and William Golding came to tea. Mr. Trested came.

As her cough hadn't disturbed her sleep too much last night, Rose felt a trifle better on waking this morning. Mamma suggested that when breakfast was finished, they should take a ride in the chaise to Town Malling as she had purchases to make there. 'Yes please, Mamma, I would like that very much,' Rose replied. After eating her breakfast, which included the fish Tom had caught yesterday, she went upstairs to prepare for the outing.

The weather had turned a little cooler today, so Rose put on warmer clothing for fear of catching a chill. Suitably dressed, she went back downstairs to find dear Mrs. Robson, along with Mr. Jennings, standing in the hall. Knowing Rose was unable to walk any distance, they had called to take her out for a ride in Mrs. Robson's chaise, thinking a gentle trot down country lanes would be beneficial to her health without taxing her too much. Rose thanked her greatly for the gesture, saying it was so kind, but must decline the offer as she was just about to leave for Town Malling with Mamma in their chaise.

'No matter, my dear,' she replied. 'You will receive the benefit of the same air in your own chaise as you would in mine, we shall go out on another day, I am sure.'

Leaving the ladies in Mary's care, they climbed into the chaise and set off at a fast pace. Mamma enjoyed driving the chaise and she handled the horses very well. Rose never liked taking the reins as she always worried the horses would bolt and she would not be able to control them. Mary, however, was not afraid to take charge and enjoyed driving the chaise whenever she was allowed. Rose longed to share Mary's spirit of adventure, but it was not to be. The chaise arrived at Town Malling in next to no time. Rose assisted Mamma with her purchases and was rewarded with a delicious cup of hot chocolate in a nearby coffee house to round off a delightful morning which she thoroughly enjoyed. They arrived home just in time for an excellent dinner supervised by Mary, who had helped Cook to prepare and serve the meal.

Tom and William Golding called after dinner as Tom was returning to Cambridge tomorrow and wished to say goodbye. Also, William and his brother Frederick were returning to boarding school the following week and wished to do the same. Mr. Trested called while they were entertaining, but having no wish to examine Rose today, he accepted a cup of tea, drank it, and left.

A jolly afternoon followed, and Mamma invited the boys to take tea with them in the drawing room. The fire had been lit as the day had become rather gloomy, so with glowing embers in the grate, they all toasted thick slices of bread before applying generous amounts of butter and Cook's delicious jam. When the toast and jam had been eaten, Cook brought in a large fruitcake with pots of tea to wash it down. The boys ate until nothing remained on the plates. Rose was always amazed to see the amount of food her brothers could eat, not to mention their two guests. She sympathised with Cook who was always kept busy cooking and baking endless amounts of food as there were so many males living in their household.

There had been much laughter around the fireplace with everyone trying to get their toasting fork to the flames first. Rose and Mary sat patiently by, quietly waiting for their turn, taught to them by Mamma as being the correct behaviour of a lady. Writing in her diary with a more cheerful disposition, Rose was happy to record a most enjoyable day.

SUNDAY, 26ᵀᴴ APRIL
Low Sunday, a day of thanksgiving in honour of Easter.

Went nowhere all day. They all went to church in the morning. Mary and Augustus had dinner at Mrs. Robson's on account of the rain. Papa George and John went to chapel. Tom Golding went to Cambridge.

Rose kept to her room in the morning as her cough had returned. When it was time for the family to go to church, she watched them all leaving from the bedroom window and felt sad to be left on her own. Mamma and Papa took Grace and Octavius in the coach while the rest of the family set off on foot.

As Rose watched them disappear down the lane, she could see a storm brewing. Soon lightning began to flash across the sky followed by rumbling thunder, then the rain started cascading down the windowpanes. Having no fear of thunderstorms, Rose found it all quite exhilarating. In fact, she rather enjoyed being outside in the elements when a storm was taking place. But with her cough being troublesome today, she accepted that it would have been foolhardy, so she stayed inside to watch from her window.

The family returned home soaking wet, and as soon as Rose heard them scrambling to get into the hall, she went downstairs to greet them. Mary and Augustus were not amongst them. When Rose enquired as to where they were, Mamma said they had taken shelter at Mrs. Robson's, as Augustus was fearful of storms. When they failed to return for dinner, Rose presumed they had dined there which indeed they had, to be brought back safely later in the day by Mr. Robson in the shelter of his coach.

The poor weather confined everyone to the house. Rose remarked, 'Poor Tom Golding's drive to Cambridge would be a perilous one in this weather.' Mamma agreed, saying his coachman was sure to take great care if the roads were flooded. Rose said a prayer for him, and for anyone else unfortunate enough to be outside in such heavy rain.

The afternoon passed very slowly, only punctuated by regular visits to the window to stare at the weather. Finally, it was time for tea to be served. Rose went upstairs to her bedroom as soon as the meal was over to find another vantage point from which to gaze out. The dark clouds had brightened a little when she noticed Papa, George, and John get in the coach below her window; they had spoken at teatime about attending chapel if the rain eased.

There was nothing particularly interesting to tell her diary tonight apart from how the weather had affected the day's events.

MONDAY, 27TH APRIL
Sir William Jones died, 1794. J. Stothard, R.A. d. 1834.

George Nash came after dinner. Mrs. Robson called to take me for a ride, I went beyond Town Malling with her. Mr. Trested came in the morning. Mr. Jennings went to London in the afternoon.

After another restless night, Rose got out of bed full of resolve to put all thoughts of what her future might have been with John out of her mind and embrace whatever the Lord wanted for her. She had spent too many hours in the dark of night lying awake in her bed, fretting about both John and her health. She felt it was now time to exclude him from her thoughts altogether and accept that their lives had changed irreversibly, and they would never be together again. She had high hopes of recovering from her illness in time, opening the possibility of letting someone else into her heart should the situation arise. With this further resolve, she dressed and went to join the family for breakfast.

Mr. Trested called quite early this morning, followed by Mrs. Robson who arrived in her chaise. The purpose of Mrs. Robson's visit was to follow up on her earlier offer to take Rose out for a drive. 'Would you like to join me for a ride? It is a beautiful day for a jaunt, Rosie.'

'Yes please,' Rose replied enthusiastically.

'Very well, my dear, but do bring a shawl to keep out any chill winds off your chest.'

Rose went hastily to her bedroom to select a warm wrap and gloves before returning downstairs, eagerly anticipating her unexpected treat.

Saying goodbye to Mamma who waved them off from the

front door, Rose and Mrs. Robson set off down the lane. Mrs. Robson, like Mamma, was good with horses, so they were soon trotting at quite a fast pace trying to avoid the larger puddles as they went along. Rose enquired as to which direction they were going. 'To Town Malling, my dear,' Mrs. Robson replied.

The weather was fine with a slight breeze making for a most enjoyable ride. Rose became a little concerned at the length of their journey bearing in mind dinnertime was fast approaching, but a short distance later Mrs. Robson turned the chaise around and they trotted back home. When the chaise came to a halt at Mill Hall, Rose alighted and thanked her travelling companion profusely for their excursion which she had enjoyed greatly. Mrs. Robson smiled at her and said, 'It was a pleasure, Rosie, it is good to see some colour back in your dear face.' Bidding her goodbye, Rose hurried inside to be met by Mamma, who was waiting in the hallway looking a little concerned her daughter had forgotten the hour and pleased to see her return.

The family were gathered in the drawing room after dinner when George Nash called to see Rose. When she told him of the trip with Mrs. Robson in the morning he said, 'You are feeling a lot better I see, Rosie.'

'Indeed, I am, George,' she answered. 'And all the better for seeing you too.' They spent the rest of the afternoon talking together when George mentioned that Grandpapa was as well as could be expected, with no need to worry about him at present. He stayed for tea then returned to Gillingham. It had been an enjoyable day for Rose who was determined to try her best in continuing this new resolve and face the future, whatever it may hold.

TUESDAY, 28ᵀᴴ APRIL
Suwarrow defeated the French on the Adda, 1799.

After breakfast, Mary and I went to Aylesford. Called on Mrs. Peppercorn, she was out. Then we went to Grandmamma's. Afterwards Mary and I called on Mrs. Robson, found her at home.

Mary asked Rose if she wished to go for a walk to Aylesford with her this morning. Mamma was unsure whether Rose was able to walk that far and suggested that Mary took the chaise. Rose's resolve of yesterday made her declare she was able, and after promising Mamma to keep resting whenever she could, they set out. It was the first walk Rose had attempted for quite a while; fortunately, the weather was still very pleasant, dry and sunny with a gentle breeze. The girls walked together arm in arm, Rose felt good to be outside with her sister again. She mentioned to Mary her determination to stop maudlin thoughts from crowding her mind and look to a brighter future instead.

'I am so pleased, Rosie,' Mary replied. 'It will make you much happier keeping pleasant thoughts in your head rather than the unhappy ones you have harboured of late.'

When the girls arrived at Mrs. Peppercorn's farm she was not at home, so after spending a few minutes talking to Mr. Peppercorn they made their way to Grandmamma's house. She was delighted to see her granddaughter up and about and said, 'I have been exceedingly worried for you, Rosamond, but I can see you are improving and not looking quite as pale.'

'Thank you, Grandmamma, I am hopeful of making a full recovery soon,' replied Rose.

'Yes, indeed you will, my dear. Did you know I was rather

sickly as a child? And now I am eighty-six years old. Because you were named Rosamond after me, I expect you will do the same.'

After visiting Grandmamma, they decided to call on Mrs. Robson. Mrs. Robson's maid answered the door and ushered the visitors into the parlour, where Mrs. Robson sat them down and instructed her maid to serve tea. Pleased to see Rose had walked from Mill Hall, she said, 'You are beginning to tire child, I can see it in your eyes, please allow me to take you home in my chaise as it would not do for you to overexert yourself.' Rose did admit to feeling rather weary and said she would be grateful for a ride home. 'Very well, my dear, I shall order my coachman to bring the chaise to the front of the house.'

Being able to accompany her sister into the village again along the familiar riverside footpath was something special to Rose, but she was now glad to be home. With no more visitors, Rose sat for the rest of the day in the comfort of the drawing room surrounded by family; even Grace, Octavius, and Seppy were present and played games for a while. It was an enjoyable day for Rose who felt much happier and hoped to remain so.

WEDNESDAY, 29ᵀᴴ APRIL
Oxford and Cambridge Terms begin.

A wet day, went nowhere all day, exceedingly dull. Took physic. Nothing particular happened. Miss Thison came down to stay with Mrs. Robson.

Not a day to remember with the incessant rain making it an extremely dull one to endure. No one ventured out, and no one stopped by to visit. Rose complained of feeling unwell, prompting Mamma to administer some of Mr. Trested's physic which she found as difficult as ever to swallow. She attempted to read in the drawing room for a while, but the heavy rain pouring down the windows seemed to make the children restless, causing them to argue over who should have which toy. All this commotion gave Rose a headache, so she sought her bedroom to escape the noise.

They received word in the afternoon that Miss Thison who lived in London had arrived at Mrs. Robson's. Rose thought it must have been a most uncomfortable journey through all the rain.

THURSDAY, 30ᵀᴴ APRIL
The first stone of London University laid, 1827.

After dinner, Mary Nash and Mary went to call on Mrs. Robson and Mrs. Haines. William Golding came after tea and stayed to supper. He sang several songs.

The rain ceased at last, but not until after dinner. Mary had hoped to go to Aylesford in the morning with Mary Nash but because of the rain, they were confined to the house for yet another day. The sun finally came out after dinner, allowing the two Marys to go on their walk at last. As Mary Nash was leaving the next day, she wanted to say goodbye to Mrs. Robson. Rose, who continued to feel unwell, stayed at home.

William Golding, who was home from school, called in the afternoon and gladly accepted Mamma's invitation to join them for tea. After a lively conversation round the tea table, the family, along with their guest, went through to the drawing room where they settled down for the evening. William sang several songs, and all were delighted to join in with the choruses. Rose had been struggling to maintain her recent resolve after feeling unwell again, but William's company and the evening's singsong had helped to raise her spirits a little. Today being the last day of April, Rose hoped winter was now behind them and they would enjoy a pleasant summer. The prospect of a stay at Manor House Farm in Frindsbury, as well as with Mrs. A. Spong of Rochester in a few weeks' time, gave her something to look forward to if she was well enough.

With the hour now late, Rose was in her bedroom with two entries to write in her diary as she hadn't felt inclined to do so yesterday. Just before retiring, Mary called in to say Miss Thison had settled in at Mrs. Robson's when they called earlier. Rose hoped to see her soon.

Jackie

2017 continued

Another bright sunny day greeted us on the second day of our trip to Kent.

'Let's walk along the lock, I'd like to take some photos,' Mike said as we strolled up and down the river for a while until I managed to persuade him it was time to head for our next port of call.

We had only just fastened our seatbelts to set off for Aylesford when I received a call from Andrew Ashbee, the historian we had met the previous day. 'I have some news for you,' he said. While looking through a book on Kent history, he had found an article in the ecclesiastical section which mentioned a young woman who'd written several diaries in which she had spoken of attending church two, sometimes three times a day. Her name was Rosamond Nash Spong.

'Oh, my goodness!' I exclaimed. 'How amazing.' My mind went into overdrive at this revelation, and I asked how we could find out where the diaries were.

'Leave it with me. I will get in touch with the author who printed it over thirty years ago, but he may still have his research notes.'

'That would be fantastic if he has,' I replied.

'Indeed it would,' Andrew said. 'I will let you know how I get on. Meanwhile, enjoy the rest of your stay in Kent.'

Stunned at this information, I didn't know what to think. Mike, who had been waiting patiently during this exchange, asked what all that was about. 'You have gone as white as a sheet, Jack.'

I mentioned to him that Andrew Ashbee had just said someone, somewhere, had a private collection of unpublished diaries by Rosamond. This news was both amazing and alarming. I was planning to write her story based on the little diary in my possession, and I hadn't considered the existence of others, so to think her earlier ones could give me so much more information about her life upset me. 'I can't continue with this, Mike,' I said.

'Don't be silly, Jack,' he answered. 'You mustn't stop now, having given so much of your time to what is obviously helping you, please don't give up,' he begged.

'I don't know, Mike,' I said. 'But seeing we are here now, let's continue looking round her birthplace.'

So off we travelled to Aylesford feeling quite deflated, but when we arrived in the village my mood changed to excitement at being where Rosamond had spent so much of her time. We parked the car and made our way to the High Street. It was just as I remembered from our last visit some twenty-one years ago. The ancient houses, some half-timbered, still looking as they would have done in Rosamond's day, raised my spirits even further. Drawn to the medieval bridge over the river Medway featured in the opening scene of *Half a Sixpence*, I stood gazing at the water flowing underneath. I then knew I had to write her story. Mike was right, I mustn't let the existence of other diaries put me off. It had become far too important to give her a voice now, and if I were to walk away from it, I would never forgive myself. With that decision now made, I continued the search with a renewed determination.

'Let's have a look at the church,' I said. 'A place where Rosamond particularly loved to be.' Out came Mike's camera to take more photos of the family vault, having walked up the hill and into the churchyard to take clearer photos of the vault standing behind an iron railing under the old Yewtree just inside the gate. Disappointingly, the church door was locked and out of bounds, so I suggested we go to the Brassey Centre located on the other side of the river.

This building was originally the village school but is now an information hub and local history centre. Luckily, we found it open and on entering were greeted by a friendly lady sitting behind a desk. We spent a pleasant hour drinking tea and talking about the history of Aylesford and the surrounding villages. I wasn't surprised to hear she hadn't heard of the Spong family who had seemingly disappeared from the area. 'Have you been to the church yet?' our hostess asked.

We said that we had but the door had been locked, to which she replied, 'Oh of course, I had forgotten they're keeping it locked as vandals are everywhere.'

Apparently, the key was now held in safe keeping by the newsagents on the High Street, and if we tell them that the lady in the Brassey centre has vouched for us, they will hand it over. Indeed, the shopkeeper duly produced the key and once again we made our way back up the hill to the church.

When we first visited Aylesford, I had very little information about Rosamond or her family and the contents of the diary were still largely a mystery, but now it was a very different experience. Unlocking the ancient door, we were greeted by total silence. Quietly closing it behind us we crept further in, speaking to each other in whispers at first as if those who once inhabited it were listening.

As I gazed at the old pulpit in its raised position over the congregation, I could imagine Mr. Staines as a tall man, towering over his flock as he preached the sermons Rosamond took such comfort from. When I found her grandfather's will on the Internet, I discovered that the Spong family owned three pews close to the pulpit. Her father Thomas had inherited them when his father died. Two were for the private use of his own family and servants, and the other for his mother and her household. Wishing to record the scene, I climbed up the steps to the ancient carved oak pulpit so Mike could take a photo. Standing there with my hands on the rail, I could visualise the families staring up from their seats as they listened intently to Mr Staines words. So much so, I had a vivid picture of Rosamond, Mary, and Mamma sitting next to each other wearing their best Sunday bonnets with gloves on their hands to keep out the cold, as it must have been freezing in the winter and not much better in the summer. No such luxuries as heating in those days, apart from the small fireplace in the vestry that most old places of worship did. Nowadays of course, radiators adorn the walls to keep the congregation warm at the risk of them falling asleep during the sermon.

Stepping down from the pulpit I went to sit in a pew and allowed the peace and tranquillity to surround me. I am not a religious person as previously stated, but I didn't want to leave such a beautiful church, so I just sat watching the sunlight streaming through the stained-glass windows lighting up the dust particles as they danced in its rays. 'I'm getting quite hungry, Jack,' Mike whispered in my ear. 'Can we go for some lunch now?' So, reluctantly standing up, we left our wonderful surroundings.

We made our way out of the churchyard through a different gate as I wanted to see the old Vicarage, now a private house but once the home of Reverend Staines and his wife Jane. Depositing the church keys back with Aylesford's only newsagent, we made our way to the Chequers public house next to the Medway, where we enjoyed our lunch sitting on the terrace overlooking the river so that we could watch the boats as they passed under the old bridge. In Rosamond's day the village would have been surrounded by meadows but now it is just part of the urban sprawl, although Aylesford remains one of the prettiest villages in Kent. The modern world may go on around it but walking across the bridge and on to the High Street is like stepping back in time.

When we finished our meal, Mike asked what was next on the agenda. 'I think it should be Mill Hall,' was my answer. Back in 1996, we were disappointed to find that little remained of the original hamlet, but this time I wanted to take a closer look.

Mill Hall sits on the opposite side of the river to Aylesford village, and as we drove slowly up, it became evident that the little hamlet is no more than a lane, with a row of old cottages to the left and small industrial units beyond. Opposite the cottages, on the right, where a random assortment of storage facilities was scattered on our last visit, tall blocks of modern flats now stand which completely dominate the area. Walking down the narrow street, we stopped and looked back up the lane to compare it with the black and white photograph of the old house John Vigar had kindly given me. I said, 'Where do you think the Mansion House stood, Mike?' Taking the photo from me, he looked at the row of cottages, and told me to look at the overhangs above each cottage door, then look at the photo again. When I did, I was astonished to see they were the same cottages as in the old photo. 'Oh, my goodness,' I said, 'that means the old house stood right in the middle of all those new flats.'

'It certainly did, Jack,' Mike replied.

Just then a resident who lived in one of the Georgian cottages came out of his front door and we managed to speak to him.

He confirmed that the Mansion House had been directly opposite his home as he had seen an old photo showing a family sitting on the steps which he understood had been taken in the mid-19th century, after Rosamond's family had moved on. If the house had survived it would have been wonderful to see, but at least we knew exactly where it had once stood. From there we walked round the back of the new estate to the path by the river Medway. It felt good to be walking on the ground she had walked on, following in her footsteps so to speak, and in doing so I wanted to believe she knew I was there.

Back at the hotel, feeling tired but happy, we had a cuppa and discussed all that had happened that day. 'Just one day to go, Jack, what shall we do with it?' Mike said. We decided that, because the lady at the Brassey Centre suggested we visit the Maidstone library for any new information, that was what we'd do.

After a good night's sleep, we woke to find the sun had disappeared and it had started raining. I received another call from Andrew Ashbee during breakfast to say he had contacted the author of the book in which the existence of other diaries was mentioned, but unfortunately, as it had been written over thirty years ago, he hadn't kept his research notes. I didn't know how to feel about this news, hearing there were more diaries somewhere had left me with conflicting emotions and perhaps, if I'm honest, at that moment I was relieved not to have to think about them. However, this is not how I feel now as I would love to see them, but I suspect I never will.

Our last morning was spent in Maidstone archive centre with rain pouring down the windows, but unfortunately, we couldn't find any further information, so Mike suggested we go for lunch. Whilst taking lunch in Maidstone town centre, I looked at my list of places to see in the vicinity. 'Aunt Brenchley lived at number 10 Albion Place,' I said. So, with help from a street map, we went in search of the house. After a considerable walk, we discovered that Albion Place still existed but not number 10. Our luck seemed to be running out. The next place to see on my list was the Mitre Hotel, where Rosamond's Papa had booked rooms for his family to witness the Maidstone County elections. After a little difficulty getting lost down a multitude of side streets and cul-de-sacs, we eventually managed to locate it, but unfortunately found it closed. I was by this time quite exhausted; we had seen much of Maidstone but had gained little information. 'Never mind,' I said as we walked back to the car, 'it's still wonderful to be here where she visited friends and family and did her shopping.'

Relaxing at the hotel with cups of tea in our hands, I told Mike three days wasn't long enough. We still hadn't been to Frindsbury or Rochester, I lamented.

'We can always come back,' he replied. 'But don't you think the time has come to start writing her story now? You can't put it off forever, Rosamond is waiting for you.'

Rosamond

1st May to 13th May

FRIDAY, 1ˢᵀ MAY
St. Philip, a native of Bethsaida. St. James the Less, surnamed the Just, cousin-german of our Lord. Holiday.

Mary Nash left us this morning. Mamma and I took her to Maidstone, we called on Mrs. Day, she was out. Not very happy after tea.

May had arrived at last, with the promise of summer now approaching. It is the month when trees are adorned with fresh green leaves and hedgerows are awash with hawthorn blossoms, with the sweet aroma of honeysuckle drifting in the evening air. May had always been Rose's favourite month, but unfortunately not even the thought of long walks in the sunshine with her sister in the coming weeks was helping to lift her spirits, as her ill health was preventing her from enjoying these simple seasonal pleasures. No matter how hard she tried to be happy and positive, she was failing greatly.

This morning Mamma confirmed that her stay in Frindsbury with Ambrose had been arranged in two weeks' time. The farm was situated near the coast across the Medway from Rochester, so the fresh sea air, according to Mr. Trested, would be most beneficial for her health. On previous occasions, Rose had always enjoyed staying with her Frindsbury relatives with their fondness for entertaining, but this time she feared the preparations and dressing up to attend all the social events may prove too much for her. However, she was determined to try her best and pack suitable garments for the trip.

Mary Nash left today, so Mamma and Rose took her to Maidstone in the coach. Rose was sorry to say goodbye to her cousin. She would miss her company as would Ann, the nursery maid, as she had been such a help to her and Mamma with the children. The two sisters would now resume their duties of childcare in her absence, but they took great pleasure in this, so it was not a hardship.

Calling at Mrs. Day's house after leaving Mary at her cousins in Maidstone, they found that she was out, so they set off home to Mill Hall for dinner.

An exceedingly dull afternoon was spent with Rose's mood worsening as the day progressed, recording her thoughts with a heavy heart.

SATURDAY, 2ND MAY
W. Hamper died, 1831.

Dear little Grace's birthday. I began to teach her letters. Mrs. Robson called after dinner. They took Grace for a ride. Mrs. R bought her a set of tea things. Ambrose Spong called. We all stayed at home all day.

It was Grace's third birthday today. She was now old enough to begin learning her letters, so this morning Rose gave Grace her first lesson sat at a small desk in the nursery. Grace was not a child who liked to sit still for long, which meant Rose had quite some difficulty keeping her on her chair. Eventually Grace began to show an interest, giving Rose hope the next lesson may be easier.

Mrs. Robson called to see Grace on her birthday after dinner and presented her with a gift. On opening it, Grace was delighted to find a little set of tea things and was soon serving everyone imaginary tea. Mrs. Robson asked Grace if she would like to go for a ride in her chaise as it was a pleasant day, 'Oh yes please,' was her prompt reply. And in no time at all, they were in the carriage on their jaunt.

Ambrose Spong called a few minutes later to discuss Rose's stay at the farm in Frindsbury, and to say how much they were all looking forward to having her there. 'Now, Rosamond, you can rest as much as you like during your stay, but if you feel inclined to join us in our social circle, you will be made most welcome,' he said.

'Thank you,' she replied. 'I am very much looking forward to my visit with you.' On Mamma's invitation, Ambrose joined them for tea before returning to Frindsbury in his chaise.

Rose spent the rest of the evening in her bedroom thinking about the trip and planning what she would need to take, as there would be several social occasions she may wish to attend. Earlier thoughts of not being able to cope were briefly forgotten as she started to get excited at the prospect of going away, until her worries returned about not being well enough and being a burden to her hosts.

SUNDAY, 3ʳᴰ MAY
Invention of the Cross. The finding of it on Calvary.

We all went to church in the morning. I stayed at home in the afternoon. Mamma, Papa, and Mary went to chapel. I was left at home in very bad spirits. Tom Golding was here all evening.

The weather today was pleasant enough to make everyone more inclined to attend the morning service at Aylesford church. Despite feeling unwell, Rose decided to go with Mamma and the young ones in the coach. To be in the house of God listening to Mr. Staines' sermon and singing hymns should have lifted Rose's spirits, but unfortunately it did not. Her beloved sanctuary of St. Peter and St. Paul's church with Mr. Staines' voice echoing round the old church had failed to cure her melancholy. It seemed that every time she began to feel a little better with the prospect of her health improving, the illness always returned to dash her hopes and she despaired of her life being in peril once again.

Rose decided to stay at home in the afternoon and leave Mamma, Papa, and Mary to go to chapel without her, not wanting to spoil their afternoon with her bad humour. When he called in the evening, even Tom Golding failed in his attempts to make her smile, so abandoning his efforts he turned to converse with the family instead.

Feeling remorseful for not responding to Tom's good intentions, Rose went up to her bedroom in tears and cried for some time. After a while Mary went to look for her and found her lying on the bed, sobbing uncontrollably. Mary laid beside her sister until the tears subsided. When Rose was able to speak, she told Mary of her worry about the forthcoming visit to Frindsbury, and how she feared her illness may become worse. Mary then reminded her of the purpose of her visit, to enjoy the sea air even if it meant spending the days sitting in a bath chair in the garden, adding, 'It could still be beneficial to your health, and you would surely return home all the better for it.' Mary offered further encouragement by saying, 'Just think, Rosie, if you are well enough to be amongst the social scene in Frindsbury, imagine how better your spirits will be because of it.' Rose, grateful for her sister's words of comfort and reason, agreed not to be so miserable and accept whatever may happens whilst away.

MONDAY, 4ᵀᴴ MAY
Seringapatam taken, 1799.

Charles Spong came in the morning. After dinner George Nash came to say Grandpapa was worse. He asked whether I was engaged to XXX. I thought it a very strange question.

Rose felt a little better today, with hope returning to lift her spirits again.

Charles Spong called in the morning to see Papa. After dinner, George Nash came to say that Grandpapa's condition had worsened. This worrying news upset Mamma greatly and she was concerned that her presence in Gillingham may be needed again. George reassured her not to worry too much, he would send word if it did become necessary to nurse Grandpapa. Relieved at the prospect of not having to leave the family to their own devices again at such short notice, Mamma went to organise some refreshments.

When Rose was alone with George, he asked a rather strange question about her relationship with John: he wanted to know if she was engaged to him. Rose said, 'Why are you asking such a question?' To which George replied he wished to know what her present position with John was, and did she still hope things may change in the future. Rose was most perplexed as to why he was asking these questions, as she thought he had been fully aware of her acceptance that she and John were now both free.

After George left for home, Rose spent the rest of the day in confusion as to why George had wanted to know what her feelings were for John, and what difference did it make to him?

TUESDAY, 5ᵀᴴ MAY
Buonaparte died at St. Helena, 1821.

Charles Spong stayed all night. Mr. Robson and Mrs. Robson called, I did not see them, only Mary saw them. Mamma was at Aylesford. Mary and Grace went afterwards.

Rose kept to her bedroom this morning, feeling unwell again. Mr. and Mrs. Robson called whilst Mamma was in Aylesford buying provisions, and they were greeted by Mary who served them tea in Mamma's absence. Rose, aware of the arrivals, chose to remain in the confines of her bedroom and left her sister to entertain them on her own.

When the Robsons were ready to leave, Mary and Grace walked back to the village with them, hoping to see Mamma and help with the shopping. They found her outside the village stores on Main Street talking to Mrs. Hunt, arranging a visit for the following evening if the weather held.

Meanwhile, Rose continued her isolation until she became bored with her own company and went to seek others in the dining room for tea. Mary asked on her return if she was feeling any better, to which Rose replied that the rest had done much to restore her, and she felt able to stay in the drawing room for the rest of the evening to enjoy their company along with Charles Spong, who happened to be staying at Mill Hall again that night. Another dull day with little to write about.

WEDNESDAY, 6TH MAY
St. John the Evan. ant. Port. Latinam.

Stayed at home in the morning. Charles Spong left. Mr. Milner called to see Papa. After tea, Mamma, George, and I went to call on Mary Hunt.

Rose was a little improved this morning and felt well enough to assist Ann with Grace and Elizabeth by taking them to play in the walled garden across the lane for a while.

After dinner, their guest Charles Spong left to return home. Shortly after Charles' departure, they had another visitor; it was Mr. Milner of Preston Hall who had called to see Papa. Hannah showed him to Papa's study where Mamma served them refreshments. Rose made herself comfortable in the drawing room and stayed there until teatime reading a book.

Mamma suggested a visit to Maidstone to see the Hunt family and asked Rose if she wished to accompany her. Rose, thinking the idea would be a good diversion from her worries, happily agreed. It would be good to see her friend Mary Hunt again. Her brother George, not wanting to be excluded from the impromptu arrangement, said he also wished to go. With the journey and its passengers decided, Wood brought the coach round to the front of the house. The three passengers climbed inside, and off they went.

The trip from Mill Hall to Maidstone took twenty minutes, a most enjoyable ride indeed, with the trees and meadows looking so picturesque in the evening sunlight. The coach came to a halt outside the Hunts' cottage, and having heard them approaching in the distance, the Hunt family were standing outside the front door to greet them. The party were made most welcome, and refreshments sent for after they were ushered into the front parlour and comfortably seated round the fireplace. Mamma and George accepted a glass of Madeira, but Rose, not being partial to wine as she found its taste not dissimilar to Mr. Trested's dreadful physic, declined and was offered a fruit cordial instead.

After a lengthy exchange of news and general conversation, Mamma's attention was brought to the clock on the mantel piece which indicated a return home was well overdue. It was quite dark when they left the Hunt's cottage, apart from brief glimpses of moonlight escaping through the clouds. It had been a most agreeable evening, particularly for Rose, and served as a reminder that it was possible to enjoy some pleasure in her life despite her constantly returning illness. Perhaps her planned visit to Frindsbury next week may not be the trial she feared it would be.

THURSDAY, 7ᵀᴴ MAY
First stone of Hammersmith suspension bridge laid, 1825.

After breakfast Mary and I went to Mrs. Robson's and took our coach. Mr. Summerfield and Miss Rixon were staying there. We spent a very pleasant day. Little Grace came after dinner and stayed for tea. George fetched us in the chaise.

It was another good day for Rose, as her ability to perform everyday tasks without feeling ill continued.

After breakfast, the girls went to spend the day with Mrs. Robson and were taken there in the coach by Wood. Mrs. Robson had two guests, Mr. Summerfield and Miss Rixon, who proved to be excellent company, providing much jollity around the dinner table.

Wood brought little Grace along after dinner so she could visit her god mamma, Mrs. Robson. Grace had her usual happy disposition, charming everyone with her sunny nature. Tea was served in Mrs. Robson's dining room with a variety of cakes to choose from. With Rose's appetite returning and having a sweet tooth, she managed to eat several of the delicious confections temptingly displayed on Mrs. Robson's table.

Brother George arrived after tea to take them home in the chaise. Rose and Mary, with little Grace between them, chatted away excitedly all the way home about what a pleasant day it had been and how much they had enjoyed it. The chaise now back at Mill Hall, Mary handed a sleepy Grace down to Ann, who then carried her straight upstairs to bed. Mary, George, and Rose went through to the drawing room to tell the family of their enjoyable day at Mr. and Mrs. Robson's home.

As Rose's stay with the Spong family in Frindsbury in a few days' time would soon be here, Mamma reassured her that she would enjoy the social occasions frequently taking place there, and to pack suitable dresses for every eventuality. Mary offered to help in selecting the correct garments when the time came to prepare for the journey.

Now in her bedroom and sitting by the fire with a mug of warm milk, Rose's mind became full of all the things she had to look forward to during her stay in Frindsbury. She had been fretting about the trip, but with her health improving every day, she was now rather looking forward to it, especially spending time with her dear cousin Fanny.

FRIDAY, 8ᵀᴴ MAY
Lavoisier, the celebrated French chemist, beheaded, 1794.

Mr. Trested called, I received a letter from Fanny Spong. The boys went to Rochester with William Golding. Mamma and Seppy went to Maidstone. I went in the garden by myself after tea. Not in good spirits. Chest hurtful.

Not a good day for Rose, particularly after her good humour of yesterday. John and Edward had gone to Rochester with William Golding, Mamma had taken the chaise to Maidstone with Seppy, Mary was out walking somewhere, and George had simply disappeared. With so many absent from the house, Rose had little or no company to distract her from the severe pains in her chest she was suffering. The return of her illness also prevented her from spending time in the nursery with the younger children. Had she been well enough they would have served to lift her spirits, but she confined herself to the drawing room and read a book instead.

Even though the weather was pleasant, her heavy heart offered no inclination to leave the house in the afternoon. Rose knew by the way her family fussed over her what a worry she was to them. After admitting to being poor company to Mamma, when tea was over, she went over to the walled garden to be alone with her thoughts. Appearing so miserable and in such ill humour must be making everyone else just as miserable, thought Rose. And with that in mind, she decided to pray to the Lord for her bad humour and dark thoughts to disappear when she went to bed but feared her prayers would go unanswered.

SATURDAY, 9TH MAY
The Corporation and Test Acts repealed, 1828.

Mary and I went to Aylesford, called on Mrs. Robson, saw Mrs. and Miss Summerfield there. We also called on Mrs. Peppercorn and then on to Grandmamma's. I went in the garden after tea and read.

It appeared that Rose's prayers were answered last night, as her mind seemed calmer when she awoke, and she was not as troubled for her future. With some relief and hopes of remaining so, Rose quickly dressed and went downstairs to ask Mary if she would like a walk into Aylesford.

'Are you sure, Rosie?' Mary said.

'Yes,' Rose replied, 'because I am much improved and resolved to be more cheerful.' She then went on to tell of her prayers the previous night, when she asked for the Lord's guidance in accepting what her future may hold, and believed he had answered her, as she felt so much better today. Mary hugged her and said how pleased she was to hear that, and yes, she would love to go walking with her, and suggested going straight after breakfast.

The two devoted sisters walked with their arms linked together in the glorious spring sunshine. It was a beautiful day to be outside and marvel at the delights of nature only the month of May can bring, with hedgerows full of May blossom and the trees newly clothed in fresh green leaves. Rose had sorely missed her regular walks into Aylesford, so today she took extra care to observe as many flowers as she could.

Walking along by the river, they stopped to gather flowers to give to Mrs. Robson. A short distance along, they came to a thick carpet of bluebells sheltering in the dappled sunlight, bunches of which were added to their bouquets. This vision of nature lifted Rose's spirits so much, she gave quiet thanks to God for his wonderful gifts. After the harsh winter and having suffered so many dark days, she never imagined beholding such beauty again.

Arriving in Aylesford, they crossed the ancient bridge into the village. Being such a sunny day, the High Street was thronged with people either shopping or simply taking the air, which caused the girls to be engaged in conversation several times before reaching Mrs. Robson's door. Mrs. Robson was delighted to receive both them and the bunches of flowers, which unfortunately by now had wilted in the sunshine and Mary's warm hands. Mrs. Robson handed them to the housemaid and bade her plunge them in water to prevent their seemingly imminent demise. Going through to the drawing room, they found Mrs. Summerfield and her daughter were also visiting. Tea was sent for as Rose, grateful to be seated at last, needed refreshment.

After resting, she felt well enough to continue their journey, so the girls said their goodbyes and went to call on Mrs. Peppercorn at Cossington Farm. On the way back from the farm Mary suggested they visit Grandmamma, who was happy to see Rose out of her sick bed and calling once again. The offer of more refreshment was declined this time as the morning was fast slipping away, so saying goodbye to Grandmamma, they walked back home for dinner. Rose's legs were very tired with all the walking she had done so she spent the afternoon resting in the drawing room. Sitting in a comfortable chair by the window feeling contented and cheerful, she was happy to reflect on the busy morning shared with her sister. Even though it had served to remind her just how frail she had become, the resolve to stay cheerful remained, at least for the time being.

It was far too pleasant an evening to stay indoors after tea, so Rose went over to the walled garden to sit and read a book underneath the pear tree until the light faded. The lamps and candles had been lit when she returned to the house. Feeling tired after all the walking, Rose yawned and said goodnight. Mamma followed her upstairs to help prepare her weary daughter for bed, and when that was done, Rose told her how much she wanted to overcome her fears of what may lay ahead and maintain a cheerful disposition no matter what she had to endure. After declaring her resolve, she added, 'I suspect there will be occasions when I fall from grace, so please forgive me if it were to happen.'

Mamma, pleased to hear these words, said, 'Oh Rose, we know how much you have suffered, and indeed still do, so all we can wish is that you find your own way. We do not expect you to do it all the time with a smile on your pretty face.' After a hug, Mamma left to attend Octavius and Seppy.

When Rose sat at her table writing of the day's events, she experienced a feeling of contentment and security in the knowledge that whatever did happen to her, she would always have the love and support of her family, a blessing indeed.

SUNDAY, 10TH MAY
Battle of Lodi, 1796.

> *We all went to church in the morning. Stayed at home in the afternoon. Mamma, I, and George went to chapel. We saw Mary Nash and the boys there.*

It was another good day for Rose as she continued to feel better and was able to join in the family's visit to church for the morning service. The familiar surroundings inside the old church never failed to give her comfort, and she enjoyed the service immensely. As the family made their way out into the sunshine, Rose took the opportunity to speak to Mr. Staines who remarked how pleased he was to see her looking much improved. Thanking him for his kind words, she mentioned that praying for guidance had helped her greatly. 'Well done, my dear,' he replied. 'God always listens to your prayers; you can always rely on him in times of trouble.'

Most of the afternoon saw Rose amusing herself in the drawing room where she played with Grace and Octavius for a while, before going across to the lawned garden so the children could run around on the grass. Mamma and Ann, relieved to have peace restored at their exit, were glad of a rest from Grace's constant shrieking while fighting with Octavius over a toy. Rose was pleased at being able to help, especially after being such a burden to everyone of late.

After tea, Mamma, Rose, and George went to chapel and saw Mary Nash there. After the service she stopped to have a chat with them, mentioning how much she was enjoying her stay in Maidstone. Rose let it be known she was greatly missed at Mill Hall before telling her cousin of her proposed visit to Frindsbury, and how much she was looking forward to it. Mary said it would be good for her to have the opportunity as she had been so ill recently. Rose agreed before saying goodbye and returning home with Mamma and George.

Arriving back at Mill Hall, she went upstairs to her bedroom. Once prepared for bed, Rose made an entry in her diary before reflecting on how improved she felt and hoped to remain so.

MONDAY, 11TH MAY
Earl of Chatham died, 1778.

Mrs. Robson and Mrs. Peppercorn, also little Miss Fantine, came to dinner. George Nash came after dinner. Very attentive. Mr. Robson and Mr. Summerfield came after tea, they all went home together. Mr. Trested came to see me with more Physic.

It was quite a busy day today with Mrs. Robson, Mrs. Peppercorn, and Miss Fantine joining them for dinner. It grew so noisy in the dining room with everyone wishing to speak while Rose found it difficult to know which conversation to listen to. Their guests enjoyed themselves so much they stayed until the evening.

Mr. Trested called during the ladies' visit with more of his unpleasant physic. Even though Rose assured him she felt much better, he still insisted she kept taking the medicine to ensure she continued to improve. It was difficult to argue against his reasoning, so she agreed to do as he wished, having no desire to become ill again. After watching her swallow the medicine with a grimace, Mr. Trested said, 'That's a good girl,' and bid her good day.

A little later, a knock at the door was answered to reveal George Nash who had also called to see Rose. After their greeting he asked her to accompany him for a walk in the garden. As it was a pleasant day there seemed no reason to decline this invitation, so the two of them made their way over the lane and through the gate.

To Rose's surprise and discomfort, George became overly attentive, and it suddenly became clear why he had been asking about her position with John previously. Taken aback by his approach, Rose rather hoped he would not declare himself to her, so before the conversation became more awkward, she suggested going back indoors as Mamma was about to serve tea, after which George returned to Gillingham. Mr. Summerfield and Mr. Robson joined the family and guests after tea, contributing to the happy atmosphere in no small measure. When it was time to go, they all walked home together. Rose had enjoyed today apart from the situation with George, which made her uncertain of what to do if he did declare his feelings for her. She had no wish to hurt him but couldn't find it in her heart to feel the same way. She rather hoped to have misunderstood his intentions and decided to discuss it with Mary tomorrow.

TUESDAY, 12ᵀᴴ MAY
Easter Term ends.

I went nowhere all day. I brushed my hair after dinner. Papa came home from London.

A dull day today, the good weather enjoyed of late had deserted them as it rained continuously. The usual place to gather under such circumstances was the drawing room, today being no exception. All was reasonably quiet with Mary sewing and Rose reading a book, and Octavius and Seppy contentedly playing with their toys. Then Mamma brought in Grace and Elizabeth. Shortly thereafter, the tranquillity was disrupted when the newcomers became fractious and quarrelsome as Grace wanted to join the boys in their game, and Elizabeth, who was now walking, toddled off with the toy soldiers. It was a relief for Rose to go into the dining room for dinner.

After the meal, she decided to go to her bedroom for some peace and quiet as tiredness began to take hold. Sitting in front of her mirror, she felt quite shocked to see how untidy her hair had become, so taking out a hairbrush, she set about the task of removing all the knots. After rigorous brushing, her hair became smooth again, falling in tresses about her shoulders. Rose vowed to repeat the process daily, as she did before her illness took hold. With all the impending social events to consider, she had no desire to appear in polite society in Frindsbury and Rochester with matted and unkempt hair. After studying her endeavours at various angles in the mirror, she thought how lax in attending to her appearance she had been and resolved not to let herself become lazy in future. Rose wanted to look the best she possibly could on her visit to Manor Farm and felt much better for her efforts.

While admiring her improved appearance, Mr. Staines preaching's about vanity came into her mind. 'We must not allow vanity to become too important,' he had said. 'If we become too fond of the looking glass, it would only serve to make us less humble and pious.' Rose's respect for Mr. Staines regarding his wisdom and piety was unquestionable, but she disagreed with his teachings on this matter. Not usually given to spending time staring at her own reflection, she nevertheless took pleasure in putting on a pretty dress and curling her hair into ringlets before tying on a bonnet. If that made her feel happy, then surely that is what the Lord would wish for, she mused. Putting thoughts of Mr. Staines out of her mind, she turned her attention on what to pack in her trunk ready for her trip on Saturday. With the decisions made, Rose went down for tea to find Papa had returned from his business in London and was now safely back home with his family.

Nothing particularly interesting to record in her diary tonight, and still determined to remain cheerful, Rose got into bed and blew out the candle.

WEDNESDAY, 13TH MAY
Peace of Teschen concluded, 1779.

Mr. Trested came to see me. I stayed at home all day. Read Hannah More after tea. Did not feel well.

Another dull day for Rose, feeling unwell again this morning meant she needed to rest before travelling to Frindsbury on Saturday and staying inside the house. The cheerful mood of yesterday had evaporated to be replaced by the same worrying thoughts that kept returning to plague her.

To ease this burden, she talked to Mary about her worries; she also told her of George Nash's inclinations towards her. Mary replied that she had noticed the way he looked at her and was beginning to wonder if he had declared himself in any way. 'Not as yet,' Rose replied, 'but he has been very attentive towards me recently and has been asking rather strange questions about my feelings for John.'

Mary asked if she was happy about this attentiveness, and whether she welcomed his interest. Rose made it clear she did not. 'But I do admit to being extremely fond of him and I have always enjoyed his company.' Mary said she was sorry it could not be different, as he could be a most suitable match. Rose replied, 'But my heart has not mended since John left me, and I truly believe it never will.'

Mary frowned, then said, 'You will find that one day your

eye will be caught by a handsome young gentleman, Rosie, it is just the nature of things.' Rose laughed and said she hoped her prediction was correct.

Mr. Trested called to see Rose after dinner and was shown into the drawing room by Mamma. After informing him she was once again feeling unwell, Mr. Trested answered, 'Do not fear, my dear. Your trip to Frindsbury will soon have you much restored as the fresh air on the estuary will help your lungs greatly, and I hear that there are many young people there and much socialising, which will be sure to cure your melancholy.' He then added, 'It was your dear Mamma's suggestion you should go, as she has been most concerned about your low spirits lately.'

Rose spent the remainder of the afternoon with the family in the drawing room, but after tea she went to her bedroom to read her latest Hannah More novel, which served to keep her mind off her troubles for a while. After reading a couple of chapters, she put the book down and began to think about her trip. Although she was eagerly awaiting Saturday, she could not help fretting over being too unwell to enjoy it.

ROSAMOND

14th May to 23rd May

THURSDAY, 14ᵀᴴ MAY
Margaret Nicholson died, aged 99, 1828.

Mr. Trested came to see me; felt very poorly all day. Went nowhere all day. Very wet. Very busy preparing to go to Frindsbury.

Rose felt even more ill than yesterday on waking this morning. Mr. Trested called to check on her ability to travel on Saturday. After seeing her current condition and considering it was raining rather heavily, he advised that it would be wise to stay indoors to avoid catching a chill. Other than that, he had no misgivings about her journey to Frindsbury. 'If you take your medicine and rest when feeling unwell, and only go outside if you are able to do so, you will do very well.' Rose assured him that these were the habits she observed at home.

'Go on your trip, Miss Rosamond, and I hope you enjoy it.' Mamma agreed, so the decision was made that she should go as planned, although Rose was secretly worried, she may find it a trial rather than a pleasure.

Mary went up to see Rose after dinner to help her choose which dresses and bonnets to include from her wardrobe. Soon multiple outfits were scattered on and around Rose's bed. Knowing Rose would want to look her best on the morning of departure, Mary offered to help with her hair. Rose packed two of her new muslin dresses; also, as summer had not fully arrived, two light woollen dresses complete with various shawls, gloves, and shoes were added to the trunk. Although relieved at making her choices, the effort had left Rose tired and breathless, but with Mary's help they finished the job and left everything carefully folded on the trunk ready to pack in the morning.

After tea, Rose retired to her bedroom where she read for a while before making a few notes in her diary. She was beginning to feel quite nervous about leaving home whilst unwell but accepted it would be to her advantage and that she must bear it with good grace.

FRIDAY, 15TH MAY
George Cuvier died, 1832.

Mary and I went to Aylesford, we called on Mrs. Robson and Grandmamma in the afternoon. Packed up to go to Frindsbury. After tea Mamma and Mary went to Town Malling.

A far better day today, thanks in no small measure to an improvement in Rose's condition which prompted a walk to the village with Mary after breakfast. The first destination was usually the Robsons' house when arriving in Aylesford, as indeed it was this morning. Whilst there, Mrs. Robson gave Rose her very best wishes for her trip and hoped she would return all the better for it, to which Rose replied it was what they were all hoping for. When the visit to Frindsbury had been discussed and the teapot exhausted, they said goodbye to Mrs. Robson and made their way to Grandmamma's house.

After a warm welcome, Grandmamma also offered her best wishes for the forthcoming journey and said, 'Your trip will do you good, my dear, as your Mamma has told me of your recent poor mood.' She added with a chuckle, 'You will have little time to feel sad while you are there, as Ambrose and Sarah are well known for their socialising.' Rose was aware of this, and if she visited Ann Spong in Rochester she would be even more busily occupied.

'I do hope you have packed some evening attire because you will certainly need a pretty dress or two for the evening parties that will surely take place,' said Grandmamma. Rose thanked her for bringing it to her attention and stated that she had packed day dresses but not evening wear, explaining that she would rectify this when she got back home, as she had no wish to appear unsuitably attired.

After saying goodbye to Grandmamma, they returned to Mill Hall so that Rose could go in search of a dress to wear for the evening entertainment. Looking through her party wear she found two dresses that could be suitable, but finding they didn't bear any resemblance to the 'latest mode' illustrations in her diary for that year made her worry. Shrugging this off, she quickly decided the chosen dresses would serve her very well and packed them carefully, together with more pretty combs and ribbons for her hair. With no more to be done, she went downstairs to dinner.

Mary washed her hair in the afternoon then, when it was dried, she styled it into ringlets. With all this completed, Rose checked Mary's endeavours in her mirror and was delighted with the results of her hard work, although she suspected it would need more attention after a night in bed.

After tea, Rose finished packing her books and the writing material requirements needed on the trip, then prepared herself for bed. Once the day's events had been noted in her diary, it too was packed away ready for her trip to Frindsbury in the morning. Despite some misgivings about her health spoiling the visit, she eagerly looked forward to enjoying this new adventure that awaited her.

SATURDAY, 16TH MAY
Battle of Albuera, 1810.

Mary and I went to Frindsbury in the chaise. Mr. and Mrs. Barker were staying there. Ellen Hale and George Spong called before dinner. Then later stayed to dinner. Mary went home after tea.

A very busy morning indeed. Following all the final preparations and loading of bags and boxes onto the chaise, Rose and Mary set out to Frindsbury after breakfast. Thanks to the weather being fair and bright, the hour-long journey to Frindsbury was a pleasant one.

Frindsbury is located on the opposite side of the river Medway from Rochester and Chatham where all the large ships are built, quite a distance from Aylesford so there was plenty of time to talk on the journey. Rose told her sister of her fears that she may become ill again during her visit. Mary tried to reassure her it would not be so, and even if it should happen, Mamma or Papa would collect her and bring her home immediately. Just as Rose was beginning to tire with the journey, Manor House Farm came into view. As the chaise went up the drive, the Spongs stood at the door on seeing them approach. Once inside the hall, the girls were ushered into the drawing room to be introduced to a Mr. and Mrs. Barker, who also happened to be staying at the farm.

After morning tea had been consumed, Fanny suggested they

go up to their room to unpack after resting, as she noticed her cousin was tiring. Rose, delighted to hear she was sharing Fanny's room, gladly agreed. The two girls along with Mary left the company and made their way up the staircase to Fanny's bedroom, chattering and laughing all the way. With Rose's trunk unpacked, all her possessions were carefully put away by Mary into various drawers and cupboards. When her hairbrushes and combs were neatly placed beside Fanny's on the dresser, they returned to the drawing room where two more guests, Ellen Hale and George Spong of Rochester, had arrived to join the party for dinner.

Manor House Farm, a substantial household employing several servants, required Mrs. Spong to have plenty of assistance for these occasions, with Ambrose having equally as many farm workers to help with the endless hours of work a farm generates. Rose always enjoyed staying at the farm when she was little, with happy memories of running barefoot through the hay meadows and playing hide and seek in the old barn with Mary. Now, returning as a young lady, she would not be pursuing these childhood pastimes even if she were able to do so.

Mary left soon after tea to return home. Rose was sad to see her sister leaving and wouldn't stop waving until she disappeared, worried that having need of her family so much lately, she would not fare well without them. With Mary gone, they all returned inside to settle in the parlour. Although Mr. and Mrs. Barker's company was most entertaining, Rose became very tired, so Fanny accompanied her up to bed. As Fanny also kept a diary, they sat together at her table recording the day's events in their little books. Rose was hoping her stay would continue to be as enjoyable as it had been today, apart from waving goodbye to her sister.

SUNDAY, 17ᵀᴴ MAY
The Thames tunnel broke in 1827.

We all went to Frindsbury church in the morning. I stayed home in the afternoon. I and Mrs. Barker went to the churchyard. George Spong came to tea.

Rose awoke this morning in much better spirits than last night, when going to bed all she could think of was Mill Hall and all those within. Knowing her immediate family was an hour's ride away in Aylesford had caused her to become quite tearful. Fanny, on hand to console her, said she wasn't surprised at her being homesick but felt sure her mind would soon settle after hearing of the plans she had made for them during her stay.

After dressing, Rose joined her hosts for breakfast. The conversation round the table soon turned to attending church at which point Rose said she would like to go with them. Out of concern for her health, Ambrose enquired as to whether she would rather rest on her first full day with them, but Rose answered she would much rather go to church with the family than stay at home. 'So be it, my dear,' said Ambrose, and off they set, walking down the lane together.

All Saint's Church is an ancient place of worship where Rose's hosts have their own family pews, as did the Spongs in Aylesford. Walking out of the church into the daylight after an enjoyable service, Rose was warmly welcomed by several parishioners whom she recognised before being introduced to other members of the congregation, receiving various invitations to call along the way. When the congregation started to disperse, Mrs. Barker asked Rose to accompany her for a walk round the churchyard. All Saints Church sits high above the river Medway, and from there you can see across the river to the Norman keep in Rochester and the shipyard at Chatham, a view also enjoyed from the Manor House Farm gardens. It was a view Rose considered to be one of the finest in that corner of Kent and one she never tired of seeing.

After strolling back to Manor House Farm, all the family sat down to a substantial dinner before retiring to the drawing room for a rest. George Spong called on them in the afternoon and stayed to take tea. An entertaining and jolly evening followed with Rose telling Fanny that she was enjoying her stay greatly and looking forward to visiting another Mrs. Spong in Rochester in a few days' time.

MONDAY, 18TH MAY
Dr. Darwin died, 1802.

Went nowhere in the morning. Mr. Trested called, he asked me a few questions about my illness. We dined and had tea with Mrs. Oakley. We rode home but walked there.

Yesterday's activities were rather tiring for Rose, so she thought it wise to rest a little this morning before indulging in any further pursuits.

Around mid-morning a visitor called at Manor House Farm. It was Mr. Trested who had travelled from Town Malling to see Rose. His visit was most unexpected and came as quite a surprise to her. His reason was that he wished to see her health after taking in the sea air. Rose replied that she had not detected any changes during the short time she had spent in Frindsbury, but hoped it would improve in due course. Mr.

Trested also thought an improvement would be felt within the next few days.

After his impromptu consultation, Mrs. Spong ordered tea to be served before he returned home. Fanny had been waiting for Mr. Trested's departure to inform Rose that they had been invited to dinner at Mrs. Oakley's home, so Rose hurried upstairs to change into something suitable for the occasion. Once ready, she and Fanny set off to walk as the day was fair and Mrs. Oakley's house was only a short distance away. On their arrival Mrs. Oakley gave the girls a warm welcome, and Rose took to her on first sight, probably because she was similar in appearance to Mrs. Robson, quite round with a happy face.

Dinner was a jolly affair for the ladies, after which they spent the rest of the day chatting away together in Mrs. Oakley's drawing room. Losing themselves in conversation made it seem like no time had passed at all when teatime was announced by the maid, for which Rose and Fanny's presence was insisted upon by their host. Happy to oblige, they readily agreed to stay. When the hour become late, Mrs. Oakley further insisted her coachman took them back to Manor House Farm having been made privy to Rose's condition.

It had been a positive day for Rose whose cough had abated somewhat, so possibly Mr. Trested was correct in his assumption about the sea air being good for her as it seemed to help with her breathing, and she prayed it would cure whatever had been plaguing her.

TUESDAY, 19ᵀᴴ MAY
St. Dunstan, a Sax. monk, Archbishop of Canterbury, died, 989.

Stayed at home in the morning, the two Miss Lynns called after dinner. Mrs. Spong, Mrs. Barker, Fanny, and I went to Strood.

It had been the third full day of her stay in Frindsbury; happily, Rose was continuing to enjoy herself immensely and appeared in reasonable health. With so many letters needing to be written, including one each to the two Marys, she decided to remain at home in the morning to attend to them.

Mrs. Spong received visitors in the afternoon, namely the Lynn twins, two spinster sisters who live close by. Rose found them to be excellent company and was fascinated by their identical appearance, including their choice of dresses and bonnets; even their shoes matched, so it was impossible to tell them apart. Even more surprising yet amusing was the fact that they spoke in unison. She had never encountered such a strange thing. There were twin girls in Aylesford who looked like each other but they were not as striking as the two Miss Lynns. Rose decided to share this fascinating encounter in the letter to her sister before it was posted.

After the entertaining Lynn sisters had left for home, Mrs. Spong invited Mrs. Barker, Rose, and daughter Fanny to accompany her on a drive to Strood. All three thought it a splendid idea to enjoy an excursion on such a beautiful day and set about their preparations. Rose went directly to her room for a shawl and a bonnet and her reticule, which contained an allowance Papa had provided for her stay. As they were sure to be visiting the shops while in Strood a purchase or two was quite likely, but the money Papa had given would have to be spent wisely. Strood High Street was full of shoppers going this way and that when they arrived. The town was not as large as Rochester, in fact it was rather small by comparison with fewer shops of appeal to Rose – even the haberdashers had little to her taste. Feeling disappointed, she decided to save her money until she visited Rochester, which was a much larger town so there was surely a better selection of shops and emporiums to explore.

With nothing left in Strood to see, the party made their way back to Frindsbury in Ambrose's coach. By this time, Rose felt rather tired and was content to spend a quiet evening in the drawing room at Manor House Farm. Once they were back in their room, Fanny and Rose were soon writing in their respective diaries. Rose was rather hoping her troubling cough, which had stayed silent for two days now, would remain so for the rest of her visit.

WEDNESDAY, 20ᵀᴴ MAY
Columbus died, 1506. Gen. La Fayette died, 1834.

Mrs. Barker, Mrs. Spong, Fanny, and I called on Mrs. Nicholson. Had a lovely walk. Mrs. Pinfold and daughter called. I went in the garden after tea by myself.

The morning sun flooding through the windows lit up the dining room during breakfast, heralding a glorious day to come. Joining Mrs. Spong, Mrs. Barker, and Fanny at the table, Rose wished for the meal to be over quickly so that she could go outside as soon as possible. Mrs. Spong was evidently thinking the same when she suggested that a walk would be in order on such a beautiful day. All agreed that indeed it was, so Fanny and Rose hastened up to their room in preparation.

Rose had been eagerly awaiting a day such as this to step out in her new clothes. Putting on the new yellow muslin dress that Mrs. Robson had bought her, she then complemented it with the matching bonnet and white gloves bought in Maidstone. Fanny remarked how pretty she looked, and when Rose saw herself in the mirror, she did indeed feel rather smart in the new outfit and couldn't wait to step out to show it off.

Mrs. Barker and Mrs. Spong were waiting for the girls at the bottom of the stairs. Mrs. Spong suggested calling on her friend Mrs. Nicholson who lived in Strood, and so they all went out together, Rose walking arm in arm down the lane with Fanny, as she loved to do with her sister Mary on their many walks. The fields were filled with wildflowers, a sight to behold. A pleasant walk was enjoyed down half-forgotten lanes, and all too soon they arrived at Mrs. Nicholson's house. After being introduced, Mrs. Nicholson welcomed Rose to her home and took the trouble to show her around. Everyone she met since arriving in Frindsbury had been so exceedingly kind and she received a warm welcome wherever she went.

Mrs. Nicholson complimented Rose on her dress by saying how pretty she looked, and how well it suited her. Thanking her, Rose said it was a present from Mamma's dearest friend Mrs. Robson. Mrs. Nicholson replied, 'She chose well my dear, as it is very becoming on you.' Rose found herself blushing at these words of praise, and it made her thankful that Mamma had suggested visiting Frindsbury for her health in the first place. Even though she had not been too disposed to the idea, she was now enjoying herself greatly and prayed it would continue. After a most agreeable morning, the party set off back to Manor

House Farm for dinner.

Mrs. Pinfold and her daughter called by whilst the Spongs and Mrs. Barker relaxed after the meal. Rose had not had the pleasure of meeting them until now. Mrs. Pinfold proved to be a delightful and friendly person, as did her daughter who happened to be the same age as Rose. Both girls shared similar interests and spent most of the visit chatting away together. Miss Pinfold had been told earlier about Rose's health problems, and said she was happy to see she was recovering well. Thanking her, Rose replied, 'Indeed I do feel better, it must surely be all the fresh air in Frindsbury that has contributed to my return to health.' Rose, declaring how much she had enjoyed her company, expressed a hope that they would meet again.

After tea she went for a walk in the garden, where she chose a bench in a pretty corner of the flowerbeds to enjoy the air for a while before returning to the house. Now settled down comfortably in the room she shared with Fanny and feeling quite content, she reflected upon a most enjoyable day and wrote to that effect in her diary.

THURSDAY, 21ST MAY
The sun enters Gemini, the twins.

George Nash called to see me in the morning. After lunch, Mrs. Baker, Mrs. Spong, Fanny, and I went for a walk. Called on Mrs. Formby and Mrs. Jones

Another splendid day, with George Nash coming from Gillingham to see Rose in the morning. After greeting the Spongs and taking refreshments, George and Rose went walking in the garden together. He told her that Grandpapa was as well as could be expected, and he had asked George to call to see if her health had improved, now she was able to enjoy the fresh sea air.

Smiling at his companion after delivering this enquiry, George said he had no need to ask if it was so, as he could already see she was much improved. Rose laughed at this remark, saying her spirits were also much better, as there was much here to distract her from gloomy thoughts. 'I am so pleased to hear it, Rosie.' he said, before they went on to talk of other things until the time came for his return to Gillingham.

Rose sought the bench on the corner of the flowerbeds when George left, to think about their meeting with a sense of relief. The conversation had been convivial and light-hearted with no references to his feelings for her, he was just the George she had always known him to be. Rose was beginning to question whether she had perhaps let her mind be tricked into believing George wished for an association, or maybe he realised that pressing his suit was a mistake, for if she refused such a declaration, it would damage their friendship and make things difficult in the future. Whatever the reason she was glad of it, having no wish to lose the closeness she shared with him.

After lunch Rose went out walking with her hosts who, in their determination for her to meet as many of their friends as possible during her stay, had arranged to call upon Mrs. Formby and Mrs. Jones. Both ladies welcomed Rose with open arms into their homes. She had made friends and acquaintances with many interesting people since arriving on the previous Saturday, with the certainty of meeting many more in the coming weeks.

After a quiet evening followed by a late supper with Fanny's family, the girls went up to bed with Rose happy to find her old self returning due to the illness receding, and her tiredness with it. Closing her eyes and ready to sleep, she prayed for her wellbeing to continue.

FRIDAY, 22ND MAY
Princess of Hamburg born.

Stayed home all day. Mr. Trested expected but he disappointed me. I wrote to Mary Nash. Ellen and John Spong called after tea. They both stayed to supper.

Sadly, Rose's prayers before sleeping last night for her wellbeing to continue went unheard, for on waking this morning she felt a little unwell again, a situation most worrying to her. When told of this, Fanny got straight out of bed to inform her mamma who was in the dining room organising the breakfast table with the maid. Out of concern, Mrs. Spong wasted no time in ascending the stairs to see her guest. She suggested that a day of rest would help Rose greatly, and breakfast was ordered to be served at her bed. Rose, more than happy with these arrangements, had no wish to join the family in the dining room feeling the way she did so, thanking Mrs. Spong for her concern, she said she would rest in her bed for a while before coming downstairs for dinner.

Mary's last letter said Mr. Trested would call by on Friday next, which was today, but to Rose's disappointment he failed to visit. She was hoping to ask his advice on whether she should return home in case her illness became severe, as it had done many times previously. Whilst in bed she wrote a letter to Mary Nash whom she believed had returned home to her family in Dover. The distance from Dover to Mill Hall was too great to make daily visits so it would be a while before they saw each other again. Rose went downstairs for dinner, and afterwards sought a comfortable chair in the drawing room to read. Fanny and Mrs. Spong went out together for a stroll so she could have some peace and quiet on her own.

Manor House Farm had visitors after tea, namely John and Ellen Spong who resided in Rochester with their mother. Fortunately, Rose felt a little better by this time and was able to stay in the drawing room and enjoy the company of their guests who stayed to take supper, and a pleasant evening was had by all.

SATURDAY, 23RD MAY
Battle of Ramillies, 1706.

Mr. Trested came to see me. After dinner Fanny and I went to Strood to meet Mr. Thorner; he walked home with us. Mr. Baker came home from London.

An improvement in Rose's latest setback this morning meant she could join her hosts in the dining room for breakfast.

While she was chatting with her cousin in the drawing room, Mr. Trested walked in. He apologised for not being able to see her yesterday, explaining that he was needed elsewhere to attend a patient who had become gravely ill. When Rose told him how unwell she had been yesterday, Mr. Trested replied, 'Well, you seem to be recovered now, my dear, so I'm sure you have no need to be alarmed.'

'Yes, I do feel much restored after my day of rest, and I am hoping to stay that way,' said Rose, failing to mention that in her heart she couldn't truly believe it would not return to plague her once more.

After Mr. Trested had taken his leave, the family settled down in the dining room for dinner. Afterwards, Fanny took Rose to meet Mr. Thorner in Strood, a young gentleman from London who happened to be staying with Mrs. Oakley. The girls stayed to take tea there, and when the time came to leave, Mr. Thorner offered to escort them back home to Manor House Farm. Rose could see Fanny was pleased with this suggestion and having no reason to decline his offer of protection, the three of them set off to walk back to Frindsbury. It occurred to Rose on the way home that their chances of meeting any vagabonds or footpads was extremely unlikely, so Mr. Thorner's wish to accompany them perhaps had an entirely different motive.

Arriving back unscathed at Manor House Farm with teatime approaching, Fanny invited Mr. Thorner to take tea with them. Happily accepting, they all went inside. Rose believed Fanny was quite taken with Mr. Thorner, as he appeared to be with her, and the fact he was a most agreeable young man and quite handsome did nothing to spoil the situation. After enjoying each other's company at the tea table, Mr. Thorner bid adieu and left for Mrs. Oakley's house. Rose felt certain he would be seen again while he remained in Strood.

Mr. Barker returned from London in the company of a Mr. Webster, another pleasant young man indeed.

Rose's diary entry tonight was a little more cheerful, as she had enjoyed the afternoon greatly and was feeling a little better. How long it would last, she really didn't know, but she resolved to enjoy her visit whilst she was able.

Jackie

2017 – 2020

Having returned home after three blissful days spent pottering around Kent, it was now time to get on with the task I had agreed to do; I couldn't put it off any longer. Mike had suggested I was looking for any excuse to avoid picking up a pen, which was perfectly true as he knows me only too well. The main reason for this was that I didn't think I had the confidence to do her story any justice, and that's why I kept putting it on hold. I am a reasonably confident person under normal circumstances, but this seemed to be a far too difficult task. After taking a deep breath and giving myself a good talking to, I did what I normally do when faced with a difficult decision, which is to jump straight in at the deep end with no clear plan. This was my usual tactic when starting a new painting. 'Here goes,' I said to myself, picking up a pen. Rosamond's early diary entries gave me little to work with, but to my surprise and relief the words began to flow. Was this by some divine intervention?

At this time, I had it in my mind's eye that Rosamond's life was like a Jane Austen novel with a wonderful house and gardens, but when I received a letter from Andrew Ashbee, her real circumstances proved to be rather different. Included with his letter was a map of Mill Hall dated 1835, which clearly showed that Rosamond's father, Thomas Spong, had owned most of the land and property in the hamlet. This couldn't have been further from the image I had in my head. An idyllic little hamlet surrounded by fields it was not, it was where her father conducted his coal business at the back of the family home beside the river. No pretty garden at the rear of the house, just a concreted yard leading down to a wharf where barges full of coal would have docked on a regular basis. As indicated on the map, this cargo would then have been lifted off the boats by Thomas Spong's cranes to be stored in the sheds ready for collection, I presume, by various coal merchants in the surrounding area.

Also shown on the map was a public house called The George, which was also owned by Thomas. It appeared that Mill Hall was dominated by his coal business, and the cottages we saw on our visit were no doubt for his employees. All signs of his coal business have long since disappeared, although traces of the old wharf can still be found behind the new housing development.

When I read Rosamond's entries, I presumed the gardens would be located at the rear of the house, but in fact they were at the front and separated by a lane. This was clearly the route the coal wagons must have travelled up and down constantly; imagine having to cross a busy lane to get into your own garden. In fact, two gardens existed, one had a large lawn with a plantation of trees at the end, the only thing remaining of it now is a small section of iron railings. The other, a walled garden, had paths and a bench to rest on. I imagine this is where the family's vegetables as well as flowers were grown. Two Victorian cottages now occupy the space where the walled garden once stood.

It would be lovely to go back in time just for a few minutes to see what Rosamond could see. I can only imagine how dirty this area must have been with all the coal dust floating around making it impossible to keep clean. I remember as a child that taking a coal bucket from our small coal shed created a fair bit of dust, so the amount being delivered constantly on the wharf behind the house would have made it impossible to keep out of the house – I can't begin to think where they dried the washing.

It must have been a hard life for Mamma, with so many children and only two servants and a cook to help.

This map was a revelation, it allowed me to understand Rosamond's situation and lifestyle, which in turn helped greatly with the telling of her story. I couldn't wait to get started, but with time not always on my side, progress remained slow, though Rosamond was never far from my mind whatever I did. The constant need to research was one of the main reasons stopping me from writing, but regardless of the time spent away from doing so, as soon as I had the pen in my hand again it seemed she had just been waiting for me to return.

A big frustration to me were the players in Rosamond's diary, her friends and family, as I had no way of knowing their personalities or what they looked like. Ancestry websites are great for giving you basic details, most important when doing a family tree, but not much use when writing a story. I discussed this point with a fellow writer who suggested I invent a character for all those mentioned and give each one a personality along with their physical attributes, eye colour, height, and so on. I wasn't entirely sure I should do this with real people, but nevertheless I gave it a try. This exercise proved to be a lot of fun, I soon had a notebook full of everyone in the diary including her siblings, parents, and servants, even Wood the coachman and his wife, the cook, had an imagined profile. Also imagined were John Jones and his parents, Mr. and Mrs. Robson, Mrs. Peppercorn, Mamma's father Grandpapa Nash and his second wife, Mamma's stepmother, whom Rosamond referred to as Mrs Nash, plus their three children, George, Albert, and Elizabeth, with George receiving special attention as he appeared frequently in her diary. For all these people who existed, both their appearance and character had to be invented by me. This was probably a long way from the truth but somehow this didn't seem to matter, because in doing this exercise, everyone mentioned in the diary sprang to life in my head instead of being one dimensional characters, or just names on a page. They were now real people who I could see and hear, so this really made the telling of Rosamond's story so much easier. I do hope if anyone reading this recognises one of their ancestors, they will not be offended by my interpretation of their distant relatives, and if they are, I truly apologise.

Next on my list to research was Rosamond's choice of reading material, as I thought that in doing so, I might get a better insight into what subject matter interested her. It had already become clear she spent many hours with her nose in a book, and I presumed that she would probably have read the popular periodicals of the day.

A favourite author of hers appeared to be Hannah More, a writer of religious subjects and a philanthropist, who was born in 1745. As Rosamond liked all things evangelical, I can see how she would have enjoyed Hannah's books. I tried to obtain some of her work but was unsuccessful, so I have never read anything by her, perhaps not a bad thing having seen a synopsis on the internet regarding some of her works which left me quite certain I would have found them hard going. However, I did manage to get a copy of 'Peter Simple', a book lent to her by George Nash. This three-volume publication was written by Captain Frederick Marryatt and is the story of a 15-year-old boy, the son of a Lord, who was sent by his father to serve in the Royal Navy during the Napoleonic wars in the hopes it would toughen him up. After reading this amusing story which I enjoyed immensely, it made me realise that Rosamond, despite being quite religious, must have had a fun side to her nature after saying how much pleasure she took from reading it.

Some of my time was spent searching old bookshops for references on social history written during the period, resulting in quite a collection on my own bookshelves. These dusty old tomes have helped me understand etiquette in Rosamond's time, as I needed to know more about the day-to-day life in the reign of William IV. For instance, what did people wear, eat, and drink, and what were the rules of their society? All this research took time, but it was important to me to have a firm understanding of Rosamond's world from her own perspective, and the only way I could do this was to constantly check every detail.

It was now 2019. Two years had passed since the start of this project, and I still hadn't completed it. Another trip to America had been planned, this time for a month, so poor Rosamond and her diary would have to wait yet again. I took my work with me in the hope I might get some spare time, but from the minute the plane landed in Orlando our feet hardly touched the ground. As soon as our cases were unpacked, they were packed again.

Two days later and we were on a plane bound for Tennessee: Graceland awaited us. What an amazing time we had in Memphis and Nashville, we even fitted in a visit to Jackson where Mike's aunt lives. After three hotels in six days, we were back in Florida with time for a visit to my oldest friend's daughter Anne and her American husband Frank who live just an hour's drive away from Iain and Sally. Anne grew up with my children and is like another daughter to me, so when I am in Florida a visit to stay with them is important. The month passed all too quickly, and it was time to say goodbye; it had been a wonderful holiday, but it offered little time to think about Rosamond.

With our adventure behind us I picked up a pen with renewed determination to reconnect with her world, and soon found the excitement came flooding back after being away for so long. Finding Rosamond helped me so much during our first encounter, so the need to finish what I started became a priority. However, Christmas was coming, and I needed to buy presents for my growing family. I now had four great grandchildren to add to the list, cards to write, and food to prepare, which meant Rosamond had to wait yet again.

Iain and Sally were arriving after Christmas, so our celebrations were to last longer than usual. Unfortunately, Mike and I picked up a nasty virus which quickly spread throughout the family; luckily, all the children managed to escape it but most of the adults didn't. We had no clue what had hit us, until we started to hear we were not the only family to be afflicted: 2020 had arrived with a bang. A few weeks after we recovered, COVID-19 hit the world. Had we already had this terrible virus? We heard later it had been discovered in December only twenty miles away in York, and in March a national lockdown followed with no idea what the outcome would be. Life as we knew it had stopped. What a frightening experience it was to see the human toll on the news as well as the heart-breaking isolation from our loved ones, the only consolation being that I could concentrate on Rosamond to escape from the reality of the global pandemic surrounding us.

At long last her story was completed, and the next hurdle to face was turning my handwritten manuscript into type. Not an easy task considering my typing skills had not improved over the last twenty odd years, so Penny kindly offered to type it up for me. However, having a full-time profession and two children proved too much to allow for the typing of over 600 pages. Our daughter Lucy then volunteered, but with similar distractions it seemed professional help was our only option. As luck would have it, Mike's cousin Diane, who happens to be an ace typist, came to my rescue on the understanding it would have to be fitted in to her already busy schedule. I explained that as it had taken three years to write, a few more months wouldn't matter. So off Rosamond went, but it was as if I had left my child in someone else's safekeeping. What am I going to do with my time now? I thought, as we drove away from her house.

Rosamond

24th May to 31st May

SUNDAY, 24TH MAY
Princess Alexandrina Victoria born, 1819.

Fanny, Mr. Barker, Mr. Webster, and I went to Rochester church in the morning. We called on Mrs. A. Spong after church, had lunch there. Went home in the afternoon to Manor Farm.

Today was the second Sunday of Rose's stay in Frindsbury. At breakfast Mr. Barker let it be known that he and Mr. Webster were going to attend the service at Rochester church and asked the girls if they wished to accompany them. The invitation was accepted, and the visit greatly anticipated. As Rochester Church was across the river Medway, Fanny's Papa offered his coach to take them there.

Rose hurried upstairs to collect a shawl and took the opportunity while there to gaze at herself in Fanny's looking glass to see if her attire was suitable. She understood Rochester church to be favoured by people of society, and therefore had no wish to look like a country mouse surrounded by peacocks. Fanny entered the room to see her posing in front of the mirror and when Rose spoke of her fears, she laughed and said not to be so silly, and reminded her how many times she had been in society and had always done so looking her best. Fanny then enquired if the fretting over her appearance had anything to do with their guest, Mr. Webster. Rose was quite taken aback at this remark and said, 'Whatever do you mean by saying such a thing, Fanny.'

Fanny replied, laughing once more, 'I saw the way your eyes lit up when you were introduced to him yesterday, do you think that your heart may be mended at last, Rosie?'

'I am sure that is not so, Fanny.' Rose was flustered but had to confess her cousin could be correct in her assumption as indeed she did enjoy being in his company. Laughing together, the girls descended the stairs to where their escorts stood patiently waiting.

After the service, the party made their way to call on Mrs. Ann Spong, who, after welcoming them, invited all to stay for lunch which turned out to be a very jolly meal. Eventually saying goodbye to their hostess and giving thanks for her hospitality, they set off back to Manor House Farm. A very pleasant afternoon was had by all, followed by an equally enjoyable teatime. The remainder of the evening passed in the drawing room conversing with the other guests, Mr. and Mrs. Barker and John Webster. When Fanny and Rose decided to retire, they both agreed it had been another enjoyable day.

When Fanny teased Rose about John Webster, Rose said perhaps Grandpapa was correct when he said that one day, she would have her head turned by a handsome swain, and it appeared his prophecy may have come true after all. They both laughed at this before settling down to write notes in their respective diaries.

MONDAY, 25TH MAY
Dr. Paley died, 1805.

Mrs. Spong, Mrs. Barker, Fanny, and I went to Rochester; called on Miss. Anderson, Mrs. A. Spong, and Miss Norton. We came back home in the chaise. George came to see me after tea, then I left to go back to Rochester. Mrs. Mansfield brought me back in her carriage.

It was a busy day for visitors and visiting alike today. Arrangements had been made for Rose to stay with Mrs. A. Spong in Rochester for a few days, and the original plan was to leave immediately after breakfast. However, they received word that Rose's brother George was to pay her a visit in the afternoon, so her arrival would now have to be in the evening. As her hosts and guests were going to Rochester anyway that morning to call on various people, Rose went with them in order to tell Mrs. Ann Spong she was not able to come and stay until the evening.

On their return to Manor House Farm, Rose started packing her things in readiness for the stay in Rochester after George's visit, albeit with a heavy heart as she had become settled and comfortable at Manor Farm and was reluctant to leave for the unknown should her illness return. But now everything had been arranged, she would have to accept it with good grace. George's arrival made Rose feel homesick, as seeing her dear brother standing there made her realise just how far away her family were – so many tears were shed on their embrace. However, when she saw the bundle of letters he produced, her tears turned to joy. Mary had written of her doings and how she missed her, one was from Mamma, and her elder brother Thomas had surprisingly put his pen to its purpose as had John. Also included in the letters were ones from Tom Golding and Mrs. Robson.

'A great deal to look forward to reading in bed tonight at Mrs. Spong's in Rochester,' she enthused to George, before handing him the letters she had written yesterday to take home. Rose went on to tell him of her meeting the Lynn twins, and when she told him of their saying everything in unison, George laughed heartily.

When it was time for George to leave, they embraced each other while Rose asked him to give everyone her love and be sure to tell them she missed them all greatly. After waving to him as he went down the lane in the chaise, she hurried back inside to prepare for the visit to Rochester before Mrs. Mansfield arrived to take her there in a carriage.

Arriving at their destination, Mrs. Mansfield helped Rose out of the carriage as Mrs. Spong and her maid took charge of Rose's luggage and conveyed it up to her designated room. Going through to the drawing room as instructed, Rose was greeted by the rest of the family with particular attention being paid by Ellen who stepped forward to embrace her. Ellen was delighted to see her and said how much she was looking forward to taking her to visit various friends, and that they would be sure to have much fun together during her stay.

Despite trying to appear enthusiastic, Rose was feeling rather tired as the day had been long, so after a short conversation she asked to be excused, and Ellen took her to her bedroom and bade her goodnight.

Rose was happy to find she had been given a room of her own, as she had assumed she would be sharing one. Putting on her night attire she climbed into bed clutching the bundle of letters and began to read them all. Very soon her eyes were wet with tears from missing home, so putting the letters on the nightstand, she blew out her candle and attempted to sleep, but sleep wouldn't come. After a while the candle was relit, and Rose got up again and took out her diary. She had thought to write today's entry in the morning but decided it would take her mind off the family and aid her sleep if she did it there and then. She hoped having Ellen Spong for company would soon make her feel better. She was also hoping Mr. Webster would still be there when she returned on Friday, as he was such a pleasant young man and quite handsome.

TUESDAY, 26TH MAY
Augustine, 1st. Archbishop of canterbury, d. 605. Don Miguel resigns to contest the crown of Portugal, as does Don Carlos for that of Spain, 1834.

I and John and Gus went to Gravesend to see if Edward was there. Ellen and I called on the Bertrams. I wrote to G. Nash and Fanny Spong. Very Unhappy day.

It was not a happy day for Rose, she was missing her home and family badly. She was even missing Frindsbury, to where she would be glad to return on Friday. Her hosts, however welcoming, were still relative strangers. Having spent very little time in their company previously, she found it difficult to settle there.

In the morning John and Gus took her to Gravesend, where she had been told her brother Edward was due to arrive on a visit to the family of a friend from his school. Unfortunately, when they arrived in Gravesend at the address given, he was still at school, so they had to drive all the way back to Rochester. Rose was naturally most disappointed.

After dinner, Ellen took Rose to call on their friends the Bertram's but being in low spirits she struggled to make any conversation. Feeling a little more comfortable by returning to her hosts, Rose decided to write to George Nash in Gillingham and Fanny Spong in Frindsbury after tea.

WEDNESDAY, 27ᵀᴴ MAY
Venerable Bede.

Mr. Spong, Miss Richardson, and I went for a walk, we were caught in a thunderstorm. Mrs. Jones and Miss Anderson drank tea here. John came after tea to say that dear Edward had arrived at Gravesend.

With great relief, Rose awoke this morning in a more cheerful disposition. Mr. Spong enquired at breakfast if she wished to join himself and Miss Richardson, a family friend who also happened to be staying there, for a walk. Readily agreeing, Rose was glad to have ventured upstairs to procure an umbrella beforehand, as they were caught out in a sudden and violent thunderstorm. With heavy rain and thunder crashing about them, the walking party had to seek shelter in an old farm outbuilding until the storm passed before returning home. Rose, quite undaunted by the spectacle, found it to be quite exciting.

In the afternoon, Mrs. Jones and Miss Anderson called. They all drank tea and chatted away in the drawing room. Rose had a visit from John, her brother, to say that Edward had now arrived at Gravesend, also that Mamma was to call on him tomorrow and would come to Rochester to see her as well. Rose was thrilled at this news which did much to lift her spirits, as she knew she was soon to see her dear Mamma.

Rose and John spent an hour talking together whilst he took some refreshment. She mentioned how dejected and sad she had been since George's last visit, but to see him again tomorrow as well as Mamma and Edward would heal her sorrow and lift her mood even further. When John finished his refreshments, he said goodbye to her hosts and thanked them for their kindness in looking after his dear sister. After giving her a hug, he climbed into the chaise and set off home to Mill Hall.

When the evening came, Rose retired to her room where she sat eagerly anticipating the visit from Mamma; and really hoping Mary would be coming too. An enjoyable day was recorded, with tomorrow promising to be even better for seeing her family.

THURSDAY, 28TH MAY
Holy Thursday. King's Birthday kept. Holiday.

Mamma, Mary, and George went to Gravesend to fetch Edward home. They called to see me, it rained, they were very wet. Ellen Spong and I drank tea at the Kent library. The two young men walked home with us.

Rose awoke this morning in great excitement, Mamma was coming to see her directly after going to Gravesend to collect her brother Edward who was staying with a school friend at his home in the town. Today King William celebrates his birthday, marking it as a national holiday.

Yesterday's storm had passed, but the sky still looked quite dark and oppressive. Ellen wanted to go outside down the lanes regardless, and would not be deterred by the weather, so she persuaded Rose to accompany her for a walk to the Kent library in Rochester town. From the moment they stepped into the library Rose was captivated by the mountain of books arranged on shelves from floor to ceiling through a series of interconnecting rooms. Having spent many happy hours engrossed in a book, this was a treasure trove to her. Ellen, however, was less interested in the bookshelves and soon pulled Rose into the tea rooms for morning tea.

The Kent library, a fashionable place for social intercourse and meeting friends, was always a rather busy establishment. Aylesford had no such building, with all or most social exchanges in the village conducted in people's homes or in the church. Ellen was a frequent visitor to the library, and introduced Rose to two interesting young gentlemen with whom they passed a most pleasant morning in conversation while drinking tea. Rose enjoyed the experience greatly and was reluctant to leave; however, when the time came to return home for dinner the two young men offered to escort them home. She was discovering that Rochester was a most stimulating place for young people and couldn't wait to tell Mary of her morning either by letter or hopefully later today in person.

The weather took a turn for the worse after dinner with heavy rain looking imminent. Rose, quite concerned that Mamma and Edward would be soaking wet when they arrived, became restless. When the rain started to lash against the windowpanes, she hoped Mamma had gone to Gravesend in the coach driven by Wood, but she eventually arrived in the chaise which offered little protection from rain, and they were all wet through. Rose was thrilled to see them, and to her further surprise and delight found that Mary and George had come along too. Ellen led the saturated travellers through to the drawing room where a fire was burning in the grate. And with warm towels sent for and a large tray of tea, they sat beside a roaring fire.

With the visitors now dry, Mamma hugged Rose and said the fresh sea air must be agreeing with her as she looked so much better for it. Rose replied she did indeed feel much restored but missed them all terribly. 'We are missing you too, Rosamond, but it is my wish you continue to stay for a while longer as it is obviously good for your health.' Rose understood Mamma's reasoning and reassured her there were many distractions to occupy her mind, so she would do well enough.

Rose told Mary the tale of the adventure that morning in the Kent Library with Ellen, and who they had met in the tea rooms.

'It would have been much more fun if you had shared it with us, Mary, as I know you would have enjoyed the experience as much as I did.' They both laughed when Rose said that Aylesford would now appear very dull after being amongst Rochester society. She then confirmed she was to return to Frindsbury tomorrow, as a large party was arranged for the evening, and confessed to being excited at the prospect of wearing one of her evening gowns at last.

All too soon, the time came for the family to part as it was getting rather late with the daylight beginning to fade. Fortunately, the rain had stopped when they went outside, and many tears were shed as she watched the chaise disappear out of sight. Going back in the house and up to her room Rose felt quite miserable again, until she remembered she was leaving Rochester tomorrow to return to Frindsbury, a place much closer to her heart, and was also harbouring the hope that a certain Mr. Webster may still be there. Rose's day ended in the same high mood as it began.

FRIDAY, 29ᵀᴴ MAY
Restoration of Charles II. Holiday.

Left Mrs. Spong of Rochester after dinner and Ellen went to Frindsbury with me, there being a large evening party there. Very glad to come to Frindsbury. Mr. B came down.

The morning was mostly taken up with preparations for returning to Frindsbury after dinner. Mrs. Spong's groom brought the coach up from the stables, then, after loading Rose and Ellen's requirements, he assisted them both inside. That done, he started the horses and off they went.

Rose felt a great sense of relief to be heading back to Manor House Farm and cousin Fanny. Ellen had received an invitation to the party to be held this evening at the farm and she was to stay the night. The coach eventually pulled up at its destination where a great deal of activity was seen to be taking place in readiness for the evening's event. Once inside, Ellen was informed she was to share Fanny's room tonight with her and Rose, so Rose led her directly upstairs to begin the process of choosing which of the two evening dresses to wear. Fortunately, the decision was easy, as her favourite was in a pale silver-grey silk with little flowers all over the skirt and long full sleeves sitting just off her shoulders. The sleeves were adorned at the top with a bow of pink ribbon to complement the waist belt in the same colour. Fanny's help had been requested to put her hair into ringlets, and to then tie them up in pink ribbons. As her neck would be exposed, Rose had thought to pack a dainty necklace to complete the ensemble. Happy with her choices, she left them on the bed and went downstairs for tea.

There was much talk round the table of the evening ahead, with many guests expected, including Mr. Barker who had returned from London, and John Webster. Rose felt quite excited at the prospect of the evening ahead; it had been quite a while since she had attended an event such as this. The minute tea had finished, everyone disappeared to their various places to attend their toilette, including Fanny, Ellen, and Rose. There was much hilarity in the bedroom with three young ladies trying to get to the looking glass first, but eventually they were ready, and all looked splendid in their evening dresses. When everyone was satisfied with their appearance, they ascended the stairs and entered the drawing room where, to Rose's delight, Mr. Webster was already there looking most handsome in his evening attire.

A few minutes later the guests started to arrive, their presence announced audibly at the entrance to the main room which looked rather splendid with its many candles adorning the wall sconces and candelabras. With the ladies in their best finery and the men looking splendid in their evening suits, it was a wonderful sight to behold. Rose was introduced to so many people she found it difficult to remember all their names. The guests made their way to the dining room when supper was announced. The large table was set with an enormous variety of tempting foods, made even more so by flickering candles placed around the centre piece. It proved to be an exhilarating and enjoyable evening, and it was quite late when everyone went home.

Fanny, Ellen, and Rose went up to their shared bedroom to discuss the evening and share their experiences. Fanny said to Rose that she thought that when Mr. Webster had been most attentive to her, she had not detected any attempt on her part to rebuff his attention. Rose blushed crimson at this statement – what Fanny said was true, she did indeed find him most agreeable.

'What a coincidence,' answered Rose, 'that it should be another John who has caught my interest. I had never thought it would happen to me again and when Grandpapa said it is the nature of things, I didn't believe him.'

SATURDAY, 30ᵀᴴ MAY
Sir J. Mackintosh d. 1832. Gen. Sir J. Malcolm d. 1833.

Went to Hythe directly after breakfast to fish. Cousin Ambrose, Mr. Barker, Mrs. Barker, Fanny, and I went in a coach, and Mr. Webster on horseback. Had a very pleasant day. Got home at five. Mr. Trested called to see me, but I was out. We all spent the evening at home. Mr. Worth and Mrs. Day called.

Ellen went home to Rochester directly after breakfast as most of the household were to spend the day at Hythe. Ambrose, Mr. Barker, and Mr. Webster were going on a fishing expedition there, and Rose, Mrs. Barker, and Fanny were going to watch the proceedings. Mrs. Spong's cook had packed a large picnic hamper for all to enjoy at midday. The fishing equipment and the hamper were loaded on to the rear of the coach and the party took their seats inside, apart from Mr. Webster who, being a keen equestrian, went on horseback.

Everyone was in high spirits as the coach rumbled along. When they reached their destination, Mrs. Barker laid a large blanket on the grass close to the water's edge so the three ladies could sit and watch the sportsmen's attempts to catch some fish. John Webster was the first to succeed, followed by Ambrose. He placed the catch in an icebox to keep cool, but the day being warm, the ice soon melted.

When the time came to prepare lunch, Fanny spread a large white tablecloth on the blanket and put out napkins and cutlery. The men, who were hungry by this time, put down their fishing poles and joined the ladies to eat. There was plenty to enjoy as Cook had supplied them handsomely with food and drink. Having had their fill of the delicious repast, the party laid down on the grass to rest after eating so much food.

Rose, sitting gazing at the water, was surprised when Mr. Webster asked her to join him for a walk along the bank. Taken aback at his bold approach, she kept her composure and replied that yes indeed, she would very much enjoy a walk after her lunch. After helping her to her feet, the couple set off to walk at a leisurely pace leaving the rest of the party languishing on the blanket. Rose felt a little nervous at his attentiveness as he had made it obvious his intentions were of the romantic kind, but she wasn't entirely against such an idea, as she found him to be quite charming, and very handsome. Propriety forbade them walking too far from their companions who remained seated whilst talking to each other, so they turned back to join the rest of the party. The men resumed their fishing and the ladies sat back to observe.

Fanny and Mrs. Barker were curious to know what had occurred between Rose and John during their walk, so Rose informed them he had asked permission to call upon her when she returned home, and her reply was that he could, and would be made very welcome. Rose then confided that she was still fearful her illness would return and spoil things again. Fanny told her not to fret as she seemed much better now and was sure it would remain so. With the day becoming late and the hamper and blankets loaded back on to the coach, they set off back to Frindsbury. It was five o'clock by the time the coach pulled up at Manor House Farm and all agreed it had been a splendid day. Rose heard on returning that Mr. Trested had called during their absence, but Mrs. Spong had reassured him that Rosamond was quite well, and he had no need to worry on her behalf.

The time passed quietly after tea until Mr. Worth and Mrs. Day paid a visit, and their stories made the evening as enjoyable as the day had been. At bedtime, Rose felt a little excited that John Webster had expressed a wish to call on her when she returned home. She truly hoped what Fanny had said was correct about her health continuing to improve, as she didn't believe Mr. Webster's interests would continue if her illness did return.

SUNDAY, 31ST MAY
Battle of St. Lazaro, 1746.

Went to Frindsbury church in the morning with Mr. and Mrs. Barker, Mrs. Spong, Fanny, and Mr. Webster. Mr. Webster went home to London in the afternoon. Mr. Barker, Mr. Spong, Fanny and I went to church in the afternoon.

Rose walked to Frindsbury Church this morning with Fanny, Mr. Webster, Mr. and Mrs. Barker, and Mrs. Spong.

After the service, Mr. Webster invited Rose for a walk round the churchyard to admire the panoramic view of Rochester. She was quite dismayed when Mr. Webster told her of his return to London after dinner; she had enjoyed his company greatly and told him so. Mr. Webster, delighted with her admission, confirmed he had taken as much pleasure with hers, and consequently would return tomorrow the moment his business was concluded. His words of assurance made Rose feel happy, a state she had been denied for some time and served to give her hope that the future she thought would be that of an invalid spinster may turn out to be a happy one after all. Rose was aware she had only known him for a short while, and that when he returned to London and her to Mill Hall his interest in her could wane, but she resolved to enjoy his company while they were together and not spoil it by worrying about what may or may not be.

After dinner they all went outside to bid farewell to Mr. Webster, who, bending down, took Rose's hand and gently kissed it, then climbing into his coach he set off for London. Rose, whose emotions were running rather high, felt quite flustered at this public display of affection towards her. She never thought she would see a day when her cheeks became flushed because a young man had shown an interest in her again.

Discussing her feelings in the garden with Fanny a while later, her cousin recalled previous occasions when young men had set their cap at her and was only flustered now because she returned his affections. 'That is why your cheeks are aflame when he looks at you,' teased Fanny.

Rose replied she did not have any such problems when courting John Jones. Fanny laughed and said, 'As you grew up with John, the situation was different as you were expected to marry one day, and any other young man who expressed an interest in you then was doomed to fail because you were already committed. Now your heart is free to go where it wants, and it would appear Mr. John Webster has claimed it.'

Rose admitted it was all so confusing but probably true, she had not expected to come to Frindsbury and find a new love, but still feared her illness would return to spoil it. 'If a man whom I truly believed loved me could not stand by me due to my illness, how can I expect Mr. Webster to, as we do not know each other very well.'

Taking Rose's hand gently in hers, Fanny answered, 'My council to you, dear Rosie, is you should cease worrying about what could occur and just enjoy what is happening to you now. No one can predict the future, so I say enjoy his flirtations while he is with us, and if it leads to a better understanding when you return home, then so be it.' Rose, grateful for her cousin's words of encouragement, gave her a hug.

In the afternoon the girls went to Frindsbury church with Mrs. Barker and Fanny's mamma. Whilst there, Rose prayed for God's guidance in the new situation she found herself in. When bedtime came and with her diary before her, Rose had a growing feeling of excitement tinged with fear about what may happen next when Mr. Webster returns tomorrow.

ROSAMOND

1st June to 13th June

MONDAY, 1ST JUNE
Nicomede. Jeremy Bentham died, 1832.

A very wet morning. Mrs. Barker busy with her muse. Left here to go to Mrs. Spong's of Rochester, with Mrs. Spong. We went down with Mrs. Barker in the chaise. Mr. and Mrs. Spong of Rochester, Mrs. Barker, Ellen, Fanny, John, and I drank tea at Eastgate House. Mr. Webster and Cousin Ambrose came after tea. Mrs. Spong and I rode home.

Rose awoke with the disappointment of hearing heavy rain on the window this morning and hoped it would not continue throughout the day. Mrs. Spong had arranged for Fanny, Mrs. Barker, and herself to call on the Spongs of Rochester and planned to leave directly after dinner.

Lying comfortably in bed, Rose thought of Mr. Webster's promise about returning today, and what Fanny had said of her worries regarding him. She knew her cousin's observations of her feelings for the young man were correct; she was aware her heartbeat quickened when he was near. Rose couldn't prevent her face from flushing when he looked at her, so much so she feared everyone in the room knew how she felt. It was a most peculiar feeling and she struggled to maintain her decorum.

Her Mamma and sister Mary would be most surprised to see how she reacted to his attentions, but she confessed to herself she was finding the situation quite wonderful, and it was doing much to lift her spirits.

With Mrs. Barker busy with her muse in the drawing room this morning, everyone was obliged to remain silent, and with no small children at Manor House Farm, Rose took the opportunity to read her book in peace.

It stopped raining after dinner, so preparations were made for the excursion to Rochester with Mrs. Barker in the chaise. Mrs. Spong informed them on arriving in town that they were going to Eastgate House to have tea there. This important building located on the High Street impressed Rose greatly. Mrs. Spong informed them it was built in the 16th century for the Mayor of Rochester, and now supported a free school for local children within its walls. As Mrs. Spong was acquainted with the owner of the house, they had been invited to have tea with her. Rochester had many Tudor buildings, although much of the city goes back centuries before that. The visit was an enjoyable one, but as Rose had no word of Mr. Webster's whereabouts on leaving Eastgate House, she began to think he may not keep his promise of returning.

Rose was disappointed to find he still hadn't turned up when they arrived back at Mrs. A. Spong's. But disappointment turned to delight when she saw a coach arrive with Ambrose and Mr. Webster inside it. Mr. Webster entered the drawing room and went to sit beside Rose after addressing his hosts. He said to her, 'I told you I would return today, Miss Spong, I trust you are pleased to see me?'

'Indeed, I am, Mr. Webster,' she replied, at the same time noticing how practised he was in the art of flirtation, whereas her own inability in this area made responding difficult.

A pleasant hour passed with their hosts until Ambrose said they must return to Frindsbury as the hour was now late. With two conveyances at hand, Mrs. Spong instructed Rose to return in the coach with them while Fanny was to accompany Mr. Webster in the chaise. Rose, a little dismayed at this arrangement, politely agreed. She was aware that Mrs. Spong only had her reputation in mind, as to be alone with Mr. Webster so soon after their meeting may be considered unseemly. Rose decided she must appear less eager in her responses to his attentions in future as she now realised everyone else was aware of his intentions towards her as neither of them had been discreet enough during their exchanges.

On returning to Manor House Farm, she resolved from that moment on to behave in a manner more in keeping with a well-bred lady of the country, at least when in company.

TUESDAY, 2ND JUNE
Charles Butler died, 1832.

Mr. Trested came to see me, he brought a letter from Mary, who told me that J.J. was coming to see me.

Today had been a day full of surprises. Mrs. Spong counselled Rose to rest for the day as they would be attending a party in Rochester tomorrow, a suggestion she was more than happy to comply with.

Rose had breakfast in bed before dressing to venture downstairs where she found Fanny busy writing letters, so she found a comfortable sofa in the drawing room on which to rest with a book. It was there that Mr. Trested found her reclining on the chaise longue. After expressing his concern at seeing her lying down, Rose quickly reassured him she was merely preserving her energies for a social event the following day. On hearing this, he enquired how she was faring with such a busy social diary, to which Rose replied that she coped well enough as her cough had left her but admitted to feeling quite tired on occasions.

'So, Miss Spong,' he said, 'it will do you good to rest whenever you can. I can see your stay here has helped you greatly and I do not feel you have need of my services anymore, so I will bid you good day, and leave you to your book, my dear.' With that, he handed her a letter from Mary. Rose thanked him for his attendance during her illness and said she sincerely hoped, with all due respect, no further ministrations would be required from him in future.

On Mr. Trested's exit, Rose felt rather strange after hearing his conclusion that she was free from her troubles, as her heart could not believe this was so. Opening Mary's letter, she read that Mrs. Jones had written to say John was planning to call on her. She could not imagine why he wanted to come to Frindsbury to see her. Rose thought her heart had recovered from his abandonment, but hearing he now wished to call upset her greatly. With no idea as to when he intended calling, she felt quite flustered not knowing exactly when it might be. Finding it impossible to concentrate on her book after reading this news, she went into the garden for a walk.

Rose took the opportunity of telling Fanny about her letter from Mary and John's intended visit as they walked to Strood together after dinner. She also spoke of her confusion over Mr. Webster as she thought their meeting had helped her heart to heal, yet now she was even more unsure. Fanny was most concerned at her distress and said she would know in time where and with whom her heart laid. Rose sincerely hoped she would.

Returning to the farm, they were met by George and Elizabeth Nash who had ridden over from Gillingham with Mrs. Nash to see Rose. Their visit was well timed as it took Rose's mind off Mary's letter. At bedtime, Rose hoped her mind would be a little clearer in the morning.

WEDNESDAY, 3ᴿᴰ JUNE
Immense sea-fight between the Dutch and the English, 1665.

After breakfast, Fanny and I went to Rochester. We dined at Mrs. Spong's. Ellen, John, Fanny, and Mr. Webster and I went to a sherry party at Captain Hobson's. Fanny and I walked home with Mr. Webster. Got home at 1 am.

Rose and Cousin Fanny had been invited to dine with Mrs. Spong of Rochester today, as had their fellow guest, Mr. Webster, who opted to make the journey on his horse. The ladies were conveyed there in the chaise, dressed in their finery as they were to go to Strood later in the afternoon to attend a sherry party hosted by Captain Hobson at his home.

After resting for an hour following dinner, the coach was brought round to take the party guests to Strood, including Mrs. Spong's son and daughter, John and Ellen. Also receiving an invitation was Mr. Webster who made the journey in his usual manner, on horseback. Rose, still confused about her feelings for him since being informed of J.J.'s intended visit, thought it prudent to be cool with him at this social event.

When they arrived at the party there were so many guests in Captain Hobson's drawing room that avoiding Mr. Webster's attentions was not too difficult. Ellen introduced Rose to so many people it made her head spin. Just as she decided to find a seat, Mr. Webster appeared at her side bearing two glasses of sherry and said to her, 'I fear you are avoiding me, Miss Spong.'

Rose, who had been attempting to do just that, replied, 'Indeed I am not.' He then handed her a glass of sherry, a drink not usually to her taste but being nervous in his company she readily accepted it and felt relieved when its effects helped calm her down.

As the evening wore on, Mr. Webster's attentions grew bolder until Rose was surprised to find that J.J. was no longer dominating her mind, and she was enjoying the ongoing flirtation. Rose accepted another glass of sherry despite thinking it was probably unwise to do so as she felt quite intoxicated, not a sensation she was familiar with, and resolved not to have another one. Just as she was beginning to feel at ease and enjoy herself, Fanny came over to suggest that with the hour quite late, they should return home soon as Mamma would be fretting about them. The night being warm and illuminated by a bright moon led Mr. Webster to suggest they walk back to Frindsbury together. Rose was surprised when Fanny agreed, so all three plus Mr. Webster's horse set off on the long walk home. Rose thought it just as well she had Fanny as a chaperone as the two glasses of sherry were having quite a pleasing effect, and if Mr. Webster behaved improperly towards her, she might have found it difficult to resist his charms. However, with her cousin keeping her company, her honour and reputation remained intact.

It was an hour past midnight when they arrived back at Manor House Farm, with Rose in a tired but happy state. She realised her feelings for John Jones had all but evaporated, as her heart had been caught by another.

THURSDAY, 4ᵀᴴ JUNE
Cambridge Term divides at noon. W. Windham died, 1810. Henry Grattan died, 1820.

I wrote to Mary. Cousin Ambrose went to Maidstone. He put the letter in the post. After tea, Fanny and I walked to Strood to get some cakes.

Due to the lateness of the hour at which Rose got into bed last night, a brief account of yesterday's events was not recorded until this morning, and even then, not until her head had cleared.

A while later, she wrote a long letter to Mary, saying amongst other things that her missive regarding John's intended visit had made her question the feelings she had for him once more. Rose then assured her that Mr. Webster's company had helped her accept that, regardless of what John had to say, she had no wish to renew any romance with him. She included in the letter how much she was enjoying her stay at Manor House Farm, and that Fanny had been a valuable companion and confidant in Mary's absence.

Rose concluded with the information she had left until last, which was that Mr. Webster had asked if he may call upon her when she returned home and she had answered his request by saying, 'Indeed, Mr. Webster, I would be most pleased to receive you.' She then admitted Mary had been correct in saying that one day her head would be turned by a handsome young man, but she had not believed her at the time. When the letter was written, Rose sealed it and then took it downstairs to Ambrose who had offered to post it when he went to Maidstone.

Rose and Fanny walked to Strood after tea to buy an assortment of cakes for Mrs. Spong who was preparing to entertain tomorrow. Much to Rose's disappointment, Mr. Webster had busied himself elsewhere today and had not been seen. At least it had been a quiet day today, reflected Rose, who found the constant socialising quite exhausting, and feeling rather tired with little to note of the day's events, the diary was put away and she retired to bed.

FRIDAY, 5ᵀᴴ JUNE
Boniface, an Englishman, bishop of Mentz, martyred, 755.

We were busy in the morning preparing for a dinner party. Mr. Sampson, Mr. Talega, Mr. Oakley, Mr. Plainly, Mr. Tarbell, and Mr. Hudson dined here.

It was a hectic day today at Manor House as Mrs. Spong was hosting a dinner party. Fanny and Rose spent the morning helping to prepare the long dining room table to accommodate six further guests who were all business associates of cousin Ambrose. The name cards at their designated places read: Mr. Sampson, Mr. Talega, Mr. Oakley, Mr. Plainly, Mr. Tarbell, and Mr. Hudson. With the preparations completed, the table looked rather splendid. Fanny, skilfully practiced in the art of flower arranging, had created a magnificent centre piece containing a variety of colourful flowers from the garden.

After admiring their handiwork, the girls went up to their room to make themselves equally presentable for the occasion. Rose put on her best muslin dress and then asked Fanny to curl her hair into ringlets, the latest popular style for ladies. She then added two pretty ribbons to complete her toilette. Rose was hoping Mr. Webster would find her chosen outfit rather fetching. She had become more interested in her appearance since arriving in Frindsbury and feared her vanity had become a habit but suspected, as Fanny had remarked, that it had more to do with impressing Mr. Webster. It occurred to her that the Reverend Mr. Staines back in Aylesford would be scandalised by the change in her.

The dinner party was a great success with much hilarity, but Rose was again disappointed not to have any time alone during the social intercourse with Mr. Webster in which to continue their flirtations, as the guests stayed for the entire afternoon. They did, however, set out for a walk in the garden in the evening, only to be joined hot on their heels by Fanny and Ambrose, who Rose suspected were sent by Mrs. Spong to chaperone them.

It had been an enjoyable day which saw Rose going to bed in a happy frame of mind as she not only felt well, but a new beau was occupying her thoughts.

SATURDAY, 6ᵀᴴ JUNE
Oxford Term ends. Carl von Weber died, 1826.

John Hopley came to see me, an old friend of mine. I had not seen him for five years. He had tea here. I wrote to Mary. After tea Fanny and I went to Rochester; called on the Spongs. Saw Mr. and Mrs. Barker.

Rose stayed at the farm all day and spent the morning writing a letter to Mary. There was more to tell of the busy life she was leading in Frindsbury and how much she wished Mary was there to share it with her. Rose ended the letter by describing her happiness at leaving the illness in the past and now looking forward to a brighter future.

After dinner, Rose had a visitor in the form of John Hopley, an old friend she had not seen for five years, so there was much to talk about. It had come to John's notice through mutual friends how much she had suffered through illness, and he was relieved to see she was now well again. Rose told him of her terrible trials and how she feared for her life on many occasions. John stayed until tea was about to be served, so Mrs. Spong invited him to join them. With tea now finished, he thanked Mrs. Spong for her kind hospitality and left to return home.

In the early evening, Fanny and Rose were taken in the coach to call on the Rochester Spongs and were reacquainted with Mr. and Mrs. Barker who were now staying there. The Barkers' usual residence was in London, but they preferred spending summer in Kent. Two branches of the Spong family lived in the Rochester area with several others scattered throughout the county. The nearest to Mill Hall was Rose's Uncle William, her papa's brother who lived at Cobtree Manor with his family.

Mr. Webster had still not returned to Manor Farm when they arrived back at Frindsbury, much to Rose's disappointment as she hadn't seen him since breakfast that morning. Feeling tired, she went upstairs to prepare for bed. Too weary to write, she closed her diary and put it away in the little drawer in Fanny's writing desk.

SUNDAY, 7TH JUNE
Whit Sunday, the time of the descent of the Holy Ghost.

We all went to church in the morning, Mrs. Spong and Fanny stayed for the testament. Mr. Webster and I came home. We remained in, in the afternoon. Mr. Webster, Fanny and I went to the church in the evening. Mr. and Mrs. Barker came in the evening, likewise Miss Norton, Miss Stabler, Mrs. Stabler and Miss Spong.

Sunday today; once again Rose's most favoured day of the week had come around when she could enjoy listening to an interesting sermon and the singing of hymns.

Eagerly looking forward to the morning service, the family and Mr. Webster set off walking to All Saints Church. The Whit Sunday service was most uplifting and did not disappoint. Fanny stayed with her Mamma for the testament. However, Mr. Webster asked Rose if she wished to walk back to Manor House Farm with him before the testament began, and she gladly accepted. Leaving their hosts behind to participate in the rest of the service they set off to walk back to Manor Farm. Rose found it more than pleasant, just the two of them walking along in the sunshine together, where Mr. Webster let it be known how he felt toward her, and how much he admired her which led to his enquiry as to whether she would be offended were he to press his suit upon her.

Rose replied that on the contrary, if he wished to walk out with her, she would indeed welcome it. So, it was eagerly agreed that on her return to Mill Hall, he would immediately seek approval from Papa for them to walk out together. Rose, although excited by his further declarations of affection, knew her papa would insist that Mary accompany them on their walks until such a time as he was satisfied of his daughter's suitor's honest intentions. Rose assured John of her sister's discretion and knew she would afford them some privacy. On her return, Mrs. Spong made it clear to Rose in a solemn tone that she disapproved of her behaviour; not only had she failed to attend the testament with the family, but she had also walked home alone with Mr. Webster, unchaperoned. 'Your dear Mamma will be most upset to hear of this, Rosamond,' she said. 'As I have failed in my duty to protect you from harm.'

Rose assured her no harm whatsoever would come to her in Mr. Webster's care as his behaviour had and always would be that of a gentleman, but nonetheless she apologised for her thoughtless behaviour, and promised she would take Fanny if they were to go walking out again. 'I am pleased to hear it, my dear, as social propriety must be upheld at all times. It is the way things should be in polite society.' Rose accepted that indeed it was, and she would endeavour henceforth to observe the social rules that were there to protect young women from harm, hoping this declaration would appease Mrs. Spong and bring an end to the matter.

Fanny was highly amused at her cousin's scolding from her mamma and giggled as they all went into dinner. Rose didn't mind being the subject of her humour, as she felt she deserved it for being so reckless in forgetting Mrs. Spong was charged by Mamma to take good care of her and would feel she had been lax in her duties. Rose's usual nature was to be shy and polite, and she felt perplexed as to why she had recently become rather bold and feared she had allowed Mr. Webster to turn her head. Nonetheless, it was wonderful to be happy once more and not so fearful of the future.

After tea, Rose and Mr. Webster, accompanied by Fanny, returned to church for the evening service, and arrived back home to find Mr. and Mrs. Barker had called, together with Miss Norton, Mrs. Stabler, and her daughter, because of which a jolly evening followed. Life will seem quite dull, mused Rose, when she returned home. She had become quite attached to Frindsbury and Rochester with their interesting society.

Fanny was longing to know what transpired with Mr. Webster on the walk this morning, so as soon as the girls were alone in their bedroom, a lengthy conversation took place. When Rose informed her cousin of Mr. Webster's request to walk out with her and how happy she was to agree to it, Fanny, delighted to hear this news, gave her a hug and said, 'When you have formally asked your Papa's permission to walk out, and he allows it, we will be able to tell my Mamma and Papa. I know they will be pleased with your choice as they are very fond of Mr. Webster.'

It had been an enjoyable and interesting day, and Rose hoped for more like it before going to stay with Grandpapa in Gillingham.

MONDAY, 8ᵀᴴ JUNE
Holiday. Mrs. Siddons died, 1831.

Very poorly all day, had a pain in my chest. Mr. Noble came, he slept here. Mr. Spong, Mr. Hall and Mr. Webster drank tea at Aunt Spong's.

After such a promising day Rose found it difficult to get to sleep and got out of bed feeling quite unwell, which put her in fear of her health yet again. As soon as Fanny was informed, she went directly to fetch her mamma who went upstairs without delay to see Rose, who was now back in her bed. When Rose told her she was feeling poorly and had a bad pain in her chest, Mrs. Spong strongly advised her to remain in bed for the day. 'We will bring your meals up to you so you can rest, and if you are not improved by the morrow, I will send word to your Mamma.'

After she had left the room, Fanny told her cousin that they had another visitor, Mr. Noble, a friend of Ambrose who had arrived and would be staying overnight.

It was the beginning of a rather unhappy day for Rose. Fanny told her she had said to Mr. Webster that 'Rose was indisposed,' and he had been to have tea in Rochester with her papa and Mr. Noble. Rose prayed to be restored on awakening in the morning.

TUESDAY, 9TH JUNE
Holiday. Dr. A. Rees died, 1825.

Mr. Stevenson called and told us that Charles Nike had cut his throat. Mr. and Mrs. Barker and Mr. Hudson went fishing. We stayed at home.

The morning saw Rose, as she had hoped, much improved, but Mrs. Spong told her to stay at home for one more day regardless.

During the morning they had a visitor. Mr. Stevenson called to tell them some sad news, he had heard that Mr. Charles Nike had taken his own life by cutting his throat. They were all quite shocked to hear this, Rose was unfamiliar with the gentleman, but was equally sorry to hear the circumstances of his demise.

Later, when the initial revelation of Mr. Nike's passing had subsided, Rose realised Mr. Webster had been out all day again. She sincerely hoped he was not trying to avoid her, knowing she had been ill. Even though her condition had improved today, in her heart she knew she was far from being cured of this terrible affliction. It was still there, she could feel it, lying in wait deep down inside her chest ready to strike her down. She had allowed herself to believe she was free of it and could live her life once more, happy at the thought of a future with John Webster.

Now, cruelly, her thoughts had become dark again, with uncertainty and confusion clouding her mind as to whether she should allow herself to continue accepting the attentions of John Webster. If she were to give her heart to him only to be abandoned again because of her poor health, she would not be able to bear having it broken for a second time.

Rose decided to write to Mary for counsel on the matter, but before putting pen to paper she discussed it with her cousin first. Because Fanny had not witnessed how unhappy she had been when John left her, or how ill she had become, she said not to act in haste, wait, and see if it really was her old affliction returning and not just a chest cold. Rose began to think it could be a possibility and agreed to do nothing for now. With the decision made, they heard that Mr. and Mrs. Barker had gone fishing with Mr. Hudson as the present clement weather was perfect for catching fish.

Rose ended her day afraid of whatever the future had in store.

WEDNESDAY, 10ᵀᴴ JUNE
Oxford Term beg. Hol. at the Exch. Duke of Wellington installed Chancellor of the University of Oxford, 1834.

Mrs. Barker dined here. After dinner Fanny went to Rochester, and after tea Mr. Webster and I went out with her. When we came home, Mr. Webster showed me some pictures. He gave me a X.

Thankfully, Rose had a much better day today. After a quiet morning spent writing letters to her family, it was soon time for dinner.

Mrs. Barker dined with them, and after dinner Fanny went to

Rochester. Rose declined the invitation to join her by suggesting it would be better for her to rest. In truth, she was rather hoping Mr. Webster would return after riding out with one of Ambrose's horses. Frequently glancing at the clock on the mantelpiece while waiting, Rose became quite restless, not knowing if she should ask him to let her go, but disappointingly he did not return until teatime when it was impossible to say anything at all.

After tea, however, he approached her and asked if she would care to accompany him and Fanny on a walk down the lane to the churchyard to enjoy the views over the Medway to Rochester. Rose happily agreed, and after placing a shawl over her shoulders, the three set out. When they returned home, Mr. Webster mentioned to Rose, having enthused about the Medway valley, that he had a set of views she may be interested in seeing.

At this point, Fanny, sensing her presence was no longer required, went up to her room. Mr. Webster also went to his room and returned to the drawing room with the views to show Rose. The pictures showed mountains in Switzerland which Rose found so fascinating; she remarked how much she would like to visit a place such as that one day. Just as she became aware how close they were as they gazed at the pictures laid out on the table, he took her hand and replied that the time may come when he would take her there. Then to her absolute surprise, he moved forward and gently kissed her on the lips. Rose was shocked at his boldness and despite her misgivings yesterday, she was inwardly thrilled, but felt it would have been most unseemly to have let him know this. Tilting her head on one side while trying to suppress a smile, she said, 'Mr. Webster, you presume too much.' But she knew he was aware she did not really mean it.

After bidding each other goodnight, Rose returned to her room with her heart racing. A short while later, Fanny came into their bedroom and was told in excited whispers what had occurred in the drawing room earlier. She said it was a good thing Mamma had been occupied elsewhere, as she would have a fit of the vapours by entering the room just as the deed was being done. They laughed so much at the prospect of such a thing, and Rose absolutely agreed it was fortunate she had not appeared. Rose was now truly unsure of her feelings and had to confess to Fanny she was enjoying Mr. Webster's attentions too much to stop them now.

THURSDAY, 11ᵀᴴ JUNE
St. Barnabas (a Levite), i.e., son of prophecy or consolation. Hol. at the Exch.

Mamma came in the morning with Alfred Nash to fetch me home, as she had heard that Mr. Webster had cut his throat, but I did not return with her. Mr. W asked to go out with us, so we left the manor house.

Rose had a totally unexpected visit this morning from her mother and Albert Nash, who had arrived to take her home.

Her Mamma was most agitated and concerned because she had been led to believe Mr. Webster had cut his throat. Rose was quite shocked at this account and said to Mamma it was simply not true as she knew he was out riding at that very moment, and the person who had committed this terrible deed was Mr. Charles Nike from London.

'Who gave you this information, Mamma?' Rose enquired. Mamma answered that Mrs. Robson had heard it from Mrs. Jones, who had been told by someone she knew in London.

'I am happy to hear it wasn't Mr. Webster who met his demise,'

Mamma said. 'But I will say a prayer for poor Mr. Nike's soul and his family.' She then made it known that Mary had told her of Rose's attachment to Mr. Webster, and therefore feared her daughter would be very upset and in need of the family's support and comfort.

'I am truly grateful for your concern, Mamma, but I am perfectly fine as you can see. Yet it is wonderful to see you, I have sorely missed you all,' said Rose, hugging her. Mamma then asked Rose if she wished to return home with her, but Rose said she was happy to remain at Manor House Farm, as a visit to Grandpapa's had been arranged for the coming Saturday.

Mamma and Albert were invited to stay for dinner by Mrs. Spong, which they gratefully accepted. Mr. Webster returned from his ride in good time and was duly introduced to Mamma. When he was told the reason for Mamma's impromptu visit, he roared with laughter and said to her, 'As you can see, Mrs. Spong, my throat is still intact.'

After a very pleasant dinner it was time for the visitors to leave. Mamma declared how glad she was to see Rose's recent struggles with her chest had abated. Rose answered, 'No more than I, Mamma, I was so worried illness would overcome me again, but thankfully it hasn't, praise be to the Lord.'

Rose felt a little tearful as she waved them goodbye until their coach disappeared around the corner of the lane. Things picked up, however, when Mr. Webster overheard Fanny suggesting to Rose that they walk out together to enjoy the fine afternoon and asked to be included, so any sad thoughts about Mamma's leaving were soon forgotten.

As the three left the Manor House together, Fanny and Rose linked arms while Mr. Webster followed at a respectful distance, but as soon as they were out of sight of the house, John Webster exchanged places with Fanny who now walked on ahead. Rose felt elated and happy to be walking beside him arm in arm, stealing an odd glance up at him as they strolled along. John was aware of Rose's visit to Gillingham on Saturday to stay with her grandpapa, and due to it not being much of a distance he had promised to call in on her, with Grandpapa's permission of course. Returning for tea in a jolly mood, Rose was certain Mrs. Spong would have surmised that social protocol would have been forgotten the moment they were out of her sight, but given her warm and friendly nature, she would well remember how it was to be young.

Rose was glad to record a happy day in her diary once again.

FRIDAY, 12ᵀᴴ JUNE
Wat Tyler killed in Smithfield, 1381.

I drew all the morning. Mrs. Beecham came after dinner. Fanny and I went to Strood. Afterwards we went to Broom Hill. Mr. W. very busy with his speech. Had a nice walk.

It was a most agreeable day for Rose; she spent the morning drawing flowers in the garden, a pastime she had neglected for a while having forgotten how enjoyable and engrossing it was.

Fanny asked Rose to accompany her on a walk to Strood after dinner and she happily agreed. Mr. Webster was in his room rehearsing a speech he had to make, so the girls were aware they wouldn't have his company today. It was gloriously warm and sunny on their walk to Strood, which required the use of parasols to protect their delicate complexions as they walked along at a leisurely pace admiring the wildflowers in the meadows and hedgerows, looking their very best in the brilliant sunshine.

Eventually arriving in the small town of Strood, they found the High Street quite busy, with everyone hurrying about their business. Rose had taken along her reticule should she find something pretty in the haberdashers, but as usual nothing caught her eye amongst the display. There was no need of ribbons or laces as she had an abundance of them at home, and a pair of white lace gloves that may have suited her were noticed but returned to the counter, as she knew she could return another day if she changed her mind.

After taking tea in the coffee house on the High Street, they decided to walk slowly up Broom Hill and seek a suitable bench on which to sit and enjoy the panoramic views of the Medway and beyond. Fanny spotted a vacant seat in a good position, so they made their way to it as quickly as they could before it was taken. Grateful to sit down and relax, the girls admired the vista until they were sufficiently rested, then retraced their steps down the hill into Strood and, from there, back to Manor House Farm for tea. It had been a most pleasant outing, but both Rose and Fanny were relieved to find themselves back home sitting in comfortable chairs with a cool glass of cordial.

Rose stayed for most of the evening in the drawing room with Fanny's family and Mr. Webster. As the afternoon had proved quite tiring for her, she excused herself then made her way upstairs to read a book. After doing so and making a few notes in her diary, she fell fast asleep.

SATURDAY, 13TH JUNE
R. E. Edgeworth died, 1817.

I left Mrs. Spong's of Frindsbury after tea. George and Elizabeth came to fetch me. They had tea at Mrs. Spong's, Miss Beecham was there. Mr. Barker came from London.

Rose was to leave Manor House Farm today in order to stay with Grandpapa Nash in Gillingham, so George Nash had arranged to collect her in the afternoon. After breakfast she spent the morning gathering up her belongings, with Fanny's help, to pack them away in her trunk. When everything was collected and ready to put on the chaise when it arrived, Rose felt quite sad to be leaving everyone, especially Mr. Webster and Fanny.

After dinner she sat in the drawing room with Mr Webster, and during their conversation he mentioned he was returning to London tomorrow but would call to see her on his return. When asked if he knew when that might be, he replied, 'That I cannot say, Rosamond.' Not receiving an affirmative answer made Rose's heart sink at the thought she may never see him again, and she desperately hoped it would not be so.

The moment he went out to the stable for a horse to ride, Fanny went in to see her, and Rose told her of her fears about never seeing Mr. Webster again. Fanny replied, 'You are just being silly, Rose, I can tell he is smitten with you. I am more than certain you will see him again.'

'I hope you are correct, Fanny,' said Rose. 'And he has not been simply toying with my affections during his stay for his amusement only.' She added, 'If I never see him again, I will know it was the case, and I will feel very foolish for letting myself believe he really liked me.'

Fanny hugged her and said, 'Please do not torture yourself with such silly thoughts, Rose, you will see him again, I am sure.' Just then Mrs. Spong came into the room to say that George and Elizabeth had called to take her to Gillingham and would be staying for tea before departing. Mr. Webster returned from his ride and went in to join them.

When the meal was done, George put Rose's belongings into the chaise as the time had come to say goodbye. Giving Mrs. Spong a hug, Rose thanked her sincerely for taking such good care of her and hoped she had not been any trouble. Mrs. Spong assured her it had been a pleasure, and she would be welcome any time. Ambrose, taking her hands in both of his said, 'Take good care, my dear.' Then it was Fanny's turn to say goodbye and, hugging her cousin with tears in her eyes, she said she would miss her greatly.

By this time Rose was beginning to weep herself and said to everyone gathered, 'I am leaving here a much more confident person than when I arrived. I was sad to leave my family behind at Mill Hall and did not know what I would do without them, but now I am sad to be leaving you all in Frindsbury.' Rose suspected Mr. Webster may also have played a part in her newfound confidence.

When all the goodbyes had been said, Mr. Webster, stepping forward, took Rose's hand and kissed it. Keeping his head bowed, he said, 'We will meet again Miss Spong, you can be sure of it,' before turning away and going back inside the house.

With no more to be said, they climbed into the chaise and set off for Gillingham. Rose, glancing back towards the house before the chaise went round the corner, could see the family waving, but Mr. Webster was nowhere to be seen. This sowed more seeds of doubt in Rose's mind about his intentions, for if he couldn't join the family to acknowledge their departure, her fears about not being important to him now she was leaving may well be true. The thought of this made Rose extremely sad and consequently she said very little on the journey to Grandpapa's. George asked if anything was troubling her, but not wishing to divulge her thoughts, she simply replied that having enjoyed her stay at Manor Farm so much, she was a little sad to be leaving it now, which was the truth.

Grandpapa stood waiting by the gate when they arrived at his home in Gillingham. Once out of the chaise and into his arms, Grandpapa said his housekeeper had prepared a comfortable bedroom where her belongings were promptly taken. After supper Rose excused herself by saying how sleepy she felt and needed to retire, and so she took herself upstairs with thoughts of Mr. Webster weighing heavily on her mind.

Wearing her night attire and sitting by a small fire which had been lit to keep the evening chill out of her room, she wrote of the day's events. It has been a troubling day and one that had included a few tears.

Jackie

2020

With Rosamond away and unable to take my mind off the pandemic I needed a new focus, so I decided to research the story of Rosamond's uncle, William Spong, and his connection to Charles Dickens. It is well documented that Charles Dickens based the character of Mr. Wardle in 'The Pickwick Papers' on Uncle William; it even appears on his memorial at Aylesford parish church.

Apparently, the young Charles Dickens happened to be skating on a frozen pond one cold winter's day and fell through the ice, plunging him into the freezing water below. Dragging himself out, dripping wet and shivering with cold, he stumbled to the nearby manor house of Cobtree Manor, the home of Rosamond's Uncle William. The story goes on to say that taking pity on the poor unfortunate young man standing on the doorstep before him, Uncle William instructed his maid to show the stranger into the drawing room where he sat him down in front of a roaring fire to warm his bones. Fresh towels and dry clothes were quickly sent for, and Charles Dickens remained there in a comfortable armchair enjoying hot tea and buttered scones, possibly followed by a glass or two of mulled wine. The two gentlemen, one young and the other more mature, chatted away by the glowing fire until the young man's clothes were dry.

As a result of this hospitality, Charles Dickens never forgot the help he received in his hour of need, and because of it, he and William became good friends. When Mr. Dickens began writing 'The Pickwick Papers' he based the character of Mr. Wardle, a convivial gentleman who entertained the esteemed members of the Pickwick Club at his cosy home by playing cards in front of a roaring fire, on Rosamond's uncle, William Spong.

Mike and I went to look for the house, referred to as 'Dingley Dell' in the story, when we visited the area in 2017. It is situated within Cobtree Manor Park on the outskirts of Aylesford, but access to the building is not available to the public. We could see through the iron gates that the original house had lost a wing and gained a new one – the whole building is now converted into separate dwellings named the Dingley Dell Apartments. I do believe that during the conversion, a large old fireplace reputed to be the one Charles Dickens sat in front of with Uncle William has recently been sold for a great deal of money. I wonder who the present owner is?

Another interesting fact to be investigated which John Vigar told me about in 1996 concerned the family's connection to Charles II. Mike took this project on and was soon able to print out the family tree of Rosamond's grandmother (Rosamond Walters). This clearly showed she was indeed directly descended from the Stuart king, and it is well recorded that Charles had a mistress called Barbara Palmer, a.k.a. The Duchess of Cleveland. The King and the Duchess went on to have five children between them. Henry, the first born, was given the title of Henry Fitzroy the Earl of Grafton, and this is the line that leads directly to Rosamond. Therefore, Charles II was her fifth great grandfather, which at first sounds quite impressive, but as Charles went on to have at least fourteen mistresses in his busy lifetime there must be many out there who can say they are related to the Stuart monarch. Being a half-Scot myself, I could also be related, as Charles was descended from a Scottish Stuart.

I wonder how many readers remember the 'Spong' mincer?

I certainly do. This kitchen appliance was invented by James Osborne Spong, another relative of Rosamond's. My parents had one of these contraptions; every Monday my mother would clamp the metal mincer to our kitchen table, and I was given the task of turning the handle for her. Sitting watching as she fed the left-over bits of our Sunday roast into it, I was fascinated by the process of a whole piece of meat going in one end, and mincemeat coming out of the other, ready to be turned into a cottage pie for Monday's tea. Although a must-have implement in my day, the only place to see them now is flea markets and bric-a-brac stalls.

The first lockdown due to the virus in 2020 was difficult, and like everyone else we missed the family greatly, but with so much time on my hands and no Rosamond to fill it, I began researching her siblings. My earlier attempts had been quite frustrating, as the information available at that time was far more restricted, but now, thanks to growth of the Internet, I did manage to trace some but not all her siblings, probably because I am still somewhat inept when it comes to technology. Weeks went by with still no sign of Rosamond, but I knew Diane was busy working from home, so I didn't really expect to see her back just yet.

Even though I had been reluctant to take on this story in the first place, now I had started I didn't want to stop; so, what on earth could I write about in the meantime?

As I lay in bed one morning pondering this question while anticipating another boring day ahead, a voice in my head seemed to say, 'What about Mary?' Many strange things have happened to me in my life, but I have never heard a voice so strong and clear. 'What about Mary' I asked out loud, feeling rather foolish as I did so. I needed to tell Mike what I had just heard, so getting out of bed and going downstairs I announced, 'I think I have just found my next venture, I'm going to write about Rosamond's sister, Mary.'

His reply was, 'Don't you think you'd better finish Rosamond's first?'

Buoyed by this new venture I returned to the computer and soon I had the outline of her story, but to learn more would require better skills than mine. It was time to contact my friend Julie, an intuitive and talented genealogist who had previously constructed an impressive family tree for me.

'I would be delighted to help,' was her immediate response, 'just let me have something to go on.' And what Julie managed to discover was truly remarkable. Not only did she add to my findings, but she uncovered more than I could ever hope to find. With all this fascinating information I spent much of the first and second lockdown immersed in Mary's world. Julie was also able to fill in the gaps regarding Rosamond's siblings, providing me with a comprehensive file of her brothers and sisters so at last I knew where they had all ended up. Our joint project helped us both immensely during those terrible days, and I couldn't have done it without her. I will always be indebted to Julie for the help and friendship she freely gave as I waited for Rosamond to come home.

What a terrible year 2020 had been, the world in crisis with COVID-19 and we all hoped it would soon be over, but the pandemic wasn't going anywhere. Diane completed the typing in December and Rosamond came home. My son Iain had installed Word on to our computer, so Diane forwarded the manuscript straight to it. It is a brilliant tool for those who know what they are doing; unfortunately, I don't. I did attempt to get to grips with it but soon gave up as my computer skills were rather limited. Mike, however, was more competent, so it fell on him to do the editing, a daunting task but to his credit he plodded on, correcting my mistakes and grammatical errors.

Christmas was fast approaching, but this year it would be radically different as no large family gatherings were allowed, only small 'bubbles,' so apart from Mike's sister Glenda, we spent Christmas without our loved ones. Thanks to Skype, we were able to exchange presents virtually, but despite our best efforts to remain cheerful it was a sad day.

The damp squib of Christmas having passed, 2021 arrived, the year I turned eighty. Where had the years gone? I was 'only' fifty-five when Rosamond came into my life, and she is just as important to me now as she was then.

January brought hopes of a safer future when the news of a vaccine appeared, and with it the possibility of life returning to normal as things progressed steadily with the editing. At this point, my own personal narrative in this project was intended to be a brief chapter at the end explaining how the diary had appeared. However, after discussing this with various friends and published authors I was surprised to hear them all saying, 'This should be your own story as well as Rosamond's.' My friend Trish also said the same when I first began this project, but I didn't agree, so when I mentioned these other comments, she couldn't resist saying, 'I told you a footnote wasn't enough.'

The opinions of these seasoned writers completely threw me as I never intended it to be about me, the focus had been on Rosamond and her family. I had no wish to write about myself, so I rejected their comments and tried to disregard it. But once an idea is planted, it grows, and to my surprise I found myself thinking about how it could work if I were to write my own story. What started out as wonderful therapy and a tribute to a young woman whose little diary had restored my life was about to become a story involving two women, separated by 180 years. Was this feasible and could I do it? I admit to feeling utterly exhausted simply by thinking about it.

This state continued for a few weeks up until one morning when I sat engrossed in a book with my morning tea, my choice of reading being a novel by an American author which I happened to be enjoying immensely. It tells the story of a slave girl in Virginia in the mid-19th century in parallel with a female lawyer living in the 21st century, both lives being interlaced throughout the book. Not a new idea by any means, but I suddenly realised that this was how my book should be presented. Setting this different course would completely change my part of the story, and in doing so I would have to revisit some heart-breaking moments in my life, and many tears would be shed during the process.

ROSAMOND

14th June to 24th June

SUNDAY, 14ᵀᴴ JUNE
Battle of Marengo, 1800.

Mrs. Nash, Grandpapa, George, and Elizabeth and I went to chapel. Heard Mr. Johnson. I wrote to Mamma after dinner. We all went to chapel again in the evening. Saw Mr. Beecham morning and evening.

As Rose laid in bed last night, thoughts of John Webster were filling her mind so much it was difficult to fall asleep. She kept ruminating over her true feelings for him. Thankfully, by the time morning came she had concluded that if he failed to call upon her whilst at Grandpapa's house, she would not be the worse for it. Her responses to his attentions towards her had shown that her heart had mended since being broken by John's leaving, so rather than regretting it, thanks should be given for the flirtations she enjoyed with him. They would never have led to marriage anyway as she did not consider him ready for the responsibilities of that institution. If Mr. Webster failed to live up to his promise of calling, or even never saw her again, she was not too concerned about her heart breaking.

Rose went to chapel with Grandpapa, George, and Elizabeth this morning. The speaker today was a Mr. Johnson who delivered an interesting if unremarkable sermon. Mr. Beecham happened to be at the meeting and engaged Rose in conversation until the time came to return to Grandpapa's house for dinner. After dinner, Rose wrote a letter to Mamma to tell her about a journey to Rochester in the chaise tomorrow with them all, where they would call on Dr. Dodds before visiting the wine merchants and grocers. A quiet afternoon was spent reading alone in her bedroom, then Rose accompanied the family back to the chapel for the evening service to find a different speaker in place of Mr. Johnson, but equally as interesting. Mr. Beecham was seen again at chapel this evening, but she didn't speak to him.

Grandpapa's home being quite different to Uncle Ambrose's, in respect of it being less populated and therefore quieter, made Rose wonder if she would find all the tranquillity rather dull. She was missing Mr. Webster's attentions already, as well as Fanny's chatter on their walks round Frindsbury, but at least she had Elizabeth and dear George to talk to during her stay.

With the family supper concluded and tiredness beginning to overwhelm her, Rose sought her bedroom to write a few notes in her diary before retiring to bed.

MONDAY, 15TH JUNE
The Spanish army defeated at Saragossa, 1809.

Grandpapa, George, and I went to Rochester in the chaise directly after breakfast. Met Mr. and Mrs. Baxter and George Spong. George Nash called on Doctor Dodds to ask him to dinner. D. Dodds dined here. George and he went out in the afternoon.

They came home for tea. D.D. felt my chest and back. Elizabeth and I went for a walk, we called on Mrs. Woods.

With the trip to Rochester in mind this morning, Rose alighted from her bed to check the weather from her window. It was a fine June day with hardly a breeze, so a light dress would be required for the outing.

After breakfast she selected the one in white muslin with little sprigs of yellow flowers all over it that Mrs. Robson had bought for her, complemented with a matching bonnet trimmed with flowers and ribbons. Looking in the mirror she felt pleased with her choice, so picking up her white gloves and reticule she ran downstairs where she found Grandpapa waiting patiently in the hall with George.

Rose had hoped to visit Mr. and Mrs. Spong while in Rochester in case Mr. Webster and Fanny were taking tea there, but she was to be disappointed. However, they did encounter Mr. and Mrs. Baxter and George Spong, with whom they enjoyed a lengthy conversation.

Now back on Rochester High Street, Rose and her grandfather sought out a coffee house, while George Nash called on his friend Doctor Dodds to invite him for dinner. After rest and refreshment, Grandpapa went to make his necessary purchases while Rose took the opportunity to visit the nearest bookshop where she spent a pleasant morning. When George returned, they collected the chaise and made their way back to Gillingham for dinner.

Rose, now upstairs in her bedroom attending to her toilette having only just removed her bonnet and gloves, saw a chaise arrive at the front door. She didn't recognise the gentleman who alighted from it, but presumed it was George's friend and dinner guest Dr. Dodds. It suddenly occurred to her that George may have spoken to him about her illness and had asked him to attend her. She was soon to find out. George duly introduced Rose to his friend who she found to be quite pleasant looking with kindly eyes that twinkled when he smiled, but knowing his profession made her worry about his reasons for being there in the first place. If George had asked his advice concerning her recurring health problems, he may want to examine her, the inference of which would suggest her family may be keeping the true nature of her past illness from her.

Rose had started to believe she had finally overcome these problems and could start to live a normal life once more, but what if her family knew her symptoms would return and were seeking the opinion of another physician? This thought frightened her greatly. Trying to be rational, she accepted it was in her nature to worry and not be so silly. However, her assumptions proved correct when shortly after dinner Doctor Dodds requested a consultation with her, confirming her worst fears. It was suggested they adjourn to the drawing room for some privacy, and as they did, she became most anxious, and her heart started to beat faster at what he might say.

Dr. Dodds sat next to her on the chaise longue and proceeded to ask many questions about everything that had occurred to her over the last few months. Rose told him of all the frightening bleeds she had to endure, which thankfully had not occurred for a while now. Listening attentively to all she said, he then asked if she would allow him to examine her chest and her back. Rose duly obliged. After his gentle examination, she falteringly asked if she were gravely ill from this affliction and likely to die from it.

Dr. Dodds gave her a kindly look and said, 'Miss Spong, please do not distress yourself so. I will help you in any way that I can, but for now I must thank you for your time as I am going out with George for the afternoon but will see you for tea.' And with that he left the drawing room, leaving her question unanswered.

Elizabeth interrupted Rose's dark thoughts by entering the drawing room to ask if she cared to go for a walk. She gladly accepted the invitation to divert her mind from what had just transpired. Rose could not believe that only this morning she was happily dressing for a visit to Rochester, and now she was in fear again, with the knowledge her family didn't believe she was cured, and certain it would return to plague her once more.

Rose and Elizabeth walked around Gillingham looking in the shop windows, then went to take afternoon tea with Mrs. Woods. After hearing Mrs. Woods' news while enjoying her tea, they set off to walk to Chatham dockyard to see the ships. On the way, Rose unburdened herself to Elizabeth who tried to give her reassurance on the matter, but Rose remained convinced in her heart and mind that what she was thinking was true.

When they returned, tea was about to be served, with George and Doctor Dodds seated at the table to greet them. No reference was made to what had transpired earlier, just an awkward silence.

With the day ending and the light fading, Rose retired to her room to ruminate on the day's events. As she sat on the edge of the bed feeling desperately lonely, her all-consuming thoughts were about the lack of information she had received regarding her illness, which was quite troubling. She had asked Dr. Dodds, Mr. Trested, Mamma, Papa, and Mary. Were they all unaware of its cause or did they simply not want to tell her? For whatever reason, they all remained silent. With no Mr. Webster or Cousin

Fanny to distract Rose from thoughts of the illness returning, which now seemed inevitable, there would be little prospect of sleep tonight.

TUESDAY, 16ᵀᴴ JUNE
Trinity Term ends. Battle of Dettingen fought, 1743.

I drew all morning, George Nash gave me a volume of poetry of his own compilation, which made me very unhappy. Elizabeth, Mrs. Nash, George and I went to Rochester in the chaise. Called on Doctor Dodds and the Beechams.

It was a difficult day for Rose who passed the entire day fretting over her health. She was terrified at the thought of dying and now solemnly believed her past illness would return with serious consequences.

With what she had read and heard of similar situations, Rose feared she was suffering from consumption, but when Doctor Dodds was asked if this was so, he would not say. How she wished Mary was there to talk to. Mary would undoubtably scold her, saying she was being fanciful and should remove all such silly thoughts out of her head at once. Rose always wanted to believe Mary's words when she counselled her as she considered her to be far more worldly wise than herself. But she thought it likely that on returning home and being able to ask her sister for an honest opinion about her condition, Mamma would have probably instructed her not to say anything and keep the truth from her.

For Rose, the most important thing now was to be returned to the family she missed and needed so much, so she resolved to write to Mamma to ask if she may return home as she no longer wished to stay at Grandpapa's. With the letter now written, she spent the rest of the morning drawing in order to distract herself.

After dinner, Rose accompanied Mrs. Nash, Elizabeth, and George to Rochester in the chaise where they called on Doctor Dodds and the Beecham's. Rose was finding it difficult to pretend that all was well in her life when as far as she was aware, it never would be again. She just wanted to go home now and ask Mamma for the truth about her condition, and when she could expect its return. Now, Rose was feeling quite well; it was her mind that troubled her now.

George gave her a compilation of his self-penned poetry, which on reading its mournful contents, did little to make her feel cheerful.

WEDNESDAY, 17TH JUNE
St. Alban, Protomartyr of England, beheaded, 303.

Stayed at home in the morning and in the afternoon George, Mrs. Nash, Elizabeth and I went to Rochester in the chaise. We called on the Beechams to invite them to tea tomorrow. Afterwards we went to chapel. Got very wet coming home.

Unsurprisingly, Rose had a very restless night and slept little, nearly falling asleep at the breakfast table. She therefore decided to stay at home in the morning to read for a while in Grandpapa's drawing room. Reading, however, failed to help her melancholy mood, nor could she concentrate, so when George suggested they took the chaise to Rochester and call on the Beecham's to invite them to tea tomorrow, she readily agreed.

The sky looked dark and dismal on the return home, but when they arrived back at the house Grandpapa wanted to walk to chapel despite his frailty, so George and Rose each took an arm and accompanied him there. The meeting started well, and the speaker would have been interesting, but as rain started to fall on the roof, steadily at first then building into a crescendo, it drowned out his voice to such an extent it was difficult to hear what he was saying.

When the meeting concluded and the time came to head home, albeit at a slow pace for Grandpapa, the three got drenched and arrived home dripping wet. Grandpapa's housekeeper hurried to the cupboard and fetched towels, then served hot drinks. Even though it had been warm lately, getting a thorough soaking had made them all shiver, and their immediate concern was for Grandpapa as he was quite elderly and in poor health. After drying out, Grandpapa was persuaded by his wife, Mrs. Nash, to retire to his room where a fire had been lit in the hope that the soaking would not give him a chill. With all the recent traumas at the forefront of her mind, Rose was similarly concerned for her own health.

The letter to Mamma asking for her to come and take her home had been posted. She hoped and prayed she would.

THURSDAY, 18ᵀᴴ JUNE
Battle of Waterloo, 1815. Don Carlos, his family and suit, from Portugal, landed at Portsmouth, 1834.

Grandpapa, George, Elizabeth, and I went to Rochester in the chaise. We left the former in Rochester and the three of us went to Frindsbury to call on the Spongs. The Beechams and Doctor Dodds came to tea. I was taken very ill. Spat a good deal of blood.

Rose's worst fears of her illness returning became a reality today when she was suddenly taken very ill.

The day began well enough with herself, Grandpapa, George, and Elizabeth taking a trip to Rochester in the coach. After walking around the town for a while, Grandpapa left them to conduct some business on the High Street.

When arrangements had been made to collect him later in the morning, they went over the Medway to visit the Spong's at Manor House Farm in Frindsbury. Happy to be reunited with Fanny, Ambrose, and Mrs. Spong, Rose delighted in exchanging news. However, much to her relief, Mr. Webster, who was still a house guest, happened to be out riding and was not likely to return until teatime. She was glad of this as she was fretting that seeing him again may upset her. Now that she thought her health was in question, she could not allow herself to become involved, and it would be unfair on him also. Rose told Fanny her thoughts on the matter, and Fanny said that perhaps she was worrying too much, but if that is how she felt then surely, she was making the correct decision.

After collecting Grandpapa and returning to Gillingham, they were soon entertaining Mr. and Mrs. Beecham and Doctor Dodds, and that was when Rose's troubles started. She began to cough quite violently, and to her absolute horror she burst a blood vessel and was soon covered in blood. Doctor Dodds went immediately to her aid, but she became inconsolable and could not stop crying. She had hoped never to see the frightening bleeding episodes again, but now felt it was her fate to suffer them forever, and the thought of that filled her with terror.

Rose told Grandpapa she wished to go home to Mamma and Mary so they could look after her. With the hour now late, it was arranged that George would go directly to Mill Hall first thing in the morning. With tears in her eyes and her heart breaking, she recorded today's terrible events in her diary.

FRIDAY, 19ᵀᴴ JUNE
Magna Charta signed at Runnymede, 1215.

Very poorly all day. Dr. Dodds came to see me three times. Grandpapa and George went to Mill Hall to fetch Mamma. Edward came also. I brought blood up many times. DD came again after tea. He stayed to help me.

When Elizabeth went into Rose's room this morning and found her to be very ill, she went straight to George's room and told him to go to Mill Hall as soon as possible to fetch her Mamma. After a hurried breakfast he and Grandpapa prepared the chaise and set off for Aylesford. Rose, meanwhile, started to bleed again, so Elizabeth sent word for Doctor Dodds to attend her. Rose spent most of the morning coughing, and every time she thought the bleeding had stopped, it would start all over again, causing her nightdress to be changed many times. She was very frightened. Doctor Dodds had to be sent for three times.

Mamma eventually arrived with brother Edward and Rose was extremely happy and relieved to see them, but when she pressed Mamma about the possibility of dying from her terrible illness, the question was evaded. The bleeding continued for most of the afternoon.

Doctor Dodds returned after tea and spent the evening by her side, trying to comfort her. When the terrifying bleeding had stopped and Rose was a little calmer, Doctor Dodds was able to leave. As soon as he did so, Grandpapa's housekeeper put a warming pan in her bed, as she complained of being cold and shivery. Mamma then went to sit with her awhile and hold her hand. Rose managed to drink a half-cup of warm milk, and after relating to Mamma what a terrible day it had been, leaving her so shocked at how quickly it had overwhelmed her and feeling too weak to write anything in her diary or even cry, she asked to be left alone to sleep.

SATURDAY, 20TH JUNE
Trans. of Edw. K. of West Sax.

Mary came in the chaise to fetch me home. D. Dodds came to see me in the morning. He stayed to dinner. I brought up more blood, he was exceedingly kind. After tea I left Gillingham. I bore my journey very well. Went to bed directly.

With little improvement in her condition this morning Rose continued to feel rather poorly, but Mamma's arrival at Grandpapa's yesterday evening had been a great source of comfort to her. Doctor Dodds visited again this morning and after displaying the same kindness and concern as he had done previously, Grandpapa asked him to stay for dinner. Rose was grateful for his continued presence when she experienced another frightening bleed after dinner. Mary arrived in the chaise to convey them home, but as Rose was still suffering with the bleeding, they could not leave Gillingham until it had ceased.

It was after tea before they set off for home with Rose worried about the journey, but fortunately there were no more bleeding attacks and she managed very well. It was with a great sense of relief that Rose arrived back home to the familiar surroundings of Mill Hall. Mamma made her go directly, with assistance, to her bedroom without seeing her brothers or the little ones. She had missed everyone so much and was so happy to be back in the bosom of her family once more. At last, in her own bed and feeling very tired, she closed her diary for today.

SUNDAY, 21ST JUNE
LONGEST DAY. The sun enters Cancer, the crab.

Exceedingly ill all day. Kept to my bed. Mr. Trested came twice to see me. He bled me in the morning. Brought blood up three times. Tom went to Rochester to ask Doctor Dodds to come and see me.

Being back in her familiar surroundings offered little in the way of relief to Rose this morning, she was far too preoccupied with trying to breathe and cough at the same time. It was the start of a very difficult day for her; the condition she was suffering from wasn't getting any better, and worse was yet to come in the form of treatment.

Mr. Trested, who had been notified that Rose had returned home and in urgent need of his services, called at the house during the morning. He was shown to her room and, following a brief description of her current circumstances, placed the bag he was carrying onto the dresser. After opening it, he produced a cup and a knife. Rose was horrified at realising his intention was to bleed her. She had never had to suffer this treatment before and had no notion of quite what to expect, but whatever it was would be unpleasant in the extreme. Mamma was present and held her hand while Mr. Trested made a cut in her arm to allow the ensuing blood to flow into the cup he was holding. Rose, finding it so painful to endure as well as witness, almost fainted. Not being able to stop the tears from falling made her realise how little bravery she possessed. Thankfully, and much to her relief, the ordeal was eventually behind her. Mr. Trested then took his leave after saying he would return later in the day.

Rose tried to sleep but once again her cough became troublesome, causing another blood vessel to burst. Eldest brother Tom was therefore instructed to take the chaise directly and call on Doctor Dodds to ask if he could attend Rose the following day. Both Rose and Mamma hoped he would be available, as they each had great confidence in his abilities, as well as preferring his kind and gentle nature to that of Mr. Trested's.

As Rose's legs were too weak for her to sit at the table and write in her diary, she had to complete the task while sitting up in bed, trying hard not to spill any ink in the process. Endeavouring to keep her spirits up was becoming increasingly difficult, especially when trying to smile and put on a brave face for her visitors while knowing how gravely ill she had become and unable to see a recovery from this terrible situation.

MONDAY, 22ND JUNE
Louis XVI. and family arrested at Varennes, 1791.

Not any better. Mr. T. came directly after breakfast. D. Dodds, Mrs. Nash and George came over. D. Dodds was with me the whole of the day. I brought blood up once. Mr. Trested bled me again. Mamma sat up with me all through the night. Remained in bed all day. Felt very ill.

Rose was very ill and frightened, so Mamma sat by her bedside all night to comfort her while her daughter was able to sleep, safe in the knowledge she wasn't alone. Her bedroom, once a sanctuary, had now become a place to be feared as darkness fell and the shadows deepened. When alone, Rose imagined demons were hiding in the shadows as she lay helplessly in bed with thoughts of death consuming her. With hardly any sleep when morning came, Mamma left Rose sleeping while she attended to the children.

She had scarcely finished the breakfast arrangements when Mr. Trested arrived to bleed her daughter again, and Rose wondered if this torture would ever end. Her salvation came a little later in the form of Doctor Dodds, who was accompanied by George and Mrs. Nash. The doctor stayed all day and was a great comfort to her. Rose did attempt to get up, but unfortunately her legs were too weak to support her. Lying in her room with the light beginning to fade, she dreaded the coming of night and having to face it alone, as Mamma needed to sleep in her own bed tonight. She prayed Mary would appear and sit with her awhile.

TUESDAY, 23ᴿᴰ JUNE
Mantua bombarded by the Allied Forces, 1799.

Extremely ill, Mr. Trested came to see me in the morning and evening. D. Dodds sent George Nash over to enquire how I was going on. I was easier in my mind. Mary Nash's friend sent to enquire how I was. Mary sat up with me.

As she hoped, Rose had her sister Mary to comfort her through the night. When she awoke, Mary told her Papa had engaged a nurse for this duty as Mamma was needed by the rest of the family during the day. The days were difficult enough, but Rose feared the night-time more as it meant being alone when everything was still and dark. This caused her to become hysterical and tearful, so to have someone near gave her great comfort.

Mr. Trested called after breakfast. Rose gave a silent thank you to God when she saw he didn't have the bag and cup used for bleeding his patient with him. At least she was saved from that unpleasant experience.

Another visitor was George Nash. Doctor Dodds had asked him to call and check Rose's condition, and then to report back to him. Although Mr. Trested was still in attendance, the fact that Doctor Dodds had taken charge of her care had come as some relief, as it meant Mr Trested was no longer her main physician.

A letter arrived this morning from a friend of her cousin, Mary Nash, asking how she was. Touched by her concern, Rose wrote a reply and asked the maid to post it. Although she remained quite ill, at least Rose had been spared another bleeding attack today.

When Mr. Trested returned later in the day he was pleased to hear she had remained stable. Although her illness remained, it had been a slightly improved day for Rose.

WEDNESDAY, 24TH JUNE
Nat. of St. John Bapt. Midsum. Day, Hol. at the Exch.

Not any better. Mr. Trested came twice. George Nash came over to ask after me. I was in much pain all day. Mamma sat up with me last night.

Rose continued to be poorly throughout the day with terrible pains in her chest and back. Mamma stayed with her during the night as the nurse Papa had engaged was not to commence her duties until the evening. Rose realised it wasn't practical for Mary and Mamma to sit with her every night and new arrangements would have to be made. Nevertheless, it would be strange to have a newcomer in the household looking after her, someone yet unknown who she must learn to accept, as Mamma could not be expected to nurse her day and night. If she attempted to do so, it would have consequences for her own health and the household would be the worse for it.

Mr. Trested called twice today, and George Nash also visited. Rose was pleased to see him, but disappointed Doctor Dodds wasn't with him.

The new nurse arrived at teatime, and Mamma led her upstairs to introduce her to Rose. Her name was Jane and she appeared to be about Mamma's age. As Mamma explained her daughter's needs, Rose hoped to find her character agreeable, and quickly wrote in the diary before her new nurse and companion joined her, feeling rather nervous about what the night would bring.

ROSAMOND

25th June to 15th July

THURSDAY, 25ᵀᴴ JUNE
Irish rebellion commenced, 1798.

Very ill. D.D. sent over to know how I was going on. G.N. came. Mr. Trested came in the morning. My cough very troublesome. Nurse sat up with me last night. Had a bad night.

Rose had a terrible night because the persistent cough she had to endure had made her chest extremely painful and stopped her from sleeping, causing more distress. At one point during the night Rose felt so ill she was in fear of not seeing the morning. Although the nurse was kind and attentive, Rose hardly knew her, and she missed Mamma, so it was hard to stop the tears from falling. Aware of the burden her illness was putting on Mamma and the rest of the family, she knew this was how things had to be. Any misgivings about Jane were surely temporary and would improve with time. She had no wish to cause further problems by being a difficult patient. With these thoughts, Rose resolved to get to know her better and keep her feelings to herself.

George Nash called again; he had now visited Rose four days in a row. Although Doctor Dodds had asked him to call in order to observe her current situation, Rose knew he would have done so anyway. George was sorry to report back that she was not improved, and very ill indeed. Rose wished Doctor Dodds had come in person to attend her, regardless of her deep affection for George.

Mr. Trested called in the morning. He was also concerned about her condition, as all the treatment he tried had been ineffective and Rose was becoming weaker every day.

Mary sat with her for a while and tried her best to cheer her dear sister up, even tales of Aylesford as told by Mrs. Robson failed to make Rose smile. She was too consumed with fear about what was happening to her to think of anything else. Mamma brought some tea and a small slice of cake to try to tempt her appetite – the tea was sipped but the cake refused. Seeing Mamma looking anxiously down at her, Rose apologised for being such a burden. Mamma sat herself down next to the bed and taking Rose's hand in hers, said sternly, 'My dear Rosie, taking care of you while you are suffering so much could never be a burden. We will do everything we can to make it easier for you to bear, as you are very precious to me and indeed to your whole family.' After hearing this and seeing Mamma's stricken face, Rose began to cry. When the tears had stopped falling, Mamma gently mopped her cheeks with the handkerchief retrieved from her rolled up sleeve and said, 'Now my dear, those tears must have worn you out, so I will leave you to rest for a while.'

When Mamma had left, Rose lay there thinking about what she had said, and how much her words had comforted her, but no words could take away the unhappiness she was feeling right now as she felt completely devastated that life had treated her so poorly.

FRIDAY, 26ᵀᴴ JUNE
King William IV. Accession. Holiday at the Exchequer. King George IV. died.

Had a bad night, Mamma was with me. Mary received a letter from G. Nash to ask a few questions that D. Dodds wanted to know. I was very ill and in bad spirits.

Following a difficult night there was no relief from Rose's troubles today, but at least she had Mamma for company. The nurse had been sent away for now; Mamma was aware her own presence during the dark hours gave her daughter far more comfort than a stranger could ever do. Rose was so grateful to have her there.

Mary appeared at her bedside with a letter she had just received from George Nash; he had written some questions down on behalf of Doctor Dodds regarding Rose's condition. She answered each one honestly and then told Mary to inform the doctor in the letter that she was very ill indeed and frightened about her plight.

Rose remained in bed for most of the day, and only ventured out of it briefly to sit by the dwindling fire to write in her diary. As Rose eased herself back into bed, she hoped someone would come to be with her as she grew so fearful when left on her own.

SATURDAY, 27ᵀᴴ JUNE
Dr. Dodd executed for forgery, 1777.

Tom went to Rochester this morning to fetch D.D. for I thought I was dying. He and George came over directly after breakfast. D.D. was with me till

8 in the evening. Mr Day and Mr. Trested came to see me; Mary was sent up to enquire after me. G. Nash came upstairs.

It had been a truly dreadful day. Mamma spent the night worrying about Rose's condition, so at first light she dispatched her eldest son, Thomas, to fetch Doctor Dodds. Rose, being unable to breathe properly, was certain she was about to expire for lack of breath. They were all very frightened by this sudden attack on her life. Thankfully, by the time the good Doctor and George arrived it had subsided enough for her to talk again. Was there no end to this torture, thought Rose? She was relieved to see Doctor Dodds, as his calm manner while attending her gave great comfort.

Two further physicians attended Rose today, Mr. Trested brought along Mr. Day. They both consulted with Doctor Dodds on the landing outside her room, and when they returned to her bedside, Rose asked for their honest opinion of her illness. Yet again, she received no clear answer other than 'she would recover in time,' making Rose believe they were only telling her what they thought she wanted to hear, and not the truth. Every time she did recover the illness returned far worse than before, causing her to become weak, frail, and in despair with the worry of it all. Doctor Dodds stayed by her side until eight o'clock in the evening, only returning to Rochester with George when he thought her settled. Rose felt sorry to see him go as he was the only Doctor who gave her any comfort.

Mary planned to stay with her tonight to prevent tears and hysteria from spoiling her sleep. She would probably get into bed beside her and draw the curtains to pretend they were little girls once more, hiding from the bogeyman. Maybe playing the game again would keep her safe from harm, she thought.

SUNDAY, 28TH JUNE
The King's Proclamation.

Very poorly, Mamma gave me her bible. Mamma stayed at home with me this morning and afternoon. Mr. Trested came. Tom and W. Golding came down after tea to enquire after me. I saw them on the lawn.

There was still no change in Rose's condition; she continued to be ill and had another difficult day.

The family went to church in the morning, but Mamma thought it best to stay at home in case she was needed. Mr. Trested called when most of the family were out to enquire whether Rose had recovered from the terrible attack she suffered yesterday. Rose told him that her breathing still troubled her as she had difficulty speaking more than a few words at a time – the lack of breath caused her to panic which frightened her. His advice was not to allow herself to become agitated with fear as it would only serve to make her breathing more difficult, so she must always remain calm.

Easy advice to give, thought Rose to herself, when you are not the one troubled by the affliction. She had grown less fond of Mr. Trested's opinions since Doctor Dodds appeared, favouring his gentle approach to that of the man before her. However, she felt a little mean in her reaction to his remark and felt that she mustn't make her dislike too obvious, so she resolved to be more tolerant of his ministrations in the future. *If indeed I have one,* she thought with sadness.

Rose managed to get up for a while to sit in her chair by the window so the bed linen could be changed. While watching people going about their business in the lane and the gardens opposite, she happened to notice Tom and William Golding talking to Mary on the lawn. Seeing them all outside together while she was trapped in the bedroom made her feel even more miserable.

When the Golding brothers had gone, Mary went up to Rose's room to say they had called to enquire after her. News of her illness must have spread as far as Ditton where the Golding family lived, thought Rose, who was quite amazed her affliction was of interest to so many people.

The Golding family lived at the Vicarage in Ditton, as their father was the vicar there. When Mary let it be known to Rose that Tom's father, the Reverend Golding, had asked for a prayer to be said for her at the morning service it made her cry at the kindness of so many people, but unfortunately it also made her realise just how ill she must be if prayers were being said for her in church. She knew Reverend Staines had said a prayer for her in Aylesford church today, because Mary had told her so this morning.

Rose ended another terrible day by writing in her diary. Again, she hoped to have someone with her in the night, but no one had told her yet who this would be. Mamma left her bible on her bedside table. Rose wondered if Mamma had left it on purpose in the hope she would be given some guidance from God on how to deal with her illness.

MONDAY, 29ᵀᴴ JUNE

St. Peter, In Syriac Cephas, a stone or rock; in Latin, Petra crucified at Rome with his head downwards. Hol. at Exch.

Mr. Staines came upstairs and read and talked to me. D.D. sent George Nash over to enquire after me. He came upstairs. Very ill and in bad spirits.

Every day now seemed the same as the last for Rose, each one following a distressing night when she tossed and turned in the vain hope of sleeping. When the morning came, hopes of feeling a trifle better were dashed as nothing changed, nothing improved.

Rose was aware her bad humour affected those who sought to help, so when Ann showed Mr. Staines into her room, she welcomed him as best she could, thinking it an opportunity to redeem herself. If she were to discuss her problems with a man of God, it may help cure her melancholy. He entered the bedroom saying, 'Good morning, Miss Spong, I do hope I am not intruding.'

'Not in the least,' she replied. In truth, Rose was grateful to see the man she held in high esteem and needed his help through spiritual guidance. Very soon she was confiding in him all her fears and worries about dying from this terrible illness.

Mr. Staines took her hand gently in his and, trying to soothe her, said, 'If it is God's will that you should leave us, he will give you the strength to accept your fate when the time comes, and if it is written that your time is not yet done, you will recover and be well again.'

Rose then told him of her ill humour at her illness, and how it affected her family, and that in turn made her feel worse. She then added, 'I also feel ashamed for being angry with God, who

I know in my heart is not to blame for the predicament I am in.' Through tears, she continued, 'I have always believed I was a good Christian, and if ever I was to face adversity it would be with good grace, but instead I have found myself to be lacking in Christian spirit and so disappointed that I have failed in my attempts to be good and graceful by accepting what God has chosen for me.'

Mr. Staines patted her hand and said, 'My dear Miss Spong, try not to be so hard on yourself, you have had much to try you, please remember you are human and therefore susceptible to errors like everyone else. God will help when it is needed most, just put your trust in him.'

Rose was still sobbing when he opened his bible and began reading to her. She laid back on the pillows and let his voice wash over her. Its effect was so soothing her eyes grew heavy and she fell asleep.

She woke up a while later to find Mr. Staines had gone. Had Mamma sent word for him to visit? If she had, it was right to do so, because Rose felt a weight had been lifted off her after confiding in him. He had spoken the truth and she would try very hard to follow his advice.

George Nash appeared on another errand at the request of Doctor Dodds. Rose welcomed him, and they talked for a while. During the conversation, Rose told him how grateful she was for recommending his friend the doctor to Mamma. His kindly attendance on her was a far more pleasant experience compared to certain other doctors it had been her misfortune to endure. At the end of an eventful day, Rose was sitting at her desk writing. She would have much to think about in the night if she was unable to sleep, as Mr. Staines' words had stayed with her and may provide some comfort during the coming days.

TUESDAY, 30TH JUNE
Earl of Argyle beheaded, 1685.

After dinner, D. Dodds and George Nash came over. The former very kind and polite. He thought me better in the morning. Mrs. Day called, likewise Ellen, John and old Ambrose Spong of Rochester came to enquire after me. I did not see any of them.

With Mary lying beside her last night, Rose was able to drift off to sleep. She also managed to eat a little breakfast which unfortunately made her feel sick again. Spending a quiet morning reading her bible, she occasionally paused to recall Mr. Staines' visit yesterday, and to give thanks to the Lord for sending him when her need for guidance was at its highest. There was no doubt in her mind that since confiding in him, she felt a good deal calmer.

Mamma went upstairs before dinner to see Rose and assess her appetite, and to say they had received a few callers again this morning to enquire after her and offer their good wishes. Included amongst the visitors were Mrs. Day and her daughter Ellen, and old Ambrose Spong who had travelled from Rochester in his chaise.

Being confined to her bed, Rose had not seen any callers until Doctor Dodds stepped into her room after dinner, accompanied by George Nash. Rose's face lit up with a smile when she saw them. After examining her in his usual gentle and polite manner, he declared her to be much improved since his last visit. It was true her fever had abated a little and she felt calmer in her mind as a result, thanks in no small measure to Mr. Staines' words. Rose was sorry when the time came for George and the good doctor to leave, she had enjoyed their company for most of the afternoon. Letting go of their hands, she bade them farewell as they left for Rochester.

She wrote in her diary that she was feeling a little more hopeful than recently. Perhaps she was starting to improve.

WEDNESDAY, 1ST JULY
Battle of the Boyne fought, 1690.

A little better today. Mr. Trested came to see me in the morning. After breakfast Mary went to Maidstone to go with Mrs Day in the evening to a concert, she is to sleep at Mrs Days'. Mr. Staines came and read and talked with me in the morning. My chest very hurtful, in bad spirits all day. George came up in the evening. He told me of poor Mr Jones death. He died last night at 1.30am.

Mary went to Maidstone today; she is attending a concert this evening with Mrs. Day and will be sleeping at her house. Rose would have to wait until the morning to hear all the news of the concert, and who her sister had seen there. She was disappointed not to be going with her and felt like a prisoner trapped in her own bedroom.

This morning saw a slight improvement, but her spirits were low all day and her chest remained painful. Rose had another visit this morning from Mr. Staines who stayed until dinnertime, but however much she appreciated his company, it did little to lift the dark mood assailing her.

Missing her sister greatly, she laid on the bed to distract

herself with a book in the afternoon, but her concentration was easily disrupted with thoughts of being left on her own tonight. Mamma called in to see her throughout the day when her duties allowed, and then only briefly as she had so many things to attend to. Her brothers made occasional visits but were not disposed to remain long. Rose was happy to see them even though they were soon fidgeting, in a hurry to escape the sickroom after fulfilling Mamma's instructions. She would have gladly done the same if only it were possible.

Rose's brother George called into her room in the evening bearing sad news – Mrs. Robson had sent a note to say that Mr. Jones had passed away in the early hours of the morning. Mr. Jones had never been less than a gentleman to her and always kind and generous, so this news made her very sad.

'I will send a letter to Mrs. Jones to give my condolences for her loss, and to ask her to pass the same on to her son John,' Rose said to her brother before he went. She suspected her illness would prevent Mamma and Mary from attending his funeral, but Papa and her elder brother Thomas would surely go. The day ended in sadness at the loss of a dear family friend, and with her eyes red from weeping, Rose had to cease writing and put the diary aside.

THURSDAY, 2ND JULY
Visitation of Blessed Virgin Mary, i.e., to her cousin Eliz.

A very warm day, I felt it very much. Mamma wrote to D. Dodds about me. Mamma went to Aylesford after tea to see Mrs. Robson and Grandmamma. Mr. Trested came.

It had been one of the hottest days of the year so far, which didn't afford Rose any respite from the searing heat. Her room being warm and stuffy prompted Mamma to open a window to let some air in, which enabled Rose to watch Papa's workers driving the coal carts up and down the lane.

One disadvantage of conducting the coal business in such close proximity to the house was the black dust that soon settled on every surface if the windows were open too long. From her window, Rose could see her little brothers and sisters playing in the lawned garden with Ann, the young maid Mamma had employed to help with the children. Rose could not help but like her, she had always been helpful and kind during her illness.

One of Ann's duties was to attend the family's laundry, and when Rose suffered her attacks of bleeding it created far more work for her, yet every time she apologised to Ann, the maid just smiled and said, 'Miss Rosamond, do not fret yourself, I really don't mind as you cannot help being ill. It's a pleasure for me to be able to attend your needs, if only to ensure your clean linen is available when you need it.' She was always smiling, and often said how happy she was to work for such a lovely family. Rose wondered how she could be so with her heavy workload. Talking to Ann and knowing how hard she worked made Rose think that although very ill, her own life had been easy compared to Ann's.

Mr. Trested called, and finding Rose to be comfortable, wished her good day and left. He seemed to have accepted Doctor Dodds as Rose's main physician. Mamma asked Mary to sit with Rose while she visited Grandmamma to tell her that Rose wasn't much improved. Mary went in to see her and sat on the edge of her bed to recount the details of the concert, and to say how much she had enjoyed the experience. She also told her that

Mamma had left to call on Mrs. Robson to discuss Mr. Jones' funeral arrangements.

On Mamma's return, she went up to tell the girls of her visit, and how understandably upset Mr. and Mrs. Robson were as Mrs. Jones and Mrs. Robson were closely related. Indeed, the Jones family were also old friends of theirs, so he would be missed by all. With the day's events recorded, Rose put down the diary and tried to sleep.

FRIDAY, 3RD JULY
Dog Days begin. Don Miguel's Fleet captured by Admiral Napier, 1833.

Got up for an hour for the second day and had my bed made again. Mr. Trested came. Mr. and Mrs. Robson went to London to Mr. Jones funeral. After dinner D. Dodds and G.N. came to see me. Brought me some flowers.

Rose was well enough to leave her bed and sit by the open window again this morning. It was another warm summer day so the slight breeze on her face was quite refreshing. While she was sitting there thinking about the day ahead, Ann came in to change her bed linen and said how pleased she was to see her out of bed, remarking that she soon expected to see her walking out again with Miss Mary. Rose thanked her for her optimism but replied that as she found it rather difficult to walk to the window from her bed, it may be a while before an attempt to descend the stairs could be made. The very thought of going outside seemed as difficult as climbing a mountain to Rose, but she kept that thought to herself as she did not want to spoil Ann's cheery disposition by making her feel sorry.

Mr. Trested entered the room moments later and seeing her sat by the window and not in her bed, assumed she was improving, but in truth Rose was extremely weak. It was Mamma's belief that her weakness was due to lack of nourishment and very little exercise, as she struggled to get her breath by doing something as simple as walking across the room.

Mr. Jones' funeral was held today in London: Mr. and Mrs. Robson went there with Papa to attend the service. Rose considered writing to John in order to pass on her commiserations at his father's death, but she didn't know what to say or how to say it. Despite feeling sorry for his loss, Rose had no wish to open the wounds inflicted by him and decided to do nothing as yet.

Doctor Dodds called after dinner with George Nash, who presented her with a bunch of fragrant pink roses from Grandpapa's garden. Rose was delighted with her gift and thanked him for his kindness, then asked Mamma to find a suitable vase and to put them on the side table where she could admire them. The guests stayed with her until after tea before returning home.

Mary went to sit with her sister until supper time, who mentioned her thoughts on writing to John. Mary thought it wasn't such a good idea to correspond directly with him now but suggested writing a letter of condolence herself and to include hers at the same time. Being too ill to compose and write such a difficult letter, Rose was much relieved at this solution and thought it a splendid idea and thanked Mary, who promised to do it as soon as she returned to her bedroom.

Rose was glad to report in her diary this evening that even though she was still feeling ill, she was certainly much better than this morning and hoped this would continue tomorrow.

SATURDAY, 4ᵀᴴ JULY
Translation of St. Martin, i.e. his enshrinement.

Mr. Trested came in the morning. I got up for dinner but went to bed directly afterwards. I was not so well today. Mr. and Mrs Layton called. I wrote this in bed.

Rose hoped her improvement of yesterday would continue. Unfortunately, there was to be no respite today, for when she awoke her fever had returned.

Mr. Trested called in the morning, but after a cursory inspection he had little to say. After seeing him out, Mary went up to tell her sister she had posted the letter to John, so she had no cause to fret, the deed was done. Rose laughed and said, 'You know me too well, Mary.'

'Indeed, I do,' she replied, 'as I know it's your nature to fret and worry.'

As the hot weather was continuing today, Mamma suggested to Rose she should sit by the open window at dinnertime and placed the side table there, complete with a vase of flowers from the garden. Ann brought the meal on a tray, then helped Rose out of bed and into her chair. Before her on the tray was a small plate of thinly sliced chicken with a portion of fresh peas from the garden, and to follow, a dish of raspberry jelly covered in thick cream. Cook had taken a lot of trouble to tempt her to eat, and Rose did try a little of each course which looked so inviting, but her appetite had deserted her, and soon, feeling sickly, she returned to bed.

As she lay there waiting for the discomfort to subside, she could hear the children playing outside on the lawn, laughing and shouting to each other as they played their games. Instead of being happy at the sound of their merry chatter on such a beautiful day, it only served to make her feel dejected and sad at having to lie in her sick bed, with little hope of ever leaving it to join in the merriment. This thought brought a few more tears to an already unhappy young lady.

Mamma quietly entered her room to say Mr. and Mrs. Layton had called to enquire after her. Rose was humbled to think that so many people were coming to their door to ask after her health, even people they didn't know very well. She ended another sad day by praying for the strength to accept her predicament with more grace than she was doing, as constant feelings of anger and resentment at the situation were making her so ill tempered with the people charged with the difficult task of caring for her.

SUNDAY, 5ᵀᴴ JULY
Algiers taken by the French, 1830.

Mary stayed at home with me, in the morning Mr. Trested came. Mamma was with me in the afternoon. She went to chapel in the evening. My cough was troublesome in the evening. Sat up a little.

Mary stayed at home to sit with Rose while the rest of the family went to church this morning. Rose had not been able to attend a church service in Aylesford since mid-May – the last time had been before her trip to Frindsbury, which seemed an age ago. In fact, she had not left her bedroom since returning from there, and now became increasingly certain she wouldn't be doing so soon, if ever, as her condition appeared to be worsening each day. Rose's prayers for courage last night went unanswered again, and she took her inability to control her resentment at being cheated out of any future happiness as a sign of weakness and feared for her very soul.

Mr. Trested called while the family were at church. Ann showed him to Rose's bedroom. He had no new treatments to suggest, and Doctor Dodds had not been to see her for two days. She was becoming increasingly worried that both physicians understood her illness was incurable, and fully expected her to die from it.

Sitting up in bed whilst struggling with a troublesome cough and trying to write in her diary, Rose put it to one side and settled down, hoping to close her mind and sleep.

MONDAY, 6TH JULY
Samuel Whitbread died, 1815.

> *Very ill all day. Mr. Trested wanted to bleed me, and Papa sent for Doctor Welch to come and see me in the evening. The doctor was not able to come. I only saw Mr. Trested in the evening. Mr. Staines came and read to me.*

Rose was very ill all day. Mr. Trested called in the morning and suggested bleeding her, but Papa refused the treatment on her behalf as it distressed her so. Rose thanked him for his intervention and was greatly relieved to avoid a very painful experience. Papa then told him he had sent for the eminent Doctor Welch, but unfortunately, he was unable to come.

However, Mr. Staines was available and called at the house after dinner. Rose was glad to see him and bade him sit down by her bed. He obliged, and very soon she began unburdening her fears to him regarding her soul, as he alone could help. After listening to her concerns without interruption, Mr. Staines answered her in his usual kind and gentle manner. 'Whatever God's plans are for you my dear, you can be sure he will take great care of you and your soul, so please do not fret, Miss Spong.' He then read a few scriptures to her before taking his leave and promising to return soon.

Rose took great comfort from his words, fully believing that what he said was the truth. He was a man of God and would not tell her falsehoods.

Mr. Trested returned in the evening for a brief visit to check on his patient. A little while later and unable to write any more, she put her pen aside to lie down and close her eyes.

TUESDAY, 7TH JULY
St. Thomas a Becket, an Archbishop of Canterbury, canonised. Oxford Act and Cambridge Com.

Papa sent the chaise to Rochester very early in the morning to fetch D. Dodds to meet Doctor Welch and Mr. Trested, but D.D. was not at home. So, I was obliged to see Doctor Welch and Mr. Trested. George Nash came over. I told him my troubles. Mrs. Hazell and June Hazell called. I wrote this in bed. I feel a little better. F.G. came down to enquire after me. I heard his voice.

Feeling a little better though still very tired, Rose kept to her bed for most of the day as Mamma advised her not to exert herself and rest. Her hopes of recovery remained low despite a slight improvement this morning, as she knew her fever would return soon enough.

Papa sent Wood off in the chaise to ask Doctor Dodds if he could possibly call to attend his daughter, but unfortunately Wood returned to say he was not at home. Papa had hoped that the doctor would be available to consult with Doctor Welch and Mr. Trested, but due to his absence Rose was obliged to see them without him. She hoped he hadn't deserted her as it had been a while since his last visit.

George Nash came from Gillingham to see her, and she was glad to see his smiling face. He listened patiently to all her woes and saw for himself the extent of her worries and fears over death and damnation. Rose had begun to rely on George's loyal support and kindness. He was always willing to lend an ear to her woes and never once made her feel like a silly young woman who succumbed to the vapours at the drop of a hat.

Mary came into her room as George was leaving to tell her that Mrs. Hazell and her daughter Lucy were in the drawing room and had sent her upstairs to pass on their good wishes for a speedy recovery. Rose returned her thanks to them for taking the time to call upon her, as the Hazell's lived some distance from Mill Hall and would have walked all the way there.

She heard Frederick Golding's voice outside and wanted to wave to him as she knew he wouldn't venture upstairs, so climbing out of bed rather unsteadily, she went to look out of the window, but he'd already disappeared inside the house. Mary went up again at teatime bearing a plate of tiny cakes and fruit jelly. Rose managed two of the cakes and a little of the jelly which was very refreshing for her throat. Mary stayed with her while she ate, chattering away about her visit to Aylesford this morning. She said, 'I didn't get very far along the road, Rosie, before people were stopping me to enquire after you. Even Frederick Golding had called at the house enquiring about you.'

'I know,' Rose answered. 'I heard his voice through the open window. I'm surprised so many people have heard of my illness, but I suppose that as our community is not a large one, it wouldn't be long before I was the talk of many a drawing room and parlour. Yet I realise our friends and neighbours are only concerned for my health, and only wish me well.'

In her usual state of tiredness Rose retired to her bed, this time employing her writing slope propped up on her knees to record the day's events in her diary while trying not to spill any ink.

WEDNESDAY, 8™ JULY
Mr. Burke died, 1797. Don Pedro takes possession of Oporto, 8 July 1832.

Had a very bad night, felt poorly all day. In very bad spirits. George Nash came over after dinner. I received a letter from John Hopley by post. Mr. Staines came over and read to me. Mr. Trested came to see me. I got up for tea. My breath very short.

As she predicted, Rose's fever returned today causing her much suffering through feeling poorly and short of breath. She thanked God for Mamma being with her last night to watch over her, but she was now so frightened and unhappy she just laid there trembling in her bed.

Mr. Trested called to attend her, but he was unable to offer any new treatment or suggestions, making Rose fear that all was now lost.

Mamma took a letter to her; it was sent from her friend John Hopley to enquire after her. She decided to reply to it later, when or if she could find some strength to sit at her desk to do so.

Mr. Staines visited in the morning. He obviously thought a great deal about her for he spent another hour of his busy time reading the scriptures which gave her comfort, but she soon fretted again after he left. George Nash arrived in the afternoon. He seemed to consider his main occupation in life as well as his privilege was to cheer up and offer comfort to his dearest Rosie, and when these endeavours failed, he paid no mind to the tears that frequently fell on his shoulder as she complained about her lot. Rose was always grateful for his loving care and companionship. She got out of bed to have tea while sitting with George at her table who tried to tempt her with sweetmeats, but again, she had no appetite. As the evening wore on, Rose reflected on not having received a visit from Doctor Dodds for some time and hoped he would call on her soon, if not tomorrow.

Unable to write any more in her diary, she put it away until tomorrow, hoping something good may happen to record as she was fully aware it made for very unhappy reading of late, but then supposed it wouldn't matter, as no one would ever read it except herself.

THURSDAY, 9TH JULY
FIRE Insur. expire. Louis XVIII. returned to Paris 1814.

Doctor Dodds, Doctor Welch, and Mr. Trested came to see me in the morning. D. Dodds stayed with me until 8 o'clock in the evening. He had tea with me upstairs. I had a very troublesome cough while he was here. He was so very kind. After my cough I had the ague.

Another difficult day, which saw three doctors attending Rose this morning. Doctor Welch and Mr. Trested arrived together, followed by Doctor Dodds whom she hoped would come today, and she was pleased to see him arrive. After privately discussing Rose's condition, the three doctors could not agree on how to treat her. Mr. Trested favoured bleeding, whereas Doctor Dodds did not. As far as Rose was concerned, she never wanted to endure a bleeding again; the whole process was unsettling and painful.

When Doctor Welch and Mr. Trested left, Doctor Dodds stayed with her, only leaving her bedside to take his dinner in the dining room. He returned to Rose's bedroom as soon as dinner was finished to continue their general conversation and enquiring into her favourite pastimes. Later in the afternoon, Ann knocked on the door to say tea was about to be served. Not wanting to be deprived of his company, Rose was happy to hear the good doctor ask if he may take his tea with her in the bedroom. The doctor was fortunately still present an hour or so later when Rose's cough came back, accompanied by a fit of the shivers. Ann was sent to light the fire, as Rose was shaking quite badly. By the time her fit had diminished it was past eight o'clock in the evening. With his patient more settled, Doctor Dodds suggested it was time for him to leave. After bidding her goodnight and promising to return as soon as he could, he left Mill Hall to return to Rochester.

With darkness approaching, Rose made her usual notes of the day's events while in great fear that the coming night would be another frightening ordeal to face.

FRIDAY, 10ᵀᴴ JULY
Camb. Term ends. London Bridge burnt, 1212.

I remained in bed all day. Did not feel well. Mr. Trested came; while he was here, I spat a little blood. Mamma wrote to Doctor Dodds. Mrs. Robson and Mrs. Hannah Jones came down from London.

With no change in her condition and too weak to get up, Rose remained in her bed for the day. Mr. Trested called in the morning and during his attendance, Rose was appalled to see she was bleeding again. Mamma was likewise concerned and went to her room immediately to draft a letter to Doctor Dodds to inform him of this latest development. When Rose managed to settle, Mr. Trested left, leaving her in the care of Mamma.

Mary went in later to tell them she had heard Mrs. Robson had returned from London today after staying with John's mother and had brought Mrs. Jones back with her. Rose imagined her to be wearing widow's weeds for some time whilst mourning the loss of her husband, then wondered if she had brought a letter from John. She didn't expect him to write as she had made it plain, she didn't want to correspond with him, but perversely she wished he would.

With little more to say for the day and too uncomfortable to sit up, Rose closed her eyes hoping to sleep.

SATURDAY, 11ᵀᴴ JULY
Oxford Term ends. Macklin, the player, died, aged 97, 1797.

I had a very bad night, coughed twice during the night. I got up and had my bed made. At eight o'clock in the evening Doctor Dodds and George Nash came. D.D. was with me until 11 o'clock. He gave me something. I slept.

Rose suffered terribly with fever and nausea from morning to night. A succession of concerned family members came and went from her bedside to comfort her throughout the day.

Mamma went into her room with Ann to change the bed linen after helping Rose into her chair while the task was completed. Doctor Dodds and George Nash came to see her in the evening. Eventually George had to leave, but the good doctor stayed with her until an hour before midnight. Before leaving, he administered a sleeping draught to his stricken patient to allow her some rest.

It had been a most harrowing day for the family and all those close to her heart, but especially for Rose herself who wasn't able to chronicle these events in her diary until the following evening.

SUNDAY, 12ᵀᴴ JULY
Battle of Aghrim, Ireland, 1691.

Did not get up all day. Mamma stayed at home with me. Mr. Trested came in the morning. Mary went to church in the morning, then went to chapel. George Nash came over to enquire after me.

Still affected by the draught Doctor Dodds had given her last night, Rose stayed in bed all day. Although her drowsiness lessened the effects of her illness, she nonetheless felt very poorly.

Mamma stayed at her side while the rest of the family went to church, no doubt to offer prayers for their cherished Rosamond. Mr. Trested called at some point and George rode over from Gillingham to see her, but apart from that, the day seemed to just drift by in a sleepy haze.

Somehow Rose managed to write yesterday's entry in her diary, but with nothing particularly interesting to record for today, the little book was put away until tomorrow.

MONDAY, 13ᵀᴴ JULY
Gordon Castle, Scotland, burnt, 1827.

Had a very bad night. Mamma received a letter from G.N. to say that he and Doctor Dodds would be here for me, but they did not come before four. I felt a little better in the afternoon. G. Nash came up and saw me. D. Dodds did not leave me until eleven o'clock. He had his supper in my bedroom. He read a chapter to me of the bible.

The effects of the sedative were wearing off, causing Rose to suffer the full effect of her fever during the night and she hardly slept.

Mamma went up to tell her she had received word from George to say he and his friend the doctor would be attending her again today. In the event they didn't arrive until mid-afternoon, when Rose's fever was not as severe. That situation soon changed when her malaise returned. George sat holding her hand for a while but went after teatime, leaving her in the care of Doctor Dodds. Rose always felt safe and confident with him in attendance. At her request, the good doctor read scriptures from her bible until supper time, taking his at her table. Sensing his patient was ready for sleep, and the hour being eleven o'clock, the doctor bade her goodnight and left. With the hour now late and her eyes heavy, Rose closed her diary ready for sleep.

TUESDAY, 14ᵀᴴ JULY
Destruction of the Bastille in Paris, 1789.

Had a very bad night, cough very troublesome. Sick twice. Felt very ill all day, as I did yesterday. Mr. Trested came in the morning. Mrs. Robson called but I did not see her.

Another terrible night to endure, with a persistent cough keeping Rose awake for the most part. Its intensity caused so much pain in her chest that she was sick twice. Mamma kept a constant vigil, so they were both very tired this morning.

Rose's turmoil through her illness wasn't helped by her anguish at Mamma's inability to rest by retiring to bed for an hour or so, as her duties to the household wouldn't allow it. While waiting for Ann to appear with the breakfast tray, Rose felt sure she would soon have to endure the ministrations of a night nurse, and if this was so, she must accept it gracefully. Mary insisted on taking care of her sister tonight after seeing Mamma's tired state at the breakfast table – she would have been only too happy to do it anyway.

Mr. Trested called in the morning to observe rather than

administer, as he still had no further suggestions or ideas to try, although Rose felt her situation was hopeless. Mrs. Robson called, but she decided not to disturb the invalid by venturing upstairs. Rose was aware of her presence, however, and felt disappointed when she didn't visit her room. After Mrs. Robson's recent stay with John's mother in London, she would have had an ideal opportunity to enquire how John was fairing after the death of his father.

Later in the evening, Mamma went in with a cup of warm milk and to pass on Mrs. Robson's good wishes for a speedy recovery. Now very tired, Rose put her diary away and had a sip of milk before settling down.

WEDNESDAY, 15ᵀᴴ JULY
St. Swithin, an early Christian, father and bp. Hol. at Exch.

Very poorly in the morning. Mrs. Robson came over after dinner. Mrs. Nash, George, and Grandpapa came; they all came upstairs and saw me. Mamma went with the boys to Holt Wood for tea. I longed to join them. Mr. Trested came. I was poorly all day.

It had been another difficult day. Mr. Trested called in the morning; he could see how ill Rose had become but remained powerless.

After dinner Mrs. Robson called, followed by Mrs. Nash, Grandpapa, and George. Rose was surprised Mamma had allowed four visitors at the same time as they all entered her bedroom together. She was happy to receive them all, but her head was soon spinning with all their lively chatter which she found quite tiring. Now unused to such noise, she was quite relieved when her company left. Rose always enjoyed socialising but now felt angry she was no longer able to appreciate the company of her family and friends.

Mary went up with her tea and mentioned that Mamma had gone to Holt Wood with Seppy and Octavius with a picnic. How Rose longed to be with them! After recording the day's events and disappointments in her diary, she felt so poorly and with no expectation of sleep, she laid back on her pillows, too tired to even cry.

Jackie

2021

Solving the mystery of what happened to Rosamond's siblings became important to me. My initial research provided little information but thanks to Julie's endeavours, the missing pieces of the jigsaw were soon in place, answering many of the questions I had.

Rosamond's father, Thomas Spong, auctioned off Mill Hall in 1852, before he and his wife Mary Eliza (nee Nash) moved to Faversham together with those who remained. Elder brother Thomas, a qualified lawyer, emigrated to Australia, sailing from Plymouth in the November of 1850 on the barque 'Anglia,' arriving in Adelaide the following March. It must have been a bitter blow to his parents knowing their first born was going to the other side of the world with the likelihood of never seeing him again. Thomas was forty-one when he emigrated, starting out in Tasmania before moving to Sale in Williamstown where he met his wife to be, Francis Robertson. They married in 1880 when Thomas was seventy-one years old. I wonder why he remained single for most of his life, another story there perhaps? He died in 1904 at the great age of ninety-five.

Just as they settled into their new home in Faversham, more sorrow came for Mamma and Papa as three more sons, namely Edward, Frederick, and Septimus, boarded another ship bound for Australia just a year after losing Thomas to the new world.

Edward, already a master mariner, became the lighthouse keeper at Cape Wickham on the remote King Island off the coast of Tasmania and remained there for twenty years. Captain

Edward Spong had a colourful and dangerous life there, as much has been written about his exploits, including reports of pirates, shipwrecks and bandits which made fascinating reading. He married Mary Lawrence in 1860, producing five children in what must have been challenging conditions. Edward passed away in 1907 at the age of ninety-one, a brave man indeed.

Frederick had a less eventful life than his brother, and seemingly more ordinary for his occupation is recorded as a stationer's assistant, rather dull after reading of Edward's exploits. He married Jeanette Watchorn in 1858 and the couple had three children. No other details came to light apart from his death in 1903 at the age of 80.

Septimus's life was more tragic. Records show he lived in Queensland and trained as an architect in 1861, before moving to Rockhampton where he set up a practice, but something must have gone wrong for him, as Julie came across a report in the Hobart Press in the July of 1874 which stated that Septimus Nash Spong had been before the magistrate charged with being of unsound mind, the sentence being a month in a lunatic asylum. Whatever happened to bring him to this is a mystery.

The next piece of information found by Julie was another police report telling us that Septimius had been remanded for yet another month for further medical care and treatment as he was deemed to be a long way from recovery and not ready to be at large. His incarceration in the lunatic asylum was extended for another three months before being released back into society. I was desperate to know what he had done to warrant being locked away in such an establishment, as during the original translation of the diary and subsequent story, I had grown rather fond of Rosamond's little brother 'Seppy,' as she herself obviously was, and to hear of his tribulations was very sad. No further clues regarding the nature of his transgressions emerged, and there is no record of him ever being married.

The next thing we found was an article written in an 1887 newspaper of our Septimus being held in a charitable institution, a place for the mentally impaired and the elderly. He was discharged the following year and eventually passed away in Tasmania in 1912 at the age of eighty-eight.

We were unable to learn much of his older brother George, born between Mary and Rosamond. The only record we found told us he had lived in Bromyard, Herefordshire where he subsequently died aged sixty-eight, in 1878.

William, aged fifteen in the diary, became a doctor. Julie found him in Faversham when he was thirty years old, sharing a house with a solicitor and now a qualified G.P. William married Martha Fairbrass in 1855, but she sadly died giving birth to their son, who was named after his father. William remarried two years later to Emily Church, with whom he had four children. He must have been held in high regard in Faversham, for whilst continuing to practise medicine he became a justice of the peace. William and Emily bought a house across the street from his parents who resided at number one Albion terrace (now demolished) with William and Emily living at number two – this building remains as solicitors' offices. William died relatively young aged only fifty-six, quite ironic considering his profession. According to his death certificate, he died from pulmonary and nephritic disease. The certificate also shows he was diabetic.

Little information was found on Henry, who still lived with his parents at Mill Hall along with Edward, Augustus, Septimus, a cook, a housemaid, and a groom, in the 1851 census. Nothing else was found until an article in a Tasmanian newspaper recorded the death of a Henry Nash Spong who had served in the Navy with Lieutenant Thomas Fletcher Waghorn. His passing and burial occurred at Mount Gambier in southern Australia at the age of fifty-four.

Augustus was easier to trace. He also went to Australia on the 'Fingal' in 1856; another loss for his parents, as now six of their sons were on the other side of the world. Our extensive research into Rosamond's siblings revealed many records of Spongs living in Australia and America, probably explaining why so few are left in England now. When he landed in Australia to join his brothers, Augustus headed for Tasmania, where four years later he and his brother Edward had a double wedding ceremony to sisters Mary and Esther Lawrence. This information came to light when Julie found their joint wedding announcement in a newspaper article in the June of 1860. By the time of his marriage Augustus had become a pharmaceutical chemist. His profile also says he was a justice of the peace just like his brother William, clearly another fine pillar of the community. Augustus and Esther had four children. He died in 1900 aged seventy-four and was laid to rest in the same cemetery as his brothers Edward and Frederick.

John's life wasn't as lucky, although he started out well enough by marrying Emily Webb in London in 1847 when the couple moved to Chatham in Kent. They had two children who both sadly died young. The census of 1851 records his profession as a shipwright, probably employed at Chatham dockyard. John and Emily had four more children before disappearing from the records until thirty years later, when the 1881 census records him as a lodger at a house in Maidstone with no sign of Emily. Did she die or had they separated? We next find John living in some kind of church refuge or hospital in Southwark, London where he was classed as an inmate, probably alcohol related, and he died there in 1893 aged eighty-two.

Dear little Octavius, who was only five years old in Rosamond's diary, is another sad case. He became a paymaster in the Royal Navy, but his naval records show he was discharged in 1860 and returned to live with his parents in Faversham. Three months later when he was thirty, he married Maria Lewis and the couple moved to Margate, taking up residence in Albert House which still stands, and is now a listed building.

No occupation could be found for Octavius, so we assumed he didn't have one. This proved correct when Julie came across an article in the Margate press dated 1864 stating that Octavius Nash Spong of no occupation voluntarily declared himself bankrupt, attributing his financial woes to the loss of his commission and pay from the Royal Navy. This statement suggested his discharge may have been dishonourable. If that was the case, what had he done?

Julie answered this question a short time later when another newspaper article emerged telling us more. It transpired that a police officer had found Octavius lying on the ground in pouring rain, and with the help of two young men who happened to be passing, picked him up realising he was in a drunken state with blood on his face. He managed to give the officer his address and asked to be taken home. When his wife answered the door, she was horrified to see Octavius slumped against it, and in fear of her life she said he was a violent drunkard and pleaded with the policeman to take him away. Maybe this was the reason for his discharge.

The story doesn't end there, because Maria wouldn't allow him back inside their home. The policeman had no other choice but to take Octavius to the Magistrates Court to be declared drunk and incapable, where he was given a fine of five shillings, quite a large sum in those days. The fine remained unpaid, but for reasons unknown he was discharged, and left the court in the direction of his home. An hour later, Octavius was found lying on the floor again, this time in a coffee house. Coming to his senses, he found himself back in the police station where he was examined by a surgeon. The question now arose of what to do with him. Maria was still adamant he was not going back to her home so there was no choice for Octavius other than the workhouse.

This sad but fascinating newspaper report goes on to say that Octavius, once admitted to the union workhouse, was put to bed whilst calling for some soda water to be mixed with a pennyworth of brandy. Two men were left to sit with him until he fell asleep on the Friday night, but at three o'clock in the morning he was found dead. After an examination to discover the cause of death, the surgeon discovered head wounds and bruises on different parts of his body. The verdict said he had died from the effects of a fall whilst in a state of intoxication. Did Octavius fall or was he beaten to death? He was only thirty-five when he died and just five years old when I first got to know him through Rosamond's writings. Was his service in the Navy so stressful it drove him to drink? Regardless of the cause, how heart-breaking it must have been for his parents. No record of any children between Octavius and Maria was ever found.

Mike and I took another trip to Kent in December 2021, taking the opportunity to stop at Harpenden to see our friends Trish and Brendan on the way. Iain and Sally had bought a lovely flat in Folkestone, quite near Sally's parents and sister, as a place to live while visiting from America and they invited us to stay.

Julie had given me a map of the cemetery where Octavius was laid to rest, so during our stay we set off for Margate with

Iain and Sally on a quest to find him. After a fruitless search we adjourned to a local pub for a late Sunday lunch. During our meal, Iain suggested we had been looking in the wrong place, so we returned to the cemetery as the light was beginning to fade with one last area to check, and after brushing away the fallen leaves we found him. Looking at the gravestone set into the ground in triumph, we marvelled at how pristine the gold inscribed pink marble memorial appeared. The lettering reads, 'Here lies the remains of Octavius Nash Spong, loving husband of Maria'. Who had paid for such an expensive memorial? It looked as though it had only been placed there yesterday. I would be surprised if Maria had. According to the records, Octavius had ended his days in the workhouse, so perhaps her wealthy father paid the bill for appearance's sake.

With all the information we could find on the boys now documented, my attention turned to Rosamond's sisters. Mary the eldest, and closest to her, got married in 1844 to a Frederick Etheridge and they had three children. She died at the age of 81. A great deal has come to light regarding Mary's life, so there will be more about her in the future.

Little Grace fell in love and married a wealthy man when she was only nineteen, and apart from a brief time in Devon they lived with their three sons in Tunbridge Wells. The 1901 census gave us a London address where her husband's death is also recorded, after which Grace returned to Tunbridge where she died in 1924 at the grand old age of ninety-two.

Elizabeth, who was the baby in the diary, also married a wealthy man and had six children but sadly her husband died in 1876. Five years later in 1881, she was found to be residing in Clapham where she lived for another ten years before moving to Surrey, passing away in that county in 1930 aged ninety-six. It was a mixed bag of fortunes for Rosamond and her thirteen siblings as you might expect, with some successful and some more tragic, but knowing what had become of a family I have felt connected to for so long through my own and Julie's research, was, and remains, very satisfying.

Rosamond's father, Thomas, died aged eighty in the year 1865, the same year Octavius passed away – a sad year for Mamma. She passed away herself in 1877 aged eighty-two, after spending the last years of her life alone (apart from her servants), quite a contrast to the hectic family life portrayed in Rosamond's little journal.

Mr Staines, vicar of St. Peter and St. Paul's Church in Aylesford, died in 1840. The solicitor who prepared his will was Samuel Powell of Knaresborough who happened to be the brother of Mr Staines' wife Jane. With no other clues as to how Rosamond's diary ended up in a house sale in Knaresborough, could this be the connection? Mike and Julie both believe that after reading the last rites to Rosamond, the diary ended up in Mr. Staines' possession one way or another. However, I do not believe that a man of the cloth could steal her diary, nor do I believe she would have given it to him, so the mystery remains unsolved.

We found little of John Jones; the man I suspect broke her heart. His father Mr. James Jones, however, ran a successful drapery business in Aldgate, London, where he lived with his wife Hannah. She was a relative of Mary Robson, hence their regular visits to Aylesford.

Mary and Thomas Robson, who were in their forties at the time of the diary, had no children. However, I imagine that given the opportunity they would have made wonderful parents, as I got the impression that this couple were clearly very important to Rosamond and her family due to the amount of care and attention shown to them.

Rosamond's maternal grandfather, George Nash senior, lived in Gillingham with his second wife, his first wife having died when Rosamond's mother was young. He remarried in 1814 to Elizabeth Hunt, the same year Rosamond was born. Elizabeth gave birth to George Nash, the young man who appears in many daily entries. Two more children followed, Alfred and Elizabeth. I soon understood after translating the diary that George and Rosamond were close in both friendship and age with just a year between them. When I first began writing this story, I took them to be cousins with nothing further to go on, as the name Nash was her mamma's maiden name, but thanks to Julie's tireless research it appears the true relationship between Rosamond and George was half uncle and half niece.

Another person to intrigue me was Rosamond's cousin Fanny Spong, the young lady who made her most welcome during her stay at Manor House Farm in Frindsbury. Fanny, the daughter of Ambrose, was two years younger than Rosamond and lived with her family in a large house attached to the farm. Its adjacent tithe barn now happens to be one of the most historically important buildings in Kent. Rosamond stayed there for several weeks in the summer of 1835.

Mike and I first went to look at the Manor house in 1996 in its elevated position over the Medway valley and were delighted to find it was still standing and intact, unlike her home in Mill Hall.

Poor Fanny's story isn't a happy one. She married in 1841 to a young man from Norfolk, their daughter Georgina was born the following year but sadly died after only seven weeks. Her husband Frederick took his grieving wife to Southampton, presumably for work purposes, but within a year Fanny also died. Mother and daughter were reunited in the family grave in All Saints churchyard in Frindsbury, close to Manor House Farm. Included in the grave are various other family members such as Uncle William Luck, his sister Sarah, and husband Ambrose Spong. I felt so sad to hear this, what on earth had happened to her? Julie sent for her death certificate which informed us she died in Woodlands, Southampton; the cause of death given was gastritis. This did not seem a satisfactory explanation to me. I know I have a vivid imagination, but I find it hard to believe that she died of a condition which is effectively an inflammation of the stomach. Another possibility could have been an overdose of some kind of poison due to grief for her lost child, a situation I am sadly only too aware of. As suicide was a crime in Victorian times, it's possible that Frederick covered it up to protect his wife's name. Whatever the reason, it remains a mystery.

Mike and I returned to Frindsbury in June 2022 to locate the grave and visit the family home where, after writing to the present occupiers explaining our circumstances, they kindly invited us to visit. We were made most welcome and given a privileged tour of the house and gardens. What a wonderful experience it was to be in the place where Rosamond had spent so much of her time.

John Webster, the gentleman who took an interest in Rosamond during her stay at the Manor remains a man of mystery, as all we had to go on was his name and the fact he came from London. He was also a guest of Ambrose at the same time as Rosamond.

Of all the people mentioned in the diary, none fascinated me more than her half-uncle George Nash, the young man who spent so much of his time with her during her illness. I really do believe that George was in love with her, but I got the distinct impression from Rosamond's narrative that no matter how close she may have felt towards him, it wasn't in a romantic way as she never gave the slightest hint of it being reciprocated, but with George, the clues were there. I began to suspect his feelings toward his half-niece when she noted on 4th May that, 'George Nash had been rather attentive,' a phrase often used in the day by a lady when a man showed a romantic interest towards her. On the 11th day of the same month, another indication of this appeared when he asked Rosamond if she was engaged to John Jones (abbreviated to XXX in her diary entry) to which her reply had been. 'I thought that to be a very strange question'. Other instances were the gift of oysters produced from his pocket, and the poems written exclusively for her that made her very unhappy. With George's love for Rosamond seemingly apparent, I thought it would be interesting to know the legality of a half-uncle marrying his niece and was surprised to learn it would have been perfectly acceptable in those days.

I sensed George possessed a kind and gentle nature, and I really wanted to know what became of him and what he did with his life. I had found little information on the Nash family during my own research, so I asked Julie to investigate it for me, and what she came up with was truly astonishing. It was during her research that I became aware of the actual family relationship between Rosamond and George. I had presumed they were cousins so when learning their true connection, several changes to her story needed to be made. I thought this was interesting enough until the next piece of information arriving on the doormat from Julie, bearing in mind the social distancing required, included an obituary for George taken from a Kent newspaper dated 1844. This article told me that my instincts about George's gentle nature had been correct, for when I read the eulogy of this remarkable man who tragically died at the age of twenty-nine, I was in tears. The entire obituary was a testament to his wonderful talent as a poet and author, his kind and friendly nature, and the fact he was much loved by all who encountered him.

George travelled to India in 1837 just after his father (Rosamond's maternal grandfather) died. While in India, he wrote several books including *The Outcast*, *The Drama*, and *A Woman's Revolt*, all of which are seemingly impossible to find. However, thanks to Julie I read a copy of *The French Prisoners, A History* on the Internet. This fascinating book printed in Calcutta in early Victorian times tells the true story of the prison ships kept in Gillingham harbour after the Napoleonic wars along with a detailed account of his father's part in this. Having been told this story when he was a young boy, it tells us that George Nash senior, a prominent gentleman residing in Gillingham, rescued a severely malnourished prisoner who had escaped from one of the rotting ships and kept him hidden until he recovered from his ordeal. Unfortunately, he was recaptured by the authorities shortly after leaving the house. The conditions in which the French prisoners were kept was horrendous, so Mr. Nash made it his business to visit them regularly in the capacity of benefactor to help the men incarcerated in the most brutal conditions. It is a harrowing account of life for prisoners of war on these terrible ships long after the war had ended, and it was clear after reading this book that George inherited his kind and caring nature from his father.

He returned to England in 1843 suffering from consumption, sadly passing away a year later. I wasn't surprised to learn that George never married, as I'm quite sure he carried a torch for Rosamond until the day he died. A sad poem he wrote about lost love allegedly regarding a man called 'Chatterton,' but so obviously about himself, seems to confirm this. It was a heart-breaking account of how he lost his only love and, now he knew he was dying, was a poignant story that produced more tears.

If you are equally interested as to where her siblings had gone, I hope most of the questions you may have had have been answered, but now it's time for me to allow the characters in Rosamond's story to go back into the past, but I do so with a heavy heart, as I feel I knew them all so well.

Rosamond

16th July to 13th August

THURSDAY, 16ᵀᴴ JULY
The Hegira, or Flight of Mahomet, 622.

Doctor Welch, Doctor Dodds, and Mr. Trested came to see me in the morning. Mrs. Robson came up and saw me. William Nash brought Fanny Spong over to see me. D. Dodds and George Nash stayed to dinner and tea. I slept very badly last night. D.D. ordered a blister to be put on my chest but cough very bad. I had the cold shivers.

Rose had an even busier day than she had the day before. After a difficult night with much coughing and little sleep, Mamma was soon showing Doctor Dodds and George Nash into her bedroom, quickly followed by Doctor Welch. The two Doctors had arranged to meet up with Mr. Trested to discuss the patient's condition, and he duly arrived a short time later. Far from being intimidated by their number, Rose was reassured to see them all, as it gave some hope that they may have found a treatment that could help her at last, but she was soon disappointed as nothing new was offered. Doctor Dodd suggested that a blister applied to Rose's chest may help with her breathing; the other two doctors agreed with this, and one was sent for. Mr. Trested wanted to bleed her again, but the other two didn't think it such a good idea. Mr. Trested's other options were his dreaded physic or, failing that, the application of leeches. Rose was truly horrified at that prospect, and relieved when those ideas were also deemed to be unsuitable. Eventually, Doctor Welch and Mr. Trested bade her good morning and left with the assurance of returning soon.

Rose was happy at having just the good Doctor Dodds and George for company, especially when they suggested staying for the rest of the day, and indeed, taking their dinner and tea with her.

More visitors were received after dinner as Mamma's cousin, William Nash of Gillingham, had ridden over to Frindsbury to collect Rose's dear cousin Fanny before travelling to Mill Hall to surprise her. Rose was absolutely delighted when her bedroom door opened and Fanny peered round it saying, 'Would you like a visitor, Rosie?'

'Oh yes please, Fanny, I am so happy to see you,' she cried. 'I have missed you so much since I left Frindsbury, how are your dear Mamma and Ambrose?' she added, also wanting to ask about Mr. Webster, and was he still staying with them?

However, she had no need as Fanny said, 'Mr. Webster sends his kind regards to you. He returned to London for a while but is back with us now.' Rose's heart jumped a little at this news, she had thought her feelings for him had disappeared along with the hope of being well again, but to her surprise, the mere mention of his name proved that it wasn't so, despite her thinking he would have no romantic interest in a very sick young woman.

They spent the afternoon happily chattering away to each other, with Fanny saying her intention was to stay the night. allowing them more time together. Her cousin's visit helped to lift Rose's spirits, as Fanny was very dear to her.

Doctor Dodds entered Rose's room just as the two girls were

taking tea together to put on the blister plaster he had previously alluded to. Unfortunately, it had no beneficial effect as Rose coughed continuously. Rose wondered if she had overdone her enthusiasm while conversing with Fanny this afternoon, as she was suffering the cold shivers again.

Even though she remained very ill and not improving, Rose ended her day thinking more pleasure was had with Fanny's visit than she had been able to enjoy for quite some time.

FRIDAY, 17TH JULY
Royal Assent given to Scotch Reform Bill, 1832.

Had a dreadful night. Mamma helped with me. Mr. Trested came to see me in the morning. He wrote to D.D. about me. After tea Fanny Spong went home with William Nash. Mr. Staines came to see me after dinner.

Last night was truly dreadful for Rose, her only comfort was to have Mamma by her side throughout the incessant bouts of coughing and the pain it brought.

Mr. Trested called and expressed great concern about her condition, telling Mamma he intended writing to Doctor Dodds directly for advice.

Fanny went in to sit and converse with her. The main topic of conversation to start with was Mr. Webster, who had asked Fanny to convey to Rose his very best wishes, and to tell her how sorry he was to hear she was so ill. Rose confided to her cousin that she had become very fond of him, and if things were different, they may have started to walk out together. She said to her cousin, 'Please return my sincere best wishes to him and be sure to say how much I enjoyed his company during my stay in Frindsbury.'

Fanny assured her she would do so. 'Are you sad it came to nought, Rosie?' she said.

Rose replied, 'Although our acquaintance wasn't a long one, I became quite fond of him, but my feelings were not as deep as my love for John had been, because when he left my heart was truly broken.' She then went on to say, 'But I will always be grateful to John Webster for showing me that hearts, however shattered, do mend in time, but what makes me really sad is knowing that I may never get another chance to make a future with someone I love, and to have a family of my own because I know if I do survive this terrible affliction, the best I can expect is the life of an invalid.'

'Oh Rosie, please do not say such a thing!' cried Fanny.

'I am sorry if I upset you, Fanny, but I am now resigned to my fate, it is the way it will be.' By this time, both girls were crying.

After blowing her nose and then composing herself, Fanny said, 'If this is how it will be, I promise to come and visit you all the time while you are lying on your sofa, giving orders to everyone like the lady of the manor.' They both laughed at the thought of Rose giving orders to anyone.

When dinner was called, Fanny went down to the dining room promising to return when she had dined, but immediately after dinner Mr. Staines arrived to read the bible to Rose and stayed for quite some time. The moment he left, Fanny returned and stayed until teatime.

The afternoon passed all too quickly, and in what seemed no time at all William Nash appeared to take Fanny home. Rose cried for a full five minutes after her dear cousin left, as she had taken a great deal of comfort from her visit and would miss her greatly. Fanny's company had been so uplifting, just being with her had helped Rose to forget how ill she had become, and now her spirits were very low again.

With nothing further to add to today's recordings, she put her diary away until tomorrow. As Rose lay in bed watching the candlelight flickering on the ceiling, she hoped the coming night would not be as terrible as the last one, when she feared not seeing another sunrise.

SATURDAY, 18ᵀᴴ JULY
Battle of Hallidown Hill, near Berwick, 1333.

Had a very bad night. Mr. Trested came in the morning. I had a blister on after breakfast. Mrs. Robson called; she came upstairs. George Nash came over after dinner from D.D. I am not in good spirits.

Her wish for a more peaceful night wasn't granted, as Rose suffered yet another dreadful time. After breakfast Mamma went upstairs with another blister plaster for her chest, but Rose was sceptical about their healing abilities as they did not appear to be making any difference at all to her breathing.

When Mr. Trested made his now daily call, Rose enquired as to why they had no effect. His answer was that she must have patience, their effect would happen in good time, to which Rose replied rather curtly, 'If a cure cannot be found soon, I fear I will not have the "good time" to be patient before God takes me, Mr. Trested.'

Rose was as shocked at her disrespectful reply almost as much as Mr. Trested was in receiving it; so much so, he was rendered speechless. After apologising for her rudeness and ill humour, and Mr. Trested had finished stroking his chin, he replied, 'It is not like you to indulge in such an outburst, Miss Spong, but considering your recent suffering has caused your sweet humour to be at a loss of late, I will choose to overlook those remarks, although I am sure it will improve when your health returns.' He then bade her good day leaving Rose to ponder over her uncalled-for behaviour.

Rose felt contrite about her truly awful treatment of the poor doctor, who did not deserve her rudeness as he was only trying to do his best to help her. She decided to ask God for his forgiveness in her prayers at bedtime.

Rose's next visitor was Mrs. Robson, who arrived bustling into her bedroom like a breath of fresh air. 'Now, my dear Rosamond, why are you crying?' she enquired. After explaining her rudeness to Mr. Trested, Mrs. Robson looked at her and said, 'Oh dear me, he would not have been too pleased by your response, but I must say, I do find his manner to be rather pompous, it's a pity I wasn't here to see his face.' They both laughed at this remark; she also found encounters with him difficult due to his lack of humour. However, thought Rose, it still didn't excuse her behaviour and she feared Mamma would not be pleased with her should she find out.

George Nash called after dinner. Doctor Dodds had sent him to enquire after her. She was happy to see him, and they talked for a while. During their conversation Rose told him of her disgrace this morning, George said she shouldn't fret about it, as he was sure Mr. Trested was aware how difficult it was for her, as indeed they all were, adding, 'It is very distressing for us all to watch you struggle so much, so it's understandable that the sweetest nature will sour when faced with so much adversity.'

In the evening as the light was beginning to fade, Rose sat by the window to watch the boys playing in the garden opposite as she wrote in her diary, thinking Mamma would soon be calling them in to bed. With the darkness came her fears of a long and harrowing night, it was the time when she was most afraid of her dreadful cough and dark thoughts returning to swirl round in her mind.

Her spirits were low during the day, but at night she was really in despair. As she laid there in bed Rose prayed to the Lord that he may grant her another chance to see the sun rise.

SUNDAY, 19TH JULY
The Turkish fleet burnt by the Greeks, 1822.

Had a very bad night. I retched till 4 o'clock. Mr. Trested came in the morning. Mamma stayed at home with me all day. After tea D. Dodds and George Nash came to see me. They stayed until 8 o'clock.

Another poor night, mostly caused by sickness continuing until the early hours. The bilious attacks were occurring more often now, making it difficult for Rose to keep anything down. The lack of an appetite had taken its toll on her body – she was losing weight and growing weaker by the day. When Mr. Trested arrived, Rose worried he may say something about her rudeness yesterday and was most relieved when he didn't.

Another Sunday came and went without her attending a service at Aylesford Church. Mamma stayed at home again to care for her, but the rest of the family left. They were making the journey to the church on foot as the day was fair, so Rose went to the window to watch them leave, waving to them as they disappeared down the lane towards the towpath. It made her unhappy to be left at home, but realised she was too ill to go with them, even if she were to travel in the coach.

Mary sat with her sister in the afternoon to keep her company and tried to raise her spirits by talking about various topics, including all the exciting things they could do together when Rose returned to health. Doctor Dodds and George arrived after tea to see her. George, taking his place by her bed, received a welcoming smile and a gentle squeeze of her hand. His presence was always a comfort to her; he willingly listened to her tales of woe and knew just what to say when hysteria threatened to overwhelm her, a situation occurring more frequently of late. They both stayed with her until eight o'clock, and she was sorry to see them go.

Trying hard not to fret about the coming night by keeping her diary up to date, she nevertheless felt certain sleep would elude her again through coughing, as it had for countless nights. Her mind filled with fear at closing her eyes lest the Lord came for her while she slept. No matter what anyone said to Rose to reassure her of a recovery, she laid in the darkness waiting for him to appear before her. In great fear of going straight to purgatory due to the lack of grace required to enter heaven, she felt unready to receive The Almighty, and therefore felt it was imperative to speak with Mr. Staines for his guidance on the matter as soon as possible.

MONDAY, 20TH JULY
Margaret, a virgin supposed to have been martyred, 275.

Very poorly all day. Mr. Trested came in the morning. George Nash came over from Doctor Dodds with some physic. Mr. Staines came over and read to me before tea. Mamma took the boys back to school.

There were no improvements in Rose's condition today. If anything, she felt even worse, and because of this she remained in bed from morning to night. Straight after breakfast, Mamma brought Rose's brothers into her room to say goodbye as she was about to take them back to school. As they leant over the bed to kiss her, she told them how much she would miss their cheery faces peering round her door to enquire after her, their appearance in all probability due to Mamma's instruction as having heard the answer, they quickly disappeared to continue their games.

Mr. Trested made his usual mid-morning visit, and a short time later George arrived with a bottle of physic from Doctor Dodds. Seeing how ill and tired Rose looked, George only stayed long enough to take refreshment with her before returning home. Mary made constant checks on her throughout the day and showed Mr. Staines up to her room when he called in the afternoon. Rose lost no time in unburdening herself by repeating her fears of eternal damnation to him once more. After listening intently to all she had to say, Mr. Staines sat quietly back in his chair to contemplate what he had heard. A little uneasy at his silence, Rose wondered if she had upset him. When he had finished stroking his chin for what seemed like an age, he took her hand and said, 'My dear Miss Spong, the doctors are doing everything within their powers to cure you, but if the Lord should wish to take you to him, I can assure you that he will give you the acceptance and grace needed to enter the kingdom of heaven, so do not fear, God will be with you, and you will find an inner peace if that time ever comes to pass. Now let me read some passages from the bible to you.'

Greatly comforted by his words, she wrote what she could in her diary before tiredness overcame her and she fell asleep.

TUESDAY, 21ST JULY
Lord Russell beheaded in Lincoln's Inn Fields, 1683.

Had another blister on. Doctor Welch came in the morning. George Nash came to dinner. Doctor Dodds came over with 2 ladies and a gentleman after dinner. I had my cough and cold. He was with me nearly all of the day. Mrs. Robson came.

Doctor Welch called this morning to attend Rose and ordered another blister plaster to be put on her chest which was most uncomfortable.

George Nash came to dinner, after which he went upstairs and found Rose sitting at her window. Whilst George was there, they saw Doctor Dodds arrive from her window; he had a gentleman and two ladies with him. Excusing himself, George went down to be introduced to them. She longed to go into the drawing room with him but was now confined like a prisoner to her bedroom, Rose couldn't ever see a day when she would enter the drawing room again. It seemed just a short time ago when she was in despair at the thought of being an invalid reclining on the chaise lounge with a blanket on her knees, but now she would accept that situation gladly. What had seemed to be a terrible fate was now something she prayed for, as it would mean being a part of her family's life again.

Her comfortably furnished bedroom had everything a young lady required but sitting in her chair or laying on her bed in solitude made her feel lonely and afraid. The family did come and go but couldn't stay with her long, and she desperately missed her games with little Grace and baby Elizabeth and running around in the garden with them. She also missed the walks shared with Mary, and it broke her heart knowing she would never be well enough to do so again. Mary told her things are not the same walking alone.

The sound of approaching footsteps took Rose's mind off her melancholy thoughts, and after a gentle knock Doctor Dodds entered her bedroom. She enquired as to who was entertaining his friends while he was busy with her, and he replied that Mary and George had been charged with that task. When his administrations were completed and he had gone downstairs, Mary went to tell her sister who the two ladies were to satisfy her curiosity. It appeared they were friends of the doctor on their way to Maidstone to attend a supper party there.

The next person to call in to see Rose was Mrs. Robson. She told Rose that Mrs. Jones, John's mother, was finding widowhood very hard. Rose went to lie down on her bed when Mrs. Robson had returned downstairs, with thoughts of John plaguing her mind. After refusing to keep him as a friend on their last meeting, she now wished she had not been so unkind to him, but all she could think of at the time was how cruel he was to her. He had been a big part of her life since they were children and she missed him so. Now very tired, it was time to stop writing and try to sleep.

WEDNESDAY, 22ND JULY
Magdalen, commemoration of casting out the devil from Mary Magdalene. The sun enters Leo, the lion.

Had a very bad night. Mr. Trested came in the morning. G.N. came before dinner. He brought some more physic. Felt ill all day. Mrs. Robson called. Mr. Staines came and read and stayed with me.

Last night was so dreadful, Rose again feared she wouldn't see the dawn. Mamma and Mary had taken turns to sit with her, and she was very grateful they were there. Poor Rose had been so ill today she was even more convinced her time on Earth was nearly over.

Mr. Trested called in the morning, but as he was not giving her any more treatment now, she failed to see why he came daily to see her.

Mamma made sure Rose wasn't troubled by too many visitors, but when George arrived just before dinnertime with more physic from Doctor Dodds, he was shown directly up to her room. Mrs. Robson called, but Rose did not see her. However, she did see Mr. Staines when he called, as his spiritual guidance was most important now. Mr. Staines' reading of the bible as she laid in bed was a great source of comfort as she absorbed every word he said.

THURSDAY, 23ʳᴅ JULY
Gibraltar taken by Sir G. Rooke, 1704.

Very ill all day. D. Dodds and George Nash came before dinner. I had a vapour bath, they left before tea. Mrs. Robson came to see me. In very bad spirits.

Today started badly with Rose suffering greatly with shortness of breath, fever, and retching, and then continued as such.

Doctor Dodds and George called before dinner as they frequently did. The doctor ordered a vapour bath to help her to breathe, but it did little or nothing to ease it. Rose was even more certain it was God's will for her to be in heaven, as all the treatments tried so far had failed in their purpose. She was hopeful that Mr. Staines was correct when he said she had nothing to fear, as God would guide her and she would find peace, but she did not feel very peaceful and in very bad spirits.

Mrs. Robson came to see her again and chattered away as well as she could having realised Rose was too poorly to contribute much to the conversation, but the distraction of listening to all the Aylesford gossip did help for a while.

With illness overwhelming her and unable to concentrate any further, she put away her diary with nothing more to say.

FRIDAY, 24ᵀᴴ JULY
The forces of Don Pedro enter Lisbon, 1833.

Had a very bad night. Mr. Trested came to see me in the morning. Grandpapa and George came to dinner. G.N. brought a long list of enquires from

Doctor Dodds. Mrs. Robson called to enquire after me. Mr. Robson and young Edward Jones came down. Received the sacrament for the first time. I had it in bed.

Grandpapa and George came to dinner today. Rose was pleased when they both went upstairs to her bedroom, and she thought Grandpapa looked quite well considering his heart troubles. She told George that Mr. Trested had only just left, and of her fears that all the doctor's treatments were failing to cure her. George replied that Doctor Dodds was working tirelessly to find a cure and had given him a list of questions regarding her symptoms and general condition that required answers. So, after leaving the list for her to read, they agreed on him returning after dinner to help answer them.

Some of the questions on the list were as follows: Did she have chest pains? Did she bleed whilst coughing? Was she taking any nourishment? Were episodes of shivering still evident? The list was quite long. Every question on the list described her illness perfectly, with each one answered in the affirmative, and on George's return, she told him as much. George stayed for a while until he and Grandpapa returned to Rochester together.

The next visitor was Mrs. Robson, who asked Rose if she was feeling any better today. Rose replied, 'In truth, Mrs. Robson, I am not, and I very much fear that if Doctor Dodds cannot find a cure for whatever is ailing me, I will never feel better again, as Mr. Trested and Doctor Welch have both failed in their search for a cure. I am sure it is unlikely the dear Doctor Dodds will be any more successful than they are.'

Mrs. Robson, quite taken aback by Rose's abrupt reply to

her question, was rather lost for words and offered no further attempt to improve her spirits. Rose had noticed that Mrs. Robson wasn't the only one finding it difficult to reassure her that all would be well, as it was now rather obvious there was to be no recovery for her, and maybe it was time to make peace with God.

When Mamma appeared, Rose asked her to request a visit from Mr. Staines on her behalf, as she wished to pray with him. Mamma, full of concern at her stricken daughter's wish, went straight downstairs to send Ann to Aylesford with a note for him. When Mr. Staines read the note, he put on his hat and made his way to Mill Hall. As soon as he arrived at Rose's bedside, she told him of her urgent desire to commune with the Lord, so he asked if she wished to receive the sacrament, assuring her it didn't matter that she was in bed. Rose readily accepted and felt greatly comforted by it.

Mr. Staines had once more produced a calming effect on Rose's troubled mind. During her prayers before sleep, she asked the Lord for forgiveness as she now felt ready to accept her fate. Whether it was life as an invalid or called unto heaven, she would try to accept either with good grace.

SATURDAY, 25TH JULY
St. James the Great, the first martyred apostle, also tutelar saint of Spain. Duch. of Camb. Birthday. Holiday.

Had a very bad night. Fanny Spong came over with William Finch to see me. After tea Mrs. Day called, she came upstairs. Mr. Robson and Mrs. Westholme called.

Last night was so dreadful, it came as a great relief for Rose to witness the dawn.

After attempting a little breakfast, Mamma and Mary made her as comfortable as possible just before Fanny Spong appeared with a companion, William Finch. Rose, although happy to see her cousin, felt a little uncomfortable receiving someone she didn't know in her bedroom. Rose wondered if he had set his cap at dear Fanny but was not sure Fanny was equally smitten by him.

After dinner, of which Rose ate nothing, she had a visit from Mrs. Robson who had brought Mrs. Westholme with her. The ladies stayed for a while, and when they were gone Rose fell asleep until Mamma appeared with Mrs. Day. It had been very tiring with all her visitors today, so the diary was put away until tomorrow.

SUNDAY, 26TH JULY
St. Anne, mother of the Virgin Mary, and wife of Joachim.

I took laudanum, but I had a very bad night. Fanny and Mary stayed at home with me in the morning. Expected D.D. and G.N. The former had not returned from London. G.N. came. Fanny Spong went home. Mary went to chapel with Papa.

Rose was given laudanum last night, but its only effect was to make her very sick, and she had another terrible night.

Today being Sunday, the family went to church in the morning apart from Mary, who stayed at home with Fanny to be with her sister. It had been a while now since Rose had attended a church service, and she did not expect to do so again. It was a most depressing thought, as she had always taken such great pleasure in attending Aylesford church in the company of family, friends, and neighbours. Should God spare her, it would be hard in the extreme to watch the family going about their daily lives from her invalid bed but having promised the Lord to bear it with good grace, that is what she must do. Doctor Dodds was expected to call on Rose today, but George informed her on his arrival that he hadn't returned from his trip to London.

Fanny and William left for Frindsbury after dinner, and again Rose was sorry to see her leave. Mary went upstairs after tea to say she was going to chapel with Papa, but she would come to sit with her when she returned. Mary was as good as her word, and comforted Rose with her company the moment she arrived home.

As night-time approached, so did Rose's worry about trying to sleep, for as soon as she did so her sickness started again.

MONDAY, 27ᵀᴴ JULY
A revolution commenced at Paris, 1830.

> *Expected D.D. all day. G.N. came after dinner to say he was still in London. Mr. Hunt came to see me, he talked about religion. Had a dreadful cough and cold feet. Mrs. Robson was here. I had a vapour bath.*

Rose's cough troubled her greatly today, and her feet were so cold Mamma had to send for a hot brick to warm them.

Doctor Dodds didn't come, just George who came to say the good Doctor had not returned from London yet. This news caused Rose to fear he had abandoned her because her illness was incurable. George told her to stop being so fanciful as he was only away on business, and would no doubt visit on his return.

Mrs. Robson called but Rose felt too weak to receive any more visitors.

Mamma gave her a vapour bath hoping it would improve her breathing in the night and ease her cough, but so far, its beneficial effects had not been evident.

Rose, unable to write through lack of strength and overcome with tiredness, put the diary away.

TUESDAY, 28TH JULY
Valenciennes surrendered to the Duke of York, 1793.

Had a bad night. Mr. Trested came to see me in the morning and Mr. Staines. Had my cough in the afternoon. Doctor Dodds and G.N. came after dinner; he altered my medicine. Mrs. Robson came to see me. Mary went to Aylesford after tea.

Mr. Trested called in the morning, as did Mr. Staines, with Doctor Dodds finally making an appearance in the afternoon, arriving after dinner with George. Doctor Dodds had brought with him a new medicine to ease her cough. Rose sincerely hoped it would work, as the last one had done little to stop her dreadful episodes which seemed to be particularly troublesome in the afternoon. She was spared the indignity of needing a change of bed-linen due to a burst blood vessel while George and the good Doctor were present.

A while later, when the two had returned to Gillingham, Mrs. Robson went upstairs to sit with her. Rose was glad of her company; she could always rely on an enjoyable chat about the doings of Aylesford and the people who lived there; it lifted her spirits for a while. Mrs. Robson, always a cheerful lady to be with, made it impossible for Rose not to laugh when she regaled her with humorous tales. When she laughed, her white lace cap bobbed up and down in unison with her stomach.

Later, Mary went upstairs to tell Rosamond she planned to walk into Aylesford after tea and would come and see her when she returned. Mary came home in time for supper and brought Rose a little on a tray but feeling sickly again, she just couldn't face it.

With nothing further to say to her diary tonight, she thought she would try and sleep as her cough had eased at last. Maybe Doctor Dodds new medicine was helping?

WEDNESDAY, 29TH JULY
The Greek festival of Martha and Mary kept.

Very ill all day. Everything I took I brought up again. Edward came home from Gillingham. Mrs. Peppercorn came to see me, likewise Laura Spong. After dinner Mr. Hunt came over from Maidstone to talk with me.

Another desperate day for poor Rose who was very ill all day: everything she ate or drank, including the new medicine, came straight back up again. She felt so wretched and frightened. As Mamma leant over to wipe her brow, Rose declared in a voice subdued by fever, 'If I cannot keep any nourishment down, death from starvation will surely claim me before this illness does.'

Edward, her brother, returned home today; he had been

staying with Grandpapa in Gillingham. Rose received a visit from Mrs. Peppercorn this morning, but she didn't stay long in view of her sickness. Another visitor was her cousin Laura Spong, Uncle William's daughter from Cobtree Manor. She also cut short her visit as Rose continued to be sickly. Her last visitor today was Mr. Hunt, a preacher from Maidstone Chapel. Rose wondered if he assumed her demise was near, as a lot of time was spent talking about heaven.

It had been quite a busy day with visitors and frequent changes of linen due to sickness, and now exhausted she bade her diary goodnight, hoping to attend to it in the morning.

THURSDAY, 30TH JULY
Jassy, the capital of Moldavia, burnt, 1827.

Had a very good night. Mrs and Lucy Hollingsworth called. I did not see them. After dinner D.D. and G.N. came over. Saw Martha Brenchley. Mrs. Robson came. Better today.

Rose slept soundly last night and woke up feeling a little improved, and even managed to eat some breakfast. Mamma, pleased to see that she had managed to eat something at last, said, 'If you continue to take nourishment, Rosie, it will help your recovery greatly.' With a good night's rest and Mamma's words of encouragement, her spirits were much improved.

Mrs. Hollingsworth and her daughter Lucy called, but they didn't venture upstairs to see Rose, much to her disappointment as she would have enjoyed a chat with Lucy who she found to be a delightful young lady.

Doctor Dodds and the ever-faithful George came to see her

after dinner. Rose happened to be sitting in her chair by the window when they entered her bedroom. Mamma had helped her wash and put on a fresh nightgown and Rose managed to brush her own hair. George went over to her and taking her hand in his, said, 'Why Rosie! I do believe you have a little colour in your cheeks, I am so pleased to see you looking more cheerful.' Rose answered that her cough had been less troublesome, and she had slept most of the night because of it. Doctor Dodds thought that the new medicine was helping at last. They had an enjoyable chat with plenty of words of encouragement. Before they left the good Doctor said he would not be able to call tomorrow but was happy that he was leaving her in better spirits than on his last visit.

Rose's next visitor was dear Mrs. Robson; she too, was happy to see the change in her. Martha Brenchley from Maidstone also called to offer her good wishes before recounting all the things that had happened in Maidstone since she was last there.

Rose ended this day in much better spirits than the one before, and with a renewed hope that perhaps she may not die after all.

FRIDAY, 31ST JULY
Baron Hullock died, 1829.

George and Edward went to London. Mary went in the coach with Mrs. Robson to Rochester. Had a bad night. Cough troublesome during the day. I am obliged to write all in bed.

After such a promising and uplifting day came more disappointment. Rose had to endure another bad night, as her cough had returned and so had her low mood. She had been so happy yesterday thinking she was recovering at last, and now the disappointment at realising this wasn't the case was overwhelming her.

Mrs. Robson couldn't make her usual visit because she went to Rochester with Mary today. George and Edward went to London on the three o'clock stage, so they were unable to show their faces, and Rose didn't know when they were due to return. With no visitors at all today, Rose felt isolated and lonely. Mamma went up when she could but being so busy with household duties meant her visits were somewhat rationed.

Having been confined to her bed all day, Rose had to employ her writing slope propped up on her knees to complete her diary entries. It had been a very unhappy day.

SATURDAY, 1ST AUGUST
Lammas Day, from tenants of cathedrals then offering a live lamb. Hol. at Exch. Bat. of the Nile, 1798.

Had a dreadful night. Very ill all day. Chest exceedingly hurtful. After dinner Mr. Hunt came to talk about religion. My breath very short. D. Dodds and G. Nash came just before tea. They stayed till 9 o'clock.

Rose had been poorly all day, and once again was unable to sleep. Her chest was painful, and she struggled for breath which affected her ability to speak. Doctor Dodds and George Nash arrived before tea. They were both very concerned to see just how much she had deteriorated since their last visit and kept a vigil with her until nine o'clock in the evening.

Unable to write all she wanted in her diary tonight through illness and sheer exhaustion, her heart broke to think the Lord was ready to take her. Rose was certainly not experiencing the aura of calmness Mr. Staines had assured her would happen when her time came to pass.

ROSAMOND

2nd August to 13th August

SUNDAY, 2ND AUGUST
Battle of Blenheim, 1704.

Mary went to church in the morning. Had a bad night. Very sick. No one went to church in the afternoon. G.N. came after tea and brought me some physic. Mamma and Papa went to chapel. I had my dreadful cough.

With her condition now worsening, we allow Rosamond to complete her story as if from her own perspective.

I was very sick in the night and continued to be so for most of the day. Although it is Sunday, nobody went to church in the morning or afternoon except Mary, who went to the morning service. It is most unusual for my family not to attend at least one service on the Sabbath, but at least Mary went to represent the Spong family. She must have been quite lonely sitting in our family pew on her own.

My cough has been truly dreadful today, and my spirits are low. I have had no visitors but am glad of it, because talking is becoming increasingly difficult.

George Nash came after tea to bring me some more physic from Doctor Dodds. While he was with me, Mamma came up to say that she and Papa were going to chapel, no doubt to say prayers for me. Everyone is very worried on my behalf, as this illness is worsening as each day passes. That is all I can write tonight because I am so ill.

MONDAY, 3ʳᴰ AUGUST
Sir R. Arkwright died, 1792.

Had rather a bad night. D.D. and G.N. came to dinner. I had a warm bath. I had a dreadful cough. Mary drank tea at Mrs. Robson's. Felt very poorly all day. They left me at 9 o'clock.

I suffered another dreadful night. Poor Mamma is quite exhausted with nursing me. It is so very hard for her, and I fear she will soon become ill herself on my account.

I had a warm bath, the first for a long time. Ann brought up a bath, placed it in front of the fire, and filled it with warm water. It was quite pleasant to lie in it for a while but I soon tired, so Mamma helped me to get out. After drying me with a warm towel, I put on a clean nightgown. I tried to brush my hair but holding up my arms became too much, so Mamma had to finish the task. I could see as I looked in the mirror just how thin I have become, no doubt because I have taken so little nourishment of late, but I cannot keep anything in my stomach.

Doctor Dodds and George came to dinner, and both came upstairs to see me after dining. As they came through the door, I began to cough rather badly, causing me to become quite breathless and frightened, feeling so poorly it was a relief to have them with me. It was nine o'clock in the evening before they left, after taking their tea and supper in my bedroom. I took nothing to eat and just drank a little water as my throat is always so dry.

It has been another truly terrible day, so I will say no more about it and put down my pen. I cannot get out of bed to put my writing slope on the table, so Mamma will have to do it when she comes up to stay with me for the night.

TUESDAY, 4ᵀᴴ AUGUST
Lord Duncan died, 1804.

Had a very bad night, felt very ill all day. Edward Jones dined here. Mr. Staines came to see me in the morning. G.N. came over. Mr. Hunt came over to see me. I had my cough.

Another terrible night with much coughing and sickness. I started today's entry sitting up in bed using pen and ink but now forced to abandon it, as I am so ill and dizzy. Mamma gave me a pencil, and now lying down to write.

Not much happened today. Mr. Staines called in the morning to read the scriptures to me. After dinner dear George Nash came. He is ever faithful in his attentions to me and says he will always be my constant companion if I wish him to be. I do believe he loves me; I have long suspected it, but he has never actually declared anything. I am very grateful he has not done so, because I love him like a brother, not as a lover. I would have to tell him of my feelings and our closeness would have been ruined forever.

Mr Hunt called to talk about God again. He is so different to Mr. Staines who is an easy gentleman to talk to, while Mr Hunt is quite serious and not fond of humour in any way, so I am finding his sermons to be quite dreary.

I have no more to say tonight, so I will close my diary and try to sleep.

WEDNESDAY, 5TH AUGUST
Earl Howe died, 1799.

I had six leeches on, which I suffered very much. D.D. came after dinner. Mary drank tea at Mrs. Brenchley's. Mrs. Hannah Jones came down.

I am becoming so weak and am obliged to write my diary in pencil because sitting up in bed is too difficult now.

Doctor Dodds called on me after dinner holding a jar of leeches. I was truly horrified when he suggested putting them on my chest and became very upset, but Mamma said I must allow the doctor to treat me. It was a truly terrible experience, and I cried all the time the horrible worms were on me. Mamma held my hand and tried to explain that they were there to draw the poison out of my blood and could help to cure me. I said, 'In my opinion, Mamma, I am beyond a cure, as it is only a matter of time before the Lord takes me, so I am resigned to my fate.' She was so upset by my words, I immediately felt sorry for saying them. At last, the leeches were returned to their jar looking very much fatter than when they came out of it.

I wish George had come today, but Doctor Dodds arrived alone. I have missed him; he would have made me feel better about what I had just suffered.

Mary came up to see me before she went to Maidstone to see Mrs. Brenchley. When I told her what had just occurred, she hugged me and said how sorry she was to see me suffering so.

I did not receive a visit from Mrs. Robson, because John's mother, Mrs. Hannah Jones, is staying with her. I expect they will both arrive to see me eventually. I wondered if John had sent a letter with her, but as he hasn't shown any concern for the terrible situation I am in, I am quite sure he won't even have bothered. I wish his silence did not hurt me so much.

I cannot write anymore as I am feeling extremely poorly.

THURSDAY, 6ᵀᴴ AUGUST
Transfiguration of Jesus on Mount Tabor.

I have been ill for two months. Today I left my room and went to Mammas for 3 hours. G.N. brought some more physic. Ambrose Spong came to see me. I had my cough.

It has been two months since I was taken ill again, two whole months since I had last left my bedroom, so Mamma asked me if I would like to go to her room for a change. My legs were so weak walking along the landing that I worried in case they collapsed, but when I did manage to get there, it was good to see something different for a while. I received George there; he had brought me some more physic. Ambrose also came down from Frindsbury in his chaise to see me.

I stayed in Mamma's room for three hours but now back in my own bed continuing to write in my diary albeit with a pencil, as I am so very weak.

FRIDAY, 7ᵀᴴ AUGUST
Name of Jesus - possibly from a catholic festival of naming Jesus.

Had a most dreadful day, went to Mamma's room and Mrs. Robson and Mrs. Jones came to see me, also Mrs. Day and Mr. John Webster. I did not see them. After dinner Mrs. Hunt came to see me and Mamma went to Maidstone to fetch Ely Hunt to stay with me. I had my cough.

It has been a terrible day. I am becoming so weak that Papa had to carry me into Mamma's room so my bed could be changed as my legs are no longer strong enough to support me.

There were many visitors this morning who all came to enquire after me. Mrs. Robson arrived first, accompanied by Mrs. Jones, who was then followed by Mrs. Day. But most surprising of all, Mr. John Webster called. Mamma did not let anyone come upstairs as I have been much too poorly to receive any visitors. I was glad Mr. Webster had come, but I would not have liked him to see me looking so ill; it is better he remembers me when I was happy in Frindsbury. I know I will never see him again as the Lord will be coming to claim me soon. I have accepted my fate at last and spend much of my time lying in bed talking to him and praying it will be an easy passing into heaven and free of pain.

Mrs. Hunt, the wife of the Methodist preacher, came to see me. Mamma went to Maidstone to fetch their son Ely, as she wanted him to sit with me. I had a very bad cough all day.

It is becoming difficult to write now, so I will put away my diary.

SATURDAY, 8ᵀᴴ AUGUST
Mr. Canning died, 1827.

Felt very poorly all day. Had a bad night. I had a very bad cough. G.N. came to see me. Then Elizabeth and Mary went and called on Mrs. Robson.

I feel extremely ill and cough incessantly. George came to see me and brought his sister Elizabeth with him. He sat by my bed to keep me company while Elizabeth and Mary went to call on Mrs. Robson. I slept for a while, and when I awoke George was still sitting there smiling at me. I fear that when I am no more, he will miss me greatly. When Mary and Elizabeth came home, they both came up to see me.

I am unable to say anymore as I feel so poorly.

SUNDAY, 9ᵀᴴ AUGUST
Leopold, K. of Belgium, mar. to Louisa, dau. of the K. of the French, 1832.

Had a very bad night. Mary and Elizabeth went to church. All stayed at home in the afternoon. Very ill all day. Mamma and Seppy went to chapel and Elizabeth and Tom went to Rochester for the day.

Last night was very bad, and the day gave me no respite from this terrible illness. I am so tired and praying God will come for me soon as I cannot fight it anymore.

People keep coming into my room, but I have no strength to talk to them. Mary sits and tells me of all the things happening around me. She told me Elizabeth and herself went to the morning service at our church, and then Tom, our brother, went with Elizabeth to Rochester. Also, that Mamma went to chapel with little Seppy. I am envious of their comings and goings no longer. It is like I am not here at all.

I cannot sit up in bed now, so that is all I can say to my diary tonight, as trying to write lying down is far too difficult for me.

MONDAY, 10TH AUGUST
St. Lawrence, a deacon, martyred on a gridiron.

D.D. came at 8 o'clock in the morning. He found me very ill. William Golding came and Algernon too. After dinner Mrs. Hunt and Mrs. Robson came to see me.

Doctor Dodds called at eight o'clock in the morning. I believe he is very shocked and saddened to see how ill I have become since his last visit. He just sat with me, and I did not say much to him. I know he believes nothing more can be done for me and that I am dying.

Everyone is most sad for me, but I am not, because the suffering I have endured for these past months will finally be over. Mr. Staines was indeed correct in saying, 'When the time comes, God will help me to accept my fate,' as I now feel calm, and ready to go.

Mrs. Hunt and Mrs. Robson came up to see me. Mrs. Robson was trying not to cry but I could see she was failing, as she tried to jolly me along with her usual chatter. I do not know if I will be writing in my diary tomorrow.

TUESDAY, 11TH AUGUST
Dog Days end. Ld. Wellington defeated Mar. Soult, 1813.

Had a bad night. Mrs. Hunt came to see me, so did Mrs. Day and Mrs H Jones. Very ill all day.

I am very weak so I cannot write much tonight. Mrs. Hunt and Mrs Day came to pay their respects to me. They probably do not expect to see me again. Mrs. Hannah Jones also came; she was very upset, but of course she tried not to show it. That is all I can write; I am too ill to hold a pencil.

WEDNESDAY, 12ᵀᴴ AUGUST
Kensington canal opened, 1828.

Extremely ill. Bad night. Mamma sent for Mr. Trested. George Nash came over. Mr. Hunt came to see me.

I have had to endure another day of suffering. I have prayed to our Lord to take me, but I am still in my bedroom surrounded by my family all looking very sad. George Nash came and sat quietly with me; he too is very sad.

Mr. Trested came, but he knows there is no cure for me. Mr. Hunt the preacher came to talk about God.

THURSDAY, 13ᵀᴴ AUGUST
The Queen's Birthday. Holiday at the Exchequer.

Very ill, bad night. G Nash and Grandpapa came over. Mr. Trested came to see me.

I have little to write about tonight, George and Grandpapa came as did Mr. Trested. I am very ill but somehow found the strength to write a prayer of reconciliation to God.

Had a dreadful night very
AUGUST ill   Engagements, &c. all   31 DAYS

day cough exceedingly painful
after dinner Mr Thirsk came
we talk of religion

August.

In honour of Augustus Cæsar.

breath very short Doctor

1 AUGUST. S. *Lammas Day*, from tenants of cathedrals then offering a *live* lamb. Hol. at Exch. Bat. of the Nile, 1798.

Dodd and Gnash came just
before tea they stayed till 9
o'clock

2 Su. Battle of Blenheim, 1704 ....
Mary went to church in the morn
had a bad night very weak none
went to church in the afternoon ?
one came after tea and brought

3 M. Sir R. Arkwright died, 1792 ....
had a ?? I had my dreadful
?? a good night I ??
?? came to supper after ??
?? very drunk tea on the
?? felt very poorly all day
they left about 9 o'clock

4 Tu. Lord Duncan died, 1804 ....
had a very bad night felt very
ill all day toward ?? ??
here Mr ?? came to see me in
the morning

5 W. Earl Howe died, 1799 ....

6 Th. *Transfiguration* of Jesus, on Mount Tabor ....

7 F. *Name of Jesus*,—possibly from a catholic festival of naming Jesus.

Mary

14th August to 17th August

Rosamond, with her strength almost gone, is lying in bed and no longer able to write. Her sister Mary, seeing the little diary on the bedside table, picked it up. Her heart started to break as she began reading of what her precious Rosamond had had to endure during the last few long months. With an overwhelming sense of pride in her sister for keeping such a faithful record of her trials and tribulations, she vowed to continue the task on Rose's behalf until the end, however long that may be.

FRIDAY, 14TH AUGUST
Drogheda taken by Cromwell, 1649.

Mamma and I sat watching Rosamond as she slept, waking only to sip some water. It is so hard to watch over her, knowing we will never laugh together again, or sit gossiping in Mrs. Robson's drawing room as she tells us of all the scandals of Aylesford. She would be amazed if she could see the number of visitors wishing to pay their respects to her that have come to our door today.

SATURDAY, 15TH AUGUST
Assumption of Virgin Mary, her miraculous ascent.

The day has been long, with so many callers wishing to see Rosie and say their goodbyes to her. Mamma was very strict in who she allowed into the bedroom to see her.

Rosamond's room is quite dark as Mamma closed the curtains to keep the light from hurting Rosie's eyes, but Rose asked for them to be drawn back so she could see the visitors gathered there. My sister is so weak now, but nonetheless she thanked her guests for coming.

After they had left, Mamma declared that we must not allow anyone to call upon Rose again, as we fear it is too tiring for her. So only family are permitted in her bedroom now, apart from Mr. and Mrs. Robson, whom the servants have been instructed to show upstairs if they come to the door.

SUNDAY, 16TH AUGUST
Flushing surrendered to the English, 1809.

It has been a heart-breaking day watching my dear sister grow weaker as she struggled for breath. I was so scared her breathing would suddenly stop and she would be gone from us.

Grandpapa, George, and Elizabeth came from Gillingham, even our elderly grandmother Spong came to see her. Mamma drew the curtains which made the room dark again, but when Rosie woke, she asked for them to be drawn back as she wanted to see the sunlight. I cried when she turned her head to the window, as I knew she was aware that she was dying and would never feel the sun on her face again.

All our older brothers came in to spend time with her, but Mamma told Ann to keep the younger ones in the nursery. The room was almost silent even though it was full of people. I saw Mrs. Robson quietly crying in her chair. Mamma and I stayed very close to Rosie's bed along with Papa and George. She looked very pale as she slept, and as the day wore slowly on, she did not wake again.

Mamma said that we should send for our vicar, Mr. Staines, as her breathing had become quite shallow. So, he was duly sent for, and he made all possible haste to be there as quickly as he could.

I knew she was dying but somehow it didn't seem real to me, and when I heard Mr. Staines reading the last rites over her it broke my heart.

It is now ten o'clock in the evening and Rose is still with us. It is just Mamma and I who are sitting with her as all the family have gone to bed. I expect we will stay here all-night listening to the ticking of the clock on her mantelpiece, reminding us that time is running out for Rosamond.

MONDAY, 17TH AUGUST
Duchess of Kent's Birthday.

When the sun rose this morning, it looked like the day would be bright and sunny, although nothing but sorrow awaited us as we gathered round Rosamond's bedside. Holding her hand as she slept, I watched her breathe until she opened her eyes and looked directly at me and smiled, then fell into a deep sleep.

As I sat there in the gloom of her bedroom, I could not stop thinking about how much I will miss her. We have been so close all our lives and have always shared our hopes and fears with each other. Who will I turn to when she is no more? My brothers are very dear to me, but nothing can take the place of a very treasured sister, and my heart was breaking as I watched her slowly slipping away from me.

Mamma asked me to go and tell the boys to come upstairs as she felt her time was drawing near. We all watched as she slept, each of us with our own thoughts, on just what the loss of our dear Rosamond would mean to us. She looked very peaceful as she lay in her darkened bedroom, and as I sat there with tears in my eyes, I prayed that she had made her peace with God, as I know she had struggled with her faith during this terrible illness.

Mamma asked each one of us to say our goodbyes, as she was sure that Rosamond was now slipping into the arms of Jesus. Everyone was crying, even Papa and the boys, but I felt a calmness in the room, despite all the tears. It felt very peaceful, and as I sat watching my dearest sister and confidante lying still in her bed, it was clear to me that she had gone to a better place, now no longer suffering with the terrible affliction that had made her life so miserable. She is with God now, but we who are left will mourn the loss of our precious Rosamond forever. Mamma, standing up from her chair with tears rolling down her cheeks, went over and drew back the curtains to open the windows wide, allowing Rosie's spirit to fly up to heaven.

There was much to attend to, and one by one the family kissed her goodbye and left the room. Mamma had gone to write notes to everyone who needed to be notified of Rose's passing. Only I remained, reflecting on all we had enjoyed together during her life, knowing mine had now changed forever. My heart is shattered into a million pieces, but I must be strong for Mamma as she has just lost her precious daughter and will need me to help her carry on. Then I too kissed Rosie goodbye before going to my room. As I sat looking through her diary, I discovered a prayer scribbled in pencil in which she was asking God to save her soul, which read:

Lord Granting, Show Me God,
His Mercy to Me, A Sinner.
Lord Jesus Save My Soul.
Lord Granting Me
And Enlightening My Mind.
Lord Take the Sting
Out of My Flesh,
And Give Me a Heart of Flesh.
Lord, After I am Me,
Lord Help Me to Love Thee
More And More.
Oh, Teach Me to Love Thee
As I Ought.

I then knew she had finally accepted her fate with peace in her heart, so kissing her little book I said, 'You are at peace now my dear little sister, where there is no more pain and fear, so may God bless your soul, I will always miss you'.

I believe this prayer to be the last thing Rosamond wrote in her diary.

Jackie

2023

Now you have read Rosamond's story, you will know she sadly passed away on Monday, 17th August 1835. Her struggle with what was undoubtedly tuberculosis was now over, and on 24th August her broken-hearted family laid her to rest in the family vault at Aylesford parish church. As they all made their weary way back to Mill Hall, I am sure as a deeply religious family they took some comfort from knowing their precious daughter was now free from pain and anguish, and safely in the hands of the God she had loved so dearly.

I was aware Rosamond had suffered from a serious chest ailment, but it wasn't until we went to Maidstone County Hall on my first visit to Kent that we realised why no more entries after 13th August were made; she had passed away just four days later. This became known as we searched for her identity in the archives using microfiche.

I have previously described how my sister and I found baptism records of a Rosamond and her siblings, a possible match, but when we turned to Mike and Iain to tell them of our discovery, Mike told us they had found a burial record dated a week after the last diary entry. The name of the internee was a Rosamond Nash Spong, late of Mill Hall; the officiating vicar of this internment at St. Peter and St. Paul's church in Aylesford was a Mr. Staines. This information proved beyond doubt we had found her, but at the same time it saddened me greatly to discover she had died, almost like knowing the end of a book when you have just started reading it or losing a friend you had just begun to know. This was going to make completing the transcription harder for me, as I now knew there would be no happy ending. I therefore decided it would be prudent to leave out this piece of information until the conclusion, so you, the reader, didn't know her fate too prematurely. I was in awe of how she managed to continue writing up to just four days before her life ended, albeit in pencil as she must have been aware the end was near.

Because Rosamond's last entry was abrupt and inconclusive, I couldn't leave it there, so I decided to bring her sister Mary into the story and allow her to narrate the last few days. It was a bold move for me as I no longer had Rosamond's words to guide me, but after a little uncertainty I began to discover a freedom from the restraint I hadn't realised was there until it had gone, and the experience of describing her last four days was amazing and heart breaking at the same time, so quite a few tears were shed as my pen flew across the page.

I was in the room as she lay in her bed, the curtains drawn to keep out the sun's rays. I could almost smell the flickering candles as they illuminated the faces of her grieving family gathered round the bed as they waited for God to take her. I have been involved in Rosamond's life for so many years that she has become very dear to me, so the writing of her demise was truly heart breaking. However, I needed to say goodbye to a young woman who had borne her illness so bravely, as I never had the same opportunity with my own daughter. So, when it was over, I dried my eyes, feeling strangely calm. There was nothing left to say: I had done what Trish had asked me to do, I had given Rosamond a voice, she was now at peace, and in writing my own story, I also felt a sense of peace. Rosamond had indeed worked some kind of magic.

It is hard to believe that twenty-five years have passed since I first received her little diary, with life at that time in turmoil and unable to see a way out of my misery, but 'Finding Rosamond' has given me a lifeline on two occasions, something to cling on to when all else had failed. I will be eternally grateful to whoever guided this wonderful piece of social history to me through Glenda, and I really want to believe it was my own daughter, Allison.

One wish remains now, and that is to find Rosamond's previous diaries which are probably languishing in a private collection at the back of a drawer somewhere. As I have her last diary, to read of her happier years would be wonderful, but as all attempts to locate them have so far proved fruitless I suspect it will never happen.

Many entries in this little book touch my heart, none more so than the prayer she wrote with an unsteady hand in pencil when Rosamond realised she was dying and wished to make her peace with God. Another poignant record of her ordeal is a tiny drawing she did of herself sitting up in a four-poster bed with her initials, R.S., written underneath.

I do not claim these next words to be my own, they were texted to me by my dear friend Trisha while out walking her dog, Sammy. They are included because they are wonderful. Here are Trisha's dog walking thoughts:

'The traces and small shadows invisible to many, are signs we leave through our life's journey, many of which we do not realise we leave behind. Did Rosamond write her diary just for herself or did she, as her illness progressed, write it with the thought that it might be read by someone else, and if so, will they be touched by her words? It is amazing that through all her suffering, she brought so much healing to you. What a wonderful legacy for Rosamond's life to have such an impact on another person, and I am certain that if she only knew her scribblings written so long ago would have the power to help someone living two centuries later, she would be absolutely thrilled, but then again, she probably already knows.'

Thank you, Trish, for persuading me to take on this project and for sharing the journey with me, also for all the help you and Rob have given me throughout the process of the story, for without you both this book would never have been written.

Many people have helped with its telling. My thanks go to Diane for typing out so many badly handwritten A4 sheets of paper, Penny and Lucy for their valiant attempts to help before Diane came to my rescue, Julia Holmes for giving up so much of her time with the research, you are incredible Julie, I will forever be in your debt. My appreciation also goes to Kent historians John Vigar and Andrew Ashbee for all their invaluable help during our time there. My love and thanks must also go to my wonderful family, David and Carole, Lucy and Dan for all the love and support they have freely given over the years which I know will continue in the future, whatever that may hold. Iain and Sally for all the wonderful holidays we have been on together, and for taking on the editing, formatting, and proof-reading of the book. Without their help this story would never have been published, you have both been amazing. I must also give thanks to my sister-in-law Glenda for finding Rosamond's diary in the first place and bringing it to my attention, if it had stayed in the bookshop window who knows what might have become of me, or Rosamond's story.

Finally, the one person I could never give enough praise to is my husband Mike, who has been by my side throughout this entire process. His encouragement during the many times my lack of confidence threatened to overwhelm me was the one thing that kept me going, not forgetting the many hours he spent trying to decipher my terrible handwriting during the editing of this book. He is the brightest star in my universe.

It is with sadness and regret that the time has finally come for me to let Rosamond and her family go, they have been part of my life for so long it is difficult to say goodbye as I have got to know them all so well. So, these following words are just for you, Rosamond. I hope you did not mind me poking my nose into your world and I really hope you approve of what I have done with the words written by you in your little 'Present from Papa,' Trish believed you should be given a voice and I hope I have managed to do that. Now our journey together is over, I will miss you and your little burgundy leather diary, it helped me come to terms with the worst trauma that can befall a parent, the loss of a child, and for that I will never be able to thank you enough, so rest in peace my dear girl.

With all my love, Jackie.

And now the next chapter of my life begins, I may be an old lady now, but I have no intention of slipping quietly into the world of daytime television. Nothing wrong with that, I have been known to indulge myself when over-tired or ill, but the thought of it being my only reason for getting up in the morning fills me with horror. Despite all my aches and pains, I cannot wait to retrieve Rosamond's sister Mary from her hiding place in the drawer, so watch this space, I will be back.

The End